Infectious

By
Elizabeth Forkey

Published by Entrada Publishing.

Printed in the United States of America.

Contents

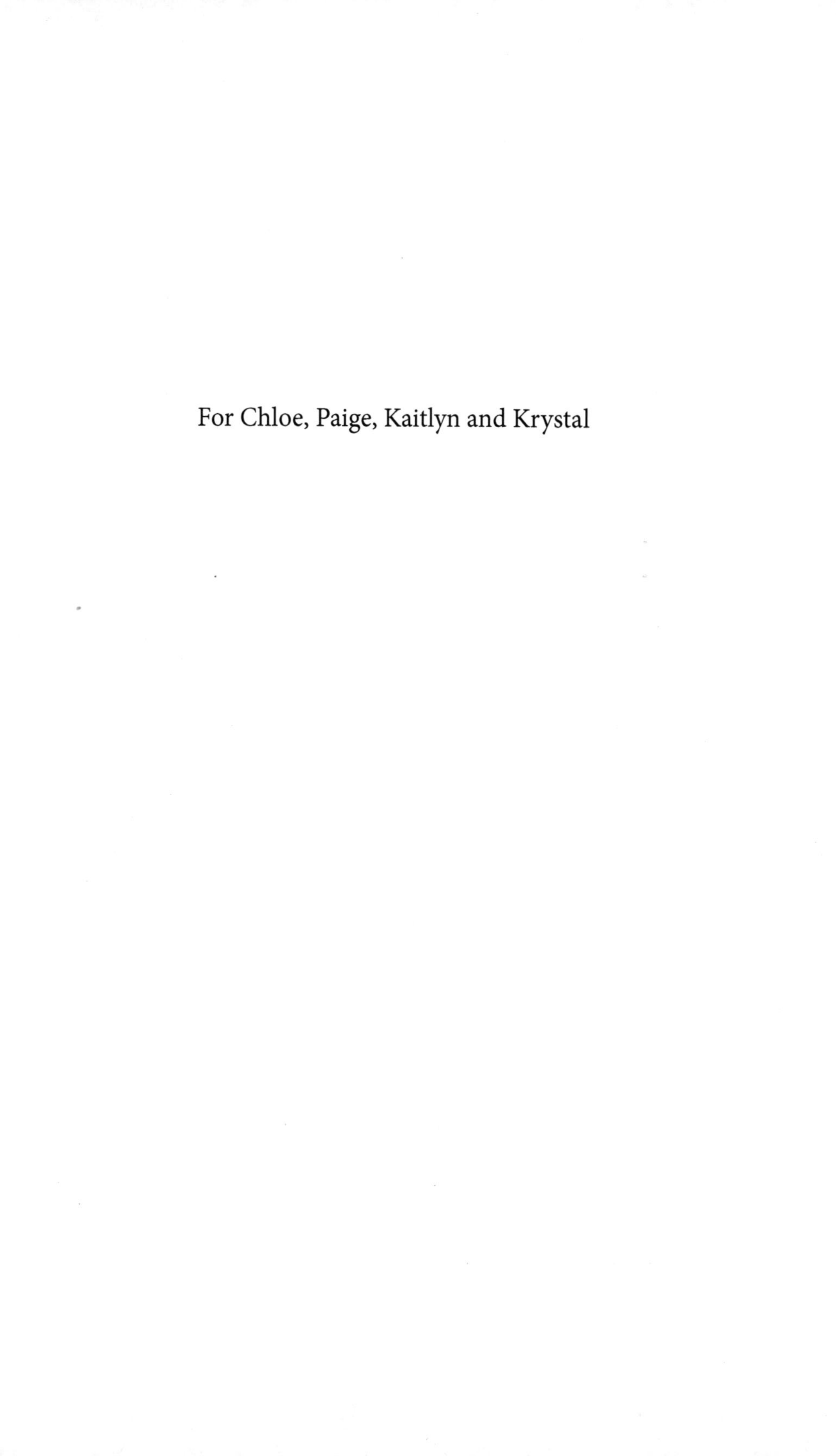

For Chloe, Paige, Kaitlyn and Krystal

First and foremost, this book is dedicated to my Lord, The Risen One, The Miracle Maker, Conqueror of Death, The Most Exciting Love I've ever known. He really wrote it, not me. He put this story in my heart for anyone who is dreaming of an exciting life - something more than the ordinary – a storybook kind of love. The stuff of "once upon a time," the kind of love that the imaginary Edward and Bella share, really does exist – and then some! It is ours for the taking! We must simply put our hand in His and run with abandon down the path he is paving before us.

Second, I dedicate this book to Chloe, my daughter and best friend. She read along as I wrote and encouraged me every day. She critiqued, she laughed, she said, "Hurry up and write some more!" every time she caught up with me. She is an amazing part of this great adventure and I'm so thankful for her.

Prologue

His bald head flashes a momentary reflection in the passing moonlight as he slinks through the shadows, hurrying towards, yet dreading, his secret rendezvous. A violent shiver seizes him. He trips but doesn't slow, the stumble propelling him even faster, looking like a small child who has lost control of uncoordinated feet. He weaves in and out of the buildings and alleys down memorized paths. He has traveled this route on darker nights than this. He does not fear the black darkness.

And yet, fear consumes him.

He struggles to breathe. The exertion of his moonlit race isn't the cause of the sharp pain in his side or the ragged way he draws in breath. The chill in his bones has nothing to do with the freezing night wind. They can't touch him on this side. They can't kill him or maim him if he stays here. Not directly, not physically, no. Much worse, they will punish him by hurting *her.* His heart and soul ache raw with constant tortured thoughts of *her. Her* agony, *her* fear, alone and ravaged by their filth because he is weak—a failure! It has been weeks and he is no closer to giving the doddering, loathsome man what he wants.

She has been his best friend and dearest love since childhood. It is an unthinkable tragedy that they will not spend their immortal days together. It's unfair. But he can no longer stand the wicked whispers with their relentless buzzing in his already guilt ridden heart. They promise him that his betrayal will spare her and he is desperate to believe the whispers.

Though the night is dark and starless, the winded runner senses that they are already there—waiting for him. He can make out at least five shadowy bodies coming into focus through the coiled fencing.

His stomach turns as he closes the last few feet between himself and the inky group. Memories of the last time he met the doctor here play like a horror movie in his head. Last time he came empty handed and left with a small brown sack. Taking the featherweight mystery bag back to his apartment, he agonized the rest of that long night over what he would find if he opened it. When the sun began to light his dirty windows, he begged the silent sky for courage and stared into the dark brown shadows of the bag.

He found her beautiful hair.

Shaved and stuffed into the small sack in knotted clumps. After crying like a child until his sobs ran out and screaming at the heavens until his voice was gone, he tried to gather the messy strands into a bundle. He wanted to smell her and stroke the familiar soft strands against his lonely cheek. This closer inspection showed skin and blood on the tips of the beautiful auburn and gray locks. Had they ripped it from her head? Their cruelty knew no bounds.

He has to do whatever they want, even if it costs him his soul. His legs shake as he stands before them in silence. He hopes against hope that what he has to offer them tonight will buy him a little more time. A little more time to do what he must. The safety of this cursed fence feels like prison to him now. Trapped. He is a bird in a cage, powerless against the evil without.

Free, on the opposite side of the fence, the old doctor stands waiting—anger and loathing written in the wrinkles of his scowl. The doctor always wears the same thing, the tight shimmering bodysuit of his learned organization. Its silver spandex fabric seems to glow in the sparse moonlight. And gloves. They always wear gloves. The grayish-white gleam of the bodysuit matches the grayish-white hair on the old doctor's small head. He is short and pudgy and the spandex suit accentuates his soft middle and his spindly legs. Despite his unimposing appearance, he emanates dark intimidation. It's his eyes—eyes that look inhumanly black in the dark.

The small crowd of taller beings around the doctor also wear the silvery suits. They look sleek, strong and capable. They stand in stoic silence, their faces hidden behind simple white masks. The plastic masks, plain and nondescript, are haunting. The bald runner looks down at his feet to avoid the empty black eye holes.

The haughty doctor saunters forward until his silver belly is pressed against the holey fence. Though his voice is shallow and sickly it is still thick with hate as he barks, "You are late!"

The frightened runner cringes, alone on his side of the fence, but keenly aware of the nearby homes and their sleeping inhabitants. If anyone hears them, all will be lost. If he is caught, his wife will die.

"Please forgive me," the runner whispers. "Don't hurt her! I was in—"

"I don't care!" the white-haired doctor rasps even louder.

The runner gasps and stumbles backwards, shooting frantic glances at nearby windows. He's never seen the decrepit one this riled. Why is this deal so important to them?

Squinting through the chain links, the runner studies the panting geezer. Beneath that shock of white hair, the doctor's face and neck glint with the wetness of open sores. His ears are covered in more bandages than the last time.

They are getting sicker.

They'll never find what they are looking for and it is the lonely man's only consolation. He takes comfort in the sureness that they'll rot to death and then go to hell where they belong.

Forcing himself to be brave, the runner steps closer to the menacing group, his voice quivering with telltale fear as he holds up what he brought for them, "I brought you this."

His hand shakes with trepidation as he pushes his fingers through one of the fence links and hovers, trembling on their side. But no one moves to take the proffered piece from the quaking hand until a nod of command is given. Only then does the largest of the masked men step forward to retrieve it. The runner shivers as the body guard's gloved hand enfolds his own and takes the crumpled image. Bravery sapped, the runner snatches his hand back unharmed. An abbreviated prayer of thanksgiving whispers through his cracked lips—old habits die hard.

Accepting the small, crinkled square from his body guard, the doctor squints at the image. He holds it up and turns the picture to catch a beam of moonlight for a better look. With the back of his gloved hand, the pudgy doctor wipes a drip of ooze from his bandaged brow as he considers the photo with quiet fury.

"Meet us here again in three Mondays and bring what we want," he enunciates through the sticky phlegm in his throat, "or I will have your wife handed to you piece by piece through the links of this fence."

The bald runner whimpers and bows, nodding with exaggerated enthusiasm, hoping that his submission to their will is obvious. If they are sure that he will do the job, maybe they'll stop hurting her.

With a discomforting smile of yellow teeth the doctor adds, "Here's a little something for all of your trouble."

Dropping a small black box through the fence links, they turn and dissipate into the buildings on their side, disappearing like snakes into their holes.

Alone and trembling, the terrified man glances all around him and then stoops to retrieve the black velvet jewelry box. He stares transfixed at the box in his upturned hand. His palms drip with sweat, the freezing night wind unable to dry them. The bile in his stomach churns and threatens to surface. The abysmal man acted as though it was a payment or a gift.

Could it be?

No. It can't be good. They don't do good.

With a trembling finger he flips open the rounded black lid. His anguished scream goes up in the night. All thought of secrecy is driven from his mind as the moon comes out from behind a cloud to reveal the contents of the open box in his hand. The diamond earring he gave her so many Christmases ago twinkles in the lunar light—still decorating her severed ear.

ONE WEEK LATER

Chapter One

I Used To Be One of Them

I am on my hands and knees scrubbing the faded-gray linoleum kitchen floor when my last decent pair of jeans rips through at the knee. My shoulders slump as I let out an annoyed groan. My carelessness has given unintentional support to her announcement at breakfast this morning. All my arguments turned to lies with a two inch long rip.

Maybe she won't notice.

Fat chance.

I should have changed into older pants for this job, but my older pants are as ugly as the rag I'm using to scrub this impossible floor. I look like a hobo circus clown in them. Their different colored patches and hastily hemmed seams are embarrassing to look at, let alone wear.

Everything I own is old. My limited wardrobe is a mismatched collection of hand-me-downs, most of which have holes and stains. My outfits span the last two decades and have been worn by several people before me—generational hand-me-downs. Homeless people wouldn't want them.

Who cares about looking shabby anyways? No one else is any better off. I am fine blending in with the rest of the equally unkempt. But she doesn't care what I want, does she? I wish she'd take someone else with her. Not that she'd find anyone else more willing. The other girls my age—who are more image conscious than me and who dream of days-gone-by and less sobriety in their lives—wouldn't dream of venturing out of the community for new jeans.

My only Living relative, Aunty Coe, is, of course, dissatisfied with what every other person in our little community has accepted. Aunt Colleen is actually my Great Aunt on my father's side—my dad's mother's sister. She took me in when I was twelve and I've been with her for four years. I love her, but I am dreading the special bonding time she has planned for us today.

Aunty is a prim and proper lady, still quite attractive for age 65. She never married. And, coincidentally, she never learned to play nice with others. She holds staunchly to the axiom "cleanliness is next to godliness." This applies to the neatness of a person's wardrobe as well. I spend a lot of my time humoring her and pretending to agree with her. Less lectures that way. I say she's my only Living relative as opposed to other family members who are hopefully still living, but probably not Living. So, she's not my mom, but she is the next best thing.

A "shopping" trip could actually be fun.

God knows I'm tired of being cooped up.

These are the things I'm telling myself as I lazily wipe at impossible stains on the floor in front of the oven. My mental pep talk is an attempt to avoid the other more pressing thoughts that come with leaving our community—mortal danger and grisly death. I'm trying to picture amazing shirts and new-in-the-box tennis shoes that are so fantastic they are worth the risk of abduction and dissection. If I'm being dragged along no matter what, it would be great if I could talk myself into some level of acceptance before she comes back with the car that will take us on our excursion.

Drawing a deep breath that works its way back out in a long sigh, I decide that I'm not convincing myself. I crawl under the table to scrub that section of the floor and consider staying there and hiding. I used to drape the old table with blankets and build myself castles and forts—imagining myself safe and hidden. Imagination was enough back then. Enough to escape from all the trauma life had thrown at me. Aunty used to play along and pretend she couldn't find me. I don't think she'd be amused if I reinstated the old game today.

Maybe I could fake the flu.

The nagging thought that a spider could be lurking on the bottom of the table above me makes me twist around to look at the back of the light yellowy-orange oak boards. No eight-legged monsters, just memories. My name is scrawled in childish handwriting and various colors of crayon.

Ivy Mae Lusato

If Aunty ever found my rebellious Crayola graffiti, she didn't mention it. A world of faded drawings hides beneath the boards we eat on every day. Framed in clouds and rainbows, my extinct dreams cover most of the table's secret side. I lie on my back and look up at the happy thoughts doodled with care so many years ago. I can't help but frown, irritated at my young, naive self. I thought my life could turn out like those pictures from my daydreams. I'm glad that little girl is long gone. She'd be heartbroken to find out how it all turned out.

Crawling out of yesteryear, I stand back up in my rainbow-less world to survey my hard work. The expression "sparkling clean" doesn't come close to an accurate depiction of this hopeless floor. Under the beige fluorescent light, the twenty year old linoleum has cracks and tears and several gross brown stains. I'm sure when it was new it sparkled, but now, even after intensive scrubbing, it still looks dirty.

I'm thrilled that I just wasted thirty minutes of my life on it.

Stinging pangs of chapped discomfort draw my attention from the floor to my hands. Already dry from the winter weather, my stubby fingers are red and irritated from the lye in our homemade cleaning soap. I forgot to wear my gloves again. I open the pantry and take an illegal dip into the last pot of store-bought lotion in town. The fancy hand cream is one of the few things Aunty has claimed as "hers." It is her favorite scent, Peony Flower, and she uses it sparingly. I may have snuck a dip or two of the precious cream over the last few years. The pink perfumed lotion heightens the burning sensation at first, but then it fades into a cool tingling. My hands lose their redness almost instantly. Miraculous. I miss modern conveniences. I miss toothpaste. I miss Kraft cheese singles. I miss roll-on clear peach sparkle deodorant. I miss normality.

Standing at the pantry and mourning the past is only making me more depressed. I've been dragging through my chores this morning and a glance at the red clock above the stove shows just how behind I am. I still need to button things up around the Inn, and Aunty will be pulling up outside the back door in less than ten minutes. The world is still dark outside, but the Living are already out and about, naming and claiming a new day.

We live in a sprawling Southern mansion in downtown Toccoa, Georgia. Trust me; it isn't as glamorous as it sounds. The old white siding is gray with dirt and age and the romantic wrap-around front porch is getting more and more dangerous to walk on. The porch's old wood is rotten and past reparable, and more than half of the termite-infested boards need to be replaced. As run down as it is, it's still the only house I've ever known to have a name. The faded wooden sign in the front yard whispers of better times and days of plenty. Framed in gingerbread cut-out embellishments, the cracked black letters almost too faded to read spell out: The Simmons-Bond Inn.

A leftover from the Victorian era, the ancient inn looks lost and out of place among the newer brick buildings that grew up around it. The house sits slumped and haggard right in the center of town, across from what used to be the Courthouse and adjacent to what used to be the Library and down the block from what used to be the Post Office. I've lived here just long enough to remember it all as it used to be—a normal American small town. Boring, but safe.

Inside, the Inn has five enormous bedrooms upstairs—each with its own bathroom. Aunty has taken the largest room upstairs for herself. My room, on the other hand, is downstairs. My bedroom is simple with none of the fancy woodwork that the grand rooms upstairs were given. Tucked in the back corner of the house, my quarters were probably originally intended for the maid or house servant. You know that expression, "If the shoe fits, wear it"?

Well—the shoe fits.

I'm more servant than niece these days.

The carved oak moldings, stained glass windows, intricately patterned wallpapers, and unique French tiled fireplaces used to be beautiful to me. I think I lost the sense of awe when it became my responsibility to clean all the nooks and crannies. The twelve foot ceilings lost their grandeur when I was given the job of dusting all the cobwebbed corners. Aunty helps some with the cleaning, but it is mostly my job now.

Aunty runs the Inn for the good of the community; offering a clean, warm place to stay for anyone who has need. There is usually at least one other family living here with us—often an orphan or two as well. I'm butler, maid and housekeeper to anyone who comes to stay. We don't have any guests in the Inn today. I would normally be relieved and spend the day tucked under my fluffy pink comforter rereading a favorite book. Unfortunately, Aunty is taking advantage of our vacancies and forcing me to take part in "Girl's Day Out."

Lucky me! I'm so happy I don't have to clean any stranger's toilets today so I can jump in the car and risk my life for a better wardrobe.

My sarcasm is Aunty's least favorite thing about me. She says I get it from my father. When I get cynical, she starts lecturing. Apparently, sarcasm is "unladylike." If you ask me, I think lecturing is unladylike. Just sayin'.

Ok, mental checklist: grab my coat, lights are all off, bars locked in place on all the first floor windows, lock the doors to our bedrooms and the kitchen, front door already locked, grab some shopping bags—Whoops! Blow out that candle. Grab the lunches Aunty packed and, finally, head to the back door. As I step outside, locking the back door and pulling it shut behind me, I realize I forgot my Taser.

Crap.

I can't go without it. I have to unlock the back door and all the other doors I locked on my way out as I work my way back to my bedroom where a frantic search finally exhumes the Taser from under a pile of dirty laundry. By the time I get back outside, with the Taser secured to my wrist band and all the doors relocked, Aunty Coe is waiting in the alley for me. Through her driver's side window I see her lift her eyebrows in that subtle correcting way she has. Translation: It's not polite to keep people waiting.

Yup. This is going to be so much fun.

I paste on what I hope is an enthusiastic smile and jump in the SUV she has borrowed for the day. Pulling the door closed, I am accosted by cheesy Southern Gospel music, Aunty's favorite. I strongly consider jumping back out and my hand lingers on the door handle. Aunty glances at me and lifts her eyebrows again. I don't have the angst it takes to be a drama queen and Aunty is just scary enough to keep me respectful; so I grit my teeth and force another fake smile. She pulls out of the driveway. This is happening.

Our borrowed transportation is a bulky, black, Ford Expedition. We've taken this same vehicle on past adventures. I settle comfortably into the seat and pull my seat buckle across me. It almost feels like it's our car. I wonder if anyone else drives it regularly and feels the same way about it. I run my hands slowly down the sides of the cold seat along my legs. The soft tan leather interior still smells new, even though the car is an older model. The heater is on high but the engine hasn't warmed up yet and it's still blowing cold air. I shiver against the cold and maybe also the thought of leaving our safe town.

"I thought you had a better pair of pants, Ivy. You said you didn't need clothes. Why didn't you wear your nice jeans?"

Let the nit-picking begin.

"These are my nice jeans," I mumble, self-conscious.

Rubbing my legs for warmth, I slide my hands down my thighs and leave them on my knees—covering the new hole with my hand. Aunty is dressed immaculately as always. Her outfit suggests a trip to some socialite function with other uppity ladies who would probably have worn fancy hats. Her snooty obsession with looking one's best is nauseating. It's not like we'll even see anyone while we are out today. Hopefully.

She purses her lips and I brace myself for her first, though—let's face it—not last, lecture of the day. I'm saved as her favorite song starts playing. I glance sideways at her and I see her face relax and a small smile replaces the scowl I caused. A throaty man is singing a duet about Heaven with a lady who warbles like she's sitting on a broken washing machine.

I smile at Aunty; I'm glad the horrible singers still relax her and bring her joy. I think her constant picking and lecturing are because she's sad that the world is broken—human civility almost extinct. She wants us to keep her old proprieties alive. Maybe because it's propriety and manners that make her feel safe in these dark days. Like if we just dress classy enough and speak kindly enough we might be able to hold the evil at bay.

I'm sixteen, but I've never driven and I have no desire to do so. I roll my shoulders and try to relax my nervous stomach as I scan the streets for anyone else out on this crisp winter morning. Aunty handles the SUV with confidence, the skills of a lifetime of driving still with her, despite how infrequent our trips are these days.

A sticker on the dashboard assures me in messy handwriting that the car has been checked over and serviced by Maintenance for our drive today. Venturing out of the safety of our community has plenty of risks and the last thing we need is an unreliable vehicle. This one has lots of safety features like dual airbags and GPS and even some of those collision bars across the front. Ironic, because the least of our worries is hitting another car. The old Ford has a great alarm system and it's high off the ground and powerful. It should keep us safe from what we are most in need of protection from.

Zombies.

I am terrified of them. I'm ashamed to admit that I used to be one of them; but that was years ago.

Chapter Two

The Natives Are Getting Restless

February is right around the corner and Northeast Georgia is still dull, brown, and freezing cold. The sun is spreading out buttery-yellow fingers of light to take hold of the new day, but I doubt it will lend us any more warmth. It may warm up later this afternoon, but it's always cold in the morning because we're in the mountains. Our trip can't wait until the afternoon warmth though. The morning is our ally—it's the safest time of day. The zombies don't come out before noon, sometimes even later.

We turn down Tugalo Street and head towards the closest security gate in our safe zone. As Aunty approaches the eighteen-foot tall electronic gate, the early morning guards recognize us, punch in the code to open the gate and wave us through. I fight against the irritation that Aunty probably had this trip planned for days and I've only just been told this morning. I hate when she does that. We weren't stopped because the guards already knew about our trip out today. It would've had to have been cleared with the Elders.

We are leaving through the Western gate of the community. No, community sounds too idyllic; maybe compound is a better word. It takes less than two minutes of driving to go from downtown Toccoa to country roads. Even in its glory days, Toccoa was only a speck on the map.

The few clothing stores Toccoa once had were picked over and emptied years ago. Very few goods are made and shipped to our city anymore, except what the government sends. They say we are welcome to our own share of the shipments—that are mostly intended for the zombies—but we don't want to wear the current fashions.

Most zombies wear long-sleeved, full bodysuits in drab colors of black, brown or tan to hide their deformities. They have special shoes with biotechnology made to compensate for diseased feet that are missing some or all toes. The shoes fill in the empty spaces and adjust to the foot providing balance that would otherwise be impossible for crippled, toeless feet. The shipments have different types of gloves that provide both comfort and concealment for rotting hands. The gloves come with anywhere from one to five fake fingers capable of lifting and holding. And, nowadays, all the shipments have masks.

The most recent trend in camouflage is to wear a mask that shows strength and personality. Funny clown faces, famous icons, and comical cartoon characters are available for purchase in each shipment. For the ladies, there are exotic feminine masks with glitter and feathers or expensive latex inlays that sculpt diseased faces into modern art. If you want to look edgy, there's always gruesome monsters left over from Halloweens past. Just picture it: a hunchbacked zombie dragging himself through the streets in a King Kong Halloween mask. It's pee-your-pants terrifying and more and more zombies are doing it.

So, since we aren't interested in wearing that, we are heading out of town to "shop." And the stores we're going to won't require the current currency in exchange for what we take. If it takes a needle to buy it, I don't need it that bad.

Aunty Coe turns down her CD and glances sideways at me. "Did you remember to pull down the bars in the kitchen?"

"Mm hmm," I ooze exasperation. She is somewhat—okay, VERY—controlling. To be fair, I am often forgetful.

"Ivy, is it possible for us to have a nice Girl's Day today?"

"Yes, I'm sorry."

"You know I love you, honey. I thought this would be a nice distraction from all of your recent duties at the U.R. You've been cleaning and studying and working double shifts to get the teachers ready for the Homecoming. I just want you to remember that you are only 16! Before He came back, a girl your age had her studies and her friends and maybe a part-time job. Sleep is still very important for a young woman. I don't think you've had more than six hours a night in ages!"

"I like to keep busy." I'm mumbling and I know she hates that.

"Oh yes, I know you like to keep busy! I'm just a little worried about why that is."

I stare out the window without an answer for her.

So I keep busy. I'm a hard worker. What's wrong with that? She has pounded me over the years with talks about good attitudes and how fortunate we are. I want to feel that way. But when I sit around, with little to do, I hate my life. I'll admit it. Life here really sucks most of the time. There are hundreds of desperate, needy, dead people living right down the street. Extreme poverty is the norm. Abandoned, lonely, lost, hurting—these are the adjectives of everyday life.

Not to mention that most everyone beyond our gates is pure evil. Rapists, thieves, and child abusers—even murder has become commonplace—and no one does anything to stop them. We are barely safe behind our high fences. When I work, I can forget about all the heavy stuff. I feel half decent about myself when I'm rolling up my sleeves and doing something to care for the Living ones who need my help. I lose myself in charity and it helps me feel right in my soul. Now more than ever, it's really important to have your soul figured out.

Aunty Coe reaches over to pat my hand. "We are still allowed to enjoy the simple pleasures in life, Ivy. Having fun with girls your age, a good book," then, in a softer voice, she adds, "perhaps even friendship with a young man."

"Ugh!" I exclaim in disgust. Here we go again!

This is the third time lately that she has tried to lure me into a conversation consisting mostly of her praising the amazing qualities of the brilliant Tim Markowitz. I was going to have a good attitude about the southern gospel music. I am trying to enjoy spending time with her. But if her plan was to trap me in a car so she can go on and on about weird, nerdy, "I act like I'm forty even though I'm sixteen" Markowitz, I'm going to open my door and jump. This "shopping trip" was nothing but a ruse and I'm sick of her pestering.

I fight back with the only ammunition I have in my limited arsenal, my tone laden with sarcasm, "I've been meaning to tell you; I saw Chuck at the U.R. last night and he asked about you. I hear he joined the choir. Won't that be nice? Maybe you two can do a duet together."

Chuck Fox has been following her around since arriving in Toccoa a couple of months ago. I guess his wife died last year. I overheard the Elders talking about him. He and his wife were living on the road, searching large cities for his wife's sister, Theo. I don't know too many details, but I know the zombies got his wife. Maybe even ate her. When he stumbled into Toccoa, still looking for his sister-in-law, he looked like a man broken beyond repair. He didn't find Theo among us; but, as soon as he set eyes on Aunty Coe at a U.R. meeting, he seemed to come back to life overnight. Like I said, she is very pretty for her age.

"I'm glad that young man has found something to involve himself with."

Oh yeah, mission accomplished. She is miffed and on the defensive. Our positions reversed, feeling triumphant, I push my case further.

"He's not young, Aunty. He's almost as old as you are!" I swipe my long curly hair over my shoulder in front of my face to hide my grin. She hates being called "old." I have what it takes to win this.

"I don't like your implication, Ivy. I'm not old."

I risk another sideways glance and get caught in her brilliant blue stare. I feign innocence and chirp with my voice syrupy sweet, "Well then I don't see why you and *young* Chuck Fox won't get along perfectly."

"Ivy!"

Lots of men have tried to catch her attention but she never seems interested. When she first took me in, I was a little kid and I thought old person romance was disgusting. I remember cringing in embarrassment when men from the U.R. would flirt with her or ask her to dinner. It's not that I don't want her to find someone—though it does seem pretty pointless. Chuck seems to hope he has a chance. He has settled down with our community and is helping with the children's program. Good luck to him. She won't go easy.

I hope I've won myself a reprieve from the dating subject for the day. Aunty is as ready to change the subject as I am. I think it's kind of weird that she keeps pushing me towards a boy. Don't most parents want their teenage girls to hate boys? I'm like the ideal teenager in that department. She should be thrilled, not trying to fix me up.

For the rest of the drive we chat with an ease I thought we had lost, and I find myself enjoying our time together. We discuss the spring cleaning that needs to be done at the Inn and Aunty offers to help with a lot of it. I suspect that she's trying to make up for the Tim conversation by buttering me up and offering to help with more than her share, but I'll take it.

We chitchat with typical feminine anticipation about what we hope to find in the stores today. We will both be picking up extra things for the other women and girls of our community. We'll grab some things for the guys, too; if we have room and a little luck. Aunty is hoping to bring home a lot of "sensible shoes." Sensible is almost always synonymous with ugly. All of a sudden, I'm glad I came. I'll get to pick out my own new tennis shoes. The less sensible the better. It's all starting to feel worth the risks.

I look out the window as we talk and take in the scenery that I so rarely get to see. We are driving windy back roads in old farm country. Though the grass is brown and the woods are bare, the countryside is still pretty and refreshing. Aunty and I exclaim with delight and she slows to a crawl when we see herds of deer peeking at us from overgrown fields. They don't dart away in fear, being so unaccustomed to human beings, but instead stand regally and look back at us as we drift by.

The sun is climbing over the distant hills of the Appalachian Mountains and we ride in comfortable silence as we enjoy the beauty of God's creation. People may have gotten messed up, but the sky and the mountains and the bare winter trees that will soon burst with spring blooms still display the glory of their Creator.

We haven't passed a single car so far. We are heading towards Commerce, Georgia—half an hour Southeast of Toccoa. Though Commerce was once a thriving destination with an outlet mall, it is now an abandoned ghost town. No government shipments are dropped there. No shipments equals no zombies. That's why it has always been a pretty safe place to "shop." The long vacant strip mall offers everything from clothes and shoes to books and bake wear.

We turn off of the back road and onto the freeway for the last few miles of our drive. It's the 85 interstate and it cuts south through Georgia towards Atlanta. Atlanta is a dangerous place and it is only an hour south of Commerce. Atlanta is one of the largest cities left in the nation and perhaps the most important one.

On the larger highway, we are more cautious and we keep a vigilant watch for any other vehicles. Highways are much more likely to have supply trucks, army vehicles, med units, or government officials. If we encountered any of those they would probably continue on without bothering us. However, that kind of traffic is valuable and bandits are also prevalent on the highways. The pirates who patrol these high traffic roads wouldn't let us pass in peace. The route we took to Commerce only puts us on the freeway for a few tense miles. Fortune smiles and we don't encounter a single vehicle. I relax a little as we take the exit for the Commerce Outlets.

"Where to first?" Aunty asks, sounding as relieved as I feel.

"The Gap!" I announce with a smile.

Ok. I'll admit it. I'm excited to be here.

Chapter Three

Spiders, Zombies, and Rapists Oh My!

Aunty was right. Being out of the house and out of Toccoa for the day is rejuvenating. The reinforced, guarded fences around our mile-wide compound are there to keep us safe. But the freedom I feel here makes home feel like a prison in comparison. Yes, our fortress keeps the monsters out; but it also keeps us trapped in our made-up world. Stepping out of the car and into real life, I take a deep breath of cold air. Is it just my imagination or does the air smell cleaner and fresher here? Healthy fear and excitement are weaving their way through my limbs, sending shivers through my muscles. I can't remember the last time I felt this alive!

My bubbling energy is in stark contrast to the eeriness of the empty stores. The shopping mall stands like a decaying monument to America's wealthy past. Not that long ago, healthy men and women filled these parking spaces on a daily basis to come and add to their collections of superfluous belongings. Today, the parking lot is devoid of life and those crowds are long forgotten. Only a few old cars remain as evidence—rusting islands on the sea of gray concrete. We are completely alone. We have the whole world to ourselves.

I think Aunty and I are the only women to leave the compound in the last year. A lot of our men come and go through the fence every day to hunt or fish. Another group leaves to maintain the city's power and water, not just for our people but also for the rest of Toccoa—which is the only reason we are still living somewhat safely "out in the open." Most of the Living that are left on earth are in hiding now.

Toccoa is a small town, overlooked by the rest of the decaying world. We've found unexplainable protection and ambivalence in her quiet streets. Our men are healthy and able to do things that the infected can't. The zombies in Toccoa need us, so they put up with us. It's that simple. Our men put their lives on the line—working in close contact with the infected—to provide us the normalcy we still have. Running water, a refrigerator, a furnace in the winter.

But none of the guys in our compound would care to spend the day here. I get this picture in my head of the macho guys from the U.R. going through the mall looking for ladies shoes and bras. The comical scenario makes me snort out loud, drawing an inquisitive glance from Aunty.

Our men are busy doing manly things, leaving the cooking and homemaking to the women. They are all more than a little chauvinistic. Except for Tim. He's probably studying something he'll never need to know and helping his dad inventory the medical supplies. I wouldn't be surprised if he knew how to sew.

I shake my head to clear away unwanted thoughts of Tim Markowitz. The best thing about being out of Toccoa for the day? No possibility of seeing Tim. Anyway, our men don't shop and our people need clothes as much as they need fresh meat and water. Aunty and I are doing the community a service. We'll bring back as many clothes as we can for the clothing bank at the U.R. Our bravery means getting to pick out some nice things just for ourselves.

Aunty opens the trunk hatch and hands me a bundle of empty bags, some recycled plastic shopping bags and some fabric duffle bags. I situate a few on each arm and with a "here goes nothing" glance at each other, we walk cautiously towards The Gap. A cold breeze blows up my sleeves and I cross my arms tight against my chest. Aunty notices that I'm cold and we pick up our pace, speed walking towards the store.

Aunty parked the SUV a few rows away from the store, just a short walk or run depending on what we encounter. The parking lot is surrounded on all sides by stores. The mall is a big rectangle with the parking lot on the inside of the box. Three sides of the mall are connected to each other, a long C shaped row of potential goodies. The fourth partition of stores is shorter and parallel to the middle of the C with access to the highway on either side—the only way in or out of the parking lot. If we stay on the C shaped side, we are able to see if anyone enters the secluded lot.

My memories of when the world was right are few and far between, but one thing I do remember is this outlet mall in all its glory. My mom brought me here to do my school clothes shopping a few days before I started the first grade. We bounced from store to store and she bought me almost everything that made me smile. I remember eating lunch, just the two of us, and sharing a milkshake. It hurts to recall her face and her smile and our happy life. That ache in my heart that comes so rarely these days flares up in full strength. I still miss her so much. My time-traveling nostalgia adds to the haunted loneliness of the mall.

Aunty, always watching, always able to decipher my private feelings, notices my sudden decline into depression as we stop just outside of The Gap.

"I'm sorry, Ivy. I just thought we could still have a nice time together. I had hoped once you got here you'd enjoy being out. I suppose I shouldn't have forced you to come."

"No, I'm happy I'm here."

Aunty raises her eyebrows in obvious disbelief, her mouth sagging with disappointment.

"I just was remembering my mom," I say with an apologetic tone.

I feel bad for missing my mom. Aunty tries so hard to fulfill that role. I try not to let on when I'm lonely for my parents. I'm afraid it somehow insinuates that I'm unhappy with her, that she's inadequate. She's an amazing aunt, friend *and* fill-in mother. She just isn't my real mother and that isn't her fault.

I don't want to ruin our day before it's even started. I meet Aunty's worried blue eyes and I make my face smile, working hard to push away the sad thoughts. I want to be happy here with her. Today. Right now. I reach for her thin hand and, clasping it tightly, we walk cautiously into the store.

Today's weather is perfect for shopping. There isn't a cloud to be seen in the cold, blue sky, and the sun is reigning overhead—offering its vitamin D filled beams for the needy world below. Those golden rays are our only source of light once inside the store. We have small flashlights with us, but batteries are scarce and for emergencies only. The door to The Gap hangs open on broken hinges behind us. Of the store's two front windows, one is shattered with not a piece of glass left in place. A good amount of light is pouring in—enough to see the color of a shirt and check the size on the tag.

The merchandise closest to the front of the store has been ruined by time and the elements. The floor is littered with garbage and the decaying remains of fashion. Dead leaves, reanimated by the winter breeze, roll gently around the clothing racks. The store's thin industrial carpeting has rotted. The cement floor beneath the gray carpet shows in patches; as though the disease that ate away at humanity ran out of victims and came here to ingest this place as well.

Winding my way through overturned racks and unrecognizable piles of decomposing clothing, I wonder if we'll find anything worth bagging here. Towards the back of the store I'm relieved to find clothes that are still in good condition. Most of them are still hanging on their hangers and folded in neat stacks. My heart beats harder in the unsettling shadows, the sunny front windows too far away to help much back here. I'm really careful with each thing I pick up because I'm sure that whatever I touch will, inevitably, have a giant spider on it. I hate spiders. Zombies are worse; but spiders take a close second on the list of things that freak me out.

Aunty Coe stands watch at the door, fingering the Taser strapped to her wrist. The Gap isn't her style. She watches the parking lot to make sure we are safe and alone here. I find a really cute pair of jeans; so I strip off my ripped ones and kick off my old shoes to try the size eight distressed flares on. We are alone and the whole store is my private changing room. You couldn't pay me to go in the dark changing rooms at the very back of the store. Not even if you had a whole package of Kraft Cheese Singles. Pitch black dark and a breeding ground for all types of carnivorous spiders, the changing rooms are the epitome of my worst nightmares. You may think I'm being a little paranoid on the spider thing; but you are wrong. Spiders are really that horrible.

The damp January cold has fully infiltrated The Gap. I'm freezing and nervous as I stand barelegged and stocking foot in the dark, pulling on the new pants. The jeans fit great and make me feel thin; so I grab another pair in my size. I stuff the old pants I was wearing into my shopping bag and then fill the bag with several more pairs of the cute jeans in other sizes for the girls at home in Toccoa. I squeeze back into my ugly tennis shoes and continue searching The Gap for treasure. Lord willing, by the end of the trip I'll be wearing a whole new outfit, shoes and coat with a lot more clothes going home with us as well. It will be fun to walk into the U.R. on Sunday feeling pretty for a change.

We move from store to store, taking turns keeping watch. After a store or two, we walk our bags to the car and dump them in the back. Rather, I would dump them if it was up to me. Since I'm with God's neatness police, we fold them all in nice organized piles in the back of the car. An Ivy pile, an Aunty pile and several piles of clothes for everyone else. I'm surprised she doesn't make us color coordinate the piles. Re-situating our once again empty bags, we move the car further down the strip and head to a new store.

Some of the stores have been picked over and are not worth bothering with. The jewelry stores look like they've been through a bombing. The glass counters are smashed to pieces, littering the floor like sparkling diamonds. Any real gems that the store had are long gone. Six years ago, when a couple million people disappeared from the face of the earth in a silent instant, all hell broke loose. People did what you'd expect: they panicked. Panicked and rioted and looted in fear-filed desperation to survive.

The jewelry stores were turned over in the search for tradable currency. The sporting goods stores were next, for survival gear and weapons. You can't really blame humanity. We've been programmed with an innate will to survive. It is human nature to care for ourselves and our loved ones at any cost. Fathers became murderers. Children became thieves. The world turned upside-down and survival was all anyone could think about.

That was before we knew about the disease. Though survival is still a common desire, pleasure has become priority one for most people. They know they are dying now.

It's inevitable.

If death is right around the corner, and you can't do anything to stop it, might as well live it up. Enjoy as much pleasure as possible in the time you have left. I guess I can understand why they are the way they are.

As we pass a recessed area of the outdoor mall, I notice the three stores tucked back into one of the corners of the big C shaped strip. One of them is a toy store. I've long outgrown toys and games but I can't help thinking of our new little friend.

"Should we grab some toys for Thomas?"

"Well—I guess we could." Aunty is cautious and the hesitation in her voice tells me she isn't sold on the idea. Staring into the corner's dirty gray shadows, she murmurs, "Oh Betty."

Her perfected mask of pleasantness slips, and her face morphs into someone I don't recognize. A heavy sadness has puckered her lips, and her brow is furrowed and wrinkled. I don't know why this place has made her think of Aunty Betty. As I study her expression, suddenly ragged with emotion, I can't help but notice how much she has aged lately. I hate how frail and small she looks. We were having such a fun time together; it figures I'd ruin it.

The loss of her sister is one of the few heartaches that she doesn't cover up with a good attitude and her normal game face. Aunty Betty has been missing, probably dead, for years now. She disappeared without a trace one sunny spring day only a few weeks after I came to live with them. That was before the fences were built. Aunty Betty and Aunty Coe were very close. Sometimes I think that I've filled that hole in Aunty's heart; but I know I can't replace her lifelong best friend, her big sister. Nor would I want to.

"What is it Aunty?" I ask in a reverent whisper as she stares into the darkened stores.

"We used to shop here together," Aunty's voice is garbled and distant and it makes me glance nervously over my shoulder. "We were vigilant, watching each other's backs and carefully going through the stores. There were still some people in Commerce then; before everyone got so sick. It was safer then. We didn't worry too much about the other people scavenging. You were home with a babysitter and I thought it would be nice to bring you some toys. You were so sad and still missing your mom so much. You've always been a serious girl."

Her eyes are soft and tender and she speaks with so much love in her voice that I can't help but reach out and hug her. She feels fragile in my arms as I cling to her. I loosen my grip, afraid I'm being too rough with her. She kisses my cheek and a tear slips down her own as she continues with her story.

"I wanted to cheer you up, and I practically ran into the toy store when I saw it there. Betty was talking to someone further down the strip and I didn't wait for her to stand watch at the door. I figured I'd only be a second. Just grab a toy or two and maybe some art supplies for my creative Ivy." Her voice gets distant again as she dredges her memories, reliving something I don't think I want to hear. "I wandered into the second row of toys. I remember tripping over something on the floor; and the fear I felt when I realized it was a body. I fell forward and felt someone grab my legs and climb on top of me." She pauses, and then stares into my eyes as she admits, "I've never been so terrified."

I want her to stop telling this story. I regret mentioning the toy store. I feel cold and nervous and too alone in this big abandoned place. It is with fear and unwanted responsibility that I realize that I am the stronger one between us. If anything happens to us out here, it will be up to me to get us out of it. Aunty is older than I thought. Aunty is more breakable today—how did this happen? When did she go from my protector to this gentle old lady? I think we should call it a day and go back home.

Aunty doesn't notice the affect her story is having on my nerves and she continues, "I tried to call out for Betty but he had his filthy hand over my mouth."

I can see disgust and loathing on her face for this man of the past. Her mouth screws up like she can still taste his dirty hand.

"Thank the Lord, Betty saw me disappear into the toy store. She was almost through the door when she watched me fall behind the row and not get back up. She was always wise, a quick thinker. Instead of running in to help me, she found a young man in the parking lot to help her and they came in together. The helpful dear had a gun and he shot it over his head as he came barreling through the door.

"The man on top of me cursed at me and hit me." She holds a hand to her cheek over the ancient sting and leaves it there as she continues, "He jumped up and ran into the shadows at the back of the store. They pulled me outside into the sun and checked me over; then the man who helped us went back in to find my attacker. He searched the whole store but didn't find him. We could only assume the horrible man had somehow slipped out the back service door of the store. It was," she pauses and then finishes the thought, "traumatic."

"I'm so sorry Aunty. I didn't mean to make you sad. I forgot you and Aunty Betty used to come here, too."

She waves at hand at me as if to say, 'It's nothing, no big deal.'

"I think I wouldn't have cared if I ever had anything new again."

We both know that's true. I'm only here because she insisted. I'd be wearing old hobo clothes with everyone else if it weren't for her proprieties.

"Life always goes on Ivy. You'll learn that. The hard times come and make you think you can't possibly move forward, but then you do."

She stares at me with wisdom and knowledge in her eyes and instead of feeling encouraged, I feel afraid. I don't want any more "hard times" to come. My life is already hard enough.

"Let's just get what we need from the rest of the stores and go home," I recant my toy store idea, no longer enjoying our adventure.

I'm nervous. I keep twisting my head to look all around us, feeling like her story will conjure up the scary man from the past.

In a quick change of mood, Aunty brightens. "We'll have to go fast and use our flashlights. Let me pull the car right up front, just in case. I let that go years ago, and I won't let it haunt me again. Thomas needs a toy or two just as much as my sweet Ivy did when she was his age."

She smiles a mischievous, devil-may-care smile at me. Her adventuresome side has beaten her cautious old-lady side. We are going in the toy store.

Chapter Four

A Killer Pair of Pumps

As Aunty pulls the car close to the store's entrance, her words are still ringing in my ears. I know what the "just in case" is. We won't find creepy bums and rapists in the store today. Something worse could be haunting the once happy aisles of the Toys R Us outlet.

The toy store's doors and windows are still intact and thick with dirt. The sun sends little light through the film. I wonder how long it has been since anyone has gone in there. Maybe Aunty and her heroic entourage were the last ones to go through these doors.

While Aunty moves the car up onto the sidewalk, right in front of the store, I try to swallow the foreboding lump in my throat and think ahead about what Thomas would like. He's been with the community for about a month now. He is pretty adorable; a funny, sweet twelve year old boy that one of the missionaries brought to us.

We rarely add to our number these days. The missionaries bring fewer and fewer converts in each time they come home. Thomas was the last to join us. He is outgoing and very bright. He's not at all athletic; so I'll look for fun games and toys, not balls or sports gear. I've gotten to know him because he stayed with us at the Inn for his first few days in Toccoa. Jose and Ellen, a young couple from the other side of the compound, 'adopted' Thomas an hour after they met him. They are the perfect parents for him; and, even if I didn't know them at all, just being members of the community would be enough qualification for me to like them.

"Ready?" Aunty asks with an overly optimistic smile as she pulls the small powerful flashlight out of her pocket. "We will only take two minutes of the batteries. Grab what you can, don't go more than one row away from me, and don't talk. Stay in the front part of the store. Ears open, okay?" She holds her Taser tight in her other hand.

"Sure. Okay. Let's go," I say not feeling at all 'sure.'

I push on the door and it seems to be locked. Am I disappointed, or relieved? Should we take it as a sign and move on to safer stores? I give it one more push to make sure, and it budges half an inch. I look to Aunty for what to do next. It's obvious this door is going to make a good amount of noise. On the other hand, no one has been in here for a long time. Zombies shouldn't be a concern. Though, there is that back door from Aunty's story; so—as much as I want to—we can't rule them out. Aunty nods for me to go ahead and we push together.

The door barely moves at first, grating and whining as we push, then it abruptly swings open with an announcing screech. The store has sat still and untouched for so long that it looks like an evil witch's trap in a storybook land. Instead of gingerbread and candy, toys line the walls and shelves to lure in foolish children. Witches don't eat children. Witches aren't real. Zombies are real. Zombies do eat children. My knees shake and my neck aches with tension.

Cobwebs hang from the ceiling in long diagonal strands. I hate cobwebs. I know they are made from dust and not spiders, but they feel spidery none the less. When I see large, lace-like webs covering the toy boxes in the cloudy display windows, my stomach lunges violently towards my hammering heart. I can't focus. I brush at my face and shoulders, sweeping away imaginary creepy-crawlers, lost in spider paranoia. Aunty makes a soft noise with her throat to regain my attention. She gives me a hard "pull yourself together" stare. I try to find my courage and focus on the reason we are here.

We move quick and quiet like shadows though the displays of toys at the front of the store, always keeping each other in sight. After a thorough inspection for arachnids, I grab some boxes from a display with science experiments for kids. I hope they aren't too childish. Next, I pick up a game with a cup and Ping-Pong ball that looks geared towards Thomas' age. I consider some multiple player board games, but none of them look fun to me. And I'm pretty sure I'd end up being the one who'd have to play them with him.

As I pull out a box that claims to have the best transforming dinosaur toy ever, several boxes that were tucked in around it topple against me and crash to the floor. I jump and shake myself, brushing at my hair and shoulders—just in case. In a normal situation you wouldn't have even called it a "loud noise;" but here, in the tense stillness, it resonates around the store. I look up in panic and see Aunty looking at me with exhausted reproof on her face. She can lecture without even using words. I shrug my apology and she nods for me to follow her as she heads for the door. She has her arms full with a skateboard and a guitar.

Score!

He is going to be so thrilled. We don't have many kids in the community right now. He's been playing with Lois, the five year old girl who lives next door to his new family. Thomas is a great kid. Lots of potential; if only there was enough time left for him to have a future. These toys will give him something fun to fill his time. I know his new parents had a few things for him at Christmas, but it was mostly homemade or used. They definitely didn't brave an abandoned toy store when they went Christmas shopping.

A lot of people disagree with Aunty and I making this trip. They don't feel it is worth the risk. What can I say? Aunty and I are two strong, brave, awesome women. We leave the toy store without incident and load the toys in the back of the car. Today has been a huge success.

*****

We've saved my favorite store for last. It also happens to be the last store on the strip. Rue 21—Teenage Girl Heaven. I love everything about it. It probably has just as many cobwebs and creepers as the toy store, but the afternoon sun has filled it with welcoming light and it seems cheery and almost untouched. I could almost pretend it was just a normal store.

One little thing in my favor is that the beginning of the end happened to be in January; six years ago. January is the perfect time of the year for shopping. All of the winter clothes are on the clearance racks and the new spring line is on the regular racks. If the world had ended in June, for example, there would only be shorts, tank tops and bikinis in the stores. I don't think I've worn a swimsuit since I was nine, let alone a bikini. So, there you go Aunty, I'm counting my blessings.

Aunty has, once again, taken her place at the front door. She has no interest in this last stop, having done all of her shopping in classier stores. I vow to still like fun clothes if I make it to old age. I stuff my bag full of cute shirts and sweaters, silly T-shirts with funny slogans, and comfy socks and yoga pants for sleeping in. I laugh out loud when I find a shirt that says "Zombies Just Want Hugs" with a little mob of cartoon zombies, arms outstretched in Frankenstein fashion. I smirk and grab one in Aunty's size.

Running this first load out to the car, I come back for another round. I keep expecting Aunty to be impatient with my frivolous choices and how long I'm spending in here, but she just seems happy that I'm relaxing and enjoying myself. Being a teenager and all. I pick out some cute necklaces and put them all on to bring them home. One of them even has a cross on it. I grab an identical cross necklace for my friend Harmony. Matching necklaces is kind of dorky, but we're dorks. She'll like it.

Then I spot the cutest, most impractical shoes ever. Pink suede wedges with stripes of black satin and a black satin strap with a round silver buckle on the ankle. I don't own anything that matches them and they are one hundred percent unnecessary—I must have them. Kicking off the brand new pink Adidas running shoes that I just took from the Adidas store, I try on the pink heels and stare at myself in the spotty mirror.

I am short and somewhat average; not Skinny-Minnie, but not chubby either. My long, curly brown hair is usually knotted in a bun on my head, but today I left it down. I'm wearing all new clothes and my new ruffled blue shirt doesn't match the hip, pink shoes. I can't think of anything I own that would go with them, but they make me look taller. Studying myself in the mirror, I feel pretty and confident. Maybe even kinda hot. Too bad the only person who's interested is Tim Markowitz. The glum feeling—that sometimes overtakes me when I think about my future among the Living—threatens to steal my pink shoe cheeriness.

A huge crash in the back of the store makes my stomach lurch and my heart fly into a panic. I run for the door shooting frantic glances over my shoulder. I can't help but think of the story Aunty just told me; and, as I look behind me, I am just sure I saw someone moving in the shadows. I flee out of the door that Aunty Coe is holding open for me. We jog to the car—Aunty facing forward, scanning the parking lot, and me jogging backwards to make sure no one is coming after us. I stumble several times in the ridiculous pink high heels. We reach the car and still no one has come out of the store.

"Clear!" Aunty barks over her shoulder at me.

"Clear!" I yell back at her.

"You forgot to lock the car, Ivy!" Her voice is shrill and full of fear.

Shoot!

I forgot to re-lock when I carried out my first load of Rue 21 finds. We jump in and quickly hit the door lock.

Before I can even hope that we're safe, I smell him. His nauseating odor reaches my nostrils just a second before he has his arm around my neck. It's the smell of rotting flesh and body odor. The two smells, though equally gross, are in opposition to each other—the smell of death mixed with the smell of activity and life. That's what a zombie is, polar-opposites coexisting. Physically alive, but spiritually dead. And cursed. He's behind my seat and his grip is an iron band across my neck.

I scream and thrash, trying to pull away from him; but he's strong, and he has all the advantage. I'm strong too, and harder to hold onto than he was expecting. I thrash and scream and he has to fight to keep me in his grasp. Something sharp pinches my neck and scrapes across my skin. I cry out in pain and pull hard to the right, pinning his arm against the door. The distraction works in our favor and, within seconds, Aunty has her Taser to his shoulder. I hear the charge build as she presses the trigger.

A standard Taser is fired from a distance. Our devices have been modified for close proximity. They can drop an attacker by pressing the electrically charged prongs directly into the skin. Almost like a short, electrically charged cattle prod. I feel a small tingle of electricity run through me, but my attacker's arms slacken as the full current paralyzes him. One shock won't slow him down for long; but I hear Aunty press the trigger several more times, rendering him limp and convulsing against the back of my seat. He's still conscious and the paralyzing effect of the shocks will only last about a minute. I'm confused and terrified when Aunty starts the car and guns it towards the highway with the reeking man still behind my seat.

"What are you doing?" I scream. "We have to get him out of here! Stop the car!"

My voice is high-pitched and weak; I can't seem to catch my breath. I feel like his arms are still around my neck, strangling me. Is this called hyperventilating? I want to fill my lungs, but they seem to be working against me! I pant, pulling tiny scraps of air into my desperate lungs. My eyes are starting to blur!

"It's a trap." Aunty's voice is flat and calm. "There are at least two of them, Ivy."

Just as unexpected as her sudden burst of speed had been, she stomps the brake; throwing me forward into the dash board. My head hits the windshield and my elbows rake against the vents on top of the dash. I slump back, dazed.

"Sorry," she says as she thrusts the SUV into park and realizes too late that she could've warned me.

This last jolt scared the wind back into me. My lungs are burning, but they are functioning again. I blink little floating lights out of my returning vision. We've only gone about a quarter of a mile, just to where the parking lot meets the highway, but Aunty is hoping it's enough distance between us and whoever was helping our attacker. She is already out of the car and coming around to the passenger-side back door.

Shaking myself free of the shock I feel—both from the predicament we are in and the hard knock I took against the windshield—I climb into the back seat to push the man out as she pulls from the other side. The zombie is slumped against the back of my seat. He is wearing a silver suit and a green, plastic Oscar the Grouch mask. His greasy black hair hangs out in dirty strands from under his mask. Before we dare to touch him, Aunty gives him one more long burst from her Taser. As we struggle to tug the moaning, convulsing monster from the tall SUV, his Oscar the Grouch mask slides to one side revealing his deformities.

His ear is rotten with almost no flesh left. His exposed cheek is covered in strange lumps of red skin and yellow sores. Near his lips there is a gaping hole, revealing what's left of his stained brown teeth. I shudder at the sight of him. He's one of the worst I've seen and this is the closest I've been to one of them for years. His odor is revolting.

Me pushing and Aunty pulling, we dump the sick man on his head in the middle of the road. Jumping back in the passenger side back door, I check the back hatch area to be sure no one else is hiding in our car. I see only our new clothes; the once neat piles toppled over from Aunty's race car driving. I climb up front and, in the rearview mirror on the passenger side, I see Aunty still bending over the man in the street.

What is she doing!

I open my door to see if she needs me; but she is finally making her way back around to her door. A second later, she climbs into the car and I lock the doors even before she slams hers shut. She hits the lock button again for good measure, and then we peel out. I don't think Aunty meant to make so much noise as she hit the gas pedal too hard, spinning the tires before they found purchase, lunging us forward. I feel whiplashed in every sense of the word. I struggle with just trying to breathe. To focus. To grasp what just happened. My muscles are still tense with adrenaline and I'm shaking.

We are okay, I try to convince myself.

Chapter Five

The Decaying Monster From Sesame Street

Aunty is glancing back and forth from road to rearview mirror; so I turn in my seat to stare out the back window. So far, no one is following us. It would be easy to see them on this clear day. I realize Aunty is talking and I have been nodding. Like my subconscious was listening and responding to her without me realizing it. All of my senses are on overdrive—each sense working to take in every detail of my surroundings without my cognitive intentional effort. It's the clarity of adrenaline that I've only read about in books and it feels surreal.

"...they were working together. One of them made the noise and the other one waited for us to run to the car. It was all planned."

She is processing each detail out loud. She glances sideways at me while she pushes the car to top speeds. She wants my opinion, my input. I am lost in my fear and I can hardly hear her.

"They were trying to take you," she says with quiet surety.

Her matter-of-fact statement grips me, and I think I might throw up. When I look at her again, I can tell she is fighting back tears. I know from the look on her face that she is trying to make a decision. Her lips are clamped tight between her teeth, and when she glances over at me, I can see it in her watery blue eyes. She is trying to decide whether or not to tell me something.

I've lived with her for over four years now, and I know her face well. I've learned all of her facial expressions. I know when she is faking to be polite. I know when she is irritated behind a fake smile. I know when she is angry and silently begging the Lord for help to hold her tongue. I have her memorized.

The face she wears now usually irritates me because I know she's hiding something from me. Normally, I would persist in pestering it out of her. Right now though, that face with its set jaw and pursed lips just scares the crap out of me. I don't know if I want to know. I'm tempted to plug my ears and close my eyes like the defiant little girl who came to live with Aunty at age twelve. Mad at mom and dad for abandoning her.

They say trauma at a young age keeps you from maturing. If that's true,

I'm probably operating with the emotions of a fifth grader because I've been through a lot of trauma in the last six years. I look out of my window to avoid looking at Aunty's face that is full of some terrible news. Aunty reaches out and grabs for my hand. She's preparing me, supporting me for something. She has something in her hand that rests on top of mine. She's squeezing me so tightly that whatever she's holding starts to dig into my skin. I wince; and, as she relaxes her hand and pulls away from me, the "something" stays stuck on the top of my hand.

It's a photograph.

Of me.

"What is this?" I ask, a cloud of fireworks threatening the edges of my vision again. "Where did you get this?"

"It's an old Polaroid Camera photo."

"What's a Polaroid Camera?"

"It's a camera that prints the photo right out of the bottom of the camera after you take the picture. It's pretty old-fashioned. I haven't seen one in years."

"It's a picture of me," I say with meek confusion.

I look closely at the picture and another panic attack hits.

Hyperventilating!

Can't breathe!

Can't think!

God help me!

In the photo, I'm standing on the porch of the Inn. Recently. Maybe this week even. I just wore that shirt a few days ago. This picture is from the zombie? This is why she didn't get straight into the car!

"But—but!" I'm stammering. "You found this picture? Where? The zombie? Why—how could he—It's not—?"

"Calm down, Ivy. We have to think. We have to keep our heads."

But my head is below water. I'm drowning in panic.

"And WHY?" I shriek. "They were actually after me? Why me? How did they know we would be there? Are they from Toccoa? Do they know someone in our community? Did somebody we know do this? Is that even possible?" I'm at champagne-glass-shattering decibels now.

"Ivy," Aunty tries to bring me under control again, but her calm voice finally breaks, betraying her true emotional state. "I don't know what I would've done honey."

I am sweating. It's running down my neck. I wipe away the moisture with my hand and realize that it's not sweat. I'm bleeding. I just stare at the blood on the back of my hand, turning my hand back and forth, hypnotized by the sight of it. The car is suddenly thumping on the gravel off on the side of the road. Aunty gasps and pulls hard to correct us and put us back on the paved highway.

"You're bleeding?" she asks, horrified. "I'm pulling over!"

"No! Don't! I'm fine. He just scratched me; it's nothing." I think it was probably all the ridiculous necklaces that I'm wearing, but I don't admit that. "It doesn't hurt; I didn't even know I was bleeding. I just felt it drip and I—if you stop, they might catch us!"

I realize how slow she's going, trying to lean over and look at me while driving.

"Aunty, go! Go faster! I'm fine!"

She pushes the SUV back up to 80 mph and stares straight ahead.

As we take the exit onto the safer back roads, we are both in shock, sick with fear, near tears—not sure what to do next. I'm all that she has left in the way of real family. She's all that I have left. I've already lost my parents, what would I do without her?

I glance behind, and still no one is following us. The problem solver in me begins to surface out of the panic, and I start to process the situation with clarity. Maybe because seeing her fear-filled, teary eyes brings out the selfless, brave side of me. I feel my rational self-start to take control again. I push the terror down and turn on the part of me that I like the best: calm, cool, collected Ivy. Not some silly, fashion obsessed 16 year old. I can handle whatever life throws at me. I'm smart. Capable. I can do this.

Confidence sweeps over me in a palpable wave of strength. It's more decision than reaction. It's an instinct that has helped me keep my sanity since the world turned upside down. Maybe I'm taking too much personal credit for it; maybe it's a gift. Whatever the case, I find myself filled with images and fresh insights. Like my brain suddenly took a gasping breath after going too long without air. My breathing is calm again, and my heart is pounding a normal tempo. I was all adrenaline and feelings, but now I'm thinking.

"Did you see what he was wearing?" The images my brain cataloged without me even realizing are clear, and I want to think about them out loud to make sense of them. "I think he was a scientist!"

He was dressed in a metallic silver, one-piece body suit with the symbol for man, a circle with an arrow pointing up to the right, on both arms. That particular body suit is only worn by Pravda scientists; the worldwide organization of scientists and doctors who are working to solve the problem of the disease. They are zombies trying to fix zombies; the blind leading the blind. Their body suits remind me of a diver in a wetsuit from Sea World. My dad took me there when I was five to see the big whale, Shamu.

My attacker's shimmery silver get-up completely covered him; except for his hands, feet and face. Of course shoes covered his feet and he was wearing that weird Oscar the Grouch mask—a strange choice of mask for a scientist. He had on a pair of their special satiny black gloves. Who knows how many of the fingers inside were his, if any. The gloves are capable of simulating up to ten bionic fingers.

Aunty starts to recall her observations as well and we work to figure out what just happened. To put the scary experience into the context of a puzzle makes it manageable. Gives us back some control over it.

"By the smell of him, I'd guess just working for Pravda," Aunty says. "Scientists bathe and wear colognes to cover the smell of the disease. And the scientists use every possible means to fight their own disease. That man was very advanced; he hasn't had the luxury of medical treatments. It's the addicts who work for Pravda and get paid in drugs that look and smell like that. He was just a hired thug."

Work in exchange for the drug that the Pravda Corporation got them all hooked on. Their "miracle" drug, Lucimer, was supposed to cure the disease.

Never mind that their "miracle" had the side effect of being more addictive than heroine. The relief that it gave at first still has Pravda insisting that prolonged doses may help with the symptoms of the disease.

"Besides, he wasn't armed and he wasn't quick," she continues. "They may have put together a decent plan to capture you; but if this old lady could take them out, then they weren't that bright. They had the advantage of surprise." Still thinking out loud, she comes up with an even scarier realization, "No weapon. He was supposed to take you alive."

Take me where? Her assessments sound reasonable and likely. I pull my feet up on the seat and press my knees to my chest. I feel small and cold. We've laid out the pieces of the jigsaw puzzle; but instead of giving me control, it has only added to the day's terrors. Pravda knows me, and they specifically want me. Why?

"Maybe he stole the clothes. Maybe he had nothing to do with Pravda," Aunty says quietly. She is terrified too. "His shoes didn't look right. They weren't biotech."

I nod. I want her to be right. I know it's wishful thinking, but I need that hope right now. The zombies are lawless, every man for himself. Maybe he did steal the suit. It's hard to know anything for sure.

"Speaking of shoes, what are you wearing, Ivy?"

I blush red; embarrassed and shamefully aware that I left my brand new, perfectly fitting, Adidas running shoes on the floor of Rue 21. I'm going home in scuffed pink platforms.

Chapter Six

As If Mondays Weren't Bad Enough Already

We ride the rest of the way home lost in our own thoughts. Aunty will have the unpleasant job of telling the Elders what happened. We'll have to tell them. It's not safe for others to attempt the trip now. Aunty said that the Elders had been against our "outing" to begin with. She'd insisted that we had safely done it several times over the years. After a long meeting that I wasn't invited to, the Elders gave in and let her have her way. Aunty carries herself with so much authority that I don't know anyone who isn't a little intimidated by her.

We didn't used to need permission for outings, but things have been getting worse. I guess the world is catching up with us. A few months ago, some of our men left the community to hunt and didn't come back. And there have been other unexplainable disappearances. People who've disappeared out of thin air—like my Aunty Betty. We thought the fence would keep us safe, but people still go missing. All of the fear and unrest moved the community to elect a Board of Elders. Aunty and I don't resent the Elders; it is out of kindness and concern for our safety that they limit us. It's less freedom though, and that's a little hard to get used to.

As the disease continues unchecked, eating away at the nerves and flesh of the infected, the morale of humanity degrades with it. I was twelve years old when the curse first hit, but I still remember those days with clarity. At first mankind didn't even know they had contracted it. It can live in a person for months before manifesting. Even when it started to present itself, it was worse in some people than others. So in the beginning, the world didn't realize that *every* living person had it.

A wave of panic swept humanity for the second time that year. The first wave of worldwide panic had been a tsunami of loss in the aftermath of the Second Coming. The church and the world's children had disappeared in an instant; and that earth shattering evacuation had already irrevocably changed the world. Many of my friends and some of my relatives—both of my grandparents—had been part of the Rapture. It felt like half of my reality had evaporated. We were left with no bodies, just questions and fear.

The people left behind were still trying to figure out where their loved ones had gone when the plague hit. There was rioting all over the world. The United States thought the disease was terrorism in the form of biological warfare and the possibility of another World War loomed over the planet.

Scientists worked day and night in a frenzied attempt to find a cure. Leprasimilis got its name when they found that it resembled Hanson's Disease, more commonly known as Leprosy. But none of the cures that had worked on Hanson's Disease had any effect on this new worldwide bane. Then the scientists had their breakthrough, and the drug Lucimer was introduced globally. The first dose of Lucimer had to be administered as a shot, an injection close to the bone—the back of the hand or the forehead.

Anyone who had symptoms of LS was required by law to have the shot, despite its limited testing. About three days after receiving the shot, the skin around the injection turned black and stayed that way. The black spot became a validity test of whether or not you had been inoculated. Anyone who tested positive but refused the injection was either given the injection by force or killed. Then the inoculation became law, symptoms or no symptoms. Every citizen of the U.S. had to have the shot.

Kids in every public school in the nation were given the shot without warning and without their parent's permission. It happened first thing in the morning, on a Monday, about a week after the new law. It was a coordinated strike, the teams of doctors and military men entered every school in the nation at the same time on the same day. Even the teachers didn't know it was coming. Students were locked inside their classrooms and systematically inoculated.

Armed military personnel accompanied Pravda's doctors into each classroom. With teachers and students held at gunpoint, Pravda administered the shot to everyone in the class who hadn't already gotten it. Kindergartners were held down for the painful shot, without the comfort of a parent by their side, under the terrifying gaze of camouflaged gunmen. Older students rebelled and tried to run. The school hallways were painted crimson with the blood of children. The media called it Red Monday. It was an unforgettable, despicable day in history.

I wasn't at school on Red Monday. My parents were paranoid people; they didn't want something that the government was forcing on them. None of us had any symptoms. They had kept me home that day to help them pack our house. We didn't even know what was happening at the school, only a mile from our house. No one knew until the students came home traumatized and weeping as they got off at their bus stops.

Through my bedroom window I watched my best friend, Kelly, get off the bus at our stop. She was sobbing and stumbling up the street to her house right next to mine. I tried to run out to her, but my parents wouldn't let me go outside. We were moving, but they wouldn't tell me where. I knew I'd never see Kelly again, and I hated my parents for that. When you're a kid, you don't realize when your hate is misplaced. It wasn't my parents' fault that the whole world had gone to crap.

That same evening, Aunty Coe showed up—unannounced—at our house. She hadn't had the shot either; and she told mom and dad that we shouldn't get it. She tried to tell them about God—about how all of this was in her Bible. My grandma, Aunty Coe's sister, had disappeared with the rest of the believers. Aunty said that grandma had been right.

I remember how scared my parents were that day. I don't know if they heard much of what Aunty said. Mom kept standing up from the couch to look out of the window while Aunty pleaded with them to listen. She invited all of us to come live with her in Toccoa. Dad said he already had a safe place stocked and ready for us. They asked Aunty to take me for a week or so while they got everything settled at the new place. They said they'd come get me. I had only been around Aunty Coe a few times in my life, and I knew she didn't like kids. I cried and begged my mom not to send me with her.

Mom slapped me.

I was twelve. I hadn't been spanked in years, and I had never been slapped. My parents had always spoiled me. I was born when they were older, and they doted on me. They adored me. I remember feeling numb—shocked and hurt—as Aunty Coe shut me into the back seat of her little, blue car.

I know that I'm Alive today because of a plan that I couldn't see or understand. I know that hard day was necessary. But every time I think of that day, the pain of that memory still rips at my heart with claws that haven't dulled a bit in four years. The last moments I had with my parents were full of anger and hate. They were mad at me and too nervous to even hug me goodbye. They never came like they said they would. I never saw them again.

I blink tears out of my eyes as I stare out the window. The fields and forests that fly by have lost their enchantments. Everything just looks dead. The barrenness of winter has chilled my heart, and I know that there is no hope left for this broken world.

Aunty pushes the car as fast as possible back to Toccoa. She keeps patting my hand and glancing back and forth between me and the bendy back roads. She probably thinks my wet cheeks are because of today; but really, my tears are for the past. For my parents. For my friend Kelly. For the wretchedness of existence in general.

The disease has ruined the world and everything in it—my life in particular—and I don't even have it. Well, technically I do have LS, but not the way the rest of the world does. For us, the Living, it's like a cold sore. You know how once you contract a cold sore it's always in your blood, but it only shows up when you are sick or too rundown? Like, your body is fighting it all the time without you knowing it? If you don't take care of your body, the virus pops up on your face and yells "Herpes!" to everyone who sees it.

The disease is that way for the Living. Our new Life in the Spirit fights the disease without us even knowing it. But if we slack off, for instance—not staying in the Word or letting anger, jealousy and pride live unchecked in our hearts, even something as innocuous as skipping church too much—our strength in the Spirit gets weak, and the symptoms will start to break out again.

In the beginning, when we were all just learning how to walk in this new Life, many of us had the symptoms right along with the rest of the world. As time went on though, we realized we weren't getting worse like everyone else. Those of us who knew the Truth were getting better. That's when the scientists first started experimenting on the Living.

At first, they assumed that we were immune. But when they ran the tests, the same disease was found in our blood too. Many of the Living have been kidnapped and tested and dissected by Pravda, but science is no closer to the cure. And they wouldn't find it if they searched for a hundred years. At least not through medical testing.

Conspiracy theorists think that we are hiding the cure to keep it for ourselves. Because we are well, we are envied and hated; and, of course, not believed. We have tried to share the Cure with them. Early on we told anyone who would listen that it was Him. He *is* the Cure but they won't hear it, won't believe.

When LS first hit, the Living lived side by side with the lost. They tried to tell anyone who would listen. They shared their faith and the Cure, just like Aunty did with my parents. But, when Lucimer came out, the Living had to go underground. They couldn't be part of society without being captured and forced to take the shot or die. I was young and I didn't believe yet. But Aunty and the others knew what the shot was and knew it was imperative that the Living not take it, under any circumstances.

Pravda was sure that the shot would cure the disease; and, at first, it brought about a massive reduction of symptoms. The world rejoiced over the successful eradication of LS. Then, weeks later, the symptoms suddenly came back, redoubled and even tripled, in anyone who had gotten the shot. Which was most everyone on the planet except for the Living.

From then on, everyone thought we were healthier because we *hadn't* taken the shot. The law was revoked, Lucimer was no longer mandatory. But, too little too late. Almost everyone had taken it, or died resisting it. It meant that the Living could come out of hiding. But, they still wouldn't listen to us. After all, we were found to have the same disease in our blood. They thought maybe if they hadn't taken the shot they'd be just as healthy as we were. They refused to see Truth.

The scientists continue to run secret tests on their captives. The government, who supposedly still cares for our interests as equal citizens, does nothing to protect us from Pravda. And for obvious reasons. The government is entirely populated with zombies, as desperate for the cure as anyone else.

We aren't sure how much longer we'll be safe living out in the open. People go missing and the government looks the other way. We are wise enough to know what would happen if we started to scream for our rights. It's like standing next to a Tyrannosaurus Rex in one of those Jurassic Park movies. If you are very quiet and still, he might not notice you. You have a good chance of making it. But if you make a lot of noise, well, you don't make it to the end of the movie. We do our best to lay low.

I've heard some of the older Living ones say that the zombies have been blinded on purpose and that they are incapable of understanding. That confuses me. If the Living who say that are right; to be honest, I find it unfair. Why do I get Life when thousands of other 16 year old girls are walking around with sparkly masks to hide the fact that their ears fell off?

Chapter Seven

You've Got A Little Schmutz On Your Ear

As we pull back through the gate and into the safety of our community, I feel myself relax. The nightmares of the past have chased me all the way home, and I've been holding on to my seat for dear life. My fingers are cramped from their desperate, inadvertent clutching. I know it's normal to be scared after being assaulted, but I'm ashamed of myself for it anyway. Aunty pulls up the narrow alley behind the Inn and stops outside of the back door. She turns to face me and starts into a speech that, I'm sure, has been rehearsed over the last few miles home.

"Unfortunately, Ivy, we don't know if someone untrustworthy has made their way into our community. We must be a little more careful than normal. I will schedule a meeting with the Elders for tomorrow morning, and I'm sure they'll want you there to give your input. This is somehow about you and we'll need to figure out why and what to do about it."

For some reason that makes me feel itchy and—diseased; like I'm bringing trouble back home to our only safe place. Are they in danger because of me? Does Pravda really want me? If we, the Living, are a body; am I a cancer?

"Keep your chin up dear," she says. "God will overcome and we are safe in His hands; just as we have been for these last six years."

Her inspirational words fall flat for me. Expressionless, I jump out and walk to the back of the car. Lifting the hatch, I start unloading the stuff from our shopping trip. Aunty still has to return the car to the communal lot; but she gets out, leaving the car running, to help me unload everything. We haul the bags and bundles of unfolded clothes to the back door of the Inn, setting them on top of the rusted porch table near the door. I close the trunk hatch when we've gotten everything while Aunty unlocks the back door. It will be my job to haul everything inside and get it sorted.

"Ivy. Stand perfectly still."

Her tone freezes me instantly. I don't even feel the panic rise this time. It's instantaneous. I was barely holding on to calm as it was. My arms lock and I remain frozen in mid step. Not because she told me to, but because my muscles are locked in fear. I wonder if I'm about to die? For some reason, the thought of dying makes me think of Him, and my terror lessens just a little.

I close my eyes.

Aunty hits my arm with her shoe.

I open my eyes.

I feel—stunned. I was expecting to be mauled by zombies, or to hear gun shots, or something—anything—other than being firmly slapped on the arm with a soft soled shoe.

"Got it," she says with confusing cheerfulness.

Seconds later, Aunty is back in the car and driving away. Disoriented, I melt like a thawing snowman; my limbs unlocking from top to bottom. As the thaw reaches my knees, I almost crumple to the ground. Looking down at the pavement beneath me, I see a humongous black spider lying dead and curled up next to my foot. I jump and scream at the sight of how large it is, dead or not. And realize that it had, just a moment ago, been crawling on me.

ON ME!

I do a freaked out, shivery, girly-scream-jump-armflap dance that only true Arachnophobes could picture and understand. I land awkwardly on the pink high heels, knowing it's a small miracle that I didn't twist my ankle. A twisted ankle would've been the icing on the cake today. My first thought that God is "looking out for me" is quickly pushed aside when I think of the zombie at the mall and the spider on my arm. If He's looking out for me, I'd like a little more attention.

Unlocking all the doors to our private quarters takes me a minute. Made even more challenging because my hands are still shaking. It is a relief to be home. I go back outside to start carrying everything in and almost jump out of my skin when I notice someone leaning against the side of the house.

"Ah!" I scream, immediately embarrassed by my obvious cowardice.

If he's inside of the gates, he must be one of us. He looks to be my age; but, as I clop clumsily towards him, I still don't recognize him. I know everyone in our "gated" community. There were 193 of us inside the fence at the last count. A count I helped with. I could tell you all 193 of their names.

I attempt to walk gracefully in my pink high heels towards the guy who must be someone I know but can't place. Why is he leaning against the wall of the Inn? Does he have some business here? I skid to a stumbling halt at the sight of the disease on his ears. His dark hair is pushed back behind ears that are bubbled, red, and crusty. He's a full-fledged zombie! He isn't wearing their clothes, just jeans and a long sleeved T-shirt. And gloves. The gloves are their thing. I back towards the door, heart pounding; all the horror of my earlier attack flooding over me.

Geez God, why me!

The terror on my face must be obvious as I reach for the door behind me. The guy, who looks close to my age, pushes off of the wall and starts towards me. He scowls menacingly and holds a gloved hand out to stop me. I stumble backwards through the open door—*I definitely hate these darn shoes*—and he yells at me as I grab for the door.

"Wait a minute!" He calls angrily as he lunges towards me.

I slam the door in his face and fumble at the lock with trembling fingers. I wait—holding my breath—for him to rail against the door in an attempt to break it down. I lean my weight against it and press my sweaty palms against the cold metal. How long will the old aluminum door hold up against an attack? There is one window next to the back door, but it is reinforced with thick metal bars. He'd be stupid to try coming in that way. A gentle rapping noise makes its way through the noise of my heart pounding in my ears.

He's knocking? What attacking zombie knocks on your door? Is this some sort of trap? Is he trying to distract me?

Aunty will be back any minute.

She'll walk right into the trap! How can I warn her? What if I go out the front door and circle around to the other side of the house? I could catch her before she starts up the alley to the back door. We could go in the front door and avoid him all together. If he's alone.

Dear God, what if he isn't alone?

Maybe he's working with someone, like the zombie in the scientist outfit. Maybe he *is* that guy's partner! They've followed us home somehow! If I go out the front door and leave it unlocked they could get in the house while I'm around on the other side. We don't have a working key for the front door because it's so old and it only locks from the inside. It's why we mostly use the back door. So, if I go that way, I'll leave us exposed and they could get in.

Then they'll hide in wait and attack us while we're sleeping! All of these panicked thoughts are bouncing loudly in my rattled psyche and no solution has yet come to mind and I realize I hear Aunty talking outside.

She's back already? I'm too late!

Any moment, I'll hear her scream. This is all my fault! I'm frozen in terror. What can I do? Then, I hear a key scratch at the door lock and I look down at the knob. It's turning.

They've gotten her key!

Of course they would; why didn't I think of that?

I turn to run. I'll go out the front door and find help. It's my only option. Hopefully, God will protect me and there won't be more of them on the front porch. I hate to leave Aunty with them, but what else can I do?

"Ivy?"

Aunty Coe walks through the back door, a pleasant smile on her lined face. I pause mid-run, looking like a cartoon character stuck in a ridiculous running position—Wile E. Coyote style. My face is a mask of panic and confusion.

"Honey, we have some company. Are you okay? You don't look okay, dear. I'll make us some tea and we can visit with this young man. This is Matthew," she says politely, introducing the scowling menace.

"Matt," the boy barks.

"Yes, Matt. He says he's Thomas' brother. Isn't that nice? Thomas will be so excited. I don't think I've ever heard him mention his family."

Chapter Eight

Interview With A Zombie

I mumble something—maybe it's "Hi"—and I reluctantly follow Aunty and the zombie into the kitchen. I look down in embarrassment as my ridiculous shoes tap loudly on the linoleum. With my eyes on the floor, I'm furious to see that Matt's shoes are caked in mud and leaving giant clods of dirt all over my newly scrubbed floor. If it was possible for me to despise this zombie any more, I do now.

Aunty shouldn't have let him in. Something is wrong here. Dragging behind them, still certain we are in danger, I catch a whiff of Matt the zombie. He smells terrible. My heart hammers, thinking of the smelly man who just attacked us, not an hour ago. Matt's stink isn't body odor but the smell of ointment mixed with the unpleasant musk of cat litter. He is musty, like he got his clothes out of a garbage can.

I wrinkle my nose in disgust and catch Aunty shooting me a reproving look. She called him company! She invited him into our home. Does she expect me to treat him kindly and have good manners? I'm afraid that's asking too much. I am certain we are in terrible danger, and Aunty's misjudgment could cost us our lives.

Aunty exudes Southern hospitality as she insists Matt try some of my homemade cookies. He grabs two gloved handfuls and devours them with no concept of manners or etiquette and no "thank you." Matt sinks into a chair at the table as he scarfs his second handful of cookies. Aunty offers tea and he mumbles something, accepting her offer. I lean against the kitchen counter behind him; my stomach is rolling and my arms and legs are tight with tension.

Aunty boils the water and strains the tea leaves into three different mismatched mugs. The tea is too hot to gulp down, and I wonder what it will look like to watch a zombie sip tea like a civilized person. I'm just staring at Matt with wide, disgusted eyes when Aunty clears her throat a little to bring me to my senses.

"So, you are here to find Thomas," she starts the conversation, talking to Matt but looking at me.

Aunty points at the empty chair beside her where she placed my mug at the table. Her eyes insist that I sit. I obey, wearing rebellious disdain like a banner across my face.

"Yes." He clips, wiping cookie crumbs from his lips with the back of his dirty gloved hand.

I'm breaking Aunty's rules of nicety by staring. As Matt takes a hesitant sip of the steaming tea, I study his face for any sign that he could be related to our Thomas. Matt's facial features might resemble Thomas', but it's hard to tell. Matt's skin is more yellow and there is damage on both of his ears. The man at the mall who attacked us today was the worst I've seen; and, comparatively, Matt is probably the least infected that I've seen in a long while.

The disease is there, you really have to look close to see it, but it's there. I think it's starting to manifest on his lips too, though they could just be chapped from the cold. LS on the lips is not pretty. Within a year or so, his lips will be mangled at best. In its later stages, the LS on his lips will eat away at them until his lips are completely gone. Matt is dressed head to toe for the cold winter day, so I can't tell if the disease has claimed any other territory. I'm glad his clothes cover whatever else is rotting.

Matt's most outstanding feature is his striking emerald green eyes. Perhaps they are similar to Thomas' aqua green eyes. Only Matt's are more brilliant, piercing even. I've never seen eyes so green. Matt meets my stare, and I shiver at the malicious glow behind his reptilian orbs.

"How is it that you and Thomas were separated?" Aunty asks, staring at him without blinking.

I realize that perhaps she's more cautious of him than I first thought. She's screening him. Making sure he really is Thomas' brother. I finger my Taser on my wrist band under the table. He's foolish if he thinks that we're defenseless.

"He left town with a freak, didn't tell me."

Nice.

By "freak" he means someone like us. I'd rather be a freak than a zombie. He stares at us with restrained disgust and doesn't offer any more information. This zombie isn't a talker. Aunty won't have much more than her gifts of wisdom and discernment to help her figure him out.

"How old are you, son?" she continues with her questioning. "I can see the resemblance. Are you and Thomas twins?"

This guy looks older than me. Thomas is twelve years old, fresh-faced and adorable. Matt's scowling, scruffy face is anything but adorable. He has shaggy, unkempt dark brown hair—nothing like Thomas' curly, cherubic blondish-brown locks. But, more than anything else, it is Matt's hardness that puts him on the other side of the Grand Canyon from the sweet innocence that Thomas embodies. There aren't any similarities. It's obvious to me that Aunty is just trying to weigh his reaction; figure out if he's genuine. Apparently, it's obvious to him too.

"Huh!" Matt snorts angrily at us, slapping the table with an angry smack. Sending my left hand to the Taser on my right wrist under the cover of the table.

"If you can't point me in the right direction, I'll keep looking. Thanks a lot."

He has figured out that he's being interviewed and his "thanks" is sarcastic as he pushes his chair away from the table.

"Young man!" Aunty's voice booms.

Aunty scares me sometimes. She carries herself with such authority it makes the zombie pause on his way out of the kitchen.

"You must understand our caution. If you do truly care for Thomas, you know that under normal circumstances your people are nothing but a threat to him."

"A threat?" he asks with genuine confusion and his consistent tone of disgust. "Look. I don't know how things work here, but I'm mad at Tom for sneaking off and leaving me. His disease is spreading, and I'm sure he doesn't fit in here. I just want to take him home with me. I'm not interested in the rest of your interview," he sneers at Aunty, "and I will eventually find him myself. Tom doesn't need your charity anymore."

He is practically spitting his words by the end of his rant. They really, really hate us. And we are supposed to "win" them over?

"Thomas doesn't have the disease anymore."

Aunty's announcement gets his attention. Matt thought he was coming here to find his little brother still sick? He didn't know? Matt squints at us, his green eyes narrowing to serpentine slits, but his skepticism immediately returns.

"I don't believe you. You don't have a cure here, you're just immune. And the last time I saw Tom, his ears were almost completely gone. His lips were so mangled it was hard for him to eat. Or speak. If we are talking about the same kid," he pauses and then finishes quietly, "you know I'll be burying him within the year. I just want to take my brother back home."

I am caught up in his words like a trance. His emotion is so real. His concern for his brother is so moving that I feel tears spring to my eyes as I hear his voice catch, thick with his emotion. Then he shakes his head and, as he meets my eyes again, his face turns back to stone. I blink.

Oh, he's good.

This show of concern is a trick or something. I look over at Aunty.

"This is ridiculous! Tell me where he is now!" he demands.

"Believe what you want," Aunty continues, seemingly unfazed by both his emotional moment and his anger. "If you would be willing to wait until tomorrow, I can arrange a meeting for you and Thomas. Obviously, there would be some chaperoning required. If you can agree to that, I will contact his family this evening and we can meet with them for lunch tomorrow."

"His family?" he asks with obvious irritation and restrained anger. "Ugh!" he growls in guttural frustration. "I'm his family!"

"Yes, a lovely young couple has adopted him," Aunty answers gently. She's good with people.

I guess if Matt is Thomas' real brother, hearing that he has a new family would be pretty upsetting. I'm not as good with people and I am holding back a sarcastic remark about Matt's angry nature and how Thomas obviously left for good reason. Matt considers Aunty's offer for a full minute in silence. Aunty and I wait, meeting his gaze, studying him for a clue of what he will decide. I'm betting it will be another angry outburst accompanied by some cursing and door slamming. I have a firm grip on my Taser and I find myself dying to use it.

"Fine." He says it quietly, with no malice.

I'm caught off guard, but Aunty looks unfazed; triumphant even.

"You may sleep in one of our guest rooms."

At this offer, I am stunned. Now it's my turn to be angry.

"What? Are you kidding?! After what happened today?"

"Ivy, I will speak with you privately. Please go put our packages away." Her voice is stern and her tone is one she seldom uses with me.

Matt stares coolly at me, and I'm humiliated in front of him as Aunty sends me away like a little child. I'm not just mad now; I'm hurt too.

I can't believe she is doing this!

I feel betrayed. Like I'm twelve years old again and my mom just slapped me. Can't I trust anyone to just be there for me? To care about me when I'm rightfully scared? I feel a tug in my heart reminding me that He is always there for me, but I brush it aside. How has He been there for me? It has been a horrible day. One of the worst days of my life, with no sign of Him anywhere.

Aunty is probably dooming us. Matt could totally be part of what happened to us in Commerce today. I have been freaking out—and rightfully so—and now she's inviting the enemy to sleep in our house? I glare at him again as I walk to the kitchen door.

"Don't put yourselves out," he glances at me. "I can find a place to sleep. I don't need your charity."

Aunty gives me a face meant to send me on my way. As I storm out of the kitchen, I hear her talking to him in that soothing, calm voice she uses to teach.

"Do you know what charity means Matthew? It is another word for love. Everyone needs love. I can't make you stay here, but we have nice rooms and it would be more convenient for you. I will understand if you decide not to stay. I won't be offended."

I can't stand outside the door and eavesdrop, she will know. Bitterly, I clip-clop outside and begin to haul the bags of clothes inside.

protein—and more fiber than a person needs in a month—all packed into one cardboard flavored cereal bar. It's one of the few things that come in the government shipments that we actually do use—mostly because they are free.

In the hallway outside of my room, I inhale deeply. I smell venison cooking. My stomach growls in anticipation. Aunty must feel bad about what happened. She's cooking what we had saved for a special occasion to cheer me up. I am so hungry and it smells amazing. A small smile starts curling at the corner of my lips.

There aren't any grocery stores anymore, and there isn't any meat shipped to Toccoa. Unless you count the freeze dried government "meat loaf" meals in their "just add water" mystery sauce. We only have fresh meat because I babysat Thomas day in and day out until Jose and Ellen decided to adopt him.

In our self-sufficient community, everyone has something to trade. We all have everything in common—-everyone works hard and everyone has their needs met by each other. We garden and share food and clothes, and it's a real self-sufficient body; utopian even.

Aunty knits and crotchets; keeping people warm in the winter with her sweaters, hats, mittens and scarves. She also runs the Inn, offering a room for anyone who needs it and food for guests who are staying with us. In her "spare" time, she helps the disabled and elderly in our community. She cooks and cleans for those who need extra help. She says it brings her great joy to clean for others. I've cleaned enough strangers' toilets to find her joy disturbing.

The elders "blessed" Aunty and me with the venison after we kept Thomas at the Inn. With Aunty off helping others most of the time, I was the one cooking for Thomas and cleaning up after Thomas and playing hours of board games and building forts. I earned this dinner. Aunty and I decided to keep the meat for some time when it could be special. A pick-me-up of real steak on a tough day like today is just what I need to feel better. My mouth is watering.

Opening the kitchen door, I stand rooted at the sight of Matt. My smile crumples off of my face in slow motion; leaving me standing with my mouth open. My eyebrows shoot up in the opposite direction of my frown. He is sitting at the kitchen table drinking a glass of *my* milk! Aunty doesn't like milk, but she gets it for me when she cleans for the Brock family. The Brocks have the only cow in town, and the milk is precious to the whole community.

Why is this happening to me?

Matt raises his eyebrows at me; and, without breaking eye contact, he chugs the rest of the glass—so fast that some milk dribbles down each side of his mouth.

I really hate him.

What a horrible waste of milk.

Aunty sees me there, stalled in the door frame and staring, and she tries to ease the tension. "Ivy, Matt is just six months older than you. He's seventeen."

Her lame attempt only adds to the awkwardness. Matt and I stare at each other until I look away from him and his uncomfortably blank expression.

Oh. My. Gosh.

Call me slow, but it is just dawning on me that she has invited him to eat with us! I am furious again. I feel my face flush red with anger and my lips purse in an attempt to hold in awful words. Aunty is shooting piercing eyes at me, her frustrated face heavy with meaning. She's subliminally insisting that I behave myself. I send angry brown eyes back at her with my own silent communication—furious loathing.

"I thought we'd share our venison with Matt," she says with too much pleasantry. "Can you please make us some fruit salad, dear?" She brushes past me to pull something from the refrigerator and surreptitiously squeezes my hand.

Her love squeeze is supposed to be encouragement, but all I can think about is the grievous injustice that is my life. She made the venison for him, not for me. My venison. Without even asking me. The conviction in my heart returns and I know I should be gracious. Pretty sure I can't muster gracious right now. Hunger moves my legs forward to the pantry where I numbly pick through the jars of fruit that we canned over the summer. I open different sized glass jars with peaches, pears, and blackberries and pour them into a pretty pink glass bowl.

Aunty has laid out the good china for me to set the table with. We only use the china when we have special guests for dinner. Not just everyone we feed warrants the use of fancy dishes. Add "catering to a zombie" to our long list of wrongs today. Using the good china is going way over the top! This jerk would eat dinner right out of the pan with no problem. He probably doesn't know how to use silverware. All this extra work is lost on him. While setting the table that is already covered with our best table cloth, I decide that Aunty has lost her mind.

When Aunty and I are finished cooking, setting the table, and pouring the drinks, we sit down. Not once during all of this has Matt offered to help with anything. He spent the time staring into space and spinning his empty milk glass on the table. Oh, and we also got to listen to him tap his foot with rude impatience.

That wasn't irritating at all.

Aunty manages constant grace and cheerfulness, and Matt and I manage to not look at each other. The minute Aunty hands him his plate, Matt digs in. Aunty clears her throat gently, and he looks up from his plate like a Neanderthal with his mouth open and full of food.

"We like to thank God for our food before we eat," she explains. "Ivy, will you pray please?"

Matt looks like a confused imbecile as he stares inquisitively at me, his mouth still hanging open. I'm not in the mood to pray, but I don't say so. Aunty and I bow our heads and close our eyes. Even with my eyes closed, I feel him staring at me while he slowly chews at his food.

"Dear Lord," I croak because I haven't been speaking. I clear my throat and keep going, "thank you for all of our blessings. Thank you for this food and for protecting us today. Please give us wisdom. Amen."

"And love," Aunty adds her request onto the end of my prayer.

"Amen," we both say again in almost unison.

Matt is staring at us, his eyebrows arching so high that they disappear beneath his shaggy hair. The small smile playing at the corner of his food crusted lips says it all—he thinks we are CRAZY. I think he would've laughed out loud at us if he wasn't already back to stuffing himself.

I shouldn't care—don't care—what he thinks, but I feel insecure anyway. I eat; but, despite my hunger, my food doesn't taste as good as I thought it would. It sticks in my throat and lays heavy in my stomach.

I'm sure it's from all the nerves.

The less than pleasant smells wafting across the table from Matt aren't helping either. If he has to stay here, hopefully he'll shower before lying on our clean guest bed. I'd bet a pint of blood I'm going to end up being the one who cleans his room. He smells like death and cat stink.

Aunty visits with Matt and gets occasional replies, usually while he's chewing with his mouth open. I just pick at my venison and mashed potatoes with gravy. I push my fruit salad around on my plate and nibble at the homemade honey rolls.

Aunty startles me out of my depressed reveries by bringing up what happened to us today at the outlets. If I felt more equal with her right now, I would argue that she shouldn't be talking about *this* with *him*. I'm still feeling the effects of her chastisement though, so I let her tell the story while I fight the cramps that keep rippling through my stomach. For some reason, at the end of her tale I'm blushing. She has left out how terrified I felt and somehow made me sound braver than I was.

When I look up from my plate, I am caught in his green-eyed stare. My eyes widen and I glance nervously over at Aunty, but she is politely cutting her meat and offers me no sanctuary from his heavy stare. I spend a few moments nervously trying to decide where to look before he breaks the silence.

"You were bleeding before. What happened to your neck?" It's the first time he's spoken to me and I wish he wouldn't have.

I look down at my lap. I know I have to be civil and polite and answer him, but I don't want to speak to him. Childish as it may be, I find myself wishing I could just stick out my tongue at him and hide under the table.

"It got scraped when he was strangling me," I mumble, still looking at my lap. I have to hold myself back from saying "Duh."

"You think they were trying to take you?" he asks with none of the sarcasm I had expected. "If you're right, they were probably junkies. Pravda doesn't fail. They get what they want no matter what. I've heard that the drugs are scarce lately; something went wrong with the last batch. I think they are running out of reliable employees."

It's really strange to hear *him* talk *about them*.

"Why aren't you on the drugs?" I throw the question out without thinking, and it comes out sounding hostile and accusatory.

"Who says I'm not," he spits back.

"Well, you don't seem crazy and desperate like the others." Believe it or not, that was me trying to sound nicer. "I mean, you seem starved, but more normal." Oh yeah, I'm a wonderful conversationalist.

"I AM normal," he says loudly, his words punctuated with even more hostility. "You people are the weird ones. Just because you're immune, you think you're better than us. And you're delusional." He makes "cuckoo" motions with his finger around his ear to show just how mental he thinks we are. "There is no God. You think because you don't have the disease that "someone" is looking out for you. There are way more of us. That should prove something. No one is *better* than anyone else."

What an idiot.

How can he miss it when it's staring him in the face? Literally. Every time the diseased look in a mirror they have to look God's judgment in the face! I'm about to start debating and ask him what he thinks the disappearances were when Aunty noisily pushes her chair back and stands up from her seat.

Finally! She's going to let this jerk have it.

Lay it on him good, Aunty.

To my deep disappointment she smiles and asks, "Dessert?"

Chapter Ten
The Undead Ate My Pudding

Aunty serves us homemade chocolate pudding—my favorite. She must have made it after I went to my room, because there are three glass bowls full in the refrigerator. She never makes pudding. It's the last straw for me. My hand comes down in a hard slap of frustration on the table; the same way that Matt slapped the table earlier today. He smirks almost triumphantly. Was it his goal to make me angry? Oh I can't stand him. He sits calmly, his arms crossed, leveling his cold, green stare at me.

When Aunty puts the smaller bowl of pudding in front of me, I stand up quickly, avoiding her eyes. "I'm full. Thanks anyway."

I stomp out of the kitchen and head for my room. I'm going to bed. It's early, but the sooner I go to sleep the sooner he'll be gone. The meeting with the Elders is in the morning. Then someone will oversee Thomas's reunion with his zombie brother in the afternoon. When Matt sees that Thomas is one of the Living, he'll be on his way back to wherever he came from. By tomorrow at dinner time, life will be back to what I call normal. It can't come soon enough.

I should've helped with the clean-up, and I feel guilty for the umpteenth time today. I hope Aunty is right. I hope we aren't in danger with a zombie in our house. She seems to feel peace about having him here, and she is already trying to save him. Which irritates me instead of inspiring me. I hate feeling like they are out there talking without me; and, worse, probably about me. Aunty is probably apologizing to a zombie for my bad manners and explaining what a hard day I've had and what a great girl I am. Next thing I know, she'll be trying to set me up with him. Look out Tim Markowitz.

Oh my gosh, I hate my life!

I am trapped in this house in this town with gross boys and no future. It's not that there aren't options here. There are some nice looking guys. In fact, there is one guy who I really like. He is super good looking and totally wonderful.

If you look in my Bible, you'll find his name doodled on scraps of paper tucked between the precious fragile pages of Truth. And yes—I'll admit it—I've written my name with his last name a few hundred times. Mr. and Mrs. Jamie Crest. Mrs. Ivy Crest. It just sounds right, doesn't it? We would be so perfect together. But, like everything else in my life, loving Jamie Crest is nothing but a disappointment. He is oblivious of my existence—even though I'm one of only thirteen girls in the compound in his age group. I'll bet you ten pints of blood he wants a blond. I've contemplated bleaching my hair to see if it helps.

With my bedroom door locked, I try on my comfy new yoga pants. Sitting on the side of my bed, I reach for my coat hanging next to the door. The picture Aunty took from the zombie is still in my pocket. I pull it out with shaky hands to stare at it again. What could it mean? How was it taken without me knowing? As I think over all the kind people in our community, I can't think of a single soul who would betray me. Their faith and love is obvious, and they all feel like family to me—even the ones I don't know very well. This picture is going to drive me crazy with its unsolvable mysteries. I stuff it back in the pocket of my coat.

I'm ready for this awful day to be over. I climb under my chilly covers and pull the old pink comforter over my head.

But sleep won't come.

I am assaulted with so many different worries that the barrage leaves me breathless. The endless what ifs and fears about what could've happened today simmer next to my deep hatred for Matt and his kind. The seasoning in this pot of crazy? Spoonfuls of guilt and shame for my doubt and my hatred. Thoughts of Matt lead to thoughts of Thomas. He's such a good kid. Will he be leaving us tomorrow with his brother? I have given up on the hope that Matt isn't Thomas's brother. Even though he's awful, somehow you can tell he cares for Thomas.

Thomas is easy to love. I'd be disappointed to see him go. I hope he'll choose us over Matt. It's not at all safe out there for a kid like him. I've even heard rumors of the Living turning back into zombies when they leave the community for too long. Thomas did leave Matt without a goodbye. He probably won't leave. Maybe I'll feel sorry for Matt if he came here just to be turned away.

Nah.

I hear voices outside of my window, and I'm immediately afraid again.

Creeping out of my bed and over to the window, I peek through the slatted blinds without moving them more than I have to—just in case someone is looking at my window. I don't want whoever it is to know that I'm watching. Just outside the barred window of my room, I see Aunty holding a flashlight and talking to several men I know. Why did I assume it would be zombies?

Shame replaces fear as I realize the men are standing guard over us tonight. Aunty isn't endangering us at all. She is, as always, taking good care of me. Wise and discerning, her gifts. One of the men follows her back inside while the others branch out around the house. As I climb back into bed, I hear the floor boards creak in the room above mine. Matt is in a room on the other side of the house, so it can't be him. Aunty must've given the men outside a room to sleep in while they take turns keeping watch. Now I have two rooms to clean tomorrow; two toilets to scrub.

I am so ashamed of myself.

Why am I so focused on me? Who promised me that I would never have to face any of this? What am I mad about? I know why we are here, on the other end of the stick, and it has nothing to do with what I deserve. I need to get a hold of myself. Be the tough girl I normally am. Maybe I have Post Traumatic Stress Syndrome. Maybe I'm a fear-filled hypochondriac. I am thinking about praying when I drift off to sleep.

*****

In my dream... It's happening again in slow motion. I'm running to the car in high heels and wearing the way-too-short sequined mini skirt that I saw in the Rue 21 window. I look ridiculous. And a bit slutty. Wow, my hair looks great.

Wait—I can't find Aunty anywhere.

I'm really scared!

Someone is after me! But who?

I'm crying and shouting for Aunty. Where did she go? Why has she left me here?

Then I see her and Aunty Betty, clear as day, struggling with a strange man on the sidewalk, but they get farther away with each passing second. As though time and space are pulling them down a tunnel away from me. I don't know what to do, so I chicken out and keep running.

When I reach the car, Tim Markowitz throws the door open for me and pulls me inside.

Tim looks terrified and his thick, nerdy glasses are smashed and crooked. His brown hair is disheveled like he just woke up with bed hair. Tim gives me a reproving stare, obviously not impressed with my new outfit. I feel embarrassed and ashamed of myself under his judgmental gaze.

Tim is yelling at me to look in the back seat but I don't want to. The car smells like chocolate pudding. He keeps begging me to look; and, when I finally peer behind the seat, I already know what I'll find. A zombie in a white plastic mask grabs me around my neck and chokes me. The attack is violent, I can't breathe, and I am sure that I'm going to die. As I'm fading, I know one thing for sure. I know this zombie hates me with every fiber of his being.

Tim lunges towards the masked fiend and I realize that Tim has a gun. I think I should stop him. We shouldn't kill a zombie. I'm sure of that, but I can't remember why. I struggle against the strong hands around my neck; and, in slow motion, I see the white mask fall off of my attacker.

I'm staring into Matt's cold, green eyes. The zombie is Matt.

With breathtaking abruptness, I'm not scared anymore. I feel sad, but not for myself or my predicament. I'm sad for this deformed creature who is killing me. I'm shouting at Tim, telling him not to shoot, when Matt pulls me in front of his body as a shield. I should be frightened, but I'm lost in a sea of deep sadness. I hear the gun go off, but I don't feel the bullet. I feel only peace.

Chapter Eleven

I Exude Grace and Poise

I draw in a deep gasp and throw off the blankets as I emerge from my nightmare-filled sleep. As the chilly room cools my warm body, a strange mix of relief and regret hangs over my first coherent moments. I am glad to be out of the murky, slow motion world that my oppressed thoughts held me captive in all night long. The feelings felt so, so, real.

It was 7:00 p.m. when I went to bed in a pout last night. And after ten full hours of sleep, I'm wide awake at 5:00 a.m. Normally, I devote myself first thing in the morning, but I'm not in the mood today. I didn't devote myself yesterday either. A trend is starting here. The longer I put it off, the more I drag my feet back to it.

I head to the kitchen and make a beeline for the pantry. I am ravenous. I love the pre-dawn hours. It's still dark outside; but, with a refreshing night of sleep, the dark of the morning is friendlier than the dark before bedtime. Something about resting my nerves and my emotions as well as my body always makes me feel optimistic and stronger in the morning. Stress from long days and dangerous surroundings often leaves me nervous and morbid when I'm tired at night. Aunty says it's very "feminine" of me. I think she means that I'm a hormonal drama queen.

I spoon Aunty's amazing homemade granola into a bowl and pour myself the last glass of milk. None left to share with the unwanted guest.

Awww, too bad.

My thoughts keep drifting to Matt this morning. I guess I'm just nervous knowing he's upstairs. I've come to the kitchen fully dressed instead of in my pajamas like I usually would. I'm sure we won't see Matt till long after the sun comes up, but I'm still careful to not be caught in a holey pink bathrobe.

Zombies stay up really late, carousing and indulging their various hungers. Night time is their day time. Then, they sleep most of the day away. Their side of the fence looks like an abandoned city with ghostly empty streets before noon. Each day, as the afternoon takes hold, they drag themselves out of whatever hole they slept in and their town of pleasure and debauchery comes raucously to life again.

We can see them right past our eighteen-foot high razor wire fence. The infected live very close. We're side by side but in totally different worlds. Sometimes an errand takes me near the fence and I'm forced to pass close by one of them on the other side. Close enough for a person to give the typical nod and smile or forced "hello."

Not that I say "hello" or smile.

When I'm forced to be within one hundred feet of a zombie, fence between us, I am bound to get one of two reactions. The men leer at me like I'm meat; something they would like to catch and devour. If they are well enough to walk, they hurry to press themselves against the fence, stretching diseased fingers through the links towards me. I feel like a caged animal, hurrying past them while they call at me and make horrible gestures. Sometimes they throw things over the fence at me.

The women, on the other hand, act like we don't exist. They *never* look at me, never nod or even acknowledge my presence. If I had to guess, I'd say they are jealous. Their men want us because we are still beautiful and healthy, and they hate us for it. Of course they'd say we are freaks and they don't want to be anything like us.

Whatever.

You'd think they'd want what we have. You'd think they'd see our healthy skin and happy lives and follow their curiosity over to our side of the fence. In the early years, there was a flood of converts to the Living; but, recently, it has become extremely rare for zombies to be healed.

I wonder if our most recent convert knows that his big brother is in town. It will probably be pretty shocking for Matt when he sees Thomas after the description he gave us yesterday. I can't wait for the whole thing to be over and for Matt to be out of my life. I wonder if he had a hard time sleeping in clean sheets in a clean house with no drugs or hookers to entertain him last night. I don't think he could've gone out since we keep the house locked up like a fortress at night. And where would he go?

Come to think of it, how did he get into the community to begin with? Our guards are stationed at the three gates 24 hours a day. They don't let zombies in without an escort and then only on official business. They wouldn't have let him in and then turned him loose. He wouldn't have been allowed to show up unescorted at our door. I don't think he came in through a gate! I wonder if Aunty has realized this yet. So, either he came over the fence—which is unlikely since it's almost twenty feet tall with razor wire at the top—or he came under it somewhere.

The thought of a hole in our security is terrifying. If zombies can come through our fence at their leisure, we'll have children going missing and women being attacked. There are a lot more women than men in the community and it's impossible to keep a guard over all the girls. The whole purpose of the fence is to protect us!

And I'm in more danger than I even realized. If Pravda is trying to kidnap me, a hole in the fence will be very helpful to them. Our meeting with the Elders feels too many hours away. Aunty and I will have to tell them about the breach. We need to find and fix that hole. My unusually morbid morning thoughts are interrupted by the kitchen door creaking behind me.

"Morning." I say with my mouth full of granola. "I have something important to tell you!" I call over my shoulder at Aunty.

She is always up early too. We often eat breakfast together. I can't wait to tell her my new realizations.

"Someone is friendlier today," a sarcastic, deep, male voice rumbles behind me.

I jump up; and, at the same time, inwardly curse myself for being so ridiculously jumpy in my own house. The chair I was sitting on turns over and falls backwards onto the floor with a loud crack—adding to my deep embarrassment. My cheeks flush red with angry humiliation. I can feel the heat on my face; which, of course, makes the whole thing even more embarrassing.

"What are you doing up already?" I shout at him.

"There she is," he says knowingly, insinuating that jumpy and mean is my normal persona.

I really resent that. I'm a cheerful, friendly girl.

Obviously.

He's the problem here and I shouldn't be ashamed of myself. But I find myself constantly feeling a mixture of fear and shame whenever I'm around him.

So, I dig myself deeper and blurt, "There's no more milk!"

"O...kay...," he says really slowly and drawn out—like he's talking to an idiot.

Maybe he is.

I don't know what to say now, so I stand there—like an idiot.

To my relief, Aunty bursts through the squeaky kitchen door, her old blue bathrobe pulled tightly around her thin frame and worry on her lined, makeup-free face. She sees the chair turned over on the floor and looks between Matt and I for an explanation. She must have heard the chair fall and came running. Matt holds his hands up in an, "I didn't do anything" pose and I glower at him, my face still hot pink with hostility.

Aunty's face fades from concern to understanding. Then, just as quickly, she puts on her hospitality face; and, turning to Matt she asks, "Pancakes?"

*****

The two of them eat their breakfast of homemade pancakes together that I staunchly turned down. Not because the granola was that filling, but because I don't want to support this behavior. Eating pancakes with a zombie. Disgusting. I'm pretty sure there's a verse in the Bible about this. Something about "throwing your pearls before swine" comes to mind. Matt fits the description as he forks big bites of warm pancake into his pig face while grunting with satisfaction.

The homemade maple syrup that Matt is excessively pouring on his pancakes was a Christmas gift from a lady at the U.R. I've only had it once since Christmas morning because it's supposed to be special and not wasted. It smells so amazing that my stomach growls audibly in the momentary silence.

That's when I actually notice how good the room smells. It should smell bad; I'm sitting across the table from someone who is rotting. I glance at Matt each time he looks down to take a bite. His hair is still damp with the proof of a morning shower—which means the bathroom in that guest room should just be sealed off and quarantined for the rest of time.

Matt's hair looks softer today and has a bit of curl, not as much as Thomas' though. His skin looks scrubbed and healthier. His ears are still red, scaly and bubbled looking, but his shaggy curls keep them mostly hidden. His lips look healthier today too, but I'm pretty sure I can see a glisten of moisture across the top like they've been treated with something. Though, that could just be syrup. Such a pig.

His shirt is different too. It's so similar to yesterdays, a long sleeved t-shirt, dark in color, which I almost didn't notice. I don't think he had a bag of any kind yesterday. Maybe Aunty offered to do his laundry for him too and came up with a shirt for him. As likely as that is, I doubt we had a men's long sleeve t-shirt in his size just lying around. He is still wearing the simple black gloves. He wore them all through dinner last night too. His hands must be where he has LS the worst.

LS acts like Leprosy. It attacks the extremities and the nervous system; the ears, nose, lips, hands, feet, and, um, other extremities. The private ones. I just threw up in my mouth a little. Matt must have it really bad on his hands or feet since the rest of him looks pretty normal. I'd hate to see what's under those black gloves He can't defy God's judgment. None of them can escape the worsening severity of the curse.

I keep staring at him while he eats—I can't help myself. He's such an oddity. I don't think we've ever had a guy my age here in the kitchen; and, just my luck, this disgusting guy would be the first. The room is quiet but for the sounds of Matt chewing with his mouth open. Aunty has put her ongoing barrage of *20 Questions* on hold for the moment to politely finish her pancake.

Of course Matt wasn't talking to begin with because he's too busy forking mammoth bites into his mouth that he can't possibly taste or enjoy at that speed. He looks up at me and—with an antagonistic wink that Aunty doesn't see—he pours *more* of my syrup on his already doused pancake. I am incredulous. I start to sputter something, but I know Aunty will only reprimand me and send me off to do a chore of some kind. I think that would be even harder on my pride, so I stifle my accusations.

I mumble unintelligibly—on purpose—to excuse myself from the table; and I stomp out of the kitchen for the second time in less than twenty-four hours. I'll hang out in my room until the morning meeting with the Elders. Behind the privacy of my closed door, I go all drama queen for a second and scream into my pillow. I've never been so disgusted and irritated by another living human being. This guy is the worst. I'd rather have breakfast with a Pravda scientist or one of the snotty zombie hookers from the other side of the fence than spend another minute with Matt.

Chapter Twelve

The Reason We're Stuck Here

Several tedious hours later, it is 8:45 a.m.—time to leave for our meeting with the Elders. I make another appearance in the kitchen looking as cool and confident as possible in some of my nicest new clothes. My scruffy old tennis shoes don't go well with the new outfit; but my other choices were socks with sandals or the pink platforms and that's an obvious choice. My hair is showered and springy with curls. I left it down again today to hide the ugly bruise on my still tender neck. Matt unapologetically looks me up and down several times. He lifts his eyebrows and winks at me again which gives me the chills.

I don't know what Aunty's plan is for him while we are gone. His meeting with Thomas and Thomas' new family isn't until later. We can't take him with us and he definitely can't stay here in the house alone. Please God, don't let Aunty be that trusting. When Aunty asks if he would be willing to wait outside of the fence until his meeting at noon, I sigh with audible relief. They both look at me and I blush and look down at my grubby shoes. I guess she's already been out today to set that up with the right people.

"Whatever," he says flatly. "I just want to get Thomas and go home as soon as possible." After a pause he adds, "You said there'd be lunch. Are you cooking it?"

I don't know if he's afraid of being poisoned by a stranger or if he is hoping for more of her good cooking. Either way, Aunty says that they'll be meeting at Thomas' house and his family will be providing "refreshments." Such an old lady word, I can't help cracking a small smile.

We all walk quietly down Alexander Street. It's another clear, cold January day. I'm not a fan of Georgia winters. They rarely get cold enough for any snow, but everything stays dead and gray and dirty looking. And it rains a lot. Cold and wet is definitely the worst weather I can think of. Today it's very cold, much colder than yesterday. My breath puffs out in vapors ahead of me as we walk. At least it's not rainy.

I'm bundled in my new thermal green ski coat—the fateful picture still tucked in the pocket—with a matching pink and green scarf around my neck. Keeping my hands tucked in my pockets, my fingers nervously play at the edges of the photo. Everything I'm wearing is new except for my hat. I've always worn the same one, since I was little. My mom made it for me. It's pink, of course, with two points on top like bunny ears ending in little yarn pompoms.

Walking behind Aunty and Matt, I am dwelling on his most recent irritating comment. His appreciative reaction to my appearance in the kitchen—not that I cared at all -turned to obvious humor when I came out of the back door in my wintery getup. He smirked and said, "Nice hat." Nice hat. It is a nice hat. I bet his mother never made him a hat. And I don't care what he thinks. I'm warm. And I like my hat.

Aunty is dressed equally warm and considerably classier. She is forever looking like a magazine ad for classy old lady clothes. She's toasty warm but not bulky looking. Matt has produced a knit hat out of thin air—who am I kidding? You know Aunty gave it to him—but has nothing warm on over the long-sleeved t-shirt and jeans. He, of course, still wears the gloves. They don't look particularly warm though. They are thin and satiny; the type of gloves made to cover up diseased hands. I wonder if all ten fingers are his or if he has some of those fake fingers in his gloves. He has to be freezing, it's like 30 degrees out here, but I'm sure he wouldn't admit it.

We walk past the old library which is now used for storing dried goods. Past the old post office, now the security building where "weapons" are kept and security personnel trained. We don't actually have weapons. We don't believe in killing, even in self-defense. We have Tasers for protection. The few guns that are in our community are only for hunting. We are not a well-armed bunch. Hopefully, the fence is all we'll ever need. If we could just hold out here for a little longer -

In a few hundred feet we see the gate looming ahead and the security guards walk towards us to meet us partway there. I guess word about Matt has gotten out, probably from the men who kept watch over us last night. The guards don't look at all surprised to see us escorting a zombie out of the community in the morning hours.

Aunty, Miss Manners, makes introductions, "Al and Tom, this is Mathew. Mathew, these two good men help keep us safe here."

Al and Tom look as awkward as I have been feeling, giving me a wonderful sense of justification. As they shake hands with Matt, I notice Al subtly wipe his hand on his pants after the handshake. I glance at Matt's face to see if he noticed and I'm pretty sure he did. Why does that make me feel like gloating?

Tom reaches out and takes hold of Matt's arm to lead him out through the gate. I'm close enough to Matt to hear the low rumble that becomes an explosive growl as he jerks his arm away from Tom, snarling like an animal that could take Tom's arm off with one bite. Normally, confrontation of any kind really stresses me out. I am definitely not myself lately because I find myself stifling a giggle in what should be a shocking and tense situation. The guards look unsure in front of Aunty, not sure how to handle her "guest."

In this small pause, Matt marches quickly and resolutely up to the gate. Al rushes up behind him and shields the key pad with his hand as he punches in the security code to open the gate. Then Matt is through, and I breathe a sigh of relief. Back on the other side where he belongs. He finds my eyes on him and winks at me one more time before turning and walking down the road, his downturned mouth making the wink seem more sinister than the previous ones. Maybe he'll just go and not be back at the gate at our appointed meeting time. Wouldn't that be wonderful?

I don't seem to have good enough luck for that lately. He'll probably be there with a whole bunch more of Thomas' family members. I bet they're all real winners.

Aunty thanks Tom and Al and asks them to treat Matt politely if he returns before we do. She only looks at Al as she makes her request.

*****

Aunty and I retrace our steps back to the Inn and continue on past it to the city courthouse building across the street. This is our meeting place, community center, hospital, and most importantly our church. We call it the Upper Room, the U.R. The Elders meet in one of the smaller rooms on the main floor. I see them almost every day because I work two doors down from them as a volunteer secretary to the teachers of the U.R. I help the teachers with classes and reports and research, and I sometimes visit the members of the community to find out what they need from the U.R. I really like my job and I have learned a lot while working under the five different teachers.

Mr. Jarvis teaches the younger kids—only twelve of them in the whole community—six of which are 5 years old or younger. They were born after the disappearances, after we were left here. The other six are 12 to 13 years old, Thomas is one of them. There is no one left on earth between the ages of 5 and 10. Every one of the kids in that age group—all over the entire world—disappeared, because at the time of the Second Coming those kids were babies and young children. They were innocent. Pretty creepy, huh? So, Mr. Jarvis has a tough job being in charge of preschoolers all the way up to middle-schoolers. Chuck Fox has been helping him lately, giving much needed support.

I'm 16, almost 17, and there are twenty other teenagers between the ages of 14 and 17 in the youth class with me. Our teacher is Mrs. Sherry LaFakis, a gentle, devoted woman in her early forties. I used to pretend that she was my mom, which I've outgrown but would still love to be true. Sherry's daughter, Harmony, is the closest thing I have to a best friend. Harmony is genuine and honest and sort-of like a sister to me. Though we are very different, I can always count on Harmony to understand me when no one else does.

The young adults study under Ms. Julia Scott. There are about fifty of them, which is a lot for her to handle so I help her a lot, administratively. I'm still not sure why she goes by Ms. She doesn't talk much about herself and I'm not sure if she was ever married or if she had kids or anything. I would guess her to be about 40 years old.

The other one hundred and ten members of our community are old like Aunty. They have two different teachers, one for the men and one for the women. Mrs. Ruth Manof leads the ladies—though sometimes I'd swear Aunty was in charge—and Dr. John Talmurf leads the men. With the older groups, the leaders are more like administrators. They teach on occasion, but there are several others who are equally capable and learned and they all just switch around and take turns. Dr. John Talmurf is also one of the Elders.

The head Elder, Rev. Ralph Depold, is both the Pastor of our church and mayor of the community. A pudgy, older man in his late sixties, Rev. Depold leads us with gentleness and—more than occasionally—tears. Intelligent and faithful, he reminds me of my grandfather; but sometimes I have a hard time respecting him on account of the frequent crying. It's probably genuine, but sometimes it seems kind of—manipulative.

As Aunty and I sit outside of the Elders' door and wait to be called in, I muse about how all these great people managed to get left behind. They are such leaders, so godly and obedient; their deep love for The Lord is evident. I've heard them stand up on Sunday morning and tell their stories. Almost all of them came from churches and Christian communities. Most of them had husbands and wives and children and grandchildren who all disappeared that awful day. They knew immediately what had happened, but it was too late. They had known God with their head but not their hearts. Even Aunty was a Sunday School teacher for twenty years before He came back. But they all missed the point. It wasn't a passion, there was no deep love. It was a job, a requirement.

And He knew.

So one by one they each grieved their losses and shook their fists at God and reminded Him of all they had done for him and how great they were. And one by one they all realized their great mistake and fell under His wing and finally clung to Him. And it wasn't too late. The fact that we don't have the disease proves that we belong to Him, even though we're still stuck here for a little while. He's giving us a second chance. He's giving all of humanity one last chance. My thoughts are interrupted when Heidi, the Elders' secretary, calls us in to our meeting.

Chapter Thirteen

Aunty Uses "The Force"

There are ten Elders in total. Nine of them are here this morning. Only seven Elders need to be present during a meeting to make a large enough group for a vote to be taken. Even though I see these men on a daily basis, I feel nervous about being the object of their judgment. I feel like I'm on trial for something.

The room the Elders use for their daily meetings is inauspicious; a small room with gray walls and industrial carpeting. The ceiling is tiled with those large lightweight white squares that are common in public buildings. Several of the squares are missing a corner or sporting ugly brown water stains from leaky pipes upstairs. The small room feels too warm, probably because there are so many of us in here. I feel sweaty and itchy. I scratch self-consciously at my face. With my luck, the heat and my nerves will give me hives.

The elders sit in a semi-circle around a large meeting table made up of two long folding tables put together to make a square. From left to right they are: Mr. Davys, Mr. Phillips, Mr. Terrell, Dr. Talmurf, Rev. Depold, Dr. Harvey, Dr. Allison, Mr. Hunter, and Mr. Todd.

Rev. Depold, sitting in the middle, welcomes us heartily. He is leaning back in his chair, fingers crossed over his wide belly, telltale hanky sticking out of his pocket. I hope there's no crying in today's meeting. After taking off our coats, Aunty and I take two chairs that are close to each other—across the table from the Elders. They all stare expectantly at me as though I should say something. Aunty gives my leg a squeeze under the table.

"Well, Colleen, tell us what happened," Dr. Talmurf says kindly, his eyes twinkling with energy despite his old age.

I know Dr. Talmurf the best since he's one of my bosses. My favorite thing about him is that he always seems excited about things that should be boring, like theology and the Bible. And his enthusiasm is catching. I love listening to him as he prepares his U.R. lessons. My little desk is just outside of his office. He always leaves his office door open just a crack when he rehearses and I'm sure it's for my benefit. He's my favorite among the Elders. The other Elders don't seem to mind that Dr. Talmurf has taken the lead.

Aunty clears her throat and begins.

"We left early, as is our custom, yesterday morning. The drive was uneventful, the car in perfect working order, and after leaving the community we didn't see another living soul for the rest of the drive. We found the stores just as they were six months ago, completely devoid of people. If my memory of six months ago serves, I'd say it didn't look as though anyone had been there since the last time Ivy and I went. We were careful none the less. We went in each store together, and we took turns watching over each other and gathering supplies."

When she says "supplies," ," I can't help but think again of my frivolous choices—the jewelry, the zombie shirt, the pink shoes—and I blush at how unnecessary some of my shopping was.

Aunty continues to recite, "In the last store of the day, after much success and no incidents, we were frightened by a noise in the back of the store. To be safe, we hurried from the store to the car. We did have our Tasers with us and we are both capable with them, having taken all the safety courses required by security to carry one. When we got into the car, we were immediately assaulted by a diseased man who had been hiding in the back seat on the passenger side."

I'm squirming nervously and hoping no one will ask, but Mr. Terrell interrupts Aunty and asks the obvious question.

"How did the man get into the car without you noticing? Was the alarm not working properly?"

"We had mistakenly left the car unlocked after a trip to the car with some of our bags."

She squeezes my hand under the table to comfort me as she takes responsibility for my mistake. I am thankful to not be on the spot yet, but I still feel the blush of shame on my cheeks.

Mr. Terrell, a very businesslike man who doesn't often show his feelings, frowns and reprimands Aunty. "So carelessness is the reason for this meeting?"

Aunty points her blue eyes at Elder Terrell with a calm, even gaze and clears her throat.

"Unfortunately, I believe there would have been an incident either way. The man attacked Ivy from behind and—"

Mr. Terrell cuts her off mid-sentence, "I'd like to hear about the attack from Miss Ivy," he pauses and then adds, "Please."

Aunty nods, mild irritation showing on her almost perfect face, and looks over at me with expectancy.

I start by saying "Yes sir," but my throat is dry and scratchy and my words are quiet and unclear. I have to clear my throat twice and say it again, "Yes sir. I got into the car and knew right away that a zombie was in the car because he smelled awful."

The nine men before me all suddenly look appalled and "ahem" a lot and clear their throats.

Rev. Depold, concealing a smile, speaks up for the first time since greeting us.

"Ivy, we do not refer to the lost as—zombies. That is a very derogatory term and we will gain no ground with them if we think of them as monsters. They are just as we were before grace. They are to be pitied and loved with Christ's love or we are no better off than they."

He nods at me while staring into my face with his gentle reproof and indicates with a wave of his hand that I continue with my story.

I'm embarrassed at how immature I must sound. I need to be more like Aunty, professional and calm. In my opinion, the story oozes drama and should be told as such. But, for the sake of credibility, I'll be business-like.

"He reached around from behind my seat and locked his arms around my neck. He was choking me, but I don't think he wanted to kill me."

Mr. Terrell interrupts again, "It is strange that he didn't restrain the driver first, isn't it?"

Rev. Depold says softly, "Let her tell the whole story Marcus, then we'll make our comments."

Mr. Terrell nods and they all look at me again.

"Anyways," I'm trying to keep my train of thought, "I struggled and Aunty quickly Tased him several times. I think he was unprepared for us to fight back and didn't expect us to be armed. He let go of me when she shocked him and fell on the floor in the back seat. Aunty pulled away from the shopping center towards the road to make sure no one else came to his aid. Presumably whoever—"

Aunty quietly cuts in and corrects me, "Whomever."

"Yeah, *whomever* made the noise in the back of the store," I take a deep breath. "So we drove a good ways away and then Aunty jumped out and came around to help haul him out of the car. She shocked him a few more times and we pulled him out and dumped him on the street. He was wearing a silver Pravda bodysuit, zomb—uh- shoes that *they* wear, and an Oscar the Grouch mask. You know, from Sesame Street?"

This gets another little grin from Dr. Talmurf. Blank stares from everyone else.

"Um, so I jumped back in the car, but it took Aunty a little longer because she was looking at something the man had and when she got back in she showed me that he had a Portaroid picture of me."

"Polaroid," Aunty corrects.

At this piece of news, they all get pretty animated, turning to look at each other and exchanging scowls.

"Do you have the picture now?" Rev. Depold asks kindly. His smile is forced now—its genuineness questionable when paired with the heavy scowl of his bushy eyebrows.

"Yes sir. Here."

I pull the photo out of my coat pocket and push it across the table to him.

"This was taken of me just last week. I remember the day that I wore that shirt. But I don't remember seeing anyone with a camera."

I can't think of anything else to tell them. There's a long pause with everyone looking at me with concern.

So I add, "Then we drove home."

I sit back in my chair and look at Aunty. I'm very ready to be done talking.

"Anything you can add to this account, Colleen?" asks Rev. Depold.

She looks sad and says, "Only that after much thought, I am very confused about the nature of the attack. I can't imagine something with any planning, which obviously there was because of the photograph, being so easily thwarted. I'm afraid it wasn't their intention to take Ivy and I'm therefore quite worried about what their intentions really were. I can't help but feel less safe here in the community. Someone here took that photograph. I don't think an outsider would've gone completely unnoticed in broad daylight and I'm worried that there is someone here in the community who can't be trusted. Unfathomable as that seems."

Everyone sits stunned and quiet at this pronouncement. This is a terrifying new thought, and I'm as shocked as they are. I wish I could think of a hole in Aunty's logic, because then I'd feel safer, but I can't. I thought we had escaped our attacker and made it back to the safety of our home and our people. But if Aunty is right, I'm still in real danger and nothing is simple anymore. I know we had already talked about who had taken the photo and the possibility of not being able to trust someone. But she hadn't told me that she thought we were *meant* to get away. That something worse than the attack was still going on. A plot of some sort that involves me. Rev. Depold and Aunty are looking at each other across the table with a mirror image of sadness and understanding on their faces. I wish I knew what they were thinking.

Mr. Terrell says, "What about the boy who spent the night at the Inn last night. Do you think that was smart? Is he possibly involved in this in any way?"

"I don't believe he is related to our shopping experience in any way. He is here for Thomas, as you know. I think it was coincidental that he showed up at our door yesterday and I truly believe he is in no way involved."

Aunty seems to put force into these words; like she's Obi Wan Kanobi, wielding "The Force." Like she can simply speak with conviction and these men will believe her and repeat back, "these aren't the droids we're looking for." Sometimes I suspect that she uses these powers on me. The other elders look pleased to hear this, but Mr. Terrell seems to be immune to "The Force."

"You likewise convinced us that shopping was safe, against our better judgment, and you were wrong about that. Be careful that you don't think yourself wise Colleen and put us all in danger with your trust of this young man."

Aunty simply returns his gaze. She has always been a strong woman.

Standing on her own without a man. I think she has a hard time submitting to the entirely male board of Elders. If women had been allowed to be elected, I'm sure she'd be on the board herself.

I suddenly remember the other thing I need to tell them.

"Wait! There is one other thing. Matt, Thomas' brother, I don't think he came in through a gate. He doesn't look much like a zomb—" I catch myself again, "like one of them because the disease isn't very advanced on him, so I guess someone could've let him through carelessly. But there should've been an escort right?"

The men all nod in the affirmative like bobble-head dolls.

"Well, he didn't explain, but I am pretty sure he came in somewhere else. And I think someone should check the fence for holes. Or maybe a ladder or a tree branch he could've used to come over it?"

"Thank you Ivy. You are a bright girl; which is why I'm glad to have you as my secretary," Dr. Talmurf says with a kind smile and a conspiratorial wink.

"We will need to discuss all of this and consider how to investigate further," says the always calm Rev. Depold. "I am very thankful to have both of you back safe and sound; and, for now, you are excused. Please don't leave the community for any reason until further notice. Also, please be available to answer more questions should we need to call you back again. Thank you."

That's our cue to leave I guess. I thought we'd have more involvement in their discussions. I don't really want to be talked about and decided on without my knowledge; without some input on my own fate. We are standing up and leaving, but I'm not happy about it.

Rev. Depold, still holding on to my photograph, calls out "God bless!" as the door closes behind us.

I hope He does. I could use some blessing for a change.

Chapter Fourteen

Sister Bear and the Evil Grannies

Filled with frustration, newfound fears, and a million questions all fighting to be heard and answered in my weary brain, I walk quickly to the front door. I just need to go. I don't know where, but I need to go. My legs need to walk. I yearn for some distraction. My emotions are raw and I don't want to cry. I wish I had somewhere to go other than the Inn.

I reach the front doors of the U.R. and realize that Aunty isn't with me. I turn around to see her heading the other direction, and she calls out for me to wait for her outside. I don't know what other business she has here this morning, but that isn't surprising. We don't feel the need to run every detail past each other. She must be coming out any minute because she would've told me to wait inside where it's warm if her errand had any potential of keeping her long.

I wait for her out on the front steps in the frosty cool air. I'm trying to process everything and the hugeness of it threatens to overload my already frazzled emotions. I want to feel afraid, but I know I need to trust. I want to cry, but I've done enough of that in the last twenty-four hours, and I've resolved to be done with weakness. I take deep breaths of the freezing air and it burns my lungs. The burn feels good; the stinging pain in my lungs somehow lessens the pain in my stomach. It's weird that pain feels good. I breathe deeply again and hold the cold air in longer—relishing the distraction of my lungs being on fire.

Last year, a girl in our community lost her whole family in a fire. It went around the community that her new guardians found her cutting herself. I remember how badly I thought of her, how judgmental I was. I remember thinking, "Doesn't she know that was God's plan for her? Why doesn't she just trust Him? He'll obviously take care of her." She killed herself not long after that. I judged her for that too. Now, I desperately wish she had made it through. If she couldn't handle life, maybe I can't either.

What if Pravda comes for me and I die in a lab as one of their experiments? As the door swings open behind me I turn, expecting Aunty but run right into Chuck Fox. His eyes bulge at me like they might pop out of his head and his normally cheerful face looks yellow and sick.

"Chuck! I'm sorry. I didn't mean to block the door. I'm waiting for Aunty. Are you alright? You look terrible."

Foot in mouth as usual. I meant that he looks sick, but I don't know if he took it that way.

"Oh—Ivy—uh, yeah, I was just seeing the Doc. I got a little bug or something. I'll be fine. How ya doing kid? I heard you had a close call yesterday."

I guess the news has gone all around. I wish everyone didn't know. It's so embarrassing.

"Good thing your aunt is quick on her toes, eh? What a woman."

He shakes his head and looks at his feet. His embarrassment is cute, so smitten with my Aunty. He seemed so lost when he got here a few months ago; still deeply grieving his wife. The first time I met him, he looked desperate. I think Aunty must remind him of his late wife or something because he fell hard and quick for Aunty the moment he saw her. In recent weeks he's looked happy every time I see him, like a man who suddenly has hope for the future. I wish I knew the feeling.

"Well, I'll see ya around Ivy. You be careful now okay?"

He meets my eyes and stares hard into them with his friendly warning. His gaze has a fatherly feel. If Aunty ever caves, I guess he'd be like a father figure to me. I would like to take comfort in Chuck's kind words, but the serious look in his eyes reminds me how much trouble I'm in and an involuntary chill runs down my spine.

"I hope you feel better soon," I call after him as he walks quickly away from me, his bald head pointing the way towards his apartment. "I'll pray for you!" I call out.

I hope he's not too sick. There aren't a lot of medicines left at the clinic and the government shipments that come to Toccoa don't have anything more than what you'd find in a first aid kit. Things like Band-Aids, Tylenol, gauze, and rubbing alcohol. The sorts of things people with oozing, open wounds might need.

We've cleared out all the local abandoned pharmacies—there were two of them within our gated sanctuary—but Aunty says we are running low on everything. A trip out of town will be needed again soon; and, in light of my recent debacle, the Elders won't want to send anyone out unless it's extremely necessary. I hope Chuck doesn't need more than some rest and some Tylenol. Maybe Aunty and I should make him some soup with the left over fat and trimmings from the venison.

I know it's not my fault that we were attacked, not my fault that it's not safe to leave town, not my fault that the compound is low on medicine, not my fault that Chuck is sick. But I feel like it all is, every bit of it. I feel like making Chuck soup will somehow make *me* feel better; assuage me of some of the responsibility. I don't know why I always feel so burdened. I would call it a God thing, blame it on convictions or something, but I don't think it is. No one else tries to make everybody else's problems their own. If anything, thinking I'm the answer to everyone's problems is prideful. I think it's called a savior complex. I wish Tylenol could fix it.

A minute later, Aunty comes out of the front doors with a bundle in her arms. It's a man's winter coat.

"I got this from the clothing bank," she looks at me as though it's obvious, but I look blankly back at her.

"That's a man's coat, Aunty. Do you need another new coat?"

"Oh Ivy, it's for Matt. Didn't you notice how cold he was? I guess you have a lot on your mind right now dear, huh?"

I am ashamed because I did notice that Matt was cold and I didn't much care, so I say nothing. I'd rather she think I was self-absorbed than know the truth of it. I'm down-right mean.

"Why don't you leave it with the Elders? Won't they be seeing him soon? Which one of them is taking him to see Thomas?"

"Oh." Long pause. "Didn't I tell you dear? We are."

She rushes into her reasoning, knowing me well enough to know an argument is coming.

"I mean, I feel responsible for the boy and I genuinely like him. I think he's a good man, you know, all things considered."

I'm about to voice my most recent rant about zombies and how much I don't want anything to do with them, when she blurts out her next reprimand.

"Oh and by the way, I can't *believe* you called that man a zombie right in front of the Reverend! Ivy, I've told you so many times not to call them that! I should've reminded you again I suppose."

She shakes her head in a loving, "tsk tsk, shame on you" kind of way. Silly, sweet, dumb Ivy. I feel myself getting more depressed by the minute. I accept my fate and slump after her towards the gate to pick up her new pet.

I remember reading a Bernstein Bears book about strangers when I was a little girl. Sister Bear goes to the park with Brother Bear and the whole world is her friend. The birds wear happy faces, the old ladies on the park bench are sweet little grannies with big smiles, and even the bunnies in their holes are smiling sweetly at her. "Hi!" she calls out to everyone she meets. Brother Bear runs home to tattle on her for talking to strangers. Mama Bear tells her that even though someone looks nice on the outside, they can be rotten like an apple on the inside. The next day at the park, Sister looks around and sees only scary faces. The birds have evil grins and dark eyebrows and they are perched in sinister looking trees. The old ladies on the bench are scary and wicked with sharp pointy knitting needles. Even the little bunnies in their holes look like they'll jump out at any moment and chew off her foot. Sister Bear runs home terrified.

That is precisely how I feel at this moment.

Leaving the meeting and the safety of the U.R. building and walking down the familiar streets of our small community, I feel as though the world has never looked so frightening. The sky is the same winter gray that it was yesterday, but today it looks ominous. As I look up at the windows of the buildings that neighbor our Inn, I feel sure that nefarious enemies are hidden behind the opaque glass, staring down at me with their scheming plans as I walk around the town that used to feel like a haven to me. I wonder if I will ever feel safe here again.

I'm walking slowly and looking all around in guarded unease. Aunty grabs my hand to pull me along. She starts talking, trying to cheer me up.

"It's all going to be alright dear. The Elders are smart men. Mr. Terrell may be rough around the edges, but he cares for the people. He cares for us—"

This is news to me. I've hardly spoken to the man.

"- and I bet he'll be the one who works the hardest to sort this all out. Even if it's partly because he'd love to prove me wrong."

She winks at me. She has an unending spring of faith in God—and in His people—bubbling up out of her. Sometimes it's very encouraging. Right now I find it nauseating. So I change the subject.

"Do you know how Thomas is? Is he nervous?"

"I haven't heard anything about him yet. Jose and Ellen simply agreed to meet with Matt. To tell you the truth, I'm not one hundred percent certain they've told Thomas yet. When I mentioned Matt's name, they already knew that to be Thomas' brother's name. I guess he's had terrible nightmares about Matt and has had guilt about leaving his family. I don't know how they'll handle this, and it is up to them how to handle it, for Thomas' sake."

We walk in silence for a minute before she speaks again.

"You could help the situation a lot, Ivy. You could treat Matt with care and concern and a smidgen of decency. I think that might defuse a lot of the tension. Hmm?"

What I think and what I'll say out loud are two different things. "Mmm hmm. I'll try Aunty."

"I'm praying for you honey. I know you have a lot going on in that adorable head of yours."

"Mmm hmm."

What I'm thinking about is the rekindled hope that he won't be waiting at the gate. I don't see him anywhere as we approach the gate. In fact, I don't see anyone at all, even the guards. As we walk closer to the gate, I hear laughter and music coming from the security building next to the gate. The door is open; and, as Aunty and I arrive at the door, we see the guards, Tom and Anthony, playing cards with Matt. They look like they are having a great time, drinking Coke and laughing like they've been friends forever. Elvis is blaring on the CD player in the corner. I've heard that Tom has quite an extensive collection of CDs.

Al must have gone home after his shift. Anthony, Al's daytime replacement, doesn't seem as grossed out by zombies as his predecessor. In fact, Aunty's request that they treat Matt kindly has indeed been respected. Anthony has his arm around Matt and is pretending to whisper something insulting about Tom.

We all hear him clearly say, "Tom's got a wife who's a...well, one of you guys."

It's an awkward moment, punctuated by Elvis starting into the chorus of "You Ain't Nothin But A Hound Dog." Aunty and I stand quiet, witnessing this strange exchange. I am cringing inside at Anthony's lack of wisdom when I realize that I've been just as tactless. I'm ready for Aunty to clear her throat like she does when she's about to start "putting things right."

Tom laughs Anthony's ignorant words off, calloused to his friend's careless banter, and makes a horrible corny joke about how *he* left her—for Jesus.

I'm embarrassed for all of us.

Right on cue, Aunty clears her throat to make our presence known. The guards jump up and both talk at once about entertaining the guest and waiting on us. Their simultaneous explanations are all jumbled together, but we get the gist of it.

Matt stands up to follow us out of the door; and, to my great surprise, turns to thank them each by name for the game of cards and their hospitality. He tips his Coke can towards them in thanks and follows us out. Respect and thankfulness is not normal zombie behavior and it definitely isn't normal Matt behavior. It makes me nervous. He is good at his game—I'll give him that.

Chapter Fifteen

Zombies Just Want Hugs

We have a longer walk this time, but everyone walks these days. The half mile to Thomas' new house doesn't feel strenuous and won't take us more than 7 or 8 minutes. The Inn is only a little over a block away from the Western security gate and Thomas lives on the other side of our community near the Northern security gate.

Matt accepted the new coat from Aunty with minimal fuss. Probably just didn't want to deal with her nagging. I can sympathize. The coat fits him well; a dark navy blue wool coat with wide lapels and big buttons. The coat is heavy and warm, and Matt's cheeks get pinker and his lips lose their blueness as we walk. I guess it was nice of Aunty to think of him. I think the clothes at the clothing bank are supposed to stay in the community, and this coat will be leaving soon. I guess if anyone here needed a coat they would've picked it up by now. It is January and winter is hopefully wearing down.

As we walk, Aunty continues to try to coax conversation out of Matt, though she doesn't seem to be as good at it as the security guards were. Maybe women make him uncomfortable, who knows? Who cares? I'm still trying not to see danger around every corner.

I keep repeating one of my favorite verses to myself in my head:

At what time I am afraid, I will put my trust in thee.

I've chanted that verse to myself many times since my healing four years ago. Aunty taught it to me the first week that I lived with her—when my parents didn't come for me like they were supposed to. There has always been something for me to be afraid of or worried about. You'd think I'd be tougher by now, but there is something so personal with this fear. It's different from all the countless fearful possibilities that have given me cause for worry over the years. Different from the one million things that a logical thinking adult would have to worry about on a daily basis in a world run by zombies. This is only happening to me.

I'm lost in my head again when we arrive at Thomas'. The little, white house with a green roof sits not far from the chain links of our security fence. Just beyond the fence, no zombies are in sight—just old railroad tracks and a broken down train car that is probably rusted to the tracks by now. We walk up the narrow sidewalk, single-file, and stand beneath the green awning over the front door. Jose and Ellen's house has a storybook cottage feel about it. I can't help thinking that we've just escorted the big bad wolf right to granny's door.

We ring the doorbell and the door is opened by Jose, Thomas' new dad. Jose and Ellen are only in their early twenties and are too young to have a kid Thomas' age. They met and married here in the community just a few years ago. When Thomas came to us just before Christmas, he was traveling with a missionary named Harvey. Harvey insisted that Thomas stay here in Toccoa. Before Harvey left, he asked the Elders to care for Thomas and find him a home. Thomas stayed at the Inn for a few days while the Elders looked for the right family.

The poor kid cried a lot those first couple of days. I think Thomas thought he'd be sticking with Harvey and traveling around with him. Missionaries live a very dangerous life. Harvey left him here to keep him safe. I'm sure Thomas was missing his family a lot too. Matt, supposedly.

Aunty and I were really considering asking him to stay with us when Jose and Ellen asked for him. They are easygoing and seem really happily married. Jose is Hispanic, handsome and athletic. He is very involved with the youth at the U.R. and is in charge of all things athletic for the teens and little kids. Kind of like a Youth Pastor/Gym Teacher. Thomas isn't very talented athletically, but it doesn't seem to matter to Jose at all. He loves the kid already. Thomas is so easy to like.

Thomas' new mom, Ellen, is a nurse at the U.R. clinic. She is a petite, Chinese lady who loves to cook. She also loves to jog. I often see her and Jose jogging past the Inn together early in the morning. Ellen is very motherly, and I love how she dotes on Thomas. He looks so happy every time I see him lately. With both of his new parents working in the U.R. building, I get to see Thomas almost every day. He comes to visit me in my little office and sometimes brings me a cup of tea. Jose winked at me last week when Thomas brought me some of Ellen's cookies. I think maybe I have a twelve year old stalker.

Jose welcomes us into their home and Ellen is standing with a smile on her face just inside. The wonderful smell of baking hits us instantly, and I realize how starving I am. I don't see Thomas anywhere. I glance at Matt;

his face exudes disappointment and frustration. His green eyes flash as they roam the small house's open floor plan, searching for his brother. As Aunty makes the introductions, it's obvious he could care less about meeting Jose and Ellen.

"Where is Tom?" he demands gruffly. "Tom! Tom!!!" he calls out louder in hopes of an answer.

"Please sit down and talk with us for a minute," Ellen says with stress in her voice. Ellen's tone makes me wonder if maybe Thomas isn't here. I don't think Matt will handle that well at all.

"We just want to speak with you before we get Thomas, okay?" Jose says as he sits down and reaches out to pat the chair next to him in an invitation for Matt to sit.

Matt does his normal stubborn thing, looking at the chair then at Jose with raised eyebrows and a stormy face that plainly says, "I don't think so buddy."

"What do you want, a copy of his birth certificate? I don't need this! I think you are holding him here against his will in your sick cult community, and I demand that you let me have him. He doesn't belong here with you! He's my brother! I'm sorry I didn't bring any baby pictures with me to prove who I am. Go get him. Now."

I'm nervous about what Matt is capable of as the threat of violence grows in his angry gestures.

Matt continues, his voice loudly echoing around the little living room, "He knows me. I'm his brother. And, let me be clear, I'm here to bring him home. I will bring an army here to tear this place apart if I have to. You have no right to keep me away from him!"

I have no giggle for the tension of this situation. Matt is scary when he's furious -so much angrier than he was during the little standoff at the gate earlier this morning. His green eyes pop with rage and his face is contorted in a mask of dark threats. He waves his arms as he rants and paces around the room. I'm ready for him to start throwing things when we hear a quiet voice behind us.

"Hey, Matt."

Thomas is standing in the doorway looking meekly at his big brother.

Thomas' blond curls have grown out, covering the telltale black spot on his forehead. I'd say he's filled out a little since arriving here, the results of his new momma's good cooking. He is wearing the Steelers sweatshirt he had on the day he came to town. I'm sure he wore the familiar shirt for Matt's sake.

Matt's flashing green eyes are angry, staring at Thomas. Then, suddenly, Matt is bounding across the room towards Thomas. My stomach lurches in fear that Matt will hurt Thomas and I see Jose hurling himself after Matt. I hear Aunty gasp and Ellen cry out in fear. The next moment, Matt is on his knees in front of Thomas and wrapping him in a desperate hug. We all stand speechless, staring at this unexpected display of love.

"Why?" Matt says angrily, but you can hear the tears in his voice. "Why did you leave me? I've been following your trail, asking everywhere, looking everywhere for you!"

He shakes Thomas by the shoulders gently. Then quietly, with awe in his voice, he asks, "You're better?"

He has suddenly noticed the lack of disease. Matt's description last night of Thomas' condition before he came to us was heartbreaking. I can't imagine watching a loved one wither away before my eyes. Matt looks amazed and thrilled at the changes in his little brother. There is no doubt that Thomas has been completely, miraculously healed.

"Yeah," Thomas looks like he'll cry any second. "I got cured and I didn't want to be trouble. I didn't want you to have to take care of me and defend me. I knew they'd send me to get tests and needles so I went with Harvey cause he was cured too and he knew all about God and why I was better and—"

Thomas dissolves into tears and Matt continues to stare at him. Turning Thomas around, Matt looks under Thomas' shirt and behind his ears, even parting his hair and checking his scalp. Matt inspects Thomas top to bottom, like a mother cat that just got her kitten back. Matt gently brushes Thomas' curls aside and stares at the black spot on his forehead. The black spot is the only evidence left that Thomas was ever one of them.

Matt turns to us with the softest face I've seen on him and whispers the words, "He's cured? How?"

Chapter Sixteen

I Spy a Shred of Decency

I can't get over how loving Matt is with Thomas. He keeps Thomas—he calls him Tom—in his sight at all times. If Matt smiles any bigger, his dried out zombie lips might start bleeding. I wouldn't have guessed he was capable of this much happy. I can't keep my eyes off of him. This new behavior is so bizarre, so unlikely—like watching a pig fly.

We spent the first fifteen minutes of Matt and Thomas' reunion trying to talk about God—explaining why Thomas is better. Matt didn't seem to care much about the mechanics of it all. He listened with poorly restrained impatience and kept interrupting us to ask Thomas something totally unrelated to whatever we were saying. At that point, Aunty signaled a halt to the heavy conversation.

The adults are visiting quietly in the kitchen, and I am nestled into the corner of Jose and Ellen's soft blue sofa—staring. Watching both of them, the two brothers in their joyful reunion, but my eyes are more on Matt than on Thomas. Yesterday's greasy-haired, foul-smelling, bitter-faced zombie has been replaced with an easy-going imposter. Today, Matt's soft brown shaggy waves cover his ears and hide his mild symptoms. In the warm, dim light of the cozy living room, you'd never guess his true nature. His black satiny gloves are the only overt evidence left. They look wrong on him today, and I wish he'd take them off.

I'd probably regret that wish if it were granted.

I'm sure he wears them constantly for a reason. I don't want to see the grotesque deformities on his hands. The menacing gloves are best left on. Seeing someone covered in sores and infection, ruined and mangled from a curse they refuse to acknowledge is something you don't ever get over. It's a sight that will fuel your nightmares for years.

The zombie men that cat-call from the other side of our fence almost always wear masks. They reek from 20 feet away and most of them are crippled and hunched over. The zombie from the outlet mall was the first one I've seen up-close, without a mask, for a while. And he looked like a rotting corpse. Hence the nick-name that I keep getting in trouble for using.

It's true though—I don't know why we can't say it out loud. Not only do they look dead, they are Dead in the same way that we are Living. I don't know how they endure it. I would welcome death if I was prematurely decomposing.

I can't even picture Thomas looking like one of them. I wonder why Thomas was so bad. A new thought dawns on me—I wonder if Matt is so much more normal for the same reason? Maybe he didn't have the shot? I thought all of them had gotten it, Matt included. When I didn't see the black mark on Matt's forehead, I just assumed it must be hidden on his gloved hand. Gloves or not, spot or no spot, I find him less evil by the minute as I watch him pin and tickle his giggling little brother.

I would be content to sit quietly and spy on them all afternoon, but the tempting smells of meat cooking and bread baking are becoming a painful distraction. My stomach moans an angry growl—so loud that Thomas turns to look with an accusing smile—and I blush embarrassed at my body's noises. Ellen is waiting to serve lunch until after Thomas and Matt have spent a few minutes catching up. My stomach is going to start ingesting other internal organs if we don't eat soon.

Sneaking away from the semi-violent tickle fight in the living room, I head to the kitchen to see if I can help move things along. Ellen has prepared a feast of Asian cuisine with so many different dishes on the table that I'm thinking we should've invited the whole Board of Elders. There's enough food here to feed Aunty and I for a week. Maybe she'll send us home with leftovers. Ohhh—I am so hungry!

"Is it time to eat, Mom?" Thomas says, bouncing into the kitchen after me, wearing his typical jovial smile.

Matt is standing close behind, and I see his eyes bulge in surprise. I'm not sure if it's because he just heard Thomas call Ellen "Mom" or if it's because of the huge feast on the table. Knowing Matt's appetite, it's probably the feast.

"Yes, I just finished," Ellen says with an adoring smile. If not for their obvious difference in skin color, anyone would assume she really was Thomas' mom. Doting, maternal love colors every word she speaks to him. "Let's all sit down. Wash your hands first, okay?"

Ellen, the nurse and new mom of a twelve year old is, of course, germ conscious. A sudden, uncomfortable situation arises, since Matt is still wearing his gloves and probably has no intention of taking them off. I glance at Aunty and we both look at Ellen, hoping she'll realize her mistake.

She does.

Ellen starts to stammer that only Thomas needs to wash up. Matt, oblivious of our nervous behavior, strips the gloves off and washes up at the kitchen sink. As he turns back around looking for a place to dry his hands, he catches all of us staring with open-mouthed shock at his hands. They look a little dry and chapped, but not at all like what we were expecting. And no black spot either.

Then, Matt does something that forever changes my opinion of him. He lifts his eyebrows at us, holds his hands up in front of everyone and wiggles his fingers in a show of health. And then, looking at me with those haunting green eyes of his, he winks.

Everyone else smiles and sheepishly shuffles to a chair at the table. The conversation resumes, and they all just go on like it's nothing.

I'm dwelling on it.

I'm intrigued by his sense of humor. Charmed by how lightly he takes himself. He's so normal. So nice. A loving big brother.

I like him.

I can't believe it, but I genuinely like him as a person. I know it's Schitzo of me because I hated him this morning. Am I really this fickle and emotional? Maybe it's just relief. Yeah. That's it—relief. I'm pleasantly surprised to find that one of them can be decent. It restores some of my hope in the rest of the world. I'm sure that's where these feelings are coming from.

Now that Matt has found his brother, the frantic way that he moved and spoke is gone. His dangerous anger seems to be gone too. He doesn't think of us as horrible people who kidnapped his brother anymore. Thomas is better than ever and deeply loved by all the people in this room. I think I'm seeing the real Matt now.

As I linger on these new optimistic revelations, brooding and smiling to myself, I don't realize that Jose is praying for our meal until about halfway through the prayer. I look up for an instant and find Matt's eyes staring at me. Blushing bright red, I drop my head and pretend to pray with the others. I can hear Matt already digging in to his food before the “Amens” are said.

Chapter Seventeen

Please Pass the Foot So I Can Eat It

Dinner might have been delicious, but I can't remember tasting my food. Yes, I was really hungry, and I inhaled it. But it's more because I was so lost in my thoughts and awkward about Matt. Now that I've decided I don't hate him, I am focused on the thought that he might still hate me. I haven't been good to him at all. He has every right to hate me. I've been unfriendly, aloof, unaccommodating, judgmental, oh—the list goes on and on. I'm trying to figure out how to start being nicer without looking totally mental.

No one else is talking much; they are listening to Thomas talk excitedly about everything he's done and seen since leaving Matt. Matt listens to everything Thomas says with an adorable crooked smile on his face. I study his face while he is safely staring at Thomas. Matt's nose is thin, but nicely proportioned to his thin face. He has long eyelashes that set off his large, emerald green eyes. Matt's thick black eyebrows seemed so menacing yesterday; but, softened by his mood, they are comically bushy today. He has two crooked teeth that stick out just slightly on one side of his mouth. When he smiles, he only lifts his lips on the opposite side. I wonder if he's self-conscious of the crooked teeth and has learned to hide them when he smiles.

Thomas mentions God several times casually in his stories. "God helped me do this, and God showed me that." I keep expecting Matt to be disgusted or to turn and yell at us for brainwashing Thomas, but it doesn't happen. Matt has so much love and admiration for Thomas that, even though Thomas is so much younger, you can just tell that Matt trusts him and respects his opinion. There is no condescension in his eyes as he listens to Thomas ramble, only genuine admiration. Another side of Matt I never would have guessed existed.

And I needed to see it.

I guess I had forgotten. Every day I think about how evil the zombies are. I've obsessed over it to the point of despising every single one of them. With this display of brotherly love, I am forced to remember that all humans were made to love and care for each other. That even zombies are capable of love. The Living don't own love. Family is still an unbreakable bond, no matter who you are or what you believe. It makes me miss my zombie parents. Makes me wonder if I'll ever see any of my family again. I had a sister once, too.

Hazel ran away from home when I was just a toddler. My parents never said it, but I think she left because of me. Mom and dad had me later in life. Hazel had been an only child and was 15 when I was born. They never admitted it, but I know she was unhappy. In the few pictures I saw that were taken of her before she left, she never smiled. When I came along and they were so in love with me, it pushed her away even more. I wish she had stayed. I wish that she and I had gotten a chance to have what Matt and Thomas have.

While they all listen to Thomas talk about tent camping with Harvey in the snow, I carry on with my ogling. Matt continues to draw my excessive gaze, partly from fascination and partly from—I don't know what. He isn't gross anymore. He's maybe almost slightly attractive. Which is crazy talk. It's just how much he loves Thomas. Like when guys are automatically cute when they are holding a baby. He's not just capable of love, he's good at it. He's kind, funny, encouraging and gentle; not just some pig-headed, overly masculine jerk. I'm attracted to his personality. Not that he's ugly. But I guess I found him really ugly just yesterday.

Can I really have changed my mind this much about him, this fast? If you had asked me a week ago if I could ever be attracted to one of them, I would have laughed at the absurdity of the thought! Just laughed and not even answered you. This is new territory for me.

I keep reminding myself he's a zombie. He's a zombie, stop staring!

And he keeps noticing me staring, so I'm trying to look at him out of the corner of my eye to figure out if he's just staring at me because he's noticed I'm staring at him or if he's actually staring at me. This is maddening.

When Ellen stands to clear away the dirty dishes, Aunty and I stand up to help. In the close quarters of the small kitchen, I find myself brushing past Matt several times during the clean up. He smells—good. Like coconut shampoo.

All of my stereotypes and negative expectations are evaporating. My stomach somersaults every time he looks at me. It's so weird to me how normal he is. He fits in just fine, like he belongs here. I wonder if he feels it too. Visiting with Jose and Thomas, he seems comfortable and relaxed.

I remember how hostile he was yesterday and how set he was on taking Thomas away from us. What if he still wants that?

*****

As the day stretches on, Matt never mentions leaving. Surely everyone else is as nervous about the confrontation as I am. I can't help obsessively wondering when it will come up. Every time Matt speaks I brace myself for it to end with, "By the way, I'm taking Thomas now and there's nothing you can do about it." I know Jose and Ellen won't let Thomas go. They'll say no for sure. What then? Do they have the right to say no?

Jose and Ellen ask Aunty to come downstairs with them to see the renovations they've been making in their basement. Jose's tone was too peppy, too persuasive for the boring subject of basement linoleum. You know, the way adults speak when they think they are fooling us kids with their obvious duplicity. I'm not an idiot—I know they are talking about Matt. I'm left alone upstairs with the boys, and I think Matt knows he's being talked about too. It's awkward.

Thomas breaks the silence. "Ivy is my best friend here."

This simple endearing statement takes me by surprise and gets me blushing again.

"I stayed with them at their house when Harvey brought me here. What room are you in Matt? Did you get the Africa room too?"

"Yeah," Matt answers Thomas but he's looking at me.

I blush even redder and look away. Stupid cheeks. I must learn to control this.

"Ivy played games with me and made me grilled cheese sandwiches and she took me for a walk all around town and she helped me make a fort under the big table in the dining room. Did you see how big that table is?"

"Yeah, it's big." Matt answers again, still staring at me and smiling his one-sided smile. "Thanks for everything you've done for Tom."

I just shrug and smile back awkwardly, barely able to meet his gaze. It's our first pleasant conversation. The first time he's spoken directly to me since I realized he isn't just a creepy zombie. It's crazy obvious that my feelings have changed. Yesterday, I glared at him with unveiled hatred. If only I could play it cool now and not look like a schizophrenic mess. But my traitorous femininity won't obey. My mouth won't stop smiling and my cheeks continue to burn brighter, betraying my new attraction.

"Really. Thank you. You've all been so kind. I was really worried," he says quietly. His tone becomes playful as he puts an arm around his brother. "Now I see that he's been living it up while I've been freaking out looking for him." Matt roughly rubs at Thomas' curly head inducing more happy giggling.

"Thomas is one of us," I say, nervously responding to his appreciation.

What I meant to say was: *It's no big deal. He's a great kid who fits in perfectly and is easy to love.* Expert conversationalist that I am, it sounded nothing like that.

Matt's face darkens and his half smile slowly lowers to match the other side in a firm line.

I should take a vow of silence. The whole world would be better off. Of all the things I could've said, that's the first and only thing I've added to the day. I alienated Matt and made it seem like Thomas belongs here with us and that Matt doesn't.

Brilliant.

Thankfully, Aunty, Jose and Ellen come back up the stairs—saving us from my destructive powers of foot-in-mouth conversation. Aunty announces that she and I have a lot to do at the Inn, indicating that we'd better get going. This is it. The moment. What will happen? Who will bring it up?

Aunty, pulling her coat on, offers, "Will you be staying with us again this evening Mathew?"

"Yes, thank you. Tom and I are going to hang out for awhile, though. Is it alright if I ring the bell when I get back?"

"Perfect," Aunty approves. "Your coat, Ivy?"

"Oh yeah," I mumble and hurry to pull myself into the puffy warmth of my coat. I can't bring myself to put my pom-pomed hat on—I guess I do care what he thinks. I ball it up in my hands and fiddle nervously with it. Matt doesn't look at me again; and, after thanking Ellen for the wonderful food, we leave. Just like that. No big moment.

As soon as we are down the sidewalk, I barrage Aunty with an assault of questions. “What do you think Matt will do? Do you think he’ll let Thomas stay? Maybe now that he’s seen that Thomas is healed, he’ll be smart and let him stay where it’s safe.”

“I hope so. Actually, we are hoping that Matt will decide to trust God and stay here with Thomas.”

I hadn’t thought of that. Why hadn’t I thought of that? Isn’t our whole purpose to bring people to God? To tell them the good news that they can be healed? Why have I never once considered Matt becoming one of us? Maybe because he is so antagonistically against everything we believe in. Will seeing Thomas change that? I kind of doubt it—but I would like it. It would be pretty great if he did change and stay. I mean great for him—and his soul.

“Thank you for trying so hard today, Ivy. You were much nicer with Matt. I appreciate your effort.”

“No problem.”

It wasn’t really an effort at all. It felt good to be nice to him. He’s pretty cool.

Chapter Eighteen

Here's Hoping He Left Out the Gas

Back at the Inn, there are plenty of chores to fill the evening. While I dust and fold, my thoughts drift to Matt over and over again. His eyes have burned an image into my mind that I can't shake. Sometimes those leafy green eyes are dark and frightening in my memories. Other times, they pop into my daydreams full of emerald expectation, and the thoughts they evoke leave me feeling breathless. I need to think less about him. I'm not allowed to like him. What a ridiculous thought, me having a crush on a zombie. Ha! I don't. I'm pretty sure I don't. Well, fifty percent sure.

When the doorbell rings my stomach does ten flip-flops.

That doesn't mean anything. I don't have a crush on him.

I run to my bathroom mirror, wet my hands and run them through my curls to smooth the frizz. My face looks pale. I pinch my cheeks a few times. That's better. A quick swipe of lip gloss, okay I'm trying too hard. I run for the door, hoping Aunty didn't hear the bell ring.

It's him; I can see him through the glass. I slow down and take a breath.

No blushing. Control yourself!

Pulling the door open for Matt, I see Jose standing just behind him on the porch. "Hi," I say to both of them, breathing hard from hurrying across the big house, "Come in."

It's gotten even colder out and the freezing air rushing in makes me wrap my arms around myself. Matt steps in past me, but Jose doesn't follow him into the house.

"I was just walking Matt back," Jose says, peeking out from behind his zipped up coat. "We'll see you tomorrow," Jose calls over his shoulder as he trots down the front steps, his shoulders hunched against the evening chill.

I'm sure Matt could've found his way back to the Inn on his own, but the community wouldn't like one of *them* wandering our streets unaccompanied. Jose waves without looking back as he starts up the sidewalk towards home. I push the big wooden and glass antique door shut behind Matt.

Alone with Matt in the golden light of the foyer's brassy chandelier, the awkwardness of our last conversation returns. I don't want to alienate him again. I really want him to feel welcome and at home here. Aunty's words have been bouncing around in my head all day. Will Matt decide to follow God and be healed and stay here with us? I smile nervously and try to meet his stare. He looks down at me from his slightly taller view. He doesn't return my smile, but his mysterious eyes are unleashing their full power on me and I get lost looking up into them.

"So -" I start with no idea what to say next. "Uh—how was your day?"

So lame.

"Great. Thanks," he says softly, staring into my upturned face only a foot or so away from me in the quiet foyer.

"I thought I heard someone. Matthew, how was your day?" Aunty asks, appearing out of nowhere.

Was she listening around the corner? The creaky old hardwood floors usually warn me when she's approaching. I should've heard her coming. I blush deep red, and step back embarrassed and insecure.

"Do you need anything in your room? More towels?"

"No. Thank you," he answers calm and confident. "Everything is fine. Thank you again for keeping me here—and for all you did for Tom when he came here. He talked about you all day."

Matt looks at me again, and I can only imagine all the info Thomas has given him about me. An unfair imbalance of knowledge lies between us. I know nothing about him.

I dig through my memory of those days with Thomas here at the Inn and try to remember if I did or said anything horribly embarrassing. I think we spent an entire afternoon making fart sounds as conversation. What are the chances that Thomas left that out of his Ivy account?

Ugh.

Aunty ushers Matt upstairs for the night, leaving me standing alone and self-conscious by the front door.

Chapter Nineteen

My Butt Hangs Out

I am snuggled under my covers, trying but failing at falling asleep. Could he be interested in me? Is it any compliment if he is? He's a zombie. He's probably interested in anything that wears a skirt. Even if I was super ugly, I'd still be more attractive than a zombie girl—by virtue of having uninfected, unspotted skin.

Stop thinking about him Ivy. Stop!

I toss and turn in frustration, looking for a comfortable position. I should be exhausted. I've been up since 5:00 a.m., and I've had a long, emotionally exhausting day. I wish I hadn't drunk all the milk. Warm milk would be nice right now. Maybe some tea.

I climb out from under my faded rose colored comforter and feel goose bumps breakout on my arms and legs. The furnace gets turned down at night, and the house gets very cold. I thought we were past the worst of winter; but, the way the temperature continues to drop, I wouldn't be surprised if we see snow tomorrow. Slipping my pink holey bathrobe on, I tiptoe to the kitchen. I'll just put on the tea kettle and make myself some of Ellen's homemade chamomile tea. That'll help me sleep.

There's a soft light seeping under the kitchen door. Aunty must've forgotten to turn the stove light off. She really is getting old. Pushing the door open, I'm once again shocked to find Matt sitting at our kitchen table. Last night my shock was revulsion. Hatred. Tonight, it's excitement, nervousness, confusion; and, mostly, extreme awareness of how ugly I am in this ratty bathrobe.

"Why are you down here?" I blurt from the doorway, my flustered self-sounding—flustered.

"Hello to you, too."

I cringe. I did it again. At least he doesn't seem to get offended every time I speak—because let's be honest, he should.

I take a breath, purse my lips and try again, "Hi."

Pulling my ugly bathrobe tighter around me, I bravely step in to the kitchen. He's reading. That's interesting. I didn't expect him to be a reader.

"You read?" I ask with too much surprise.

"Yes, Ivy. Me read," he says in a tired, cave man voice.

An unauthorized giggle bursts out, and I follow it up with a sheepish smile.

He smiles that half smile back at me. "I know you don't talk to anyone outside of your angelic town, but I'm guessing you don't have a lot of conversations with guys in God Town either. You don't seem very good at it."

He's insulting me. I feel deflated, and I ready a spiteful comeback.

"Don't get me wrong, it's actually kind of cute," he says before I can throw out something rude about him having only whores for friends.

He called me cute.

That repairs *most* of my hurt feelings.

I return his half-smile; and, cautiously, sit down across from him. "What are you reading?" I ask.

"I borrowed it from the bookshelf in my room. Little Women," he says holding up the large book with a beautiful scene on its cover. "Every other book on the shelf was religious. I'd rather get in touch with my feminine side than read about imaginary feelings of loyalty and self-righteousness. You really need some Tom Clancy or Dean Koontz."

"Who?"

"Never mind," he flashes that disarming, somewhat condescending smile.

Is it possible that this zombie is more well-read and more educated, than me? I'm sure his education and mine would have very little in common. I ignore his jab about the foolishness of my faith and change the subject.

"Do you want some tea? That's why I came out here. For tea."

"Sure. Thanks."

Standing up to fill the kettle, I remember that the biggest hole in my bathrobe is right over my butt. I turn quickly back around and find him looking down at his book and hiding a chuckle behind his gloved hand. I have pajama pants on underneath the robe. It's not like I'm indecent. Still though; so embarrassing.

I finish making the tea while turning myself at odd angles to avoid him seeing my holey butt. At the first chirp of the kettle, I pour our cups; hoping that Aunty didn't hear the kettle's whistle. I fill the small metal tea ball with fresh dried chamomile and tighten the little lid. Using the delicate chain that hangs from the strainer, I dunk the tea in his mug first and then in mine. My tea will be weak, but I don't want to waste any more of the tea. It's almost gone. Unlike my attitudes last night about the venison and the good china, I find that I don't mind giving him the better cup of tea tonight.

It's Christian maturity and nothing more, I tell myself.

"I think my brother is in love with you," Matt says with the crooked grin.

"Yikes," I say, sitting down across from him with my tea cup warming my hands.

"He talked about you *all day long*. I feel like I know you really well."

"I hope he didn't tell you everything."

"I assume you're referring to your hidden talent of making 'super cool fart noises'. His words, not mine."

I drop my head into my hands in horror and scrunch my eyes closed; I was so hoping Thomas hadn't told him about that. There is no way to control this blush. Matt could see my face glow red in the dark.

"That was really great of you," he continues softly, and I can tell he's trying to be serious. "I think you gave him more than you realize. He's happier than I've seen him in years."

"Umhphm," I mumble into my hands.

"Ivy." Matt's gloved hand is on my arm.

I jump in surprise and sit back, pulling my arms away and off of the table.

Matt just shakes his head at me. Apparently I'm hopeless and predictable. I need to get out of here before I make myself look any worse. If that's even possible. Tea in hand, I stand up and start backing towards the door—still trying to keep the big hole in the back of my bathrobe out of view.

"Well, goodnight," I say pleasantly, as though this has been a normal, completely un-embarrassing visit. "Enjoy your book. It's a good one," I say due to a complete lack of anything else to end my bungling banter.

"Goodnight," he says with his crooked smile.

I fumble with the doorknob behind my back and clumsily slip from the room.

Chapter Twenty
Eat My Heart Out

Today is so opposite from yesterday that it's hard to believe they fell next to each other on the calendar. I was thrilled when Matt beat Aunty to the kitchen again this morning and I ready this time with a smooth, "Good morning, I trust you slept well?"

Minimal blushing.

When Aunty arrived in her bathrobe a few minutes later she found us talking pleasantly at the table. No chairs overturned or anything. Aunty made eggs and toast and I enjoyed every bite while visiting almost easily with Matt at the table. After breakfast, he left for Thomas' house with Aunty as his escort.

*****

Left alone to do my chores, I alternate between humming and singing as I vacuum the threadbare oriental rugs of our sitting room—filling the echoey parlor with melody and the clacking roar of the sweeper. The high ceiling makes my voice sound bigger and more operatic. I haven't belted out in song like this in ages. I can't quit grinning about this strange, joyful optimism that has taken hold of me.

Rubbing lemon-scented oil into the carved wooden mantle above the fireplace, I smile at the curly haired, pink cheeked girl who smiles back at me from the ornate mantle mirror. Monday's horror is a fading memory—the only reminder is the scratch on my neck that seems a little infected today.

I keep thinking that I'm past the anxiety of the attack, but the cold fear continues to return when I see the souvenir welt in the mirror. The warm, puffy red cut stands out on my neck and brings back the terrorizing attack in all its horror. I'd avoid looking in the mirror altogether but—well I find myself wanting to make sure I look nice. I keep wanting to smile at myself in the mirror and then stare to see if I think the person looking back is worthy of my attention—or anyone's attention. Pulling myself from the mirror's hold, I give a focused burst of effort to the tasks at hand.

Aunty and I have been invited to Thomas's for lunch again today. I finish my chores in record time and have almost an hour to decide what to wear and how to fix my hair. Keeping the weather in mind, I put on a plush new sweater that is dark purple. The soft fuzzy weave falls almost to my knees. It would look best with tight leggings, but my old tennis shoes would ruin that look; so, jeans it is. I braid my long curls into pig tails and put a little sparkly eye shadow close to my lashes. I almost never wear makeup and I'm afraid that if I add anymore Aunty will see right through me.

*****

On the walk to Jose and Ellen's, I have to slow my giddy skipping steps to stay in pace with Aunty. She is walking slower than normal, and I wonder if it's just to frustrate me. Not even she can get me down today. I feel sure that God has brought Matt here for a reason—to save him. I know Matt will feel it too, and he'll decide to follow God and stay here with us. I just know it. I know it like I know that the cold sky is gray and the evergreen trees are just a shade darker than Matt's incredible eyes.

*****

Lunch was delicious.

I feel full, warm, and happy. Matt has winked at me several times in the last half an hour. I'm still glowing from Ellen's compliments when we arrived. Something about how "purple is my color and how gorgeous I look in my new sweater." Not that I remember it word for word and am replaying it in my head—or how when she said it I blushed and looked away, only to catch Matt staring intensely at me with that handsome half smile. I'll be honest, I don't know if I've heard a single word of anyone's conversation; I'm so lost in my own happy glow. My life is finally getting good.

Cue disaster.

The moment that I've been sure wouldn't happen, does. I am standing up to help Ellen clean up the table, when Matt clears his throat.

"I want to thank each of you for everything you've done for Tom and me," he says.

My hands fall to my sides; I can tell goodbye is coming.

I imagine everyone has been dreading it, skirting around it with pleasant conversation. Hoping, like me that it just wouldn't happen. Leaning over, Matt whispers something to Thomas and the poor kid's face falls. We could tell it was coming and we can guess what was said. Thomas looks lost and confused. I guess he *didn't* know it was coming. He shakes his head "no" and looks to Ellen.

Matt says quietly, "We'll be leaving after lunch." Then he looks into Thomas' eyes again and says too cheerfully, "Tom, pack your stuff. Just what you came with."

Does he think that his upbeat tone will make everything better and Thomas will just run off at the request of his hero big brother? I'm sure that worked when Thomas was little, but it's not working now.

"Now wait a minute," Jose says sternly, as though he's a forty year old man when in reality he's just a few years older than Matt. "We need to talk about this."

"There's nothing to talk about. He is my brother, he comes with me. I appreciate how kind you've been to him. He hasn't had parents in a long time, and you've been awful good to him. Thank you. But blood is important, and he needs me. We are going back to Atlanta. End of discussion." He shrugs his shoulders as though that pronouncement covers all that needs to be said.

Matt looks at Thomas again and says more seriously, "Tom, I told you to go pack up bud."

Thomas looks to Ellen and she nods at him and smiles sadly, "Go ahead to your room, honey, and we'll be in to get you when we're all finished talking."

"Okay," is all Thomas says, and he looks like his little heart is breaking as he obediently leaves the room.

Aunty, always to be counted on when it comes to lecturing, speaks first. "Matthew, Thomas won't be safe in Atlanta. We shared with you what happened to Ivy and me out there. They are hunting people who have been cured. Have you thought about what life will be like with Thomas living amongst the rest of the sick ones? I am sure you would do your best to protect him, but you can't be with him every moment. You have to sleep, you have to get food. I don't know if you work somewhere or how you manage, but at some point they will take him."

"I can keep him hidden," Matt says confidently. "He'll be safe with me. I'll keep a mask on him and no one will know he's different," Matt says without a hint of doubt, humoring her with his well thought out answer.

"What kind of life is that for him?" Aunty asks with the power of "The Force" behind her question. "Pretending to be sick, hiding from people? And if one person finds out, he could be gone before you even realize. Gone somewhere you can't follow and find him. We have no intention of keeping him from you. You are welcome here just as he is. We want nothing from him; we only want good things *for* him. We are hoping you'll decide to stay here with him."

I'm staring at Matt, weighing every response, looking for any clue that he'll consider staying. He meets my eyes and I see nothing behind his. They are cold and resolute. He has turned back into the guy we met two days ago. Emotionless. One of them.

Thomas bursts into the room from where he has been disobediently hiding in the hallway, listening.

"Please Matt," he begs, "I love it here. I don't want to go. They said you can stay too and that's perfect! I'm learning to play sports, and I get to go to school and Ellen's the best mom –" He trails off sheepishly as he looks around at all of us. "I love it here," he says to Matt while he's looking back and forth from me to the floor, his cheeks a light shade of pink.

I am touched to realize that I'm one of the things he likes about being here. I hope it matters. I hope Matt will reconsider. Maybe I could be a reason for Matt to stay too.

"Please Matt? Please? I don't want to go back to Atlanta. Maybe you could bring Jesse here?"

Who is Jesse?

Please let Jesse be the family goldfish.

I can tell Matt is frustrated, his emotionless facade cracking slightly. His bushy dark brows are furrowed and his eyes have a green hurricane brewing behind them. We all sit still, waiting to hear what he'll decide. I suddenly realize that I'm holding my breath and I try to let it out slow and quiet without looking like a dork who's been holding her breath.

"I have a life in Atlanta, bud," he says softly. "I don't know anyone here. I don't have a job here or a place to live. It just doesn't make sense. I've always taken care of you and you've always trusted me. You gotta trust me on this one, okay?"

Crestfallen, I blurt out, "You could live at the Inn!"

Everyone looks at me and they all have a different look on their face. Thomas looks thrilled at this suggestion. Aunty has one eyebrow way up in the air with a look on her face that says, "Excuse me?" I don't know if she's shocked at my change of heart or just not okay with my offer. Ellen and Jose glance between each other and Aunty. I think they were hoping for just such an offer. But Matt's face is the one I'm really looking at, and he is staring at me darkly. It's very obvious that he's not happy with this suggestion that came from some madness within me.

Nervous and on the spot, I start to stammer. "I mean—if you want too—it's okay if you don't—uh—you know—whatever."

"I told you," he says through clenched teeth, "I don't need your charity. I have a good job and a nice place to live that I like just fine. We are going," and then, softening just a little, he adds, "Now."

I feel tears spring to my eyes and Matt returns my watery gaze with a sad but resolute expression.

Jose starts to argue again and Ellen is crying softly. Aunty keeps trying to "talk sense" into Matt but he refuses to budge on the matter. At this point, what can we do? Matt is Thomas' real family. We can't hold Thomas here and risk Matt's threats of involving outsiders. That would be very bad for the community. We try really hard to go as unnoticed as possible by the outside world.

Matt walks Thomas to his room and helps him pack a small bag. Ellen and Jose follow behind like lost puppies at Thomas' heals, insisting that Thomas take the clothes and little things they had given him for Christmas. Somehow Jose had found Thomas an old Steelers jersey, signed by one of the players before football ended. Thomas told me about the special shirt once when he visited my office at the U.R. He holds the cherished gift now like a security blanket. Matt stands stoically by the door and, when the goodbyes seem to not be ending, he clears his throat and Thomas turns to go with him.

I am crying openly now. It all seems so wrong. I hate to think of the danger out there for Thomas. I feel so sad for Jose and Ellen. They really love Thomas and were making such a great life for him. I love Thomas too, and I know I will probably never see him again here on earth. And Matt—I like him—a lot. I'll admit it. If it would change anything, I would say it out loud right now. But I can tell by the way he avoids my teary eyes that it wouldn't. So I keep it to myself and only allow the truth to show in my tears.

As they open the door and step outside, the drop in temperature is shocking. It is even colder than it was on the walk over here, only an hour or two ago. The freezing air rushes into the house and makes Ellen cry harder. It's too cold to send her sweet boy out on a hopeless trek towards zombie town. The sky is noticeably darker, like a storm is coming, and big fluffy snowflakes are falling heavily. We all stand there for a minute, in silence but for Ellen's heartbroken sobbing, looking at the snow.

Matt voices what we were all thinking. "I had hoped for better weather. But we'll be okay. Our first stop isn't far from here."

"Come stay another night with us and maybe we can come up with something that works better for everyone," Aunty says with her arm wrapped around Matt's shoulders.

"No. It has to be now—but thank you."

"You are welcome to stay here with us, you wouldn't have to be separated from Thomas," Jose says with the desperation in his voice only thinly veiled. "Let's go back inside and keep the heat in."

"No," Matt says curtly.

"But -" Ellen starts to speak; and, when Jose puts his arm around her, she dissolves into a fresh round of tears.

Thomas wraps Ellen's tiny waist in a tight hug and then gives an equally tender embrace to Jose. Thomas' normally cheerful face is distorted in a pinched mask of confusion and grief. He loves his new parents. But his loyalties to his brother are ingrained. He's too young to be faced with such a big decision. Really, there isn't a decision being offered to him. Jose and Ellen aren't refusing Matt. They've begged and pleaded, but begrudgingly submitting to Matt's right to Thomas. Thomas is just rolling with the punches.

"I'll be back," Thomas says resolutely to Ellen. "I'm sure God is doing this for a good reason." Then turning to his big brother he asks with such innocence, "We can come visit, can't we Matt?"

"We have to go now, bud," Matt says avoiding Thomas' question.

"God will bring me back again." Thomas says to Ellen, looking up into her eyes with steadfast faith.

Thomas looks at each of us one more time and his patented smile reclaims its rightful place on his cherubic cheeks. He has such childlike faith. Something we are all supposed to carry. We aren't ever supposed to lose the faith that comes so easily to a child—faith mixed with imagination and devoid of life's long history of disappointments. Faced with such a hard situation, Thomas just assumes that God has a great plan and that it will all work out. He's more faithful than me. I'm learning a lot about myself this week—and I'm not proud of what I'm finding.

"Thanks again. You've all been great." Matt nods a final goodbye to Aunty, Jose, and Ellen. I keep my wet eyes trained on Matt's face, but he doesn't look at me again. I know I was awful to him in the beginning, but I thought maybe we were over that. I guess he really doesn't like me. I know I totally deserve it.

Matt and Thomas walk down the front walk towards the street. As they go, Aunty calls to Thomas who is following after Matt but glancing back at us every step or two, "Thomas, read your Bible and trust Jesus. We'll all be together again real soon. It's not long now. Take care of Matt. We'll be praying!" The last promise Aunty yells loudly into the wind.

As Matt and Thomas reach the street, they start to blur in the fuzzy white static of the falling snow. Aunty, Jose, Ellen and I stand in the cold and watch as the boys turn left down the road towards the gate. I can't seem to stop crying. Aunty puts her arm around me to comfort me as they disappear around the bend.

As we step back inside, I notice the coat that Aunty got for Matt hanging over a chair by the door. I compulsively grab it and dash back out into the falling snow. He should have it. It's freezing out here! I'll say I'm sorry, too. I desperately need to say I'm sorry for the way I treated him.

I run down the sidewalk, and Aunty calls after me to be careful. It should be easy to catch them since I'm running; but, as I round the bend and see the gate straight ahead, they are gone. They've vanished. I run the distance to the North gate and ask, out of breath, if the guards have seen them and let them through. They haven't. He must have gone out the way he came in. And I don't know where that could be. They're gone.

Matt is gone.

I didn't get to apologize.

Devastation sticks a knife and fork into my chest and starts to feast.

Chapter Twenty-One

The Lesser Of Two Evils

Three of the scariest, craziest, most emotionally full days of my life have turned the corner into a long, quiet, dull, depressing week. It's Saturday now. Matt and Thomas left on Wednesday. I've spent the last three days trying to feel normal and never achieving it. I've gone to work, but at work I see the Elders and they ask me how I'm feeling and if I've thought of any other valuable information about my attacker.

The "Outlet Mall Stalker" is the name I've given him.

It would make a good headline if we had a newspaper. We don't—but apparently we don't need one. Everyone has heard about what happened. Everyone I pass looks sympathetically at me. Like I'm dying of cancer and don't have long to live. Maybe they're right. If the scientists want me, what will stop them? I can't fathom a life where I never leave the compound again. At some point I will step out of these gates again, maybe just to end the incessant questions and fears that are plaguing me. I picture myself walking out and waving my arms and yelling at the sky, "Here I am, come and get me!"

Tim Markowitz stopped by the Inn on Wednesday evening after Matt and Thomas left. Apparently his only reason for coming was to say "Hi" and check on me. He brought me some cookie cutters he found somewhere—he said where but I can't remember—to cheer me up.

Aunty had a field day with that.

I think I thanked him, but I don't think I looked very thankful. And I definitely didn't look interested. I excused myself and went to my room hoping he'd take the hint and leave. I'm sure they talked about me as soon as I left. Aunty probably told him I was still distraught about the attack or something. When I came back out of my room an hour later he was still visiting with Aunty in the Parlor. It was such a nightmare. I just wanted to be left alone to cry about my horrible life. Tim stayed for one more cup of tea and some cookies before finally heeding the subliminal messages I had been screaming at him from inside my head.

"Leave!"

"I can't stand you!"

"You are totally gross!"

"Go away!"

Aunty kept shooting me dirty looks and motioning at me to smile whenever Tim wasn't looking. For one reason or another he left looking more interested and confident than normal. Inconceivable, because I couldn't be making it clearer that I'm not interested.

I can't quit thinking about Matt. I hate that I realized what a great person he was after two days of treating him with loathing indifference. No, I treated him worse than that. It was more like outright hatred. I wish I could have a do-over. I would be so much kinder. I'd ask him about himself and try to get to know him. I'm not so full of myself that I think it would've mattered or that he would've stayed. I just think maybe I wouldn't hate myself so much. And maybe he would've looked at me and said, "Goodbye." That would've been nice.

I can't fall asleep at night. I toss and turn and worry; and, when I do manage to sleep, I have horrible dreams. Ellen gave me more of her homemade chamomile tea to help me sleep. It doesn't seem to help. I've gone to visit Ellen twice in the last of couple of days. Even though we had only spoken a few times in the last year, I suddenly feel close to her because of our mutual loss.

She has cried during both of our visits. She's so worried about Thomas and misses him so much. I think she thinks I'm real sad about losing Thomas too, since he stayed with us a few days. I am sad about him leaving, of course I am—but really it's Matt I can't stop thinking about.

I haven't told anyone. They would probably be appalled. Aunty might have guessed, but we haven't talked about it, and I've been avoiding deep conversations. Ellen would never guess my true feelings, but she was there that day with Matt and saw that he had good qualities. So I feel like she's the only person who ever would understand. At least more than the others would.

I know it's stupid. What do I know about him? Very little. He's a zombie who loves his little brother. He is handsome. He has a good sense of humor. His green eyes are mesmerizing. That's not enough information to form such an attachment is it? I'm sure there are a bunch of classic psychological things playing into this.

Such as: The attack at the outlets has left me feeling mortal and vulnerable. I'm trying to make up a relationship to feel secure.

Or: I've bonded with someone who reminds me of my attacker like that Stockholm syndrome thing.

These reasons make more sense to me than actually falling in love with the first zombie boy I've spent a total of two days with.

I haven't devoted myself in at least a week, and I *know* that's a big part of my deteriorating mental state. I keep meaning to. I know it would make everything better; but, for one reason or another, something else comes up or I doze off.

Whatever.

I am pretty un-devoted right now. I've heard of people losing their healing and their faith. I won't let it get that bad. I just need to stop moping. The only solution I can come up with for the moping is napping.

Chapter Twenty-Two

A Doodle Makes Me Cry

The doorbell wakes me and I groan in frustration. It took forever for me to fall asleep and it feels like that was just a moment ago. I pull the covers over my head. I'm sure Aunty will take care of whoever it is. It rings again a minute later. And again.

Ugh!

I crawl out from under my warm, velvety pink comforter and put on some old flip-flops. A quick check in the mirror shows that my hair is still somewhat in place. I rub my cheeks and chew on a dry mint leaf. I don't want whoever is at the door to know I was napping in the middle of the day. I know that people nap and there's nothing to be embarrassed about. It's a privacy thing—it's no one's business but my own if I want to nap.

The doorbell rings a fourth time and I hurry to the front of the house a little irritated. It better not be Tim again. I think my good manners have run out.

Through the curlicue leaded glass pattern of the front door, I see my friend Harmony. I've been avoiding her, too. She already stopped by once this week, and I told Aunty to apologize for me—I had a bad headache.

My convenient headache wasn't really that bad; I just don't know what to say to her. She'll probably want all the details of what happened. I don't know how to talk about it. I like to go fix other people's problems. Honestly, other than the post-apocalyptic life I'm stuck with and the traumatizing childhood memories, I rarely have any serious problems of my own.

At least I still have my sense of humor.

I try to look happy to see Harmony as I unlock the door and invite her in. She looks shy and uncomfortable as she walks into the foyer, her tall, bony frame slumped over in bad posture. That's just her usual way though—humble and unassuming. She's wispy and thin with long wavy auburn hair and gray eyes. She would look like a ballerina if she carried herself with more confidence and better posture. She doesn't care about fashion, but somehow everything she wears looks good on her. She's a year younger than me, just 15, but she is several inches taller than I am.

I think her best feature is her lips. I wish I had lips like hers. They are full and beautiful and when she smiles, she's gorgeous. She stands awkwardly on the foyer rug as I shut and lock the door behind her. We smile unsurely at each other for a second, and then Harmony reaches out and gives me a quick hug. We don't usually hug. I wish so badly that things could at least be normal with her.

"I'm fine," I say with a shrug and a smile, easing out of her skinny arms. "Sorry, I guess I've been hiding."

"I know," she says softly. "And I know you don't want to talk about it. You don't have to okay? Just let me come over and we'll act like everything's normal." She puts her hands up in a non-threatening, "I surrender" gesture.

Wow, the girl knows me well.

"My mom sent you some stuff. Homemade chocolate to cheer you up and some papers she wants you to look over."

Harmony's mom, Sherry, is fun to work for and always extra nice to me. The chocolates are just one example of the many ways she dotes on me. The papers are probably for next week's lesson. Because Sherry is the teacher for our age group, I often see the lessons beforehand, help put them together, and then hear them again in my Sunday morning class with the other teens.

"So—show me what you got!" Harmony says enthusiastically, referring to my fated shopping trip. "Did you bring me anything?"

"Yeah, I did," I am smiling already. "It's in my room."

I model everything I got and Harmony does the best friend thing and tells me it all looks fantastic on me. I brought her a bunch of things and she blushes with each new thing I hand to her. But I know she genuinely would've been okay if I hadn't brought her anything. If I had gotten tons of new things and nothing for her, I don't think she would have been anything but happy for me.

Harmony seems overwhelmed with all of the new clothes; and, when I show her the matching cross necklaces I got for us, she gets teary. Making her so happy is helping me feel good again. Who needs a boy anyways? If we don't have much time left here, there's no point in crushes. No time for dating when dating's main goal is marriage. I just need to get back into my regular pattern, and that crazy couple of days with Matt will eventually fade into a bitter-sweet memory.

Harmony and I hang out all afternoon. I, of course, end up telling her every scary detail of our trip. It feels better this time, cleansing somehow, the second time I tell it. I trust her with my life, and I know she's not weighing my words in light of how they'll affect the community—unlike the Elders. She cares about me. I somberly tell her about the picture of me that we found in the zombie's hand. She is horrified when I tell her what Aunty concluded about Pravda allowing me to get away. We brainstorm for awhile about what it could mean.

"Show me the shoes," she says with a derisive tone that she can get away with because we are best friends.

I haul the pink heels out of the back of my closet and notice the bags of toys we got for Thomas but never delivered. It's for the best that he didn't see the toys. He would've had to leave them all behind. It would've only been more disappointment for him. My heart has that stabbing pain again.

I model the goofy shoes and let down my pride and laugh with her and let her make fun of me. They still make me feel taller—and thinner.

When we're done giggling, I ask my closest friend the question that's been plaguing me all week, "Why me? What makes me special from all the other people here? I'm not important to the community, not unique in anyway."

"Of course you are important!" Harmony says, her full lips in a pout—defending me. "Everyone here is important!"

Her enthusiastic encouragement makes me think of a line from a kiddy superhero movie we watched once at the U.R. The mom says to her superhero son, "Everyone is special." He in turn mumbles, "Which is another way of saying no one is." I remember thinking that line was clever. We talked about it after the movie. We are all unique and special in God's eyes, yadda yadda. But there's a ring of truth there. If everyone is special, then really no one is *special*, you know?

"Who could've taken the picture?" I have wracked my brain for the answer all week.

I try, again, to remember that sunny afternoon. What had I gone out on the porch for? It dawns on me suddenly—Harmony brought the reminder that I needed.

"The doorbell!" I shout at Harmony. She looks at me confused, wondering if I just heard something that she didn't. "That day! Someone had rung the bell and I had been napping! I was hoping Aunty would answer it. When it rang a second time I jumped up and fixed my hair real quick; but, by the time I got outside, no one was there."

Harmony is staring at me with wide eyes as I unravel my mystery.

"I walked down the side of the porch to look for whoever I had missed, but didn't see anyone! It wasn't a big deal, so I had forgotten all about it! I just figured I had taken too long to answer the door and whoever it was left thinking we weren't home!"

I realize, now, that it had been a set up. Sitting across from me on my bed, Harmony's gray eyes are huge. She stares at me with concern as we realize we've come across a very important clue. I look down at my hands. The seriousness on her face is freaking me out.

I haven't gotten to the Matt part of the story yet. I decide to tell it because of Matt's secret way in. It might be being used by someone other than Matt. I quickly fill her in about his time here, leaving out the gambit of feelings I ran through over those three crazy days.

"The key thing is that I'm certain he came and went from the community through some secret way in that he found," I sum up after telling her that he had disappeared around the bend and the guards confirmed he hadn't left through the gate. This is scary news to her too. The gate is the only thing that helps us feel safe living so close to our hostile neighbors.

"Is it possible some other zombie found the same way in? Are you really sure Matt doesn't have something to do with it?" she asks.

Just like the elders had.

"It seems way too coincidental to me," she continues reasoning, "him showing up within an hour of your, uh, attack. I bet you were so scared to see him standing there at your back door."

"I guess I was a little scared."

Don't judge me for leaving out my terror. I'm not good at being vulnerable.

"So then, maybe it isn't anyone we know at all," she says hopefully.

We both want this theory to be true. While it's scary to think that zombies can come and go from our community unnoticed, it is worse trying to imagine that one of the Living would do this. Really it's impossible. If one of the Living was working with zombie scientists to hurt me, they'd have to be living out of fellowship and they'd risk losing their healing. The disease coming back would be a dead giveaway. Surely someone in the community would've noticed and reported it to the elders.

"So what was it like, being around him? He was right upstairs while you slept?" she asks looking horrified.

"It was—weird."

I just can't talk about him with her. How would I explain all the confusing feelings? That first night, falling asleep, I had been so mad and scared. And then I had that horrible dream, reliving the awful moments in the car at the mall. But the next day, everything changed. I found Matt more and more fascinating. I found myself liking him. When he left, it was hard to believe how much of a turnaround I had done in so short a time. It physically hurts me in my chest when I think of him. My heart actually aches.

Harmony and I are both quiet, lost in our own thoughts. All the talk about Matt brings that hard day when he left back to me with clarity. I keep thinking the memories will fade but they only get stronger.

I see it all again—Aunty and I left Ellen and Jose so they could cry and console each other in peace. We walked home through the falling snow in tear filled silence, me still holding Matt's coat. I'm sure Aunty was thinking of others—praying for Thomas' safety, praying for Matt's soul, praying for comfort for Jose and Ellen. I was lost in my own self-centered thoughts. I wanted Matt to come back. I at least wanted a chance to apologize. Let's be honest, I wanted him to stay with us, find Life, and ideally marry me next week.

Halfway back to the Inn, I realized that no one had been up in his room yet. I needed to go up there alone. Maybe he could have liked me? There was all that winking. Oh, I missed the winking. Maybe he had left something behind? I was suddenly desperate to get in there. I quickened my pace without realizing it, filled with the desperate hope of finding something. Aunty assumed I was afraid to be outside and that I was hurrying home to safety. I let her think that, it had been true just the day before.

When we got back to the Inn, I had my speech ready. I told her I was ashamed of my bad attitudes—which of course I was—and that I was so thankful for her and her patience—once again totally true—and that to thank her I wanted to clean the dirty guest rooms by myself. So that she could have a break. This part was less truthful. But she bought it and, really, she did seem exhausted.

I grabbed some cleaning supplies and practically flew up the stairs. Matt had been in guest room number one; our smallest, manliest room at the top of the stairs. Room One's golden walls make it feel sunny and inviting on the cloudiest days. Someone painted an African mural on one of the walls years ago—a serene scene of a boat on a river with silhouettes of trees and a sunset on the horizon.

The other unique thing in the room is the bathroom. It is hidden behind a bookcase door. I glanced around the room and decided to clean the bathroom first. Pulling open the bookcase door, I found that the bathroom looked completely untouched. At first glance, it looked as though he hadn't showered or used any of the towels—they were all folded just the way Aunty and I leave them. Only a closer inspection proved that he had showered. Then he had wiped down the shower and refolded and rehung the towels perfectly. So he was not only a funny and endearing zombie, he was also neat as a pin. I opened the shampoo bottle in the shower and breathed in the coconut smell. The smell brought new lonely tears to my eyes.

After wiping down the bathroom, I began a careful inspection of the bedroom. I was meticulous in my search. I stripped the sheets from the bed—that he had remade perfectly—and shook them to be sure there wasn't anything tucked in them. I almost wondered if he had ever been there at all. There was no trace of him. At that point, I might have even liked it if the sheets had smelled like he did the first night, that cat litter odor. I had been so disgusted that first night at the thought of cleaning up after him and now here I was burying my face in his pillow hoping for some evidence that he had been there at all.

I dusted the furniture and knickknacks, my disappointment growing with each swoosh of the dust cloth. There was nothing there. It was like a ghost had stayed in that room. There wasn't so much as a stray hair left behind. With the room thoroughly clean, even under the bed, my depression overwhelmed me.

He was gone and I hadn't been anything more than an irritation to him. I looked the room over one last time to be sure it was ready for the next guest who came our way. On my way out, I noticed some books sticking out a little on the bookshelf door. I walked back in to push them back into place. One of the books was Little Women. I pulled it out, thinking maybe I'd read it again. A piece of paper tucked in between the pages fell to the floor. I had already given up any hope of finding anything from Matt, and I almost crumpled it up to throw it away.

Then I noticed what it was.

It was a simple sketch done in pen. Not much more than a doodle, but someone with talent had drawn it. It was of a girl with long curly hair. It was just her head and neck and all around her were beautifully sketched vines, ivy vines. Around the sketched girl's neck was a small cross. It was me! The ivy, the cross, I knew it was me. He doodled me. He thought about me. My heart was pounding, my stomach felt sick; my eyes filled with tears of happiness, sadness, and relief that maybe he cared -

"Are you okay, Ivy?" Harmony asks with concern etched into her face.

I snap out of my memories and brush away the tears that had carried over from daydream to real life. Harmony, assuming my emotions are still from fear, leans over to give me her second hug of the day. I accept the hug and the comfort and try to quit sniffling. I need to pull myself together. I can't tell her about him. She wouldn't get it, and it's pointless. He's gone. If I talk about my feelings, it will take longer to get over them. I need to move on to the bigger, more important issue at hand.

"I think priority number one is finding this hole in the fence and reporting it," I say with more gumption than I feel.

To be honest, the last thing I feel like doing is walking the perimeter, which may or may not have a dangerous hole somewhere, while enduring the catcalling that always ensues from the zombies on the other side.

"I'll come with you," Harmony offers bravely. "I don't have to be home for a couple hours. Told mom I'd be searching for a new book in the U.R. library, but that can wait."

Thank God she's coming with me. I'd be too scared to do it alone.

Chapter Twenty-Three
Afternoon of the Living Dead

After Harmony and I bundle up and go through the process of locking up the Inn, we walk down the main street of Toccoa, silent and overwhelmed. It's still cold, but not as frigid as Wednesday was. The snow fall became a raging storm the night that Thomas and Matt left us, leaving our grieving little group worried sick. My heart stormed all night in chorus with the moaning wind. The next morning, the storm had passed leaving several inches of fresh white snow on the ground. My insides were left empty and dark, no blanket of peaceful white in exchange for my mourning.

I've only seen snow a few times in my life. If I hadn't been in the depths of depression that day, I'm sure I would've enjoyed it. I heard the other kids in town went sled riding down the big hill behind the old Elementary school. None of them had sleds, but that didn't stop them. They made due with garbage can lids and flattened cardboard boxes. Aunty told me that Tim was there too, forsaking his responsible-old-man behavior to play with the rest of the kids.

That snowy night is just a pleasant memory for the rest of the town; but I find myself still lost in the stormy haze. The snow is mostly melted now and the sky is a vibrant blue. There are still little patches of snow left here and there in the shade of buildings and bushes; but, for the most part, the ground is back to its normal brown muddy winter ugliness.

The agoraphobic feeling of being outside of the Inn; and, therefore, unsafe returns. I feel like maybe Harmony and I should've told someone where we're going. We don't normally have to ask permission; but, in light of recent events, I feel a little nervous that no one knows what we're doing.

Harmony and I decide to start at the Western gate just down the street from the Inn. After all, the Inn is where Matt was first seen. As we approach the security gate, I'm happy to see that Anthony is one of the guards on watch today. He was kind to Matt, ergo I like him. That's how my logic is working these days.

"Hey!" I call as we walk over to him.

"Hey pretty girls," he says in his deep southern drawl.

Harmony blushes and stares at her feet. I'd better do the talking.

"Um, we are going to walk around the fence and check it for holes," I say with made-up nonchalant confidence in my voice.

"Ohhhh," he says, real slow and drawn out, his lips scrunched in a pucker as he weighs out whether or not this is a good idea. "You sure dat's smart? I don't dink dat's a job for two young pretty girls. You know, da Elders already had a group of guards go around two days ago and nobody found nuttin."

"Yeah, I know," I lie. "So, then it's perfectly safe for us to go around and get some exercise right? It'll just make me feel better to see it myself."

I hold my breath as he considers my plan, hopeful that there will be no reason to argue. We could always start somewhere else on the fence and avoid the guards and gates. I hate to be sneaky, but I really need to do this. I'm surprised to hear that the Elders took me seriously. That's pretty cool. It's comforting to know that security has already checked around. But they didn't know where to look, and I have a suspicion about where the breach might be. I think I'd be more likely to spot something out of the ordinary. Anyway, Anthony doesn't really have the authority to deny me my walk—fingers crossed.

I'm right because Anthony's face says "no," but he nods his head slowly in the affirmative, "Please be careful Miss Ivy. I don't tink it could hurt ta walk around, but stay aways back from da fence. We seen some real ugly groups near da fence lately. Less and less supplies in town. Day're short on da drugs and meaner dan ever. Everybody getting sicker. I don't tink anyone is helping us on da outside anymore. We on our own now," he says quietly while staring into my eyes with a warning. "I know dat all sounds pretty scary, but I mean for it. You girls gotta be careful now. Can't afford ta be naive anymoe, ya understand?"

Harmony looks terrified.

"Yes sir," she and I answer in almost perfect unison.

I add, "Will you radio to the other gates that we'll be coming through? Then we'll know people are watching for us and expecting us. That would be even safer, right?"

"Dat's a good idea ma'am. How 'bout you come all da way round ta me so I know when you're back."

"Okay," we wave and head down the fence in the direction of the North Gate.

Harmony and I walk and talk and periodically check the fence for any weaknesses. The guards were probably very thorough—I'm sure we won't spot something they didn't—but it doesn't hurt to double check. We look for any holes in the ground near the fence and also watch for any trees that stick over. Sometimes we have to go around a building instead of walking along the fence. There are a couple of buildings that go right up against the fence on our side, with a mere inch or two of space between.

We've been walking for about twenty minutes when we come within view of the North Gate. We wave at the guards stationed there, but don't stop to talk. They wave back, and it's nice to know that they were watching for us. They'll radio ahead to the South Gate now, and someone else will be waiting to wave at us.

We spend a lot of time around the Northeastern side, near Jose and Ellen's house. That's where Matt and Thomas disappeared, and I feel certain that Matt's way in is somewhere around here. We are disobeying Anthony's warning, walking right up against the fence so we can pull on it regularly. About a half mile down the fence from the North Gate, we pass a large group of zombies who aren't far from the fence on the other side. This isn't out of the ordinary. With minimal apprehension, we walk past quietly; hoping to get by without being noticed or harassed.

I glance through the chain links and unexpectedly lock eyes with one of them. The no-big-deal moment explodes into a living nightmare. The infected man's eyes look crazed as he holds my terrified gaze. He shrieks a loud cry of rage, and my stomach twists violently inside me.

The entire group of zombies sparks to life and runs at the fence en mass. Some of them are limping badly, but the lame ones seem to drag themselves to the fence almost as fast as the ones with healthier limbs. They are alive with fury. Mutilated faces scream and rail against the fence, and I can see the chain links strain against their force. Harmony and I stumble backwards away from the buckling fence, stunned by their sudden violent fervor.

They form a besetting, aggressive wall—grabbing the fence and shaking it while howling at us. Is it the drug shortage that's making them crazy? Though the noise is cacophonous, I can still hear how slurred and nonsensical their speech is. Some of them curse and shout sloppy obscenities at us like victims of Tourette's syndrome.

Harmony pulls at my arm, begging me to run; but I can't seem to unlock my legs. Though I'm scared out of my mind, I still find myself searching the crowd for Matt's face. The zombies are horrifying to look at. Many of them wear the full body suits, but a lot of them don't. In the chaos of moving limbs, I see bare areas of skin covered in sores and oozing blood. I don't know which is scarier, the ones with masks or the gruesome raw faces without masks.

Screaming masked faces is the stuff of nightmares, but the unmasked are grotesque. I see skeletal holes where there should be noses. Bloody lumps of tissue replace their ears and make them look more alien than human. One man's lips have shriveled up to reveal the toothy snarl of a predator. They look dead. Like, if we had arrived just moments earlier, we could've watched them climb out of their graves. How can anyone act shocked or appalled at the name that best describes them?

How can Rev. Depold even speak of winning these awful animals? If they could reach me, they would kill me—I have no doubt. The strained lace of metal wire is supposed to continue to protect us from them?

Harmony finally succeeds in pulling my attention to her terrified face and we run past them as fast as we can. Hiding behind the closest building, out of their sight, we wait for the screaming to stop. It takes me a while to convince Harmony that we're safe and that we should keep going. She might not be girly, but that doesn't mean she's tough either. She survives by living in her own little world of books and imagination. This is too much for her to handle.

After begging Harmony back onto the trail, we carefully resume our mission. We don't go back to check the section of fence where the group of zombies rushed us. If there was a weakness in that section of the fence, they'd surely have come through it.

We search the bushes, yards, and houses near where Thomas and Matt must have been when they suddenly disappeared. Just around the bend from Jose and Ellen's house, I find some cinnamon gum wrappers trapped in the melting remains of muddy brown snow under a large clump of bushes. I know Thomas loves cinnamon gum, but really, he could've dropped the wrappers there forever ago. They could've been blown there by the wind. Maybe he shared his gum with the little neighbor girl, Lois and she dropped the wrappers. It's nothing like a solid clue. We give up on that area and keep going down the fence.

The fence runs along the railroad tracks for awhile; and, though we check every possible place there could be a weakness, we find nothing. The occasional storm drains running under the tracks between our side and theirs have all been filled in with cement and show no sign of weakness. This search is turning out to be fruitless. I should be relieved, but instead I am fighting back disappointment and, strangely, loneliness.

Chapter Twenty-Four

5 Foot 2 Inches. Brown Curly Hair. Answers to the name Troublemaker.

When the third and last gate comes into view, I see a lot of commotion. There are more guards than normal standing around. Harmony and I exchange curious glances as to what the new trouble could be. When the guards spot us, two of them come running to meet us. I only recognize one of them—the younger guy, Terry, just recently graduated out of our age group and joined the security team. Terry and I haven't talked since he graduated, but he's a good guy and a friend. I don't recognize the older guard at all, though he seems somehow familiar. The looks on their faces makes anxiety flare up like fire in my chest. Something is very wrong.

"What happened?" asks the man whose name I don't know. I can't fathom why, but it seems like he's really mad—at me.

"Huh?" I answer with confusion. "What happened here?" I ask in return, with a scowl to match his.

"Where have you been?" No-Name demands.

"What do you mean?" I ask somewhat dumbly. "We were just out walking?" I say it like it's a question instead of an answer.

Harmony is looking terrified and embarrassed next to me and I'm really hoping she'll pull it together and be a united force with me here.

"What is going on?" I demand.

No-Name stares me down and spits his words at me, "You're telling me nothing happened? You just took your good old time getting here with no thought to the fact that we've all been radioing around all afternoon watching for you?"

Oh. This is about me—Again. Crap!

We took a long time between gates. I guess we were looking around for almost an hour. I didn't realize they were this preoccupied with my schedule. I didn't give anyone a specific time that I'd be back, and I had no idea anyone was "watching out for us" that seriously.

"Um, I'm sorry?" I say with an irritated lift in my voice.

Which probably sounds disrespectful and isn't going to help my situation.

"I didn't mean to be a pain. It wasn't my idea to get everyone all upset and watching for us. We haven't ever needed permission to walk around our own community in broad daylight before, you know?" I'm getting louder and more assertive. Aunty always asks me when I'll learn that humility is always best. Probably not before the fast-approaching end of time.

"We aren't here to babysit troublemakers," says No-Name with pompous disgust.

I lose what cool I was holding on to and sputter incredulously, "Troublemakers! We were doing a community service! There is a hole out there, a way in through the fence that YOU missed!"

"You found a breach?" Terry, joining the conversation, asks skeptically.

"Well, no, I haven't found it yet—but it *is* there! You know Matt—the zombie?—Left days ago with Thomas, and he didn't go out any of our gates. How do you explain that? Why isn't everyone upset about this? Doesn't anyone else see the obvious here?"

"Go home," No-Name commands with teeth clenched in quiet frustration.

"We aren't done yet!" I argue. "We still have to finish the loop back to the West Gate. I told Anthony we'd finish there."

"You are done, and Terry is escorting you each home. If you give me anymore problems or take any more of my men's time with your games, I'll speak with the Elders about it. We are here to keep all the families in this community safe, and it's a tough and time-consuming job. We don't have time to keep daredevils from getting themselves snatched by an outsider. Do we understand each other?"

"Yes sir," says Harmony.

Her first words in the whole dispute and they do nothing but undermine me. I flush red with anger and stare the guards down—defiantly.

"Come on, Ivy," Terry says, turning away to lead us towards home. He sounds tired and older than the nineteen-year-old that I know him to be. Only three years older than me. He was playing basketball and watching Disney movies with us last summer. His new job seems to have aged him ten years.

As we walk, I start to cool down, and I feel a little guilty. I know they were just trying to keep us safe. I really was just trying to help, and I didn't mean to get everyone all freaked out. The stress induced age lines on Terry's face give testament to the fact that the guards carry a heavy load watching over all of us.

I wish I had handled that better. I cringe when I realize Aunty is going to hear about this, one way or another, and I can only imagine the lecture I have coming.

Harmony and I walk quietly behind Terry without talking. He glances behind at us to see that we're keeping up and periodically responds to the static-filled conversation over his radio. I'm not mad at Harmony for not being more help. Really, she handled it all the right way. Respectful, humble, obedient—all the things I know I should be but just haven't been lately. It's in there somewhere though. I need to dig it out again. Terry suddenly takes a right turn two blocks before the Inn.

"Where are we going?" I ask.

"We are taking Harmony home first," he says as though it was obvious.

"Oh. I figured you'd be taking us both to the Inn."

"No, Harmony is going home. You are going to the U.R."

My shoulders sag. I'm glad Terry continues to lead the way a few steps ahead of us as I wipe the tears of embarrassment and unfairness from my leaky eyes. I furrow my brows and let my heart run wild with frustrated prayers to the One who let all this happen to me.

Thanks a lot God. Are you even paying attention? Have you noticed all the crap that's been happening to me? Now this? What did I do wrong? Why are you punishing me?

I figured people were going to treat me differently since the attack. I shouldn't be surprised. Life really sucks lately.

I hug Harmony at her front door. Might as well finish the day with a hug. She returns my embrace with her skinny, wispy arms and retreats behind her faded blue door. I hope I didn't get her into trouble too. I'd die if they didn't let us hang out together. She's the only person who helped me feel like myself this week.

I walk the last two blocks behind Terry without my accomplice. The town feels gray and unfriendly again. But, instead of picturing enemies behind the glare of the windows, I imagine the faces of the people I call family. I imagine them watching me. Whispering to each other about the problem I've become. Judging me. Staring at me as I'm lead towards whatever punishment they think I deserve. I slump my shoulders and burry my face in the collar of my coat, despising the shame.

When we arrive at the U.R., Terry escorts me to Rev. Depold's office; and, after seeing me through the door, leaves me there without a word. Terry used to be my friend. So much for that. I sit anxiously on the edge of one of the leather chairs that faces Rev. Depold's desk. The ornate cherry wood desk fills the small room and has the effect of making the owner of the desk seem powerful and important.

The walls of the office are papered haphazardly with faces. Faces of children in Africa and faces of happy worshipers in Asia. Faces of people praying and singing and lifting their hands collectively in praise. Faces from every nationality and every race. The posters are full of the vibrant colors of the different costumes of each exultant convert. Rev. Depold has surrounded himself with a cloud of witnesses. Barely any paint shows through the sea of smiling, emotional believers. It's overwhelming in the small space, and I feel like they are all staring at me. All of them are wondering why I can't be more like them; joyful and content with their Maker. I look down at my feet and wait for the Reverend.

I chew all of my nails down to nothing and move on to picking at the dry skin of my cuticles. Finally, Rev. Depold struts his large self in and sits down at his desk, the quilted wing-backed desk chair sighs under his weight. He's smiling, but he's always smiling so I don't allow myself any hope.

"Hello Ivy."

"Hi."

"Soooooo, I think we need a better strategy."

"Sir?"

"How are you doing Ivy?"

"Sir?"

"How's your heart?"

"Oh. Well, I have been a little scared since, uh, everything. And I was sad when Thomas left. I feel better today. Well, I felt better until we got yelled at. I really didn't do anything wrong! We were only walking. Is there a new rule about not walking in our own community?"

"No, Ivy, no new rules. We are free here. We do want to be wise though, and we don't know yet what's going on with that picture you found. I would hate for us to not take it seriously enough and have something happen that could've been avoided with a little wisdom. I'd like you to stay at home until we figure some things out. In fact, I am specifically asking that you not leave the Inn, except to come to the Sunday morning meetings. Ok?"

"Please Reverend!" I can't handle this level of punishment. "What about my job? My friends?" I'm pleading, but I manage to keep my tone respectful and sweet this time—even if it's fraudulent.

"I'll arrange for someone to deliver the teachers' papers and work assignments to you at the Inn. Someone can set up a computer for you there. And your friends may visit you any time you'd like."

The Reverend's face is pleasant but resolute. There is no point in arguing. I wish I could kill myself and be done with this awful life. I can't stand the thought of being on house arrest. I didn't do anything to deserve this. The Reverend can tell by the quivering, scrunched look on my face that I'm trying not to lose it.

He tries to soothe me, "We just want to keep you safe, Ivy. We've never had a security problem like this before and we are all trying to figure out what to do. We don't fight our neighbors and we don't believe in defending ourselves by force. The fence and our wits and godly wisdom are all the defense we've ever needed. There may be a time coming soon that we'll need a new plan. I hate to consider it, but we may need to move the community somewhere safer." His pleasant smile slips away as he stares over my head at something farther away than the jubilant walls of his office, "This might be nothing—but it might be the start of the end of our freedom in Toccoa."

Angry as I am, a chill of goose bumps runs up my arms from his ghostly wonderings.

Then he brightens and finishes with the normal Pastor preachy pep-talk, "Whatever the case, the Lord will guide us." He says this with complete conviction and faith.

I want to feel the same way. I know I have felt that way in the past. Why can't I pull it out of me now?

Rev. Depold stands up from behind his desk and comes to sit by me in the other leather chair on my side of the desk. He puts his hand on my shoulder and squeezes it kindly. "He has a perfect plan for us and for the salvation of as many as will receive him. May I pray for you Ivy?"

"Yes sir." I say begrudgingly. I'd rather he didn't, but I would never dream of saying that out loud.

"Father, thank You for Your goodness to us, Your sheep. Thank You for bringing Colleen and Ivy home safely to us. Give us wisdom in this new dilemma. I know, Lord, that You know the answer. Your plans for us are only good, plans to give us hope and a future. Watch over Ivy and protect her, please Father? Send your Spirit to encourage her and draw her ever nearer to You. Help her to find purpose in You. Thank You Father, Amen."

His prayer felt like it was meant to chide me more than encourage me—reminding me that I'm falling short in my dedication and trust. I wonder if he meant it to be a hidden lecture or if I'm just paranoid.

"So, I guess I'll be going home now." I say, more than ready to get out of this office.

"Yes, your Aunt is waiting in the lobby to take you home."

Great.

That's probably the only thing he could've said that would make me want to stay here for as long as possible. My face is as telltale as ever, shame and dread cloud over my proud demeanor. With an irritating chuckle, the Reverend catches that I am in no hurry to see Aunty. He gives me a consoling pat on the back and then gently shoves me out of his office door.

Chapter Twenty-Five

I Get Rid Of That Cold Sore

There is no lecture. Aunty doesn't speak to me at all on the short walk home. Somehow, this is worse. I'd rather a lecture. Even Aunty and I are damaged. My life is literally falling apart. We used to be close, telling each other everything. I never went through the "difficult teenager" phase. We've never even had a fight. Sometimes I'm emotional, and sometimes I'm irresponsible; but Aunty is always understanding, and I always apologize later. She's never been anything but patient with my moods and immature moments. I've had the hardest week of my life and she picks now to get fed up with me? I feel like she could be a little more understanding. I've been through a lot. She's the grown-up. She could bear with me. I'm sorry I haven't been perfect enough for her lately.

Back at the Inn—otherwise known as my new prison—Aunty heads straight up the stairs to her room without a word.

"Aunty?" I ask, despite my prideful plan to stay aloof.

When she pauses on the fourth step, it seems like she's considering continuing on up the stairs. She takes another step; and then, sighing, she turns towards me and stares at me with ice in her blue eyes. For the last four years, Aunty's eyes have been the eyes of my adoptive mother. Her blue eyes have been soft pools of warmth that have refreshed my heart and liquid kindness that I could bathe my wounds in. Tonight there is only ice. This is the first time I've ever felt chilled by her gaze.

With a sad, tired face that robs her of her youthful look and shows all the weight of her sixty-two years she says, "We're supposed to be a team Ivy. I've lost someone this week too." Her ice cold eyes stare me down and I realize that she means me.

She thinks I haven't been there for her? What the heck?

She's breaking out the big guns now: guilt tripping. She turns away and slowly finishes the climb to her room. I hear the door lock click tight on her bedroom door. She's in for the night.

Angry, lonely, depressed and hungry, I stomp to the kitchen for something to eat. There isn't anything on the stove, and I realize that tonight was my night to cook dinner. We usually eat together around 5:00 and I'm always the chef on Saturday evening. It is now 6:00.

Crap!

Geez Louise I'm batting a thousand.

I pour some of the peaches we canned last summer into a bowl and grab a Gov Bar. I balance my lousy dinner on a tray with a cup of chamomile tea and head for my room to eat and sulk. I eat alone in total silence. The winter evening is quiet with no wind. There aren't any sounds from birds or crickets, not even the hum of the furnace to keep me company. The cold hibernation of outside is too much like the cold I feel taking over my heart. The frost in my spirit snuck up on me. My heart is cold, and sins of omission have dulled me.

I scarf my peaches and nibble my Gov Bar. Alone and lonely, I pace my room. I look out the window, lie on my bed, stare into my closet, and rub bacon grease on my dry hands. I am almost crazy with anxiety when I remember that Mrs. LaFakis sent me work to do. And chocolate!

Chocolate sounds sooooo good.

I find the little pile that Harmony set by my closet earlier. Eating two of the five precious pieces of chocolate, I start leafing through the pages Sherry sent. A letter is attached on top.

Dear Ivy,

I have a lot going on this coming week in preparation for the missionaries coming in. I handled this week's lesson without you. I know you had a lot going on. I'm glad you are safe, dear. You know that we all love you. I was hoping you'd help me prepare the Sunday School lesson for next Sunday morning. I'm sending you a few devotionals that I'd like you to read over and combine for me into a lesson format. They have minimal scripture attached and I'd like you to dig in and find some more scripture to go with them.

Thanks Hon.

Love,
Sherry

P.S. Enjoy the chocolate

Sounds easy.

I need something to fill my time and distract me anyway. With a notebook and pen in hand, already missing my computer at work, I start reading the first devotional. It's by Charles Spurgeon. I've read his work several times before in my secretarial duties to the teachers. He was a pastor in England in the 1800s. He was dead long before The Lord came to collect His own, and I'm sure he will be a fascinating person to meet when we're done here. It's a little hard to read his writings; they're very old fashioned and very intellectual.

A lot of the kids my age aren't intellectuals.

Bible study aside, each family is responsible for the non-Bible schooling of their own kids. Some of the families care a lot and some don't care at all. Aunty teaches me some things, mostly things like cooking, cleaning, and of course proper speech and grammar. Her tutoring helped me to get my job at the U.R. where I've had to teach myself a lot about typing and filing and office work.

Tim's dad, Dr. Markowitz, is one of the ones who cares a lot. He keeps Tim busy all day long, five days a week learning math, science, history, the whole shebang. Tim is a genius by today's standards.

Most of the other guys our age are helping with hunting, fishing and building or repair work for the community. They learn a bit about the Bible on Sunday under Sherry's teaching, but they are pretty lost when it comes to anything more than basic math and reading. High speech and Old English might as well be Chinese.

For most of the Living, it's hard to see the point of higher learning. We are nearing the end. There are different interpretations and opinions about how much time we have left here. Most people think we may only have a year or so of time left on earth. So calculus is kind of silly at this point. Most of the Living have a "let's just get through this" mentality.

Sherry doesn't have to do much teaching with Harmony. That girl loves to learn. She reads constantly. Harmony does a pretty good job with her own education. I really hope she isn't mad at me. I don't want today's trouble to affect my relationship with Sherry either. If she felt like I was a danger to Harmony, I'm afraid she won't let us hang out anymore.

I'm getting distracted. Back to the Charles Spurgeon. When Sherry wants to quote him or use one of his devotionals, I have to go through it and make it easier to read for the kids who aren't as studious. I actually enjoy the challenge of studying his writings.

The Spurgeon paper is based on Psalm 120:5. It reads: "I'm doomed to live in Meshech, cursed with a home in Kedar."

Okay.

I've never heard of either of those places. I look up the rest of the Psalm so I can try to figure out what the heck that means. Both names are completely unfamiliar to me and I've read my Bible front to back.

> Psalm 120
> The Message (MSG)
> A Pilgrim Song
>
> 120: 1-2 I'm in trouble. I cry to God,
> desperate for an answer:
> "Deliver me from the liars, God!
> They smile so sweetly but lie through their teeth."
> 3-4 Do you know what's next, can you see what's coming,
> all you barefaced liars?
> Pointed arrows and burning coals
> will be your reward.
> 5-7 I'm doomed to live in Meshech,
> cursed with a home in Kedar,
> My whole life lived camping
> among quarreling neighbors.
> I'm all for peace, but the minute
> I tell them so, they go to war!

So it sounds like whoever—I mean whomever—wrote this Psalm hated where he lived too. He says he has lived his "whole life" in close proximity to his enemies. As I keep reading, I am hit with how much it applies to me. Did

Sherry know? Or is it just God? I don't know why I'm surprised, it's happened so many times before. Goose bumps run up my arms in anticipation of hearing His voice.

Then I feel the fight begin.

There is a part of me that says, *Put this away and go to bed!* I know it's the zombie in me. With a deep breath, I turn my back on that degenerate girl and set my eyes on Spurgeon's words.

Spurgeon writes about verse 5:

As a Christian you have to live in the midst of an ungodly world, and it is of little use for you to cry "Woe is me."

I've been doing a lot of that.

Jesus did not pray O that you should be taken out of the world, and what He did not pray for you need not desire. Better far in the Lord's strength to meet the difficulty, and glorify Him in it. The enemy is ever on the watch to detect inconsistency in your conduct; be therefore very holy. Remember that the eyes of all are upon you, and that more is expected from you than from other men. Strive to give no occasion for blame.

I can't help but think of the horrible example of Life I was to Matt. If he never wanted anything to do with being healed, finding Life, would it be totally my fault?

Let your goodness be the only fault they can discover in you. Like Daniel, compel them to say of you, "We shall not find any occasion against this Daniel, except we find it against him concerning the law of his God." Seek to be useful as well as consistent.

I have gotten really good at being useful, but for who? Am I doing it to give glory to the God who gave me these skills and abilities or to make me feel better about my sinful self? Have I been losing myself in doing good and hoping to find my worth there instead of the only place I can really find any worth? My only worth is in the love of God who made me and bought me with His own blood. He gave me healing and Life when all around there was death and that death was what I deserved! Then when it came time to put my money where my mouth was, to be like Jesus in the hard times, well, that didn't go well at all.

In the last week I've been assaulted, terrified, filled with hate and self-pity, heartbroken, made to feel like a pariah in my own community, and, now, imprisoned in my own house. I can't think of any other time in my life with that much trial and drama; a test to be sure. Who is Ivy? What is she really made of? Who does she really value? Oh, it's so obvious. I'm full of me.

Perhaps you think, "If I were in a more favourable position I might serve the Lord's cause, but I cannot do any good where I am"; but the worse the people are among whom you live, the more need have they of your exertions; if they be crooked, the more necessity that you should set them straight; and if they be perverse, the more need have you to turn their proud hearts to the truth. Where should the physician be but where there are many sick? Where is honour to be won by the soldier but in the hottest fire of the battle?

Was Spurgeon clairvoyant? Did he look into a crystal ball and write this specifically for me? How could anyone describe the zombies any better? Or my trapped position in the town of Toccoa in the midst of all the hate outside of our gates!

And when weary of the strife and sin that meets you on every hand, consider that all the saints have endured the same trial. They were not carried on beds of down to heaven, and you must not expect to travel more easily than they. They had to hazard their lives unto the death in the high places of the field, and you will not be crowned till you also have endured hardness as a good soldier of Jesus Christ. Therefore, "stand fast in the faith, quit you like men, be strong."

All week I've been asking the wrong question, "Why me?"

Really the more appropriate question would be, "Why not me?"

I can hear the warriors and saints of old asking me, "Who do you think you are? Hundreds of thousands of saints have suffered much worse than you and persevered and won their crowns. How wussy can you be?"

Yes, I can picture St. Paul saying "wussy".

The shame of my failures in the past week—I don't know, maybe it's been going on even longer—makes me fall on my face in the carpet next to my bed. I have been a complete failure. I have been muddling along on my own, without going to Him each day, each hour, like I need to for the right perspective, the right attitudes, the strength to face the tests that come at me. I have done it all on my own instead, and the fruit of my efforts has been fear, anger, resentment, foolishness, fickleness, and loveless results.

I was a horrible example to Matt and a bad friend to Aunty Coe who has cared for me so faithfully all these years. I was disrespectful to the guard who is putting his life on the line for me daily, and I drug Harmony into all of it with my lack of wisdom and careless disregard for anything but my own agenda.

I totally suck.

Tears spill over and wet my carpet. I've cried all week long, but tonight's tears are not made of fear or anger or loss. They are the refreshing tears of repentance, and they flush out my sin. The carpet in my room is very old and it always smells like wet dog. I usually avoid putting even my bare feet on it. Now, wet with my tears, it is even grosser, but I continue to lay my head against it and cry. I am humbled and ashamed and finally willing to submit to my loving God.

While I'm crying, He reminds me that everyone sucks. That if I didn't suck, I wouldn't need Him. If anyone was capable of saving himself through hard work or charity or goodness, Jesus wouldn't have had to come; wouldn't have had to die. We suck. It's the best thing we've got going for us. It's how He shows us how much he loves us.

I love Him so much; and, for the first time in ages, I feel His love for me. I've known something was wrong. I've sensed but avoided the truth that I was slipping. You'd think if you recognized that you were dying that you'd hurry to stop it, to heal whatever is sick. It's innately human to struggle for life. But for some reason, though it makes no sense, it's also innately human to lean away from eternal life. I should feel ashamed, but I feel—grateful. His grace and peace and joy have moved back into their rightful place in my heart. I offered my heart to Him years ago, but then I pushed him into a corner and let myself take the Master Bedroom. With Him back on the throne, everything fits like pieces of a puzzle back into perspective.

I sing Him some of my favorite songs about Him. He warms me all over, and I feel life in my soul again. It is cold outside, cold and drafty on the floor of this old house; but I'm brimming again with His love, and I feel warm. It might sound crazy, but my whole world is crazy. The cursed who live beyond our gates are the dark side of my story, but you'll only understand them when you meet Him; the Hero that my heart desires—my Savior. I belong to an awesome, loving God.

Even the disease is His goodness. He has done everything to restore His creation, to bring His people back to Him. When they still wouldn't turn back, He made the curse of sin even more recognizable and even more obvious through the disease. And He gave even more proof of his goodness by curing anyone who would come to him. Miraculous Healing on display for all the world to see. The outsides cured with the insides.

And still. Still most of them refuse to see it.

And it's *my* purpose to do my best to show them with the time I have left. I can't run away afraid. If they come for me, I'll show them love. I'll show them till they kill me and send me home. This is why we don't kill zombies. We were born to love them for Him. If I die, my fate is set and secure. Their fates still hang in the balance and we are all running out of time.

A transformed Ivy stands up in place of the guilt ridden girl who fell woefully down on the musty carpet. With joy in my spirit, I go to the bathroom to wash my salty cheeks. A glance at my face in the mirror makes my eyes go wide with shock. My skin looks radiant and new—glowing. I haven't looked this alive in ages! Had it gotten that bad? Was I decaying and not even noticing? It looks like I just came back from a week of spa treatments and facials.

And it's not just my face; I feel the rejuvenation in my limbs and in my bones. Energy. Vigor. I shudder to think of how bad I would've looked a month from now if I hadn't been cleansed. I was so awful to Matt—and so grossed out by him and his kind—and I was unfathomably close to seeing my own skin rotting. I'm blown away by my God; overwhelmingly thankful for another fresh start. It's my one thousandth fresh start. It's my umpteenth clean slate. His grace is amazing.

Before I climb into bed, I need to go talk to Aunty. It's late and I haven't knocked on her door after bedtime in years, but this can't wait until morning. I know her well enough to know that she'll forgive me. She's probably praying for me right now. After I make things right with her, I think I'm going to have the best night's sleep I've had in ages.

Chapter Twenty-Six

Pancakes Always Give Me the Sniffles

After a night of restful, dreamless sleep, the first thing I do this morning is open my Bible. I won't play it that close again. I have to do this every day; visit with Him, focus on Him, or I'll fail again. Who knows what the consequences of walking away could be next time? I don't want to take anyone else down. I must stay on task. I decide to keep going with the material Sherry sent instead of picking up my normal devotional book. I do as she asked and look up more verses to add to the Spurgeon study. There are a lot of ways Sherry could go with this one, but the most obvious to me is bravery to live among our enemies and what our purpose is here in the midst of them. So with that in mind I find:

> *Matthew 5:16 "Let your light shine before men in such a way that they may see your good works, and glorify your Father who is in heaven."*

> *1 Peter 2:12 "Live such good lives among the pagans that, though they accuse you of doing wrong, they may see your good deeds and glorify God on the day he visits us."*

I wonder if Sherry would notice if I wrote zombies instead of pagans in that one.

> *Philippians 2:15 "So that you may become blameless and pure, children of God without fault in a crooked and depraved generation, in which you shine like stars in the universe."*

> *1 Peter 4:16 "However, if you suffer as a Christian, do not be ashamed, but praise God that you bear that name."*

> *Proverbs 29:27 "The righteous detest the dishonest; the wicked detest the upright."*

Very nice of God to understand: We hate them and they hate us. But God wants us to be the better person here and love them because He loved us back when we hated Him.

> *John 16:33 "I have told you these things, so that in me you may have peace. In this world you will have trouble. But take heart! I have overcome the world."*
>
> *John 15:18 "If the world hates you, you know that it hated me before it hated you."*

I decide to write them each down and memorize them.

Praise God, today is Sunday! Even though I'm stuck with this horrible house arrest, I already get to go out today. Rev. Depold said I could still come to U.R. meetings with Aunty. I'm looking forward to worshiping, and I can tell Sherry how much her stuff helped me. She loves hearing about the cool things God does in our lives. I pray for a minute, and then head to the kitchen for some breakfast.

Aunty, of course, forgave me last night. She probably had forgiven me even before I knocked on her door. We hugged and chatted for almost an hour before our yawning had us laughing, and I climbed out of her bed and found my way to my own. We used to hang out in her bed all the time. It's nice to know that even though I'm pretty much a grown woman, I'm still welcome there.

I'd never admit it to her; but, last night in her nightgown with no makeup on, Aunty looked so old. I guess I've been so self-absorbed that I wasn't even noticing her aging. I'd be lost without her. The end is near for all of us. We're almost done here. If we can just make it another year together, we won't ever have to say goodbye to each other. This world will end and melt into the next, and we'll be healthy and young and beautiful together for all of eternity.

When I get to the kitchen, Aunty is there waiting for me with coffee and pancakes. I'm sure she thought I'd be thrilled to enjoy pancakes and syrup since I missed out the morning she made them for Matt. But Matt—that antagonistic smile when he poured my syrup on his flapjacks, his beautiful green eyes and the special wink he always gave me. The memories sink into my chest and resonate with that familiar dull ache. I look up into Aunty's blue eyes, warm again today, and I know she is reading me like her favorite book. My eyes glisten with a new layer of held back tears.

"I thought so." Aunty sighs. "I wasn't sure, I of course suspected, but this confirms it."

"I miss him," I blubber, "and I treated him so awful, and then it was too late."

I am such a mess.

I'm usually more together. I must be PMSing or something. Aunty wraps her arms around me and clucks her tongue at me. It's slightly condescending, but appropriate I guess. She's older and wiser; and, as it turns out, I am just a silly girl after all. I've been so out of character this week with all the crying and all the hugging. After a somber pancake breakfast, we clean up and head to different parts of the house to get ready for the Upper Room.

*****

Twenty minutes later, Aunty and I are strolling down the jagged, pitted sidewalk towards the U.R. arm in arm. I left my depressed heart behind at the Inn, trading it out for a fresh spirit from a little Bible reading before we left. Aunty and I are wearing our best new clothes and coats, and I feel chipper and elated to be out in the cold fresh air of freedom. The sky looks glorious. The blue is so fresh and deep that it's almost the same turquoise of my new coat, and the clouds are piled over and over on top of each other with peachy pink shadows to differentiate each puffy shape.

Aunty opens the door for me when we arrive at the front of the U.R.; and, with a deep breath and a wink, we enter and split up towards our different Sunday School classes. Aunty walks slowly and gracefully upstairs in her pretty red high heels, and I turn towards the basement steps, comfortable in my old tennis shoes.

Sherry's class is mostly full when I arrive, and everyone gets quiet as I walk in and sit down. Harmony isn't here yet. Sherry gives me a little smile, but it isn't full of her usual warmth. Insecurity and nerves pound the first crack in my confident, peppy spirit. Sherry starts right in with the lesson, the last in our series study on the book of James. It's good. Her teaching is always great. Harmony sneaks in a few minutes late; and, even though there isn't anyone in my whole row of chairs, she sits down somewhere behind me.

Wow.

So I guess she's mad at me.

Great.

The self-esteem my new clothes brought and the joy I felt on the walk here both shatter along the fault line that Sherry's half smile started. I fidget through the rest of Sherry's lesson, missing most of it. At one point, I glance behind me and catch a scowl from Jamie Crest—my last week crush. He's friends with Terry, the guard. Terry probably told Jamie all about what happened yesterday. And, from the judgment in Jamie's scowl, I'm guessing Terry didn't tell it quite like I would have. During Sherry's closing prayer, I duck out like a coward, hurrying out the door and up the stairs to the Sanctuary.

I am relieved to run into Aunty in the lobby, and I cling to her side like a little girl. I work here! I help run this building! I've always felt so at home here, important even. But today I feel distinctly not welcome. Am I paranoid or does everyone here think badly of me?

I'm absolutely certain that they're all talking about me. I try not to hear our friends' whispers as Aunty and I walk to our usual seats near the front—my face red with shame and frustration. I'm dressed nicer than anyone here. Aunty brought the clothes we got for the clothing bank days ago. I thought the other girls my age would be wearing the new clothes we brought. But everyone else's clothes look old and bedraggled; their Sunday best barely nicer than my cleaning clothes. Are they intentionally not wearing the clothes? Is this some sort of show of disapproval?

My new clothes, that I was so excited to put on this morning, fit my body nicely and make me feel so pretty. Last Sunday, I would've been proud to have these new things and thankful. I would've walked past Jamie Crest and felt confident that he might have noticed me and liked what he saw. Today, I realize belatedly that I should've worn my hand-me-downs. These stupid clothes are the reason that all of this is happening.

We must look so vain—so selfish—to put our friends at risk for new clothes. It's so unfair. I didn't even want to go! Aunty made me. But they don't see it that way. I look like the spoiled rich girl who lives in the mansion and has to have the best of everything. I wish they knew how much I worked. I clean that place all week long. I cater to the constant needs of strangers in my own house, having almost no privacy and never a day off! They don't know me. But I wish they did. It would be vindicating.

The music starts, and I ask Him to help me focus on worshipping Him. He answers, and I'm lost in His grace for the rest of the singing. We sing a lot of the old hymns. They are so full of meaning and depth; written by men and women who lost much in their service to The Lord. We studied them once, some of the most famous of the old hymn writers, and their stories were tragic. Dead children and wives, terrible health, blindness, and they chose to write praises to the King who allowed it all to happen. I admire those people a lot.

Ms. Julia stands up at the small podium in front to give a few announcements about the missionaries' homecoming next week. There are preparations to be made for the extra gatherings we'll have, and volunteers are needed. I thought I'd be a big part of the homecoming, but now I'm not sure I'll even be allowed to go. I'm not sure I even want to go.

My eyes wander the large room we meet in as Ms. Julia continues on in her monotonous, business-like tone. The U.R. used to be the city court house. This was the main courtroom, and the wooden pews we sit in were meant for those attending trials. The judge's seat still sits in its prominent place at the front of the room, but no one sits there. It's very symbolic to us though. That seat is for Jesus. As the blameless, perfect Lamb who died for us, He's the only one who can sit in judgment over us. And even though we are constantly sinning and Jesus has every right to condemn us—all of us deserving the death penalty—He considers our debts paid because He paid them for us. He met our bail. He rescued us from the prison we deserved, and He looks at us with incredible Love from His place in the Judge's seat.

When this building was just a courthouse, all the offenders got their due. No human judge ever offered to take the sentence of murderers and thieves. Those of us who sit here today know what's been done for us, and we try our best to live our lives to please Him; to thank Him. Incense burns in a little dish at the Judges desk. It is always burning there, and its smoky wisps are just visible in the bright florescent light. The smoke rises with our praises to bless the real Judge where He sits in Heaven. The spicy, smoky smell fills the whole building and I'm so used to it that I hardly notice it anymore.

Finally Rev. Depold stands to deliver this morning's message. "Zombies," he says and then pauses for effect.

Oh no.

Please no. Please don't let the sermon be about me. I can't handle this!

I want to crawl under the bench and hide.

Chapter Twenty-Seven

The Devil Made Me Do It

Rev. Depold booms from the pulpit, "It was recently brought to my attention that some of our number call the diseased, 'Zombies'."

My face is a bright red beacon. It's chilly in this big room, and I'm certain there must be obvious steam emanating from my warm, humiliated face. I sneak a glance at Aunty. She isn't looking at me, but she has a pained expression on her face and her lips are pressed in a hard line.

Our Pastor continues, "Obviously, a very derogatory way to think of and refer to our neighbors. But it stuck with me. I spent some time thinking and praying about that term. And, believe it or not, friends, there is some unique truth in that word. Not just for them, but also for us. Let me share with you what the Spirit has laid on my heart.

"Before The Lord came back for His own—leaving all of us here and changing the world forever—people used to watch television and movies about zombies. Zombie movies were one of the most popular ways to pay to be terrified.

The undead.

The walking dead.

Reanimated corpses crawling out of their graves.

And what did zombies do? They ate the living. Hits us close to home doesn't it?

The comparison is easy to make. The world out there is getting sicker. And I don't mean the disease. Murder is commonplace here in Toccoa. Babies are being aborted and sold as delicacies to the rich. Pravda is harvesting and selling stem cells and umbilical cords from aborted babies, promising healing and rejuvenation to people desperate enough to buy and eat them. Such dark times," he says with tears forming in his eyes.

Out comes the hanky.

I listen and silently beg God for my name to not come up in this sermon so pointedly meant for me.

Rev. Depold continues and clears his phlegmy throat, "They have lost all respect for human life. In Roman's Chapter 3 verse 10 we read:

> *There is none righteous, not even one.*
> *There is none who understands, there is none who seeks for God;*
> *All have turned aside, together they have become useless;*
> *There is none who does good, there is not even one.*
>
> *Their throat is an open grave, with their tongues they keep deceiving,*
> *The poison of asps is under their lips;*
> *Whose mouth is full of cursing and bitterness;*
> *Their feet are swift to shed blood,*
> *Destruction and misery are in their paths,*
> *And the path of peace have they not known.*
>
> *There is no fear of God before their eyes.*

"I'd say that's a pretty fair commentary on our neighbors. Some of you have been sheltered within our community, but many of you know well of what I speak. We live in dangerous times my friends. Our missionaries are out there, on the battlefield, seeking to save that which is lost.

"But the word zombie isn't only for the lost. It's for us too. How you ask? How can I compare Christ's beautiful bride, the church, to a decaying reanimated corpse? We are Living, but we have the same disease. The curse of sin waits in our members looking for an opening to strike. We are not as safe here, inside our fence, as we would like to believe.

"Romans Chapter 7 verse 14 speaks about the Living, not the lost. Paul is talking about the church in this passage. Paul is speaking about *our* sinful nature. When the scientists test the Living, what do they find? They find the same LS in our blood. No less of it than anyone else. We have been healed, but we still fight the sickness. We still need our Healer on a daily, hourly, minute by minute basis. We read:

> *...I am flesh, sold into bondage to sin. For that which I'm doing,*
> *I do not understand; for I am not practicing what I would like to do,*
> *but I am doing the very thing I hate.*

"This is Paul, the great apostle, speaking! Paul who wrote much of the New Testament. Paul who saw our Savior on the road and was struck blind at the sight of His glory. He says:

> *For I know that nothing good dwells in me, that is, in my flesh; for the wishing is present in me, but the doing of the good is not. For the good that I wish, I do not do; but I practice the very evil that I do not wish. But if I am doing the very thing that I do not wish, I am no longer the one doing it, but sin that dwells in me.*

"Paul is almost calling "sin" a thinking, sentient being that lives in us and exercises its own will against us, causing us to sin. That old phrase, 'The devil made me do it' could find defense in these verses."

Rev. Depold pauses and scans the faces of his congregation, "I want to be perfect for my Lord. Don't you? If you could somehow never sin again, whatever the cost, wouldn't you take it? I would. Or at least my heart, my brain, my belief would. But my friends, it's not to be. We still live in these bodies for a while longer. And these bodies are married to sin.

"Our hearts are alive in Christ, but our bodies are dead in sin. We are zombies. What does that look like for us?" Rev. DePold stares straight at me.

I swallow hard and look down.

He looks away and continues, "Zombies are committed to the fulfillment of one desire 0 eating the living. When our zombie comes out, we are that irrational. We are selfish, with only ourselves in mind.

"Zombies disregard their own wellbeing and the wellbeing of others to get what they want. They would dive off the side of a hundred foot cliff if they smelled human flesh at the bottom. And we can be that careless with our own lives and each other."

I know what Rev. Depold is saying. I know I'm guilty of selfish moments. But so is everyone else in this room. As guilty as the whole congregation is of their own zombie tendencies, I feel certain that everyone else is thinking just of Aunty and I and our shopping trip. Our focus on fashion has seemingly brought a new danger home to them. If they knew the whole story, they'd know it was a danger that was already here. I didn't bring it to them. It lives here among us. If anything, our going out brought that danger out into the open. Mine and Aunty's run-in with Oscar the Grouch has prepared our whole compound for what could be coming.

We did them a favor.

Lost in my inner rant I've missed some of the sermon. I pick it back up on Rev. Depold's final point on zombies.

"More than just scary, zombies make you sad. They are someone's mother or brother or husband or daughter. They are a shell of what they used to be. Back then, watching a zombie flick, you could feel sad about the little girl, alone on the screen, a lonely zombie. I ask, brothers and sisters, maybe we could come up with that for each other? Be more patient with each other's inner zombie?

"And, more importantly, could we find the same heartbreak that Christ felt for the lost? Yes, they hate us. Yes, they long for our blood. But Christ died for those who hated Him. They screamed for His blood, the blood that bought our healing. I'm not asking you to die for them; though God might ask that of you.

"What I'm asking is for you to fall in love with them. To see in them the potential that God sees. To ask yourself, 'What can I do to reach them in the little time we have left?'

"My friends, we need to become infectious to the infected. Our lives should draw them. Our love should be obvious, setting us apart and making them want what we have. Someone who belongs to God should walk in a way that makes the lost want to have what we have been given. It is a gift we could never deserve. Are we behaving as those indebted, or have we had the gift so long we have begun to think it was our right all along?

"Let us pray," Rev. Depold bows his head; and, wordlessly, the congregations follows suit. "Father, may we be honest enough to face the zombies within, and may we have the courage to forgive the zombies around us. Lord, give us compassion for the dead around us and grace for the dead within us. Amen."

Chapter Twenty-Eight

I Can't Handle Any More Markowitzs

I can't believe how relieved I am to be back in the Inn. After ten minutes of strained post-sermon conversation and a short reflective walk home, I am back in the house for at least the next week. I know I have permission to go to meetings; but, after the debacle that was this morning, I don't know if I want to go for awhile. Maybe time will heal the rift between me and the rest of our people.

Aunty and I are only home a few minutes when the doorbell rings. We are cooking lunch together in the kitchen when the melodious chimes sends Aunty scurrying to the front door, leaving me up to my elbows in flour, kneading biscuits.

Within seconds, Aunty reappears in the kitchen, her face lined with the concern of some new disaster. She barks, "I have to go, I'll be back."

"What happened?" I yell after her as she heads out the back door, but the only response I get is the door slamming shut.

She's gone with no explanation.

Curiosity and suspense eat at me while I wait for her to come back. I'm not allowed to leave the house to go find her. I pace back and forth in the foyer; staring out the front windows for clues of what could be happening out there. Is someone sick? They sometimes call for Aunty when Dr. Markowitz and the two nurses aren't enough. Aunty has no real medical training, but she's calm and cool under pressure—and not afraid of blood—so she's helpful in situations where they need more hands. Maybe something happened with the zombies?

Yes, I'm still going to call them that.

Is there some new development in the Outlet Mall Stalker investigation? Has there been another attack?

*****

I finish cooking lunch. And eat. And send up countless prayers. And wait. I wish life was perfect. I wish that all that rejuvenation and great time with my Bible had left me with nothing but joy, but I'm only human. I'm already struggling with renewed feelings of hopelessness. I'm mad about being trapped here. I'm afraid of what is hunting me out there. Why is it so hard to trust Him?

The big house is empty and unsupportive. Even though it's still sunny outside, the nerves that usually only come over me at night begin to creep in. I feel painfully alone. I was hoping that Harmony would visit me a lot; but, after the cold shoulder in class this morning I'm not getting my hopes up.

So much for BFFs.

I remember that Rev. Depold said someone would come set up a computer for me and bring me work to do. I guess it won't be that much different than working in my little office. It's not like I'm surrounded by people there either. I doubt anyone will come today though. It's Sunday. Tomorrow is the earliest I can expect to be back to work in full swing.

*****

I'm napping in the comfy chair in the Parlor—or, as Aunty would say, "resting my eyes"—when the doorbell scares me to death. I jump up, and it takes me a second to remember where I am and what's going on. I hurry to the door and see Harmony pressing her face against the glass. I unlock and open the door, grabbing her arm and pulling her inside.

"Do you know what's going on?" I demand a little frantic, "Where is Aunty?"

"Okay. Just don't freak out okay?"

"What?" I freak. "What is it?"

"They're back," Harmony says darkly.

"Who is back?!"

"Thomas and his brother. And, Ivy, Thomas is hurt."

"Matt? Matt is back? Is he ok? Oh my gosh, he's back! What happened? Is Matt hurt?"

"Huh?" Harmony is looking at me like I'm crazy. "Ivy, Thomas is hurt. Who cares about his zombie brother?" She pauses and stares hard at me, "I'm confused. You are worried about him?"

"Is he hurt?" I grab her by the arms and shout the question in her face.

"I don't know," she answers with quiet anger in her timid voice.

Harmony pulls away from me. I let go of her arms, and she rubs at them like I bruised her.

"Is that where Aunty is? Did they need her? Thomas must be hurt pretty bad. Of course that's a big deal," I say to show her I get it; and that I'm not, despite her worries, insane. I mean, of course I care about Thomas being hurt. I can prioritize.

I start again with forced calmness, "I wonder what happened. Do you know?"

"I know less than I realized," she says with a sour twist in her full lips.

"Please Harmony, I'm sorry. Please?"

"Ugh." She sighs and starts to spill what she knows. "I know they showed up at the North Gate sometime this morning. Matt," she enunciates his name with disgust and a glare, "was carrying Thomas and demanded to be let in. The guards didn't know what to do. Your boyfriend told them to call Ellen and Jose or Miss Colleen, but they refused."

It sounds like Matt is okay, and I feel a guilty sense of relief.

Harmony continues, "Anthony was the guard on duty at the West Gate. I guess he overheard what was happening on the radio. He came to the North Gate and escorted Matt and Thomas straight to the clinic. Thomas is really badly hurt." Harmony takes a gulp of air before saying, "I think he maybe lost his arm or something. Jose and Ellen are really upset. Matt," the scornful way she says Matt's name is getting old, "is being held somewhere until the commotion settles and they can figure out what to do with him."

"What to do with him? What do you mean they are holding him?"

"I don't really know anything else."

"Harmony, I'm sorry. I just—of course I'm super worried about Thomas. I just, I mean, I care about Matt a little."

She looks at me with a mixture of confusion and disgust, and I know this will change our friendship. We've never talked about boys because Harmony has held onto her childlike disgust for boys and crushes. I'd never even told her how I felt about Jamie Crest because I knew she'd think it was weird and gross. And now I've fallen for someone way off limits.

"Do you know where Matt is?" I ask. "I really need to see him. Please Harmony? You must have some idea where they have him?"

"First of all, you aren't allowed to leave the Inn, remember?" she says with a scowl on her thin, freckled face.

"Ugh! What's second of all?" I ask, not caring one bit about Rev. Depold's restrictions.

I'm pretty sure Harmony will have to sit on me if she knows where Matt is and expects me to sit here and do nothing.

"Second of all, you aren't going to like where he is," she says with a look on her face that promises that her next sentence will be bad news. "That guy we didn't know, you know the guard you ticked off? Turns out, he's the new head of security. He's Tim's older brother."

"Tim Markowitz?" My turn to look disgusted at the mention of a boy.

"Yeah. So, I guess he was leading a group of the Living near Atlanta and the Doctor asked him to come home. His name is Andrew. He's only been here for like a week and they put him in charge of all our security. He's keeping Matt at his apartment. He lives in one of the apartments they made in the old police station."

Harmony was right. Second of all was worse. I already had "apologize to no-name" on my recent list of things to do. I can't go barging into his apartment when he knows I'm supposed to be at the Inn. First of all, because it's not respectful of the Elders or of no-name—I guess I should call him Andrew now. And secondly, because that kind of behavior isn't going to get me out of my house-arrest any sooner. The new head of security already thinks I'm trouble. I'm going to need to prove I'm not if I ever want out of here.

My thoughts are running a mile a minute. Matt is back. Will he stay? What if he leaves again before I'm allowed out of here? I will die if I don't at least get to see him and say I'm sorry. He's independent, not to mention sneaky. I know he won't like "being held" anywhere by anyone. He'll probably be out of that apartment by tonight and back through whatever hole he's been using. Apparently, it's a hole that he couldn't carry a hurt Thomas through, forcing him to use the gate.

Will his love for Thomas keep him around? Maybe he'll stay to make sure Thomas is okay. What if Thomas isn't okay? If Thomas dies, I know for certain I'll never see Matt again. I sink back down into my napping chair; full of worry and questions. Maybe God is giving me a second chance with Matt. I will do better this time. Please, God, let me have another chance to show Matt the Truth? Harmony is back by the front door. I look up to see her leaving. Just like that. With all of the wreckage still smoking between us. Life is so complex all of a sudden.

"Harmony, wait! Please don't leave. I don't want to be here all by myself," I finish quietly.

"I guess you should've thought of that before you got us into trouble."

"You got in trouble? Oh my gosh, I'm so sorry! Forgive me?" I ask in a small pleading voice.

I feel terrible. Harmony is practically perfect in every way. I can't think of a time she's ever been in trouble. She considers my apology while looking down at her feet. She kicks the toe of her brown boot back and forth along the fringe of the Oriental rug just inside the door.

Her face is softer when she meets my eyes again. "Yeah. It's okay. I know you didn't mean to."

She lifts her little matching cross necklace from inside of her coat and says, "Best friends, no worries," with her full lips spread in a smile.

Her smile looks a little forced, but I'll take it.

"I gotta go," she says apologetically. "I'm not allowed to be out alone for more than an hour now. I still have to go to the library."

"Oh. I'm really, really sorry. Can you come back tomorrow? Maybe you could get permission to study here part of the day?"

"Maybe."

"Well—thanks for coming. I'm sorry."

"I forgive you. Really. You don't have to say you're sorry again. It's really okay. Nothing to do around here anyways, right?" She smiles at me and turns to leave.

"Yeah. But even Toccoa beats house arrest," I say glumly, standing up to see her out.

"I'll be back," she says as I close the door behind her and lock it.

I'm alone again. If Thomas' injuries are that bad, Aunty could be gone all day. Now that I know Matt is back, and being held right across the street, being trapped in the Inn feels unbearable. I stare out the front windows at the old police station, searching each window. Where is he? I have to see him again! Is he staring back at me from behind one of those dark windows? I see no sign of him and my heart sinks low.

In an effort to fight off the crazies, I look for something to do. I decide to run up and down the stairs for some exercise. Exercise gives you endorphins and endorphins make you happy.

The expansive Inn has a front staircase and a back staircase. The wide front staircase winds and turns up four different levels, twenty-one steps in all. The front stairs are honey colored oak with a patterned red carpet running up the middle of the steps. At the bottom of the stairs is a beautiful carved oak post with an antique, three armed bronze lamp built into the top of the post. The globed lamppost looks like something you'd see in an old train station. At the top of the stairs, a spindled oak banister looks over the drop at an 8 foot tall arched stained glass window.

It's beautiful—I guess—but I've lived here so long now that all the fancy windows and antique oak are nothing more than difficult places for me to have to clean and dust. I've lost most of my appreciation for the house that so awed me as a little girl. I jog up the stairs, taking some of them two at a time.

At the top of the stairs, the upstairs hall stretches before me with five different doors leading to five different guest rooms. Jogging to the end of the hall, behind the second door on the left is another hallway. Just inside this back hall is a narrow door leading to the back staircase. These stairs aren't as wide as the front steps and they are plain and un-decorative. Like my room downstairs, they were probably used by the maid back when the house was built. There are nineteen steps here.

I spend less than ten minutes running up the front stairs, down the hall and down the back stairs. I make the loop over and over until my legs are burning. I'm in fairly good shape due to having to walk everywhere. But stairs are harder than just walking, and I'm disappointed at how quickly I'm too winded to keep going. I slump down on my butt on the bottom step in the back hallway and lean against the wall.

I hope those endorphins kick in soon. I really need some happy.

I think I'll go eat another piece of chocolate.

Chapter Twenty-Nine

What Has Two Thumbs and Four Fingers?

Aunty finally comes in the back door at 8:00 p.m. I scurry from the kitchen where I was filling my time with cleaning and washing dishes. As Aunty enters the kitchen, I stifle a gasp. She is covered in blood. Her hair is disheveled and standing up on one side. Her face is as white as the guest room sheets. She looks haggard as her eyes meet mine, and she watches me appraise her. I've been planning an onslaught of questions for her, but they are forced aside by the tsunami sized wave of concern that floods through me.

Aunty, the queen of good posture, slumps uncharacteristically through the kitchen door, and I hurry to pull out a chair at the table for her. She digs into the plate of leftovers that I had waiting for her. The dinner I cooked and ate by myself—venison in gravy over leftover biscuits from lunch with home-canned green beans—isn't warm anymore, but Aunty devours it. We sit in the kitchen by the light of homemade candles and kerosene lamps. The oily, pungent smell of kerosene used to make me wrinkle my nose, but I've grown used to it.

We've always eaten the Sunday evening meal by candle light. Our tradition dates back to the first Sunday I spent here at the Inn. Aunty was trying to make those hard days special and fun for mc. Shc always says it was the first time she saw me smile that week that I came to live with her. The flickering lamps are usually cozy and relaxing on a cold winter evening, but tonight my muscles are tense with worry. Aunty sighs and takes a long sip of her tea before finally speaking.

"Thank you, Ivy. I know you've been worrying all day. I really needed to eat; I haven't had a morsel since breakfast." Even her voice sounds exhausted as though she's been screaming all day and her throat is strained.

"How is Thomas? Is he going to be alright?" I ask in a whisper to match hers.

Her tired eyes lift in surprise, and she tilts her head with a look of reproof and suspicion. "How did you find out? You didn't leave the house did you?"

"No. Harmony came by to tell me." I fight the defensive, insulted feelings that rise up in response to her accusing eyes. I haven't given her enough reasons to think the best of me lately.

"Ahh. Of course." Her face softens and she sips at her tea. "Well, yes and no. Thomas will live, but unfortunately we weren't able to do much about his injuries. He lost most of his right hand."

"What happened? I heard Matt is back too?" She must hear the hope and longing in my voice because she looks suddenly grave.

"Yes, he is. But Ivy, even if you weren't confined to the house I would insist that you not go looking for that boy. He isn't for you. If he turns to The Lord at some point then we can reconsider. But for now, I don't want you to even consider the thought. He was very angry and violent with the guards, and I'm not sure exactly how this happened to Thomas.

"Matt would NEVER hurt Thomas!" I'm so sure of this that I adamantly defend him. "He brought Thomas back to us, didn't he? And just last week you were the one defending him and asking me to treat *him* kindly!"

"Yes, he brought Thomas back, but I wouldn't be at all surprised if he intends to take him again when he's recuperated. Either way, he's made it clear that he won't be staying long. I just hope he'll leave Thomas when the time comes. Without his right hand, Thomas will have to learn to use his left hand which will take time. He'll need to be watched for infection until the deep wounds are completely healed. He'll need constant care. Hopefully Matt will realize the foolishness of taking him now. And yes, I asked you to treat him with decency and kindness, not fall in love with him! I do believe that he was sent here by the Lord and that God is calling for him. But he may or may not respond. That's in God's hands."

"Did he say when he'd be leaving?" I ask with misty tears in my eyes.

"He didn't say much that I could repeat. He was very angry. Apparently, he blames us for Thomas' condition. Though I'm certain he's really upset with himself for letting Thomas get hurt. He had to wait outside the gate while Thomas lost more and more blood. The guards on duty didn't know him and didn't know what to do. There wasn't a protocol for what to do when one of the infected stands yelling and cursing at the gate, demanding to be let in, all the while holding a bloody boy in his arms! They refused to let him in. Apparently Anthony was on duty and overheard what was happening on the radio. He ran to the West Gate and insisted that Matt and Thomas be allowed in. Anthony brought them to the Doctor and then sent for me and Ellen. Unfortunately, the other nurse, Joy, was home with a bad flu and wasn't able to be any help to us. Thomas was completely unconscious by the time I saw him, and very near death." She pauses to take several sips of tea and I realize she's holding back tears of her own.

As always, her tears make it even harder to hold back my own. My voice thick and quiet, I ask, "Is he still unconscious? Is Matt still with him? Harmony heard that Matt is being kept at this new guy Andrew's house? How come this Andrew guy is suddenly in charge of the town and I've never even heard of him?"

My questions would've kept coming for as long as Aunty kept sipping, but she puts her tea down and holds her finger up to quiet me. I learned long ago not to interrupt her while she's explaining something, she really hates that. Harmony and I can have long conversations where we interrupt each other and overlap each other and change the subject three times in two minutes without realizing it. It's how we work. But I have to be careful not to do it when Aunty is talking because she takes it personally. Interrupting is "unladylike" and "disrespectful." She'll clam up until you apologize and beg her to continue whatever it was she was saying. I'm desperate for info, so I wait patiently for her to speak again.

"Thomas was still unconscious when I left. He had lost a lot of blood and needed a blood transfusion. The only one there with compatible blood was Ellen. Actually Matt had the same blood type as well, but he refused to give Thomas his blood."

"What!" I exclaim, despite my efforts to not interrupt. "That doesn't sound like the same guy who was desperate for his little brother last week!"

"He was afraid he'd give Thomas back the disease. He begged us to find someone else's blood. We tried to convince him that Thomas wouldn't get the disease again, that Thomas still has the disease in his blood, but he wouldn't listen. He was watching his little brother slip away with grievous injuries, and we weren't really dealing with a rational Matt at that point. So, even though Ellen was the only trained nurse there, her blood was compatible and, of course, she was willing. It meant even less help from her and more required of me—and I'm no nurse. It was very trying for all of us."

She sips.

I wait.

"Hale had to work frantically for many hours at what would've been hard for several doctors. He has Tim very well trained as a nurse aide, and Tim was invaluable to us today. The two of them worked as quickly as possible to get blood back into Thomas while trying to repair all the injuries. The poor dear had been stabbed seven times, and his hand was just hanging off," Aunty clucks her tongue with disapproval. I know she is wondering how the world has gotten this bad. Wondering who would do such a thing to a sweet boy like Thomas.

She continues, "Thomas got more stitches than I could count and I did a lot of the stitching. Hale wasn't able to repair all the nerve and bone damage in the hand. We are hoping that the thumb will heal, but even that is a long shot. Thomas lost the other four fingers and some of the hand itself. We've given him the last of the strong pain medicine. He'll probably wake fully sometime this evening because of the pain, and we'll only have Tylenol for him. It's going to be a hard recovery. For now, they are keeping him at the clinic, but I'm sure Ellen will want him moved home to her house as soon as he's able. She's sleeping at the clinic with him now. Jose is there, too. Pray for them, Ivy. Pray that God will ease Thomas' pain."

Another sip of tea.

She knows I want to know more about Matt. She's choosing her words for me—selectively—and I just wish she'd tell me everything!

"Matt was taken, by force, to Andrew's house. He was very angry. Yelling and knocking things over at the clinic. Blaming us for taking too long to let them in. We had to get him out of there so Hale could concentrate. It took several guards to pull him away. He has a lot of rage and hate in his heart, Ivy. I know you saw the good in him," she preemptively holds up a finger to silence my next round of arguments, "and so did I."

My heart sinks at her word "did." Not "I do see the good in him," but "I did see." Matt changed her opinion of him today.

"He is not Living, Ivy," she continues as my eyes fill with tears. "He is his own man. Full of sin. I don't know what the plan for him is. I only just learned where they had taken him as I was leaving. Andrew is Dr. Markowitz's oldest son. He was with a small group of the Living somewhere near Atlanta. They were attacked and killed two weeks ago, everyone but him. Andrew came here because his father and brother are here. The Elders were impressed by his testimony and his skill in security and knowledge of Pravda's dealings. They asked him to help make us more secure here. That's all I know. Dr. Hale Markowitz has raised some intelligent, impressive sons."

She looks me pointedly in the eye with this statement. I look away. I'm not particularly fond of either son.

"Well dear, I'm exhausted. Thank you for that lovely dinner. I must say I am very glad to have you back."

She smiles and her warm blue eyes are the only thing that looks right on her haggard, pale face. Hugging me to her, she kisses the top of my head. I lean away from the dried blood on her shirt. She looks down and seems to notice the gory state of her appearance for the first time.

"We are so blessed to have each other Ivy. Family is precious. I kept thinking of you today and counting my blessings that we are together. That we have Life!"

I smile back, but my thoughts are running wild—longing for a glimpse of Matt's crooked smile.

She starts to clear her dish from the table, but I jump up and take it from her, "You go, I know you're tired. I've got this."

"Thank you, honey. I am very tired. I think I'll go to bed early."

Aunty limps out of the kitchen and I watch her go.

I'm alone again. Loneliness and worry fight to tear me out of God's peace-filled hands; tempting me to listen to their whispered lies. I finish the dishes quickly and take my tea to my room. I have a lot to pray about.

Chapter Thirty

The Bones Are Full Of Flavor

It's Monday afternoon and my in-house work station is almost completely set up right outside of my bedroom door. This comes with good news and bad news. Which do you want first?

I'm a bad news first kind of girl, so I'll lead with that.

The bad news is they've sent Tim to set up my computer.

BLAH.

He probably volunteered. I've had to spend the entire afternoon with him hanging out right outside of my bedroom. I had to feed him lunch, too. But really, the bad news isn't that bad since it brought the good news.

The good news is that Tim has spent the morning with Matt. Tim knows all about what's going on and it is information that I am desperate for. So, I'm being a little sweeter than normal with Tim, because I am dying to know everything he knows about Matt. And Thomas.

Judge me if you want, but I'm supposed to be sweeter and nicer. Just because I am more interested in his boring conversation than normal doesn't make me a bad person.

"I brought you some ice water," I say, returning from a quick break in the kitchen with my smile fixed in place.

"Thank you, Ivy," he says with obvious surprise and unmasked glee. He pulls himself up from the tangle of cords on the floor, his too-big brown glasses sliding down his nose.

"Sure," I say, fighting to maintain my smile as his hand lingers a moment on mine when he reaches for the cold glass. "It'll be great to get back to work. I'm going stir crazy here already. It was nice of you to come over and do this for me. I am a trouble-maker you know," I add sarcastically.

"They just want you to be safe, Ivy. We all do," he adds with so much concern in his voice it makes me nauseous.

Keep that smile on, Ivy.

"Well, you've been hanging out with zombies lately, too." I try to encourage him to bring up Matt again on his own. "Maybe they'll lock you up next."

"You aren't locked up, Ivy. We're just worried for your safety. I'm not being threatened by Pravda."

Rub it in.

I scowl at the mention of my mysterious enemies and Tim continues, "And I'm not hanging out with anyone. My brother has to be out most of the day with the other guards, so someone has to check on him in his cell and feed him."

"In his cell? You have him locked in a cell!" I say this with way too much emotion, and I see Tim furrow his brow and look sideways at me over the computer monitor. I try to recover by dialing it down a notch. "I mean, why not just kick him out? Let him go back to wherever he came from?"

"I don't know what they are going to do with him. He's definitely dangerous. Anyways, I'm just trying to help out. I don't spend much time there. Your aunt gets more out of him than I do."

I'm sucker punched.

She had been out all morning, but I assumed she was helping with Thomas. She never mentioned Matt when she came home for lunch.

Tim studies me and assumes the stormy emotions he sees on my face are fear or worry. He actually puts his arm around me and says, "Don't worry Ivy. You're safe here. He'll be gone soon and everything will be okay again. My brother is working hard to figure out who tried to hurt you. It's his number one priority. I've told him how great you are."

I think I'm going to be sick.

I mumble, "Thank you," and go in my room and shut the door.

*****

A little while later, Tim knocks on my bedroom door, "Ivy? I'm done. Do you want me to show you?"

"Uh, I'm busy. I'll come check it out later," I lie because I don't want him to see my red eyes—heaven forbid it might lead to him trying to touch me again.

"Oh. Okay," Tim sounds disappointed. "Bye," he says pitifully into the door, and I can picture him leaning against it in dejection.

I wait five minutes to be sure he's gone, and then I go out and lock the front door.

I hear pots and pans banging around. Aunty must be cooking dinner. An inner mental debate ensues. Should I just come right out and ask her, "Did you see Matt today?" I doubt she'd lie to me. Or should I wait and see if she brings it up? She knows how interested I am, how much I want to know what's going on with him. If I don't ask and she doesn't say anything about him, then what? I don't want to be pouty or angry. We just repaired our relationship. I decide to be direct. It's the healthiest course of action.

She's cooking vegetable soup with venison scraps. I walk over to the stove and inhale deeply. The aroma of fresh dried herbs mixed with the earthy smell of the potatoes and carrots and the savory scent of venison makes a magical concoction that threatens to pull my stomach out through my nose. The bones sticking up out of the pot look gruesome, but they'll make the broth rich and delicious. I'm not tired of venison yet. We've been eating it almost every night to use it up while it's fresh.

When we have meat we use every last bit of it. We'll even use the leftover fat for making tallow candles. Tallow candles work as well as the kind we've salvaged from stores over the years with one distinct difference. Tallow candles make you hungry. They smell like meat cooking. I'd rather smell rosy candles or vanilla candles or unscented candles than candles that smell like pot roast.

Aunty is humming to herself as she bustles around the kitchen. She scoots me out of her way to add another ingredient to the simmering pot.

"You saw Matt today?" I ask while her back is to me as she stirs the soup.

I see her shoulders slump. She was hoping I wouldn't find out.

She sighs and answers me, "Yes. Tim told you?"

"You wouldn't have?"

"Ivy, I really wish you could focus your thoughts somewhere more productive."

She means she wishes I'd focus them on Tim.

I feel misunderstood and frustrated, and I can't help the little rant that bursts out unchecked. "Just last week you were lecturing me about my over-productiveness. YOU wanted me to be a normal teenage girl who likes boys. I like one and I'm still wrong."

"Let's not fight Ivy. I'm too tired."

"Why is he in a cell?"

She sighs again. I'm informed and not going away.

"He's made several threats against the community. We have to take them seriously. We are on thin ice, Ivy. We might have to move the whole community; which I don't even know how we'd accomplish without a miracle."

"Will you tell me what he said?"

"He threatened to kill the guards who wouldn't let him in. He says he'll bring Pravda here if we don't let him out and give him Thomas. So, we aren't sure which threat to be more worried about. If we don't let him out and he should escape, we'll have to consider that he may be telling the truth and might bring Pravda here. Since our recent brush with them, we already know they are interested in us. If we do let him out, how do we ensure the safety of the two guards? And I'd imagine that he's not too thrilled with Captain Markowitz either."

"Captain Markowitz?"

"Andrew, dear."

"Captain Markowitz?" I repeat again this time rolling my eyes. "So what did he say to you? Just more angry threats?"

"No, he was decent with me. He let me tend his wounds in exchange for information about Thomas."

"He's hurt too? How hurt? And why did you need information about Thomas?"

"Yes he had several deep cuts and his face took quite a beating. He can barely open one eye. He needed to be cleaned up, and I even gave him a few stitches," she sounds proud of her medical prowess.

"But why did you need information about Thomas?" I ask again.

"I didn't, he did. I had to bribe him with information about Thomas' condition to get him to let me care for him. He was refusing care, and I hated to see him all bloodied up. Captain Andrew stood guard with a Taser the whole time, so I was relatively safe."

"Of course you were safe! This is ridiculous. Matt wouldn't hurt anyone; he was just worried and upset about Thomas. He wouldn't do any of those things he said. You know that, Aunty! Can't you tell them to let him go?"

"You are going to have to trust me, Ivy. I've never exaggerated the facts before have I? Do you find me embellishing other people's stories and looking for drama where there is none?"

"No."

She's right. If anything, she always down-plays a serious situation; looks for the best in people. It must be pretty bad if everything she's saying is true.

"I'm taking some of this soup over to the clinic." She pauses and then adds, "I'll bring some to Matt and Andrew too."

I think she's doing it just for me. And if I can't see him, I do like thinking that he'll eat some of our soup. Maybe he'll think of me.

"Thank you Aunty," I say as I hug her tightly.

"You're welcome dear," she says while shaking her head at me. "You really are a teenage girl aren't you?"

I smile sheepishly.

Chapter Thirty-One

The Only Thing That Could Make Toilet Cleaning Exciting

I'm eating dinner alone again. Aunty told me she might have to stay awhile with Thomas this evening to give the others a break. I guess I've spent this much time by myself before; but, because it's forced on me, each lonely minute feels like ten. I clean up and go to my room to finish the work Sherry sent me. Hopefully the other teachers will send work soon. Everyone is extra busy getting ready for the missionaries' homecoming.

At the last count, there were one hundred ninety-three people in our community. Andrew Markowitz makes one hundred ninety-four. If Matt counted, it would be one hundred ninety-five. But he's not Living, and he doesn't plan to stay. The one hundred ninety-four Living people who are here by choice aren't the only members of our body. We have about thirty more people who have answered the call to go out and tell the zombies that they can be healed. They travel to different assigned areas, risking their lives, to hopefully save some. Three times a year the missionaries come home for a week to catch up, stock up on supplies, and share the news of what's happening outside the gates.

The last time they were home, the news wasn't good. We heard a very bleak report of a scattered few converts, most of whom fell back in with the zombies shortly after converting. Between all thirty of them, they only brought four people with new Life into the community last time they were home. One of those converts was Thomas.

The missionaries told us stories about rising lawlessness and unbridled hatred towards our kind. One missionary didn't come home for the last homecoming. He's MIA. Missing In Action. That's when the board of Elders was elected. They met for several days to decide whether or not it was safe to send out the missionaries for another term. The missionaries themselves unanimously voted to go back out, so they were allowed to leave again. We are all anxiously waiting to see each of them make it safely home from another term. They will trickle in all week, and this Sunday will be a big celebration. We'll stay at the U.R. building all day long, eating meals and worshiping together. The missionaries will each take a turn sharing where they've been and what they've seen. It's always an exciting, emotion filled day for everyone.

I can't decide if I'll go or not. On the one hand, I'll be allowed to be out of this house all day long! On the other hand, no one seems to like me much right now. An entire day of trying not to notice their whispers, avoiding conversations and clinging to Aunty's side like a child doesn't sound worth the time out of the house.

I'm sure we'll fill all five guest rooms upstairs with at least ten missionaries. Filling all five rooms would normally exhaust me with the thought of all the impending chores; but, for a change, it sounds really nice. Lots of people in the house means someone to talk to, an end to my boredom, and firsthand news from outside our sheltered town. Even better, they're people who don't know about my recent problems and won't judge me for my mistakes. It will be a much needed distraction from my constant thoughts of Matt. Company sounds heavenly.

*****

I can't go to bed until I know Aunty is home safe. She finally comes in, long after dark, at 9:00. I've had the teapot simmering and ready for her for an hour. I had to add new water twice to keep it from boiling away to nothing. I stare at her while she drinks her tea, and I can't help but worry about how unhealthy she looks. Her face is thin, the wrinkly skin beneath her eyes looks baggy, and her hair looks dull gray instead of lustrous silver. She looks older than her age- and she normally looks so much younger. It's been a stressful week for sure, but I'm worried that maybe something worse is draining her. Surely one tough week couldn't take her down? I need to take better care of her, take some of the work off of her shoulders. Make her rest.

"I look pretty bad, huh?" Aunty startles me, and I meet her eyes guiltily.

"What? No! You're beautiful!"

"Ivy, I know you so well. I read you like a book. You are scowling at me and looking me over. You should see your face."

"No really, Aunty. You are as gorgeous as always. You look tired that's all. I'm worried that you are working too hard," I say wondering if God is offended by little white lies that make someone else feel better.

"I am tired, Ivy. Very tired. I'm sorry dear, you are probably lonely and wishing for someone to visit with, but I'm dead on my feet. I promise we'll spend some good time together tomorrow," Aunty says standing up. Our short visit is over already.

Putting her cup in the sink, she shuffles towards the door. Shuffles—like an old lady. I feel a stab of fear at the thought that if she were gone I'd have no one.

As she's leaving the kitchen, she turns and says, "By the way dear, Matt said thank you for the soup. To you. I mean he thanked me for bringing it, but he asked me to thank you, too. I still don't want to encourage your feelings towards him, but I wouldn't feel right not telling you. Love you sweetie. Goodnight."

Chapter Thirty-Two

How a Missionary Ruined Spaghetti for Me Forever

Well, I asked for it; so I can't be disappointed about it. I'm swamped. Everyone has sent me something to work on for this coming Sunday. I'm compiling lists, typing lectures and sermons, looking up scripture, and tons of other secretarial type things. Mr. Jarvis even has me cutting out little fabric animals and people for a felt Noah's Ark project for the little kids. Not to mention all the baking and cooking Aunty and I are doing.

Everyone has to contribute as much as possible for the potluck lunch and dinner at the U.R. for over two hundred people on Sunday. In my "spare" time, I'm trying to dust and sweep the whole house and make sure the guest rooms are ready for whoever comes. I keep intentionally trying to take as much of Aunty's work as I can. She looks a little less tired; so I'm hoping it's helping. I can't wait until she's back to her speed-walking self.

Thomas has been moved to Jose and Ellen's house. Aunty says he's in a lot of pain and we pray for him together at every meal. They are giving him Tylenol around the clock. Aunty says Thomas is asking relentlessly to see Matt. Thomas is such a tender-hearted kid, and Aunty says he feels like what happened out there is his fault. He doesn't know Matt is in a jail cell. Thomas thinks they are keeping Matt somewhere to be safe. It's too much to explain to a little boy who loves his brother and is already dealing with more guilt and pain than he can handle.

I hear very little about Matt. Aunty has only seen him one other time. I know because I've pestered her for info every day. Aunty says Tim is always there. I can't even picture the two of them together. I wonder what worldly, exciting Matt thinks of boring, nerdy Tim's company.

Harmony has only come to see me once this week. She brought more papers from her mom and only stayed about half an hour. She looked at her watch a lot and wasn't herself. I can't even remember what we talked about. It was awkward. I felt extra lonely after she left.

This afternoon, the first missionary arrived back in town. Aunty says the whole community is thrilled to see him, but everyone is worried that more of the missionaries haven't arrived by now. By the way, I'm getting *really* tired of getting all my info through Aunty.

The missionary, Ben Morvose, is friendly and handsome. I checked him into his room here at the Inn shortly after he arrived today. Ben is in his early twenties, maybe 22 or 23. He's tall and thin with a summer tan complexion. He's already starting to lose his hair. For a guy so young, I can't help but wonder if his receding hairline has to do with how stressful and dangerous his life is.

Ben is boisterous to say the least. As I showed him around the house and let him peak in the different rooms, he exclaimed and complimented the smallest details. His joy and enthusiasm are infectious; and, watching him enjoy the simple things like a comfy bed and clean sheets, made me think of Rev. Depold's sermon. Ben is so enjoyable to be around, I can't imagine any zombie not liking him. He's a great advertisement for our great news.

Ben chose the small room at the top of the stairs to stay in; the same room that Matt stayed in. Ben hasn't stayed with us before. He's always been one of the last missionaries to arrive and has stayed with other families in town because we were already full. It's always been first come first serve for rooms at the Inn. Once we're full, families start volunteering their guest rooms for the rest of the missionaries.

Ben is eating dinner with us tonight. I'm looking forward to being the first to hear Ben's stories of life out there. When he found out that none of the other missionaries had arrived yet, it took his spirited vigor down a notch. The missionaries are like family to each other since only they can really understand what it's like to be out there alone with the zombies.

Aunty and I gave Ben some dinner choices for his first meal back in civilization. He chose spaghetti with homemade sauce and garlic bread—Italian comfort food, true to his Italian last name. I've been working all day and dinner is just about ready; so I jump in the shower and take a few minutes to get cleaned up. I put on a little lip gloss and braid my hair to the side. Satisfied with my appearance, I run upstairs to knock on Ben's door and call him to dinner.

*****

Ben follows me into the kitchen all the while emitting enthusiastic sighs and moans over how good dinner smells. After another round of exuberant exclamations about how good the food looks, Ben prays a blessing over the meal and our home.

"Father," Ben begins, "Thank you. Thank you for your goodness. Thank you for Colleen and Ivy and this beautiful home. Thank you for bringing me home safe."

With my eyes closed, I smile. I'm glad Ben feels at home here. It is so soothing to hear a man of God pray at our table. I feel God's blessing emanating from the encouraging man whose head is bowed across from me.

"Father, protect this place and these women who belong to you. Thank you for their humble hands that serve this community. Thank you for their service to me in sharing this amazing feast. Jesus, care for the lonely and lost who suffer tonight. The little children who have no food and no home. Minister to the innocent tonight, Creator."

Ben's voice, thick with passion and concern for people outside our walls brings tears to my eyes. I never think about the babies. I forget that there are innocent children out there in the broken, rotting world. Ben says, "Amen," and Aunty and I meet each other's glistening eyes. Ben's prayer carried weight and authority. This man of God lifted me and my safety up before the King of Kings. I know God hears everyone's prayers, but I feel like he especially honors the prayers of a missionary.

I'm starved for the homemade spaghetti, but even more starved for news and a glimpse outside of our limited existence. Aunty and I make pleasant conversation and take small polite bites of pasta. Ben nods and "uh huhs" while vacuuming up slurpy bites of spaghetti. Aunty keeps leading the conversation towards what is happening on the outside. Ben knows we're dying to hear all his news, but he seems reluctant to talk. Looking up from his plate, Ben sees me staring at him with wide eyes like a child waiting for Santa. With a deep sigh, he starts to tell us what his last term was like.

"It's gotten—insane out there. I don't even know how to describe it to you ladies without being offensive. Even after the disappearances, the United States was still a nation with a Christian heritage. For my first several terms out there, people were still people. Of course, people were terrified back then—especially when the disease first hit. But, in those first few years, people were more receptive. They wanted to hear good news. They were willing to change."

He pauses and his deep voice sounds spooky when he says, "Now, everyone is so far gone. Almost everyone is drug addicted and not in their right mind. The disease is causing such serious nerve damage and disabilities that people are dying in large numbers. The streets are full of bodies. All hope is gone. Most of them have given up on Pravda.

"Instead of making them more interested in what's after this life, they avoid talk of death or spiritual matters with a sick desperation. They are desperate to soothe themselves with as much happiness and pleasure as possible. They exist for a good feeling, numbness to the pain, with nothing else on their mind but where to get their next fix. I didn't have a single convert this term," he says quietly with sadness etched into his handsome face. He looks down at his food as though ashamed.

Aunty immediately tries to encourage him. "Ben, what you are doing is so brave. It's not your fault that they won't come. You are giving your life out there; living with danger and want. We are all so proud of you. The Lord knows how hard you try. You know as well as I do that unless He calls them, they can't come. It's His job, not yours."

"Yeah." I add lamely. All the happiness and encouragement that I felt when Ben prayed is gone. I feel depressed from the heavy news Ben has shared. Why do Ben's words make me feel so bi-polar? How can he have me smiling one second and loathing existence the next? Maybe Ben has a dose of "The Force" in him just like Aunty.

Ben smiles at me and swallows a mouthful of garlic bread. I look down when I realize I've been staring at him and scowling.

"Tell us what it's like here in Toccoa, you know, just outside the fence," I ask.

After slurping in a big bite of spaghetti, he obliges me, "Well, really it's just more of the same. Pleasure is god to these people. The government has people living together in large compounds now. With everything they want provided for them. It's not free by any means though. They pay in blood. The lines are hours long every day."

"What do they do with the blood they collect? Why does Pravda need so much blood Ben?" Aunty asks.

"They recycle it," he answers. "People line up to give their blood in exchange for credit. They spend the credit on drugs, sex, food, clothing and shelter; in that order. The government provides entertainment and cheap sustenance for free. The entertainment is unspeakable, and I won't even allude to the depravity of it. The very poor get by on the free food, choosing instead to buy drugs and sex. But not everyone is poor. Anyone with means buys their food."

"They have grocery stores?" I ask with the possibility of tasting cheese singles again on my mind.

"No, not at a grocery store," Ben says, his face clouded with anger.

His dark expression makes me feel bad for asking. I have no idea why the mention of grocery stores would be so infuriating. Throughout his report, I've watched him. Ben gets more and more tense with each sentence, like he's crumpling up on the inside. Shrinking in terror as he stares wide-eyed at the monster he has faced outside our walls. His fear is contagious, the itchy chills that I usually only get from spiders are moving up my spine.

"The food that's for sale now, well, it's beyond comprehension."

We stare at him with an equal mix of expectancy and horror, waiting for him to swallow another bite of spaghetti.

Sauce on his cheeks, he keeps recounting as though desperate to get the terrible knowledge off of his chest, "There's no beef or pork or fresh fruits and vegetables to be found in town. No one farms; no one makes or sells anything locally. And people are hungry for meat."

He pauses and takes a deep breath, "Less than a mile from our gates, people are being murdered and eaten."

Aunty and I gasp at this blunt statement and the chills finish their climb to my neck. A shiver shakes my shoulders, but neither Ben nor Aunty takes any notice.

"It's commonplace now," Ben says with irritating calmness about the murderers and cannibals that live just down the street from me.

"Surely the family members care?" Aunty asks. "Just this week we've had our own close call with an infected boy who came looking for his younger brother. Young Thomas ran away to join us when he was recently brought to Life. He came in with one of the missionaries last fall. Thomas' older brother searched for him and tracked him here. Matt, the older boy, displayed great love for the boy. It was very touching."

"Which missionary?" Ben asks, more interested in his fellow missionary than Aunty's speech about the loving zombie who stole our hearts. Well, my heart for sure.

"Harvey Johns. I think he's the oldest missionary still out on the field," I answer him, glad to add to the conversation. "Older than Aunty."

"Ahem," Aunty clears her throat at me. I smile at her.

"Harvey is a great man of God. I hope he's still okay. Hopefully they'll all arrive soon," Ben says, his voice dripping with worry for his comrades.

"So, like Aunty said, don't the family members freak out when someone is, uh, killed? How can it be just okay?"

"They murder the orphans, the loners, and the old. With the world so out of touch from one place to another, if you have no family in the community you are living in, there's no one to complain that you are missing. And of course abortion is the nation's largest source of meat these days. Women are paid more credits to carry longer and abort later in the pregnancy to ensure the aborted are large enough to eat."

As Ben describes the baby selling market, I think I'm going to be sick. I put down my fork, and I know dinner is over for me. Ben keeps filling his mouth, talking with his mouth full, throughout his account. The white noodles covered in red sauce, dangling from his lips look suddenly gory—like little baby guts. Not only am I done eating this dinner, I think spaghetti is ruined for me forever. Aunty, too, has put down her fork and we are both staring at Ben wide eyed and openly disgusted.

"How? Why?" we ask in shock.

"I've almost lost my sense of shock." He says in response to our horrified faces. "It just is what it is out there. Saying it all out loud reminds me how horrible it all is. I've seen it on a daily basis for months now."

"We have meat here," Aunty says. "Can't they hunt? There are deer in the mountains and cows that have lived roaming free. Our hunters bring us pheasant and duck and even the occasional wild chicken. Why can't they eat dogs or squirrels for heaven's sake?"

He nods, "Of course there is still some meat out there, mostly wild, but not enough to feed the masses. And anyone healthy enough and entrepreneurial enough to hunt it is selling it at very high prices that only the very rich can afford. Most everyone out there is very poor. There is no industry now, except the Pravda industry. Blood and drugs. That is the only economy. Pravda is running the show with the government's help. The very poor are kept content with mostly free food, free entertainment, and inexpensive drugs. It's every man for himself and the poor don't fight the system because they all know they are dying. There won't be another generation."

Aunty and I nod. They are right, there's little time left. It's good news for us. Bad news for the dying.

Ben says emphatically, "This is it for earth. It's over. Human life means nothing. No one believes in anything. People and babies are the last marketable commodity. Aside from blood, a baby is the only thing a woman can make and sell easily. And with sex being the number one source of entertainment and pleasure, babies are made every day."

"Ahem," Aunty clears her throat again with a reproving look for Ben. She doesn't want me to hear about the birds and the bees.

Ha!

The birds and bees sound too cute for what we are talking about. More like the vultures and the flesh eating wasps.

"Sorry," Ben answers Aunty's reproof without feeling. "It's just the way it is. The other reason for the big boom in the baby market is stem cells. The scientists say there are documented cases of stem cells slowing, though not curing, the disease. I think it's a lie. What I do know for sure is that the people believe whatever they're told out of sheer desperation. So now everyone in Toccoa is trying to get their hands on stem cells.

"What are stem cells?" I ask, embarrassed at my own naivety. Tim would know.

"Cells found in the umbilical cord," Aunty explains. "What do they do with them?" she asks Ben.

"They inject them into their diseased flesh, eat them raw, you name it."

I'm kind of surprised Aunty hasn't put a stop to the whole conversation by now—insisted we speak of saner things at the dinner table. But that tired look is all over her face, she seems weaker than yesterday.

I take charge. "Can we talk about something else? Like the weather or something?"

I feel like Aunty and I have switched roles. I feel more like her care-giver these days. I'm suddenly doing more of the work, while worrying about her fragile appearance and failing health. I feel like the grown up. With these terrifying new images that Ben has put in my head, the compounded fear of losing her threatens to steal my sanity.

Ben nods his head and says, "I know. I don't want to know about it. Don't want to have seen it. But it is reality and it is right down the street. We don't have the privilege of being sheltered anymore. They are getting more and more depraved. More violent by the hour even. I must make you all see this before I leave again."

"The elders won't send you again," Aunty whispers. Then her voice gets stronger and stronger with each word as she tries to persuade, "You must stay here now Ben. You may stay with us at the Inn until they find you a good apartment. You are welcome for as long as you need."

"I have to go." He takes a deep breath and then exhales, "And so do you. You aren't safe here anymore. Our time in the open is over." Then, tearing off a mouthful of garlic bread, he mumbles while chewing, "God save us."

Aunty and I don't speak. We clear our half eaten plates, emptying them into the garbage. Ben stares off into the distance and puts a third helping on his tomato stained plate.

All I see is blood.

Chapter Thirty-Three

Passing Love Notes

It's Friday. Matt has been being held across the street for five days. Homecoming is only two days away now, and I'm reconsidering going. Maybe I could slip away during the day and sneak up to see Matt. Would anyone notice if I excused myself to use the bathroom and took a little long in returning to the meeting? Seeing Matt again would be worth the stares and whispers I'd have to endure.

Ben is still the only missionary to have arrived. He's been in his room all day today and hasn't eaten any meals with us. I think he is fasting and praying for his fellow missionaries.

After a quiet lunch with Aunty, I begin cleaning up while she sits and sips her tea.

Aunty clears her throat and makes an announcement, "They are escorting Matt out of the gates in about an hour."

"What! Why? Has something happened?"

I had grown used to the current situation. I knew he was safe, even if it was behind bars, just down the street from me. I couldn't see him, but I at least knew where he was and the future held endless possibilities.

"No, nothing new has happened. Tim has spent a lot of time with him and so has Andrew. They are fairly certain he isn't a threat to us, despite his early promises to the contrary. So, they have asked Matt to leave us in peace, and he has agreed. We feel somewhat safe knowing that Thomas will be staying here with us. Everyone agrees Matt would never do anything to hurt Thomas. If he wanted Pravda to have his brother, he wouldn't have brought him back to us after they were attacked. So, we are hoping he will let us be.

"Will you please do something for me Aunty?" I was prepared for this possibility.

"No dear. You can't leave the house. I'm sorry, but you can't be part of this."

"No, I know that. I just—I wrote him a letter."

Aunty's gray eyebrows shoot up, and I can tell she doesn't like where this is going.

"It's just an apology really. I felt so awful for how I treated him, and I know it was such a horrible witness, and I need to tell him I'm sorry. I have an apology letter for Andrew, too. Would you just deliver them for me before it's too late? Please?" I silently plead with my eyes, putting all my energy into looking as innocent and desperate as possible.

If I've inherited any of the powers of "The Force," now is the time to find out.

Aunty is quiet for almost a full minute—staring back at me and considering my request. Finally, she nods in the affirmative, and my heart leaps with joy and triumph.

"I had better get ready to go then. I wasn't planning on seeing him again, and they'll be leaving shortly. Don't be disappointed if they have already taken him."

"Thank you, Aunty. I love you so much! I'll go get the letters."

*****

We meet at the front door a few minutes later. Aunty has been going out the front door more often—now that I'm always home to lock it behind her. I think it's because she's out of shape and the front door is twenty steps closer to the U.R. building. I hand her my letters. One says "Captain Markowitz" on the front and the other says "Matt." She puts them in her coat pocket and walks slowly down the front steps of the Inn. I wish she would hurry for me. If I didn't already know that she wasn't feeling well lately, I'd have thought she was stalling on purpose. I'd think she was hoping to miss them, leaving my "Matt" letter undelivered.

From the front window, I watch her cross the street, pass the U.R. building, and walk down the alley that leads to the entrance of Andrew's apartment—the old Police Station. My stomach is full of butterflies at the thought of Matt reading my letter. It's so personal. I think I can trust Aunty not to read it first. It wouldn't be the end of the world, but I'd rather she didn't read it. It says:

Dear Matt,

I am sorry. I'm ashamed of how I treated you while you were staying with us. I think what you've done for Thomas is incredible. You reminded me what love looks like. I truly admire you. I regret deeply that it took me too long to realize that and you were gone before I could say it. Thank you for drawing it out of me.

Your friend,
Ivy

The last sentence was kind of a code. I don't know if he'll get it, or maybe he'll just think I'm a weirdo. Hopefully he'll figure out that I found the drawing that he made of me and that I liked it. I sketched a few ivy leaves next to my name at the bottom to make it as obvious as possible. I don't think anyone else reading it would ever imagine what it alluded to. So, if Aunty reads it, I think she'll still give it to him. To her eyes, it will simply seem a heartfelt apology.

The letter to Andrew reads:

Dear Captain Markowitz,

Thank you for all that you do to keep us safe. I'm sorry that I caused you trouble and then was disrespectful. Please forgive me.

Respectfully,
Ivy Lusato

No ivy leaves doodled on that one.

*****

I'm working at my new computer workstation just outside of my bedroom when I hear Aunty come in the back door. It took her much longer than I thought it would, and I hurry to find her in the kitchen. I'm desperate for details.

"Not much to tell," she says. "They hadn't left yet, I gave each of them your letter. Actually, Captain Markowitz insisted on reading Matt's letter before I could give it to him. But then, seeing that it was simply an apology, he gave it to Matt and that was it."

I was ok with the thought of Aunty reading my personal apology. I hate that Andrew read it. It's embarrassing.

"Did Matt say anything? Did he look at all—you know, happy or anything when he read it?"

"He didn't read it in front of us. I'm sorry, dear. He put it in his pocket, and I left a few minutes later. I'm sure he will read it though. It was good that you apologized, Ivy. I'm proud of you."

"Maybe he won't read it. I think he might hate me. I deserve that."

"Don't be dramatic, Ivy. I'm sure he doesn't hate you." She stands to leave the kitchen and says, "I'm going to take a nap until dinner. Okay? It's leftover night tonight. Can you fend for yourself if you get hungry before I wake up?"

"Uh huh."

And I'm alone again.

Chapter Thirty-Four
Angels and Demons

Howling wind wakes me early Saturday morning. It sounds like hell's inhabitants have been unleashed on the earth—here to warn any who will listen to repent lest they share the same fate. The mournful keens give me the creeps, and I reach for my Bible before going to the kitchen for coffee. Little gusts of cold air find their way through my bedroom window's old frame and ruffle the pages of my Bible. I struggle to focus and find comfort in His presence. The wind's ominous wail makes me think it might be best if I climbed back under my covers and just skipped today. Tomorrow will be friendlier.

I am only halfway through my devotion when the doorbell rings. It is still very early in the morning and dark outside. No one ever rings the bell this early. Could it be another emergency? Has Matt brought the trouble he threatened? I thought we could trust him. Maybe I'm foolish, but I really felt like he was a good person. Not just a zombie. I hope it isn't another medical emergency requiring Aunty's help. She looked beyond exhausted yesterday, and she never did come down for dinner. I'm almost getting used to eating all my meals alone.

Throwing my bathrobe over my pajamas, I hurry to answer the door. I don't want the bell to ring again and wake Aunty. Flipping lights on throughout the house as I go, I reach the door just as the bell sounds again, bonging its chimes throughout the quiet stillness of the house. Aunty will have heard it for sure.

Oh well. I did try.

Mr. Terrell is standing outside stomping his feet for warmth, puffing cold vapory breaths and wearing his usual stoic expression. Just behind Mr. Terrell stands a bedraggled, hairy man. Movement draws my eye to a dirty little girl, dressed in rags, peeking out from behind the hairy man's legs. I usher them quickly inside and push the door closed against the wind.

"Good Morning, what can I do for you?" I say graciously like Aunty taught me.

It takes effort to be gracious because of the early hour and my insecurities in my holey bathrobe. I look to Mr. Terrell to give introductions. Trying to warm up, Mr. Terrell is vigorously rubbing his arms. It's freezing outside, and he is dressed in only a sweatshirt. The ragged man and child stand quietly looking at me. They seem more tolerant to the wintery morning chill, though neither of them have coats on either.

Mr. Terrell dismisses my greeting with borderline rudeness, "Where is Colleen? Go get her please, Ivy."

I force my face to remain pleasant. Mr. Terrell pushes all of my buttons. He is such a rude man! Smiling a fake smile, I turn and reluctantly head upstairs to see if Aunty is up yet.

After knocking on her door several times and getting no answer, I tiptoe into her room—my concern growing. It takes me a full minute of gently shaking her and saying her name to rouse her. That minute is a telling one for me. Something is wrong with Aunty. I can't deny it anymore. It's not just her age or over activity. I turn on the lamp next to her bed. Aunty's skin is sallow and her hair looks flat and thin. I notice there is a lot of hair on the pillows of her bed.

She's losing her hair?

Aunty looks so frail; and, when she finally opens her eyes, I feel like she doesn't even know me at first. She blinks a few times and her mouth hangs open as she takes a few moist shallow breaths.

Then, finally, she asks, "Is something wrong, Ivy?"

"I'm sorry to wake you Aunty, but Mr. Terrell is here with a man and a little girl. I don't recognize either of them. He told me to go get you. They are waiting in the parlor." I pause when she doesn't immediately say something, and I ask, "Would you like me to tell him you aren't feeling well?"

I know she'll swing her legs out of bed and argue with me that she's fine.

But then, she doesn't.

Aunty nods her head and closes her eyes again. I don't care about Marcus Terrell waiting downstairs anymore. I don't care who the people are who are with him. I am terrified for Aunty and for myself. Something is really wrong.

"Aunty," I shake her shoulder gently again.

She slowly opens her eyes again and whispers, "Yes, dear."

"Aunty, something is wrong isn't it? Should I go get the Doctor? Please tell me what's wrong. This isn't LS, it's something else isn't it?" My words squeak with fear and worry, and I feel tears on my cheeks.

"Take care of -" she heaves a long breath, "- the guests, dear." Her speech is slow and quiet. "When you have them settled, come back to me—and we'll talk." She closes her eyes; and, after a long pause, she adds, "Don't bother Hale. I'm fine for now."

Fine for now?

She's not fine. I've been watching it happen and hoping it was nothing and now my worst fears are realized and something is very wrong. I don't want to leave her side now; I just want to sit with her. But she asked me to go take care of the guests. I don't want her to open her eyes and worry that I'm not handling things here. So I slip out of her room and wipe the tears from my eyes. I try to mask my feelings in the quick minute it takes for me to rejoin the guests downstairs.

"I'm sorry;" I address the man and little girl, avoiding Marcus Terrell's stern eyes, "Aunty is not feeling well this morning. She needs rest, and she asked me to care for you," I say with a confidence that I don't genuinely feel.

Mr. Terrell scowls, his busy black eyebrows drawn together. He recovers and decides to settle for me, "This is Mr. Ialongo."

"Jack," the man says, offering me his hand to shake.

"Hi. I'm Ivy. I think we've met before actually."

He's one of the missionaries, and I have seen him several times over the years. I barely recognized him. He's lost a lot of weight—he's all skin and bones—and his beard and long hair hide most of his face. Even his eyebrows seem to have joined the rebellion, sprouting off in crazy directions. If I'm remembering him right, when I last saw him he was a clean shaven, clean cut kind of guy. This half-starved Mountain Man before me bears no resemblance to the young man he used to be.

"This is Rosa," the Mountain Man Jack says gently, squatting down to eye level with the tiny girl and pushing jet black straggly bangs out of her eyes.

"Hi Rosa," I say in a sweet little kid voice.

Carmel skinned Rosa buries her head in her tattered shirt sleeve and doesn't respond. She's wearing a mismatched collection of stained rags; the jury is out on whether they were ever clothes to begin with. Even if they were clothing at one point, they were never her size.

"She's had it rough," Jack says in her defense. No other explanation is forthcoming and we all stand there staring at her for a few awkward moments.

"Do you have a room ready for them?" Mr. Terrell asks somewhat impatiently, reminding me of my job and making me feel like I'm not a very good hostess.

This man really gets on my nerves.

"Yes of course. We have a nice room with two twin beds, will that work?"

"A bed of any kind sounds amazing," says the Mountain Man.

"Follow me, the rooms are upstairs."

"I'll leave you in Ivy's capable care," says Mr. Terrell, dismissing himself.

That was almost a vote of confidence.

"We'll see you tomorrow morning," Mr. Terrell says as he goes out the front door mumbling something about misplacing a perfectly good coat.

I take the Mountain Man Jack and Rosa, his shy little shadow, upstairs to guest room number four. It's one of our prettiest rooms. The walls are dark blue with blue and white stripped wallpaper running around the top near the ceiling. A beautiful fireplace fills one wall, and I hurry over to light the logs that have been waiting for the next guest. The kindling catches with one match and Rosa's dark brown eyes light up with the orangey glow.

I light the kerosene lamps on the antique dresser and bedside table, and the room fills with light and warmth. Now that I know how bad everything is out there, beyond the gates, I realize even more that our Inn is a beautiful haven to all who stay within her walls. Days gone by come alive in the old fixtures and plush Victorian carpets. Gazing at the gilded picture frames of the past, you can forget for a moment that the world is almost over.

"Look, Rosa," I say as I show them their bathroom with its deep porcelain claw-foot bathtub, "You can go for a swim in there!"

She peers around Jack's legs and takes the tub in with a quick glance.

"This is just wonderful," Jack says appreciatively gesturing towards the room and its two separate beds. "I'm not her father, I rescued her," Jack says awkwardly. "I wouldn't feel right giving her a bath. I hate to be a bother—I'm sure you're very busy—but if you had time to help me bathe her—that would be more appropriate. Maybe you know where I could find her some clothes too?"

"Of course. I would love to," Aunty would be pleased with my gracious white lies. I've never bathed a little kid, and I don't think this wild, terrified little girl will be easy to clean off. "How long have you had her?" I ask.

"About two weeks. Two very stressful, cold, challenging weeks. I took her from a butcher outside of Atlanta." He says with a piercing stare, as though willing me to understand what he's implying so that he doesn't have to say it out loud in front of Rosa.

My legs go weak and I stumble a step backwards, both from shock and the sudden anger clouding the Mountain Man's dark eyes. The missionary Ben just told us about this. This sweet little innocent was to be butchered and eaten. My eyes swim with tears, and I give a small nod to show him I understand. He nods back curtly.

Now his voice carries the anger I saw in his eyes, "She's an innocent, not a convert. Still too young to have the disease but not old enough to understand Life. We don't normally take children, but—I couldn't leave her there! Not when I could save her."

Jack looks out the window; the light of dawn is finally showing in the distance. When he turns back to face me, his voice turns genteel and mannerly again, "So, we've been camping out and making our way from Atlanta, trying to avoid any contact with them. I've asked Marcus to find a good home for her, so I'm sure she won't be staying here for more than a day or two. I'd appreciate any help you can give me. I'm not very good at little girls."

"I'll help in any way I can. Just let me know what you need. For now, I'll let you rest and get settled. I'll go make us all some breakfast. After breakfast maybe we can see if Rosa would like to try out that big tub," I say with a smile at the girl.

"Thank you," Mountain Man Jack says collapsing onto one of the beds, his filthy clothes leaving indelible marks on the pretty white antique bedspread. I sigh to myself and pull the door shut.

I hurry down the hall to Aunty after leaving Jack and Rosa. Aunty is still sleeping and doesn't stir when I come in her room. It's almost 7:30 a.m. now, and she is normally up by 6:00 every day. Her breathing sounds strange and thin to me. I don't know what to listen for, but everything about the way she looks and the way she is sleeping looks to me like someone on their deathbed. I sit next to her and cry quietly, she still doesn't wake.

I pet her face and hair and pray for her. I beg The Lord to heal her. I know He can. I believe with all my heart that He can. He has healed all of us from LS; His healing power is still at work more than ever in these last days. Healing is a miracle that the old church saw only on occasion. But we, His last church, see it every day when we look in the mirror. It is almost a commonplace thing to us. God heals. End of story. I am going to believe in that healing for Aunty. I'm not going to panic, not going to accept "no" for an answer.

"Lord, please do your thing," I ask with my hands laid on her. "Restore her please? I need her."

I'm crying; begging Him.

"I have lost so much, please don't take her away. I'll be all alone."

I lay my hand against her face; she doesn't feel warm or fevered. I don't think this is a bug or a virus. She looks like a shell of herself; old and weak and small under her covers. She is still sleeping, and I know I have to go cook breakfast. I have to keep things going around here. Pretty soon she'll be better.

God will hear me; I'm certain.

I brush the tears from my eyes and try to think positively. I don't want to have to explain to her later why none of the guests are fed and the house is falling apart. I smile at the thought of another lecture from her. I would die if I never heard another Aunty speech.

I am believing Him to heal her. We've seen lots of prayers for healing answered over the last few years. God is doing great things all the time. About a year ago a little girl fell from a second story window. She broke her back in the fall and would have died. Rev. Depold prayed over her, and she was completely healed right then and there. God hears our prayers here. Aunty will get better. I should see if the Elders can come pray over her today.

First breakfast. Then I'll send for the elders.

Chapter Thirty-Five
Jail Break

I cook a huge breakfast. French toast made from homemade potato bread, baked apples, and scrambled duck eggs. I set the table for Ben too, hoping he'll join us for meals today. I'd like him to come down and carry the conversation with his fellow missionary. I don't want to eat alone with the Mountain Man and the mute girl.

I knock on both doors, Ben's and Jack's, and call out "Breakfast is ready."

Within minutes they are both downstairs. The minute they see each other they embrace in a long hug with a lot of back slapping. Both look happy to see the other, but their eyes both wear the same heavy sadness. I know it's the other missionaries they are thinking of. Only two out of thirty have made it home. Will more come today?

I hope so.

Ben and Jack visit and eat and eat and eat. I'm worried that the huge breakfast I made might not be enough. When the serving plates are almost empty, I offer to cook more, but they both turn me down, insisting it was the perfect amount and they couldn't hold another bite.

Little Rosa sits up on her knees in her chair and eats with her hands. She is like a little wild animal. I would guess her to be maybe three years old. She doesn't speak at all, but I watch her closely. When her eyes fall hungrily on one of the serving dishes, I stand and serve her some. I smile at her a lot and cut her food into small bites to make it easier for her. She is making a huge mess. But the sight of her eating is so tragic that I hardly think about the stained tablecloth or the food all over the chair and floor. I feel blessed to have what we have, and I'm happy to be feeding this pretty little wild thing.

I think she is either Indian or Hispanic. I wonder if Rosa is her real name or if Jack named her that? Under her long black eyelashes, dark intelligent eyes dart around the room taking everything in. When she is finally full and bored of the table and the food, she hops down and starts wandering around the big dining room, exploring.

I leave the men to talk and decide to give Rosa a bath now, while Jack is out of the room. I can clean up breakfast later. Aunty wouldn't let the mess sit out like that, but I'm in charge today. I think it might be best to clean up this sweet little mess first. I hold out my hand to her, and she looks hesitantly at me. Then, with a tiny shy smile, she scampers over to me.

When her little hand finds mine, something happens in my heart. I've never felt anything like it. It's like a bomb has gone off in me. I suddenly feel certain that I'm meant to love this little girl. Her smile fills my heart as she peers up at me from underneath those beautiful fluttering lashes.

I have never really cared much for other people's children. I've never wanted to have a child of my own. Why long for something that is most likely impossible? But this little girl is meant for me. I stand stalled at the foot of the steps just smiling at her. Does she feel it too? This strange connection? With no indication that she has shared in my epiphany, Rosa pulls me up the stairs. She happily bobs her head back and forth, her messy black curls swaying.

Partway up the stairs, I hear Aunty talking downstairs. I pick Rosa up and hurry back down. Aunty is in her old bathrobe, her hair a disheveled mess, talking to the missionaries in the dining room. I'm a little embarrassed of her appearance, and not used to her being so—old. I hurry over to her and ask her to come help me with something in the kitchen. She shuffles slowly behind me to the kitchen and sits down gingerly at the kitchen table.

"I thought you were going to come get me," she says slightly annoyed.

"I did come, Aunty. I couldn't wake you." I pause, unsure of what to say next.

Questions like, "What's wrong with you?" and "Why is this happening?" are popcorning in my head. Aunty doesn't offer any explanation.

"I figured you needed the rest. Are you feeling better?" I ask hopeful. Maybe God has already healed her!

"I'm sorry Ivy. I—I had hoped never to have this talk with you."

I slump down into a chair across from her, absentmindedly handing Rosa a pencil and paper to color on.

"Whatever it is Aunty, it's going to be okay. I prayed over you, and I'm believing in faith that God will heal you. Do you feel any better yet?"

She smiles softly at me and clears her throat. "Ivy, I have cancer. I've had it for quite some time now. I'm so sorry dear, but I'm dying."

She's apologizing to me for being sick?

This is why God will heal her. She is such an amazing, godly woman. The world needs her. I desperately need her.

"How do you know?" I ask, my eyes filling with tears despite my pronouncement of faith for her healing.

Hearing the word "cancer" plants a seed of doubt in my recently replanted garden of faith. Last week it would've put me over the edge. My garden was a desert last week.

"Hale diagnosed me several months ago. It is most certainly cancer. I have a large lump in my breast, and we are fairly certain it has spread to my bones and organs. I have very little time left."

"You can't know that for sure!" I insist.

Rosa is squirming, so I stand up and dig out a few crayons from a drawer. I show Rosa how the crayons color on the paper and her eyes light up.

"I know, Ivy. I've known for a while, and I have peace. I've already been anointed and prayed over by the Elders. Twice actually. The Lord has given His answer. I'm not to be healed of this."

They've already tried and it didn't work?

Maybe my prayer will be different. I cling to that hope. "He will heal you still Aunty. I'm positive. Maybe He wants to heal you from my prayer? Wants us to see how great He is and that He is still there. Still listening."

I must believe. If I listen to Aunty and let doubt into my heart then my prayer won't work. I refuse to hear it. I won't be sad.

I am believing!

Aunty smiles knowingly at me, as though she knows what I'm thinking, and says, "Just promise me you won't walk away, Ivy. No matter what His answer. I need you to promise me that you'll always trust Him."

She is suddenly too choked up to continue and tears spill over and run down the deep wrinkle lines that have recently changed her face. I set Rosa in the chair and hurry over to Aunty. I grasp Aunty's thin, frail hands. They feel too cold.

"Of course I'll never walk away Aunty! But you don't have to worry. You'll be here to lecture me right into the Pearly Gates, okay? Let's just get you back in bed. You just need some more rest. Should I get Dr. Markowitz? Isn't there anything he can do to make you feel better?"

"No," she sniffles, "but I guess I will lie back down. I'm hurting a lot lately."

"Let me get you something for the pain, some Tylenol?"

"No, Thomas needs it. I'm fine. It isn't that bad," she lies bravely, with a forced smile.

"Are you hungry? Can I feed you?"

"No dear, I'm afraid I haven't been hungry in quite a while. It's what the body does when it's sick. I should feel starved, but I just feel—tired."

Rosa comes over to stand next to us, and Aunty seems to notice her for the first time.

"Who is this child?" Aunty asks. "Do we know her?" she asks pitifully.

It almost seems as though Aunty's afraid that she's starting to forget things; afraid that her memory is failing her along with her declining health.

"Her name is Rosa." I say smiling at little Rosa as she does playful little hops across the square tiles of the old kitchen floor. Rosa looks up when she hears her name and smiles back at me. "I want to ask the Elders if we can keep her," I tell Aunty quietly.

Aunty frowns. I hope she'll feel better about it when she regains her strength. Even if God doesn't take the cancer away, he could give us more time together. Just one more year, that's all we need. She has lived with the cancer this long, why not just a little longer?

Please God?

"Let me walk you back to your room," I lead Aunty out of the kitchen through the door to the back hallway, avoiding Ben and Jack. "I'm going to make you some soup, and you are going to eat lunch in a little while and feel better."

*****

After tucking Aunty back in—and making a mental note to change her sheets and freshen up her room next time she's up—I head towards the tub with Rosa. Jack and Ben are still talking at the table. It seems that Jack has not conjured up any paternal instinct at all, because I've had Rosa for at least half an hour now and he doesn't seem to have noticed. I run Rosa a bubbly bath in the big tub and help her strip off her clothes. I fall back on my heels, robbed of breath, at what I find underneath her dirty garments.

Scars.

More than I can count.

Some of them are old, but some of them are still healing. I can't tell what made the offending marks, but they are all over her tiny body. I ache at the thought of what her short life has been like. What she has gone through. The fact that she took my hand, that she can smile at all, is a miracle. Rosa sinks into the bubbles of the tub and they mercifully hide her scars from my teary eyes.

I find in myself a desperate desire to make her feel loved and safe. I pet her long hair and sing to her and teach her how to splash around in the tub. She's hesitant at first, but then she takes to the water joyfully; swimming and kicking and splashing me back. She's having fun. I can't help but wonder if it might be the first time she's ever had fun. I wonder if she's ever had a warm bath before.

"Do you like the water?" I ask her.

She smiles at me.

"Can you tell me how old you are?" I ask. "How old are you?" I hold up three fingers, then four, then five.

She just smiles at me. I wonder if she even understands English.

After half an hour of splashing in the tub, I get her out and wrap her in a big towel. I sit on the bed in her room and rock her in my arms, singing a mix of little kid songs I learned as a child and some of my favorite hymns from church. She falls asleep wrapped in the towel in my arms. I don't want to put her down, but I need to find her some clothes and I still need to clean up from breakfast. So I gently lay her in the bed and cover her up.

*****

I feel exhausted as I head back downstairs. I've already done so much today and going up and down these stairs so many times isn't helping. I'm overwhelmed and trying to hold on to my faith. Afraid that if I allow a moment's doubt, He might not answer my most desperate prayer. I can't do this by myself. Who would run the Inn? Could I realistically care for little

Rosa without Aunty? And why is this happening now, when everything else in life is already so hard?

Pravda wants me for some unknown reason. I found something in Matt I never knew I wanted, only to have him taken away from me—twice. If Aunty leaves me, I'll be alone. They won't let me keep Rosa, I won't be able to run the Inn, they'll put me with some family in town—and no one in town even likes me right now. I keep thinking of that girl who killed herself. I don't want to be her, and I'm sacred that my life is barreling in that direction. My legs feel weak underneath me, and I consider crumpling down on the stairs and crying.

I sit down on the bottom step and lift my hands up to The Lord.

He says to praise Him in the dark times, and He'll be the Light.

I spend a precious minute telling him everything He already knows—and I do end up crying. But it's not a "poor me" cry of desperation, just an overflow of too many emotions being held in check too long. I ask for a lot. Aunty's restoration, Matt's safety and a chance to see him again, Rosa's short but important future, and strength. I ask for lots and lots of strength. When I stand back up, I feel Him there and I know He has a plan. A plan that I want. My own plans are shortsighted. His will get me where I need to go.

Jack and Ben are still at the table, so I decide to conquer the problem of clothing Rosa before the breakfast clean up. I can't help but smirk; Aunty would be appalled at how long I've let that mess sit there. Being my own boss isn't the worst thing ever. I pull on my coat; and, without even thinking, I hurry out the door to the U.R.

*****

It's not until I'm across the street, standing in front of the U.R. building, that I suddenly remember my house-arrest.

Whoops.

Well, I'm here now. I'll be quick and hopefully no one will care.

Please God don't let me run into Andrew or Mr. Terrell. Or Tim.

I walk quickly down the stairs to the room with the clothing bank. The ladies in charge of clothing keep it fairly well sorted, so it's only a minute before I've found the little girl clothes. I grab several warm things that look like they might fit Rosa. None of the coats seem warm enough, more like jackets. That's disappointing because what she was wearing was little more than a ragged shawl. A sign is hanging up on the wall that reads:

"Need more coats, especially Men's.

Please donate any you are not using.

Thanks, Jean Hosche Jan. 10th"

Some donations must've come in since then, because Aunty found that nice coat for Matt after this sign was written. Mr. Terrell had no coat this morning. I have this strange thought that Aunty may have stolen that coat from Mr. Terrell. And then reason kicks in, reminding me that Aunty would never steal.

Surely not?

Just imagining Aunty tiptoeing away from the Elders' coat closet that day makes me grin.

I find Rosa a cute winter hat with Mickey Mouse on it. I'm sure it will make her smile. I also take a pair of boots and a pair of shoes, hoping that at least one pair will fit for now. I remember to pick out some little panties and socks too. My bag is bulging with what I hope will be a new wardrobe and a new life for that baby girl. I don't sign the sheet with my name or what I took. I'd rather no one knew that I was out of the house against the Reverend's orders. These few little things won't be missed, and I'm only taking them for a little girl who desperately needs them.

Climbing the stairs and walking past the doors to the clinic, I change my mind. I need to talk to the doctor. Who cares if anyone knows that I left the house? What are they going to do to me? My life is already a living punishment. Maybe Aunty is being stubborn. Maybe she's intentionally not using something that could help her in an attempt to selflessly save it for someone else; like she did with the Tylenol for Thomas. I bet the Doctor can do something to give her more strength and more time. Tim's dad is one of Aunty's closest friends. It's only right that Dr. Markowitz knows what's going on.

Please don't let Tim be here? I ask The Lord in desperation. *At least do that for me?* I plead silently.

I take a deep breath and open the door to the small clinic. Tim is sitting at the front desk. I promised God that I wouldn't question Him anymore, but I yell *Why Lord?* in my head before I can control the impulse.

"Ivy! What are you doing here? Is something wrong? You aren't supposed to be out!"

"Yes, I know."

And really it's none of his business.

"But Aunty is—not well. I need to ask your dad how I can help her." I fight my emotions and keep my eyes dry. I do not want to look vulnerable and hug-needy.

Tim stares at me and then stands up to go get his dad. His pitying look and the way he hurried away makes my heart sink. Tim knows how sick Aunty is, and I found no hope in his eyes.

Chapter Thirty-Six

I Bear My Soul to Sasquatch

The wind is stinging my cheeks; and, again, I find relief in the pain. Alone on the sidewalk on this windy, God-forsaken day, my faith is wavering. Dr. Markowitz was kind but direct. The way he described Aunty's cancer and her present condition made it clear that he has given up hope for any medical turnaround.

"She's in the final stages," he said.

I didn't understand much of what he said about cells and malignancies and growth rate, but I understood that. Final stages means death's doorstep. He said her speedy sudden decline means that she probably doesn't have much longer. He told me what the end would probably look like. What to watch for.

I can hardly stand to think about it. I told him that I had prayed over her and that I am believing God for healing. He didn't say anything, but his emotionless face spoke volumes. He's a doctor and one of the Living. He believes in healing as much as the rest of us, maybe more. He made it very clear that he does not expect Aunty to get better. I wish he would've lied to me. He offered to have Tim walk me home. I emphatically insisted that wasn't necessary.

My legs feel like wood as I reach the steps in front of the Inn. My feet are suddenly too heavy to lift, too stubborn and unresponsive to carry me the last few steps to the door. My faith is slipping out in wet drops down the front of my cheeks. Maybe I should sit down on the front steps and give the cold wind a chance to do what it wants, to freeze me over, inside and out.

The branches of the tall shrubs next to the Inn's old front porch shake with more than the wind's power. I turn my head expecting to see a squirrel; but, instead, Matt steps out of the evergreen wall of pointy Holly leaves. I'm too numb inside to jump or be startled. I slowly meet his green eyes with my wet brown ones. As we appraise each other, I dig around in my heart to find some emotion that hasn't already been used up.

I thought he'd look worse from the way Aunty described his injuries of only a week ago. There aren't any stitches showing, and I realize that Aunty didn't say where he needed them. His wounds must be hidden by his clothes. Around one eye is a fading muddy-yellow bruise that spreads part way down the bridge of his nose. Other than that, he looks healthy and not at all like a zombie. He defies both faith and science with his lack of disease.

"What's eating you?" he asks pleasantly. I'm sure he expected me to be my jumpy self. He was probably looking forward to startling me.

"Hey," I reply.

He frowns, puzzled, and says, "Well, I thought you'd be happier to see me. After the letter," He lifts his eyebrows up and down at me, giving me his most handsome flirtatious look yet.

I shrug. I need to get back inside to Aunty and Rosa, and I don't have time for his sparkling eyes today.

"You reminded me what love looks like," he trills in a mocking, girl voice, reciting the words I wrote in my letter.

My love goggles have temporarily slipped off to one side, and I remember how irritating he can be.

"Aunty is dying," I say bluntly.

"I thought you people couldn't die," he returns jokingly.

"She has cancer."

He finally accepts my mood, and his quirky half smile fades. He nods knowingly. Like he had already figured out something was wrong with Aunty. Did everyone but me know? Was it that obvious? But I did know, didn't I. I knew something wasn't right. I just didn't want to believe it.

"I'm sorry," Matt says sincerely.

"Thanks. I'm still hoping God will heal her. I know He can."

Matt shrugs. "You know where I stand on that theory," is all he says.

"Yeah," I nod.

"I thought they had you cooped up. So you're allowed out of your house now?" he asks with an antagonistic smile. "I thought I was going to have to break in and steal you."

"I—no. I just had to get something."

I remember Rosa sleeping inside in nothing but a towel. I need to get back inside before she wakes up and doesn't know what to do. Neither Ben nor Jack will be comfortable caring for a little naked girl. I wonder if Jack even knows about all the scars on Rosa's body.

I need to hurry.

"I'm sorry, I have to go. I have a lot going on right now and I'm—really sad," I say, my eyes brimming with tears again.

"I'm sorry," Matt says in turn.

Then, he is suddenly holding me.

I go rigid with shock! So many feelings fight for precedence. The desire to be comforted. The thrill of being close to him. The reality that I'm being hugged in front of our house on the main street of town in broad daylight by a zombie.

That feeling wins.

I stand tense in his grasp; and, after a second or two of embrace, he releases me with a sad look on his face.

"I have to go back in." I say, looking around to see if anyone was out on the street to witness that.

"Sure," he says with disappointment in his voice. "How's Tom?" he asks.

"In pain," is all I can think to say. I'm a real Debbie Downer today.

"Can you give him this?" Matt pulls a lump of black shiny fabric out of his back pocket, and I realize it's a glove. One of their special gloves. "When he's healed enough, this will help him. It has all four fingers. I need you to tell him that I'm keeping an eye on him. It'd be nice if you didn't say that to anyone else. It just makes things harder for me."

I nod, "Okay."

He melts back into the bushes. I remember, momentarily, how much I had been missing him and I call out, "Will I see you again?"

"Course," he says, closer to me than I realized, just behind the closest bush.

A small smile plays at dry lips as I climb the front stairs and go back inside.

*****

Rosa isn't in the bed when I get up to her room. Panic is my first emotion, but I keep it in check and do a quick search of the room. No Rosa. I check the bathroom. I find her hiding under her towel in a little puddle of water down in the big tub. She is shivering, and I'm not sure if it's from fright or cold. She has her head down and is completely covered by the towel. I don't want to scare her.

"Rosa," I say sweetly, calling softly over the side of the tub. Her shivering lessens a little, so I say it again, "Rosa?"

She peaks at me from under the towel, and I smile at her. She smiles back. I hold up the Mickey Mouse hat, and she squints quizzically at it.

"Hat," I say, and I make a silly face and set it on top of my head. It doesn't fit, and it falls right off. She giggles.

I coax her out of the tub and dress her warmly. Some of the clothes are too big, but I've guessed close on most of them. The shoes fit perfectly, and the boots are only a little too big. She looks thrilled with all of it. She loves the hat and keeps looking at herself in the full length mirror behind the door.

I know nothing about her. Did she ever have a mother who loved her? Someone must have nursed her and brought her safely through those fragile newborn years. If she had only been intended for meat—the sick thought makes me almost throw up—she would've been killed at birth. Someone kept her safe. But those scars -

What was done to her? Was she kept safe only to be repeatedly hurt? What abuses has she suffered? I vow before God to keep her safe; to show her the special, wonderful things in this life. Beautiful flowers, chocolate cookies, Disney movies, fancy dresses. Just like Aunty did for me. And, most importantly, I will raise her to know Him. I lean over and kiss her cheek. She looks at me with wonder in her eyes.

"Kiss," I say with a smile.

She leans close to me and stares seriously into my eyes, like she's searching for something. Suddenly satisfied, she brushes her lips against my cheek and then sits back to weigh my reaction.

"Thank you," I say as I pull her close and hug her.

"You sure have a way with her," Jack's voice startles me. "She is more human with you. With me, she was like a little animal. She would hide in the corner of my tent and only dart out when I offered her food. She needs a mother. I'll be relieved to see her with some nice family."

"I want her," I blurt out. "I think God wants me to have her. I've never felt like this before. I love her already. Could you tell the Elders for me? I'm not allowed to leave the house."

In retrospect none of that sounded like the right way to convince him to let me keep Rosa. I've proclaimed myself a crazy shut-in who is desperate for someone to love.

"I mean, I can leave the house, just not lately because Pravda is hunting me."

This wasn't a recovery. It made things worse. I can tell by the tight furrow of his sasquatchian eyebrows. He thinks I'm a crazy, desperate shut-in with a death sentence.

"Why is Pravda hunting you?" he asks quietly.

I can't make things any worse than I already have, so I launch into the whole story. He nods and asks occasional questions. I'm getting pretty good at telling it. I was careful not to call them zombies this time.

"Did the man cut you anywhere?" he asks after thinking quietly for a few moments.

"How could you know that?"

I never even mention that part when I tell the story. It wasn't worth mentioning, just a scrape that happened in the struggle.

"They cut you?" He can tell by the look on my face that they did.

"It was just a scrape on my neck. It wasn't anything. It just happened in the struggle."

"It was everything. It was the whole point. Blood, Ivy. We live and die by blood these days. Blood purchases health. For us it's the blood of Christ. For them, it's the blood treatments. Pravda takes all the donated blood and cleans it. They sell the cleaner blood to whoever can afford it, and it slows the progress of the disease. But Pravda doesn't want to just hold the disease at bay; they are looking for a cure. For some reason, they think that your blood is special. That man was sent to obtain a sample of your blood. The question is what did they find? They may have found nothing. In which case, you are safe. They only want you if they have some reason to believe your blood will help them find a cure."

This is an extreme "good news, bad news" scenario. The good news would mean that I'm already safe. They have no use for me and are no longer interested. Long gone. I could be free again. The bad news means that they'll never stop hunting me—to the ends of the earth. And there's no way to know.

Jack lets me take Rosa downstairs. I want to keep her close. Even if they won't let me have her, I will love her forever. If someone else is chosen to adopt her, I could still be like a big sister to her. But I desperately hope they'll consider Aunty and me. If Aunty gets better.

I have to stop saying if.

WHEN. *When* Aunty gets better.

But what if she doesn't? I can't stop thinking about where I would go if I no longer had a home here. I'm sure the Elders wouldn't kick me out of the Inn, but I would never want to live here with someone else running it. All the memories of Aunty that I have here—my eyes threaten to leak for the tenth time today. I couldn't stay here.

*****

After finally cleaning up the breakfast dishes, I take Rosa to my room. My thoughts are tangled in a hazy quagmire. Every time I try to unravel the mess, it is Matt's face that emerges out of the fog. I wonder when I'll see him again. I dig through my closet for some of my old toys and put them on my bed with Rosa. She is instantly engrossed in them. I decide to finish devoting myself. Was it really just this morning that the doorbell interrupted my quiet time bringing a new wave of chaos into my already frayed life? Today has been full of a week's worth of energy and emotion, and it is only lunchtime.

The devotion book I'm reading is one of my favorites, written as though God is speaking directly to me. Today's date, January 20th, reads:

> *Approach this day with awareness of who is Boss. As you make plans for the day, remember that it is I who orchestrates the events of your life. On days when things go smoothly, according to your plans, you may be unaware of My sovereign Presence. On days when your plans are thwarted, be on the lookout for Me! I may be doing something important in your life, something quite different from what you*

expected. It is essential at such times to stay in communication with Me, accepting My way as better than yours. Don't try to figure out what is happening. Simply trust Me and thank Me in advance for the good that will come out of it all. I know the plans I have for you, and they are good.

Isaiah 55:9-11; Jeremiah 29:11

I told you, He does this all the time. It's as though this little book was written just for me, just for this day in my life. He might not be making things easy for me, but I know He loves me. He's promising me, always promising me, that it's going to be ok. I don't need to make plans for myself, He has already made them. I cry at the thought that He might still take Aunty. Like the book says, sometimes He doesn't work the way we want.

The verse at the end, Jeremiah 29:11, is every teenager's favorite verse. Looking forward to the future, wondering what you'll become, who you'll be, it's a promise you want to wrap your arms and legs around and refuse to let go of. Even when it feels like it couldn't be true: *'For I know the plans that I have for you, declares The Lord, plans to prosper you and not to harm you, to give you a future and a hope.'*

Chapter Thirty-Seven

Aunty Gets Her Way

I made homemade potato soup for lunch. Aunty's recipe. Soup wasn't the best choice for Rosa's second meal in civilization. She's going to need another swim in the tub at some point. After feeding everyone else and asking Jack to keep an eye on potato-faced Rosa, I'm in the kitchen cleaning up.

After getting the kitchen almost as nice as Aunty keeps it, I finally get a chance to bring a tray of food to Aunty's room. She is unresponsive. After several minutes of trying to rouse her, I dissolve into tears. I won't disobey twice today, so I ask Ben to go across the street for the doctor.

*****

I'm sitting on Aunty's bed when Dr. Markowitz arrives a few minutes later. His tall muscular frame fills her doorway, and worry is written in the age lines on his square face. An attractive man for his age, he's always been singularly focused on caring for the people of our town and uninterested in replacing his late wife.

"Not good," he says after checking her pulse and her heart with the stethoscope that is always around his neck. "It's happening faster than I thought it would."

"What does that mean?" I ask through small sobs.

"I'm sorry, Ivy," he says with genuine heartbreak on his face.

He and Aunty were good friends. This is hard for him too. Dr. Markowitz comes around to where I'm sitting on the side of Aunty's bed and gives me a half hug. "Colleen told me the details of what's going on and I promised her I would keep you safe. We'd like you to come stay with us."

We.

He means Tim. Of course Tim would like that.

Then, like fire from heaven, it hits me. Aunty has had her own solution planned for me. Her persistent efforts to make me interested in Tim—she *was* trying to set me up with him. And not just on a date. She was hoping to be around long enough to see me married to Tim. Safe with people she trusted. Aunty admires Dr. Markowitz, and she wanted to see me become part of his family. Aunty gets her wish after all, even if it's not my choice. The Elders will probably make me go there. I wouldn't be surprised if Aunty had it all in writing already. It will be just as bad as being married to Tim if I have to live there.

"Ivy?" Dr. Markowitz asks again, waiting for me to respond to his offer.

I don't answer my Aunt's friend. I just cry harder.

"It might be another week of this, it's hard to tell," Dr. Markowitz graciously changes the subject. "She might not last the night. I don't have the right equipment to make a real diagnosis. If I had it, maybe I could've done something earlier. I'm so sorry, Ivy."

She would want me to tell him it's not his fault. I force myself to say it; for her sake, "I know you did everything you could. Aunty always said, 'All you can do, is all you can do. And all you can do is enough.'"

He smiles a little and says, "That does sound like her."

I glance at Aunty, and she wears a peaceful smile in her sleep. I wonder if she can hear us. I'll talk to her when the Doctor leaves. I'd love to think she could hear me tell her what's on my heart. Before she goes.

It isn't looking like God will answer my prayers the way I wanted. The Living always say 'If God doesn't heal here on earth, He gives perfect healing in Heaven.' I know it's awesome of Him to do that, to have a place for us with Him when we leave here; a place with no more tears and no more pain and no more death. But it's really only nice for the person who gets to go. The ones left behind still hurt. I know it's better than the alternative. I know for sure I'll follow shortly behind her, and we'll be together again. But, right now, I'm heartbroken.

"Catheter or bedpan?" Dr. Markowitz asks.

"Oh. Uh. How does the catheter work?"

After a short explanation on how to change a catheter bag, I choose that over the bed pan. Aunty will be horrified. If she wakes up again. I leave the room while he puts in the catheter. I couldn't stand the indignity of watching. Aunty was always so dignified, such a lady. Watching her decline is as hard as the thought of losing her.

Dr. Markowitz calls me back into her room and says, "I'm going to send

Tim over to sit with you. There's little I can do right now, and there are others who need me today. Tim can do most everything I could in this situation."

I want to argue, but I know he's probably right. I don't want to be alone if she starts struggling for breath. And I don't want her to be alone, but I'll have to leave occasionally to care for our guests. I guess normal people would call in someone to help with the Inn. But I don't want anyone else in our home. It's Aunty's kitchen.

*****

Tim arrives only a few minutes after his dad left. I didn't hear the bell ring, and I assume one of the missionaries must have let him in. He found his way to Aunty's room where I've been sitting alone with her, trying to talk to her and not sure what to say. He has a small bag with him. I guess they had planned for this. He was packed and ready to come.

Tim looks with concern into my depressed face and asks in a whisper, "Do you have a room for me to sleep in?"

I didn't realize he'd be living here around the clock until it happened.

"Yeah," I answer and lead him out of Aunty's room.

I walk him down the hall to room number 5. It's a smaller room, down the back hallway that attaches to the back staircase. It's directly above my room downstairs. I show him the back staircase that we don't normally give guests access to.

Aunty's room needs a little rearranging if we are going to be sitting in there around the clock. I have no idea how long this vigil might last. I haul two chairs in and open the shades on the windows. It's already very clean in here, of course. But, despite how immaculate Aunty keeps her private space, there is still an unmistakable sick smell. It's too cold to open a window for fresh air, so I bring in a few candles and light them. It helps with the smells, but gives the room even more of a funeral home feeling.

I hear Tim coming down the hall so I straighten Aunty's blankets and make sure she's well covered. I want to preserve her modesty as much as possible. She would be horrified at all of this. The catheter, the smelliness, men in her bedroom, people staring at her while she looks so—old. She was always completely together. It's painful to see her so completely not together. I love her so much. I flop down in a chair and Tim finds me crying when he comes in the room.

"I wish you didn't have to go through this, Ivy"

I nod appreciatively and blow my nose.

"I'm lucky to have my dad and my brother. Not many people have that much family anymore."

Is he trying to make me feel better? I wish he'd go away. I don't need his help right now.

"What were your parents like?" he asks, oblivious to my desire to be alone.

Without thinking, I talk. I tell him about where I grew up and what mom and dad were like. About our little house and our big yard. I tell him about Hazel. I haven't ever told anyone this much about myself. Not even Harmony. Only Aunty knew all of this. When I finally run out of stories and grow quiet, Tim takes a turn.

He tells me about his childhood. I had never heard about his mom who died in a car accident with his little sister. He's had hard, sad things to overcome, too. It's a comfort to me. Not that I'm happy about his misfortunes, just—it puts things in perspective to remember that everyone has to go through stuff.

*****

Hours pass. Jack has run out of patience with Rosa and she sits on the floor near Tim and I while we talk. I find her a coloring book and a few more crayons which delights her. Tim says Ben and Jack have been invited to Mr. Terrell's for dinner. I'm relieved to not have to cook for all the people in our house. I bring some apples and bread and butter to Aunty's room for Tim and Rosa to eat. I'm not hungry.

Tim asks me about what happened in Commerce and I continue with my transparent babble and tell him the whole story. Even the part about being terrified of Matt when he showed up at our back door. Then, for some reason, I tell him the rest of the Matt story. How much Matt loves his Thomas, how surprised I was at Matt's humor and normal-ness. Tim doesn't respond or ask questions, he just lets me talk.

*****

Sometime after dark, Rosa climbs up in my lap and falls asleep while I stroke her hair. She never did get that bath and she's still wearing the potato soup. Tim and I are quiet now. He seems tired.

"You can rest," I say. "I will probably stay in here tonight."

I'm kind of hoping he'll leave so I can have the chair he's sitting in. Mine is super uncomfortable.

Tim checks Aunty's pulse and listens to her breathing. He doesn't say so, but I think she's gotten weaker.

"I'll stay awhile longer," he says, taking his glasses off and leaning his head back in the comfortable chair.

With his eyes closed, I can't help but study him. I have mostly avoided his gaze all day. He always looks at me with such ga-ga eyes. I know he likes me a lot. Maybe loves me. As annoying as his obvious attraction is, Tim makes me feel like he likes me for who I am. Which is surprising, considering I've never been at my nicest when he's around. What is there for Tim to like about Ivy Lusato?

With his thick nerd glasses off, he looks better actually. I never see him without his glasses, and they do nothing positive for his appearance. With his eyes closed, and his face relaxed, I decide he's decent looking. Really it's his personality that ruins it for me; so, irritatingly grown-up all the time. In the dim light, his short blondish brown hair looks darker. It comes to a point on his forehead that accentuates his nerdy demeanor.

Tim has filled out lately—he's less gangly—and I can see facial hair starting to grow on the square chin he inherited from his father. He is wearing those faded green clothes that nurses wear. He's been wearing them all the time lately; ever since his dad "promoted" him to his new status at the clinic. I think it's a little much. I guess he's proud of his new job, but it wouldn't hurt to dress normal once in a while.

He opens his eyes and sees me staring at him. I blush and look down. We've never spent this much time together before. It's very intimate. Even with Aunty there. And if she were to wake, she'd probably be thrilled to see us sitting here together.

"Do you need anything?" Tim asks in a sleepy, husky voice.

"Could you help me make Rosa a bed on the floor?" I surprise myself by asking for his help. Rosa is asleep in my arms and my arms are falling asleep too.

"Sure." He stands up and comes around to my side of the bed, squinting a little without his glasses.

I direct him to the linen closet with extra blankets and pillows, and he builds a nest on the floor for Rosa.

Standing up slowly, I gently set Rosa in the soft blankets and tuck the warm covers around her. Tim is squatting right next to me, helping. I feel his closeness in a nervous way.

"You are so sweet with her, Ivy," he whispers with peppermint breath. "I never pictured you being a kid person, but you're a natural mom."

His kind compliment reminds me how much I am hoping that the Elders will let me keep her. Maybe Tim could put in a good word for me; all the grownups in town respect him. If I was willing to live with the Markowitzs, maybe they'd let me keep Rosa. It might not be *that* awful.

"You look nice without your glasses," I blurt in a whisper.

What is wrong with me?

I don't want him thinking I have any interest in him whatsoever. I stand up quickly and avoid looking at him as I back towards the door. "I better go make sure everyone is in for the night, turn off lights, lock up -" I stammer.

I tuck my head and hurry from the room. I need a break from the smells and the heavy thoughts in Aunty's room. I walk downstairs and jump at the sight of a strange man sitting at the window seat in the foyer. After a double-take, I realize it's Jack, all shaved and cleaned up. I won't miss the Mountain Man.

"I didn't mean to startle you. I'm very sorry about your Aunt," he says.

Tim must have told them she's—she's—dying.

"Let me know if I can do anything for you," he offers.

"Thank you."

"Where is Rosa?"

"Oh, I made her a bed with me tonight. Is that alright?"

"Yes," he says with a smile. "I hereby pass the torch to you. You are in charge of her for the time being. I hope she's a comfort and not more stress."

"Thanks. She is."

"Ben and I are going to sit downstairs for awhile and plan what we'll say tomorrow."

Tomorrow is homecoming. Still only Ben and Jack. It won't be a celebration at all. It has turned into a time of prayer and mourning. I won't be there.

"There is one thing you could do for me," I say. "I'll set out all the food that Aunty and I made for the dinner at the U.R. Could you and Ben take it over when you go in the morning? I won't be going."

"Of course. And we'll make sure the lights are off before we go to bed tonight."

"Thanks. I'll set out something for you to eat for breakfast too."

"That isn't necessary."

I nod and walk back up to Aunty's room.

Chapter Thirty-Eight

Free At Last

Sometime during the night, something wakes me. The candles are still burning; and, by the soft light, I see that Aunty's eyes are open. She's awake.

I climb quickly onto the bed by her side. She glances over at Tim asleep in the chair beside her bed and looks back at me with a small smile.

"Are you okay?" I whisper quietly, full of concern. "I'm so glad to see you awake! Are you hurting? Can I get you anything?"

"Water," she whispers.

I hurry to the bathroom for a glass and fill it with cold water. Back at her side, I tip it slowly for her, helping her drink. Some of it dribbles down the sides of her mouth, and I wipe her chin with the blankets.

"Ivy," she rasps and I worry that she'll wake Tim.

I'm not worried for his sake, but for my own. I want her to myself. There's so much I want, no I *need*, to say and I don't know if this might be my last chance.

"Aunty, I love you," I breathe. My eyes are swimming with tears and one slips out and falls down my cheek, landing on her neck.

I had so much to say, but I can't find words for any of it. I feel the clock ticking, I know I'm running out of time, and it makes it even harder to think.

Of all the things I've wanted to tell her, "Thank you," is all I can come up with. It's okay because "thank you" sums up all the little things I would've said. All the millions of things she's done for me and given me.

I brush the tears from my eyes and see her nod her response to my gratitude. Her eyes are full of tears too.

Her face gets serious, and she entreats me again, "Don't fall away, Ivy"

"I swear I won't," I promise again. She looks worried for me, and I wish I could think of something to say that would ease her mind. She lays here in pain, dying, and her most precious thoughts are for me. I need her to know that she's raised me well. That I could never leave this Life she's led me in. I think of something, and though I'm not sure I can carry through with it, not sure my emotions will let me, I sing softly:

> *"Sing the wondrous love of Jesus,*
> *Sing His mercy and His grace;*
> *In the mansions bright and blessed*
> *He'll prepare for us a place."*

Aunty closes her eyes, but I can tell she's listening. Through my tears, and very off key, I sing the chorus of the old hymn:

> *"When we all get to heaven,*
> *What a day of rejoicing that will be!*
> *When we all see Jesus,*
> *We'll sing and shout the victory!"*

The old hymn is supposed to be joyful and victorious, but my heart is breaking and I can't stop weeping. I hope she understands now that I will be there with her. I can't keep singing, my sorrow is so deep.

She opens her eyes again and smiles, understanding my song and my message to her. I'm not going to miss out on being there in Heaven with her. I am sure in my faith. I belong to Him, even if He's taking her. It hurts so badly, but I won't allow myself any anger at Him. I can't afford even the smallest resentment. I almost walked away last week and He brought me back. I know how dear that is.

Losing her is the hardest thing I can imagine. To live without my rock, my security, my best friend is terrifying. I don't know how to take care of myself. She always did that. I lay my head on her chest gently and hold her. I hear how labored her heart is, and I count the beats. I want to will the cadence to keep going, to get stronger. But the gentle beats get fainter, and I'm lying against her chest when they stop.

I let out a gasping sob, and I feel Tim's hand on my back. In a beautiful baritone voice he softly sings the last verse of the song over us while gently stroking my back as I weep.

> *"Onward to the prize before us*
> *Soon His beauty we'll behold;*
> *Soon the pearly gates will open;*
> *We shall tread the streets of gold."*

She's gone. My life might as well be over. I want to go with her. My heart is chanting, "Don't leave me here." I lie against her and cry for a long time, oblivious to anything else.

Chapter Thirty-Nine

I Like Muscles As Much As the Next Girl

I'm still lying next to her in the morning. I cried myself to sleep beside her. Tim is gone and Rosa is tapping on my arm to wake me. I don't want Rosa to be scared, so I pick her up and hurry from the room without looking back myself. I don't want to look at Aunty—can't bear to see her robbed of her beauty and vigor. Robbed of life. She's gone. What is left is the body that served me and cared for me and loved me. And I don't know what to do about it. I'm suddenly in charge of it. Her body. I need help. I feel so lost.

I walk down the hallway with Rosa in my arms and knock on the door to the back hallway—the door that leads to the back staircase and Tim's guest room and bathroom. I don't hear anything, and no one answers my knock. Maybe he went to the homecoming service. His job is over now. I thought he would stay—be there for me. I opened up to him and bared my soul. I'm already consumed with grief, but the hurt is even stronger when I realize that Tim is gone. I feel abandoned by everyone.

I open the door and start down the hall towards his room to make sure. Suddenly Tim is stepping out of the bathroom wrapped in just a towel. Even in my distress, I can't help but notice how muscular he is. I've never seen a boy my age in just a towel, and the distraction makes me feel guilty. Tim's hair is sticking up in wet spikes on his head, and he isn't wearing his glasses.

I feel confused and suddenly angry. Mad at Tim for standing here looking like this in a towel. I don't know why I'm mad at him because it's his room, but still, it's not decent. I'm so embarrassed to have walked in on him. I duck my head down into Rosa's hair and hurry back up the hallway.

"Sorry," I say over my shoulder, trying not to look at him. "I thought you left. I knocked."

"I'm sorry that you thought I would leave you," he apologizes gently.

His apology is more sincere. His quiet tone exudes the tenderness behind his words. I don't know what I think of him or his endearment, but I am relieved to not be alone.

I hear a door shut, and I glance behind me to see that Tim has disappeared into his room. I don't know where to go. I feel worried that he's gone as much as I feel relieved. Is this what grief feels like for everyone? I feel like I'm losing my mind.

I step through the narrow door into the back stairwell and pull the door closed behind me. Holding Rosa close to me, I sink down on the top stair. I can't help but cry, my grief is still new and raw. Rosa looks closely at me and tries to wipe each tear as it falls. She has seen many tears in her little life, and it has made her compassionate. She leans over and kisses my cheek and looks at me expectantly.

"Kiss," I say softly.

She smiles and kisses my other cheek. I find a small smile for her and her intense loving gaze. She is my reason to keep going. I promise myself again that I'll be there for her and give her what Aunty gave me.

I hear Tim leave his room and, still sitting on the top step, I gently knock on the hallway door again. He opens the door and looks down at me as I sit there pitifully. I'm not embarrassed that he's seeing me be vulnerable. He has earned a trust that I hadn't intended to give.

He sits down next to me on the stairs; and, after a moment of silence, he says, "I have to go tell my Dad. Would you like to come?"

"No," I snuffle. "I don't want to see anyone else."

"I thought maybe I'd bring Rosa to the U.R. It's Sunday morning, and I thought she could play with the other kids in Mr. Jarvis' class. You could probably use the time to yourself," he offers.

"I guess that would be okay. Do you think she'll go with you? She might be scared."

"Would you mind if I hug you?"

"What?"

"She trusts you. Maybe if she saw that you trust me it would be easier for her."

"Oh." I guess the logic is sound.

"You just lost your aunt; your best friend. I think you could probably use a hug right now of all times."

I nod and we both stand up. It feels weird and staged. I'm still holding Rosa and Tim wraps the two of us in his arms. I know the hug is for Rosa's sake, so I try to feel relaxed. It isn't too hard. He smells clean like soap. He is wearing a sweatshirt and jeans instead of the scrubs and his shirt is soft. The comfort of Tim's closeness brings more tears.

I let him hold me while I cry. He puts his face against my head and sort of rocks us. If I had any sarcasm left in me right now, I'd make a comment about how this was devious of him, or how he was enjoying my pain. But I know it's not true. I know this hug is for my sake and not his. I can tell he really cares, and I feel like he's hurting with me. Aunty was right. He is a great guy. Not that I want to marry him, but I can see why she wanted me to.

I pull away after a minute long hug. That's plenty long enough. Tim reaches over and takes Rosa from my arms like it's nothing at all—intentionally not making a big deal of it.

"Let's get her some breakfast before you go" I say as we head back down the stairs.

After Tim and Rosa leave, Rosa proudly wearing her Mickey Mouse hat, I am once again completely alone at the Inn. I take a long shower and get dressed. I sit down to read my Bible, desperately hoping God will send me special words of comfort this morning. I flip through the pages, unsure where to read, and I hear a tap on my window.

Another tap.

Another tap.

I look out between the closed blinds, and a rock hits the window right in front of my face. It startles me and I jump back from the window in momentary confusion. I open the slats of my dark green plastic blinds so I can see better. I see Matt sitting on the ground behind a bush right beneath my window. He waves. I slip my shoes on and go around to the back door.

"Matt?" I call in a whisper.

"Hey!" He pops up from the bush. "Nice of you to finally notice. I've been stoning your window all morning. I figure with everyone at 'church'"—he makes air quotes again—"and you stuck in the house, now would be a good time to go for a walk."

"I can't."

"Why not? Your aunt isn't going to beat you. She'll never know."

I look away and my eyes swim with tears. I take deep breaths to keep from crying. He looks at me in confusion.

"She died last night."

"Oh. I'm sorry, Ivy."

"Yeah, thanks."

After a long, long awkward pause—neither of us knowing what to say—Matt says with forced cheerfulness, "Come on. Go for a walk with me. I'll show you my secret way in. I know you're dying to know how I get in."

I am dying to know that.

And I realize there's no one to answer to. I am in charge of my own life now. Surely the Elders wouldn't begrudge me the fresh air today. I need to get out of this house. Being here alone with Aunty's body upstairs was freaking me out.

"Let me get my coat."

"Don't forget that goofy hat, it's cold out," he calls after me.

Chapter Forty

The Exact Opposite of Wisdom

I can't help but glance all around as we walk down the street. I'm not supposed to be out of the house, and I'm walking with a zombie. If anyone saw us, I'd be in a lot of trouble. What can they really do to me though? I'm on my own now. I can make my own choices. I guess they could ask me to leave the community, but I doubt they would.

Besides, I'm already strongly considering that. If it weren't for Rosa, I might have left already. Without Aunty, what do I have here? I feel like I'm supposed to do something more with my life. I can't stand to sit here and wait for Pravda to come for me. The particulars of where I'll live and how I'll support myself and Rosa can come later.

"You're awfully quiet."

"My Aunt just died. You're awfully unaware of what a big deal that is." I'm angry at his self-centered lack of concern. Tim was so—No, I'm not going to compare them.

"People die," he says with a shrug. "You're the one who's unaware. If death is that big of a deal to you, you haven't been living in reality. You're going to have to get tougher if you're going to come with us."

"Come with you? Come with who? What are you talking about? I thought this was just you and me going for a walk?"

"Right now it is."

"I'm not going anywhere with you."

"Decided to stay and have a fairytale with Tim?" he asks mockingly.

I stop walking and glare at him. What does he know about Tim?

"I had Lover Boy as my only company for days while they had me locked up. Wanna guess what he talked about ALL day long?" He pauses and then answers his own question, "You."

I make a disgusted sound and resume walking in the direction he had been taking me. Towards Thomas' house. I knew the hole was somewhere near there.

"Ivy this and Ivy that. Ivy is so kind. Ivy's so amazing. Ivy's so beautiful. Jeez. He's a nice guy, but I don't think he knows you very well."

"What's that supposed to mean?" I stop walking again. "If you don't think I'm nice then why are we walking?"

"I think I saw the real you."

"Which is?"

"When you first met me, you were dying to use that little Taser of yours. You weren't willing to trust me. That was smart. You can't trust anyone. You wouldn't have had me stay at the Inn that night. Also smart. These people are naive, Ivy. Dumb. They won't last long, and I think you have spunk. I think you have what it takes to survive. I respect that." And then he adds, "But I do agree with Tim that you are beautiful. So we have that in common."

I blush, slightly less irritated at him now, but not at all happy about the rest of his assessment. Aside from my looks—which let's face it, isn't much of a compliment because any healthy girl would look good to someone who normally hangs out with zombies—he likes everything about all the bad attitudes I had, and he thinks those are the real me. Technically, they are the real me. But I want to Live above myself. I will do whatever it takes to deny the real me and not let her out again.

"Didn't you read my apology letter? That was the real me. I was awful to you in the beginning, and it was wrong. I really meant how sorry I was."

"So did you give Thomas the glove yet?"

He has an irritating habit of changing the subject whenever you try to talk about anything serious with him. I am starting to realize that there is more to loving someone than the admiration I felt for him that day at Thomas' house. Just because I saw good in him, and it genuinely impressed me, doesn't mean he's right for me. Sure he's handsome and exciting and funny and smart and -

Stop it Ivy.

"Did you? Give him the glove?" Matt asks trying to read my distracted face.

"No, I haven't seen Thomas since the day you left. I'm not supposed to leave the house. Then everything else happened."

"Think you could go in and check on him for me?"

I look at Matt like he's crazy.

"We're going right by there," he says. "I'd go in and check myself, but I don't want to set the alarms blaring." He nods upward towards the high fence just coming into view in the distance.

He's right, we do have alarms. They are spread out periodically at the top of the fence all around the compound. But they don't sound over unwanted houseguests or burglars. They are only for something big like an invasion. They only go off if a whole section of the fence goes down. They've never been used. To be real honest, I'm not even sure if they work.

When I don't say anything, Matt steps in front of me, stopping me, and looks into my face with those sparkling emerald eyes. "Please Ivy. I need to know how he is. I thought I could keep him safe, and I almost lost him. He's everything to me. I know you know how that feels. I really am sorry about your Aunt. She was a good person. I understand why you miss her so much."

"Why the change of tone? Are you just trying to manipulate me or something? A second ago 'people die, end of story,'" I say in a dumb macho voice.

"I need you to check on him for me!" Matt's manipulative smile slips, and I see the frustration behind it. "Please Ivy? If you care about me at all?"

So there it is.

He's basically asking me if I care.

And I do.

So I will.

"Okay. What do you want me to tell him?"

"Tell him I said 'hi.' But, more importantly, I need to know how he is. Is he healing? Is he walking? That kind of stuff."

"Just 'hi?'" I ask with renewed suspicion about his motives. It sounds like I'm more spy than messenger. "You aren't trying to take him again are you? Because that didn't work!"

"Ivy, I promise you, I wouldn't take him from somewhere that's safe for him. I don't want to see him in danger ever again. I want him here for as long as he wants to stay."

"You promise?"

"I promise." He looks me in the eyes, and I see sincerity in his.

But I'm not dumb. I heard how carefully worded that was. He doesn't think we'll always be safe here. It's starting to be a recurring theme.

*****

At Jose and Ellen's house, I knock on the door. Ellen has stayed home from the morning meeting to care for Thomas, as I expected. She looks puzzled to see me, but invites me right in.

"Are you allowed to leave the Inn now, Ivy? Have they figured out what happened to you?"

"No, we don't know anything new. I just needed some air, and I wanted to see Thomas." I pause when she frowns, and then I tell her the rest, "Aunty died last night."

Ellen gasps and leans back against the kitchen wall. "Oh, Ivy. I'm so sorry. How did it happen so fast? I knew she was sick, but I just saw her the other day. She thought she had more time."

I don't say anything. I wonder how many people knew Aunty was dying. Because I didn't. She waited so long to tell me, and then there was no time. I treated her terribly after the attack in Commerce. She knew she was dying, but I was so self-consumed that I practically abandoned her. She spent some of her last days feeling alone and let down by me.

I am thankful that God helped me fix it at the end, but it wasn't enough time. We should've had more time to talk about everything. I would've thanked her so much more for all her sacrifice. I would've asked her what I should do with myself when she was gone. Where I should go. There is so much that was left unsaid.

Ellen gives me a long hug and tells me I'm always welcome there. Then she takes me to Thomas' room. I'm thankful when she doesn't follow me in. I wouldn't have been able to relay Matt's greeting if Ellen was there.

Thomas is propped up against fluffy white pillows on his bed. He has a notebook and pencil, and he's trying to draw with his left hand. His right hand and arm are tucked inside a big sling around his neck. He has stitches on his cheek and on his head. His new glasses are scratched on one side and look like they've been taped together. Thomas' curly head has been shaved, so the wounds are dark and noticeable. I know from what Aunty told me that he has even more wounds that are hidden by clothes and bed covers.

The black spot on his forehead stands out now without his cherubic curls to hide it. It's the most tragic mark on him, the other wounds will heal with time, but the black spot will never fade.

"Ivy!" he exclaims when he sees me standing in his doorway. "You came!"

"Hey kid. You look great," I lie, trying to be nonchalant and light hearted. In truth, seeing him so hurt makes me really upset.

"I'm getting better," he says enthusiastically. "I've been asking Mom if you could come visit and she said you were really busy."

"Yeah. They've been keeping me busy." I don't know if I can keep up the peppy tone of the conversation. I suddenly don't want to tell Thomas about Aunty. That was my excuse coming in here, but this kid has been through so much. And he keeps smiling. No wonder Matt loves him so much. I don't want to give him anything else to be sad about. So I say, "Everything is going real good. I just finally got a break to come see how you're doing. Are you in a lot of pain?"

"It's not too bad," he says bravely.

I think we're both lying to each other.

"Are you riding your bike and running circles around Jose yet?"

"Naw," he looks embarrassed, "I can't walk much yet. Mom wants me to stay in bed and get better. I am practicing writing with my left hand though. I'll be back to my school work soon!"

"You're awesome, Tom," I say, realizing belatedly that I've called him "Tom" instead of Thomas, just like Matt—and Thomas notices it too.

"Matt hasn't come to see me," he whispers with obvious sadness showing on his scarred, innocent face. "Did he leave? Mom and Jose won't tell me."

I wink at him and say, "I have a sneaking suspicion that he's never too far away from you." Looking over my shoulder to be sure that Ellen isn't near the room, I lean in close and whisper, "Can you keep a secret?"

He nods excitedly.

"Matt says 'Hi'."

Thomas smiles a toothy grin, happy to know that his big brother is still out there. I lean the rest of the way towards Tom and give him a quick hug. I can tell he'd like to ask me a million questions, so I make up a reason that I have to be going and say my goodbyes to him and Ellen.

*****

I meet Matt right up the road, where he is, once again, in the bushes.

"It's starting to feel normal to find you hiding in someone's shrubs. And I don't think that's a good normal."

"Just keeping a low profile," he winks, stepping back out to join me on the road. "So, how is he?"

While we walk, I recount my short visit, and Matt listens quietly. I feel bad for him. The weight of his guilt over Thomas' terrible injuries pulls his typical half-smile into a solid frown. Matt turns abruptly off of the road and into an overgrown backyard. I don't remember if anyone lives in the little house on this property. The shaggy lawn doesn't mean the house is empty. Lawnmowers went extinct shortly after Better Homes and Gardens magazine went out of print.

Matt motions for me to follow him. He bends down and pushes an old piece of rotten plywood off to the side, revealing a well in the ground. Bending down to look closer, I see that it isn't a well at all. It's an old sewer pipe entrance. Matt drops down into the hole and disappears.

"Coming?" he calls up to me.

I have serious misgivings about this. I shouldn't even be walking the relatively safe streets of our community with Matt. And I should not, under any circumstances, go down into this hole with that boy alone. I should walk myself straight back home and report this to Captain Markowitz. This information might even buy me my freedom and reestablish trust with the rest of the community. Matt pops his head back up through the hole in the ground and smiles that crooked smile at me.

"It's perfectly safe. Trust me."

I climb down inside the dark hole.

Chapter Forty-One

Body Parts

Matt puts his hands around my waist and lifts me down from the short ladder. I let out a little shriek—surprised at how easily he is able to lift me. My squeal echoes loudly in more than one direction off into the darkness. I stand next to Matt about ten feet below the ground in a small, smelly cement intersection of underground tunnels.

It's shadowy here at the bottom, and the three tunnel openings around us lead into pitch black darkness. Matt produces a flash light from somewhere, and I blink in the sudden light. The round openings to the tunnels are low; dark, ominous sewer pipes that were long ago buried beneath our streets.

If Matt and I are going down one of them, which I assume we are, we'll have to hunch over to walk through them. I completely regret coming down here. No amount of respect earned from Matt could compensate for the fact that millions of spiders must live down here. And most assuredly rats too.

Matt gives me a confident smile in the light of his flashlight; I'm sure he sees the fear and regret all over my face.

"It's not far at all. And not too dirty. Just follow me okay?"

I shake my head "no."

I want to go back up.

"You can hold my hand," he says reaching out a gloved hand for mine.

I don't think I'll take any comfort from gripping a zombie glove while being led into that black abyss. I shake my head "no" again.

"I thought you wanted to know," he says encouragingly, with just a trace of impatience.

"Could you take the gloves off?" I ask pitifully.

He smiles crookedly at me; and, putting the flashlight between his legs, quickly strips off the scary gloves. He holds out his big hand, and I take it, gripping it tightly. And, whether I'm up to it or not, he's suddenly pulled me into the middle tunnel. Following close to him, we begin to make our way through the frightening echoey darkness.

"Why do you wear them?" I ask one of the many questions I've been dying to ask him. My voice quivers slightly with fear, and an embarrassing chill runs through my body and shakes my arm. He squeezes my hand in encouragement, and the tender gesture gives back some of the confidence that the darkness has stolen.

"I like them," he says simply.

I was hoping for some deeper reason. After a minute of silence, listening to just the sound of our feet and a far-off dripping of water, he rewards my silence with a better answer.

"I fit in better with them on. I'm not as sick as most people."

"Yeah, I noticed. Is it because you didn't get the shot?"

"That's one reason," he replies.

Vague as usual.

After another minute of silent trudging he surprises me with more info, "I went a long time without ever taking them off. Thomas was getting so bad, and he had to wear gloves. He was so sick, and I wasn't and I hated it. I wanted him to think my hands were as bad as his. Now that he's better -" He doesn't finish the sentence.

"Aren't you thrilled?"

"Yes. I'm happy," his voice sounds empty and casts suspicion on his professed happiness. "Tom was near death before he ran away. I was gone. I had left him alone."

He sounds so angry, and I don't have the courage to speak words of encouragement. His dark tone in this inky black tunnel makes my heart hammer against my chest and pound out a warning in my ears. So much darkness.

I shouldn't be here!

I instinctively slow down and put tension between Matt and I as I slightly pull against his hand that is clamped with Goliath-like strength over mine.

He must take my fear as reproof because he holds tighter to my hand, making me wince, and pleads with me, "I had left him because I was trying to find some way to help him!" He sounds like a man on trial, and I know it isn't me he needs to convince. He's defending himself against his own inner demons.

"How could you have helped him?" I ask, successfully hiding the tremble in my voice this time.

I am intrigued by his secrets, but I also want to calm him and pull him back out of his self-inflicted prison.

"There are ways."

"Don't tell me too much about yourself." I say sarcastically.

After a silent few seconds, he chuckles and we resume our march. My senses heightened in the dark, I feel him relax and it relaxes me. He gently strokes my hand with his thumb, and new sensations take over. Fear is swallowed up in anticipation, excitement and attraction. He chuckles to himself again, and I listen as the pleasant sound bounces up and down through the tunnel.

That's one difference between him and Tim. Tim is so sincere. So intense. Anytime I'm sarcastic with Tim, he looks hurt and confused. Matt has my sense of humor. I find conversation with him to be—easy. Even in this awful place. He doesn't want anything too serious out of me. He likes to laugh and have fun. He won't look down on me if I'm not perfect. It's very exhilarating, spending time with him.

I realize that I'm comparing them as though they are both options. So strange how fast life changes. A few weeks ago, Tim was a creepy nerd and zombies were terrifying. Now—I feel differently about both of them.

We only walk a minute more before reaching another juncture. Matt shines the flashlight up above our heads, and I see another ladder leading up. It starts about four feet up, around chest level for me. I don't have the upper body strength to hoist myself up there, and I'm not about to be picked up again. Matt jumps easily and catches the fourth rung up. He walks his feet up the wall until finding the bottom step with his foot. Then he lets go with one hand and leans down to offer me a hand up.

I'll give it a shot. I've come this far.

It's probably not going to look very smooth though. I give Matt my hand, and he pulls me while I step up the wall and pull myself up the lower rungs with my other hand. It's easier than I thought, thanks to Matt's strong arms; and, with minimal embarrassment, I'm quickly climbing the ladder behind him.

I expected to come out somewhere outside; but we come out indoors in a dark room. Matt shines the flashlight around, and I see we are in a cellar of some sort. It's a small bare room, cement floor and walls, with nothing in it but some old pieces of garbage. Off to one side is an old wooden staircase leading up into sunlight and more mystery.

"Where are we?"

"You are out in the real world, Ivy. Past your fence. You're in my kingdom now," he says with a wicked smile.

If he hopes to make me nervous—it's working. I hear the warning of my conscience telling me again that I shouldn't be here. Instead of obeying that inner, wiser, voice, I try to muster the bravery Matt seems to think I'm capable of. "How did you find this place? Does anyone else know about it?"

"No one else knows."

He sits down on the cement floor and I join him, relieved that we aren't venturing out of the supposed safety of this room.

"I knew Tom was in Toccoa. I had tracked him that far. He left only hours before I got back from my run, and I was on his tail the whole time. Just never caught up to them until they got here, and then I was stuck. I did try just asking to come in," he says with mock politeness, "and when manners didn't work—I spent a few weeks studying the fence, looking for weaknesses, asking around about who you people were. How well armed, that kind of thing.

"I couldn't come up with a good way in, and I didn't want to involve anyone else. I could've probably gotten a lot of them to storm the fence with me; but I didn't know what I'd find when I got in here. Didn't want to put Tom in any danger. One day, I found this place." He points upstairs. "It's an abandoned house, Kudzu grown all over it. It sits all alone near the railroad tracks. Quite a ways from any of the Pravda compounds.

"I was just looking around for a good place to sleep for the night and I found this hole down here. I followed the tunnel in to your side that night. But I didn't know where Tom was. The irony is he was only a few houses down the street from where I came out. So, the next day, I explored around and saw you getting out of the car. You did that little spider dance in your high heels, and it made me laugh. You seemed real enough, so I thought I'd give asking another try. You know the rest."

I remember that day with clarity. He scared the crap out me. I hadn't realized he saw me scream and jump in spider terror. That's pretty embarrassing. I'm glad it's too dark in here for him to see me blush.

"You smelled terrible." I say playfully.

"Sorry to have offended you, your highness," he retorts with a smile.

"I distinctly remember the smell of cat litter. Am I going to smell like cat poop now that I've spent the morning with you?"

"One can only hope," he says feigning animosity.

"I have to get back. Tim and Rosa will be back at the house soon."

"Tim sleeping over now?" he asks with a surprising amount of irritation in his voice.

"Why? Are you jealous?"

"Who's Rosa?"

"I'll tell you about her on the way back."

When we emerge from the tunnel, safely back inside the compound, Matt turns to take my hand again, and I look up at him in confusion.

"Ivy, I hope you know that things aren't going to last much longer here. If you're ever in trouble, meet me here in the tunnel. I'll be there."

"Are you going to live in there from now on? Should I knit you a housewarming gift?" I ask sarcastically. "Why aren't you heading back to Atlanta like you said? Your place, your job, your Jessie?"

My turn to sound blatantly irritated and suspicious.

"Jealous?" he mocks, the shoe on the other foot. "I'm not leaving until Tom is better, and I know he's safe. You'll all have to move soon."

Ben has already insisted we aren't safe. Now hearing it from someone on the other side too, I'm worried that they are both right.

"How long do you think we have?" I ask.

"Not long."

That's incredibly vague and unhelpful.

"Okay. Well, uh, I guess I'll be going back home now."

He doesn't offer to walk me back.

So chivalrous.

I'm almost home when Mr. Terrell emerges from an apartment building right in front of me. He is holding something under his arm, wrapped in what looks to be a tablecloth. I wonder who he could've been visiting during the morning meeting. I know this isn't his apartment building. Maybe someone is sick and he was making a friendly house call during the service? I can't picture Marcus Terrell doing friendly visits.

There's no way to turn around or hide, he's seen me already. I almost made it home, too. Why couldn't he have been at the U.R. with everyone else? The Homecoming meeting and the dinner should last at least another hour or two, even with the day shortened due to only two of the missionaries coming home.

I expect Mr. Terrell to question me about why I'm out of the house, but he surprises me and puts his hand out to kindly squeeze my shoulder.

"I'm so sorry for your loss, Ivy. Colleen was an incredible woman. I respected her, perhaps more than any woman I've ever known. "

"Thank you," I mumble still caught off guard by his gentleness.

"Ivy, I hate to bother you today, but we need to speak privately as soon as possible. I will gather the other Elders after the meeting. Can you meet us in the Elders' room around 3:00?"

"Sure," I say, now more confused than ever. "Just me?"

I remember again that I'm all alone now. No one will sit next to me at that imposing table or squeeze my leg with reassurance.

"Yes, I'm sorry. Just you." Then Mr. Terrell says softly, "You aren't alone, Ivy. We care for you. We are the Body. We care for each member. The Bible says, "The eye can never say to the hand, 'I don't need you.' The head can't say to the feet, 'I don't need you.'" He leans over to look into my eyes and says emphatically, "You will never be alone."

I nod at him, feeling awkward and having nothing to say in return. He squeezes my shoulder one more time before letting go and walking quickly away. He turns down the street toward the U.R. building and calls over his shoulder, "Don't be late! 3:00!"

As I walk the last block to the Inn, I wonder to myself which part of the Body I am. Aunty was the hands. She was always helping, ready to serve. I decide I'm quite possibly the appendix. My life is rupturing and the Body can live just fine without me.

Chapter Forty-Two

To Catch A Predator

Tim and Rosa arrive at the Inn within minutes of me. The Sunday Morning meeting was short, and Tim skipped the meal to come make sure I was okay. It's a good thing I was back before they got here. Tim wouldn't have understood my need for a walk. Or approved of my companion. While I was out with Matt, in another world, I somehow stepped away from the sadness. Now that I'm back home, it hits me again in full force. I wish I could just walk away from here and not ever come back again.

After getting Rosa a snack and laying her down on my bed for a nap, Tim and I sit on the hallway floor outside of my room, each with our own Gov. Bar. Tim has talked to his dad and they've decided how to handle Aunty's passing. I'm not surprised or offended that I wasn't consulted. I'm relieved to not be responsible for her body or her funeral.

"Some men will dig the grave this afternoon," Tim says quietly, filling me in on the basic details. "My dad is coming here in about twenty minutes with a gurney to take her over to the clinic. He'll keep her there overnight. Then tomorrow morning, there will be a viewing and a funeral for the community. After the funeral, only those closest to her will meet at the grave for a few words and the burial. Jamie's dad is making her a casket."

They've thought of everything I guess. Jamie Crest's dad is an excellent carpenter. Aunty often commented on his workmanship. We have a beautiful oak bookshelf that was made by him. It's strange to think that she'll be buried in his craftsmanship. I guess she would like that.

"Ivy?"

"Sorry. Yes. Thank you. That all sounds—good." It all sounds terrible really, but I'm sure nothing could sound good.

"If you are up to it, we should go get her ready before my dad comes."

I look up at Tim in surprise, a deep frown on my face.

"If you can't, someone else will do it. They'll completely understand. I just thought you might want to be the one."

I don't know what I want. What I can handle. I don't want to do it, but

I don't want anyone else to either. I want her to look like her. I don't think anyone else could do her hair the way she did. I think about seeing her tomorrow, done up with makeup by someone else, looking wrong. It should be me. Somehow, I have to make myself do it.

"Will you help me?" I can barely get the words out before the tears come again.

He nods and stands up to help me up from the floor.

*****

I cry the entire time. Fixing Aunty's hair, putting color on her cheeks and lips, picking her favorite dress; it's the most painful thing I've ever done. Her closet smells like her and I want to hide in amongst the clothes and smell her and pretend everything is okay again. I don't have what it takes to undress and redress her. It's just too creepy. It was hard enough to stare at her lifeless form and try to make it look lifelike again. I just can't rob her of her dignity. Someone else will have to put her dress on. I find jewelry, stockings and shoes to go with the dress. And then they take her.

My heart feels like it's being ripped in half as Tim's dad and Ellen wheel Aunty out of her room and away from me. Tim holds me again and I let him. We sit on the edge of her bed, and I lean into his shoulder and cry for a long time. I sob and shake and Tim holds me, and I feel him crying too. My stomach hurts, and my tears finally run out. Still we sit there. Tim finally stands up and helps me to my feet. It's time to leave her room, and I don't want to come back in here ever again. I look around, searching her sanctuary for something to remember her by.

My eyes wander around the room, stopping lovingly on each treasured item. On the nightstand is a silver picture frame with a photo of her and Aunty Betty when they were young. Slung over the carved bed post is the red hat that I picked for her on our first "shopping trip" together. On her dresser, there are antique glass perfume bottles that belonged to her grandmother and the bracelet that I made for her last Christmas.

I spot her Bible lying on the floor by her bed. These last two items are what I choose. I slip the bracelet on my wrist; it's simple, but she had acted so thrilled when I gave it to her. I pick up her Bible from the floor and walk quickly from the room. Tim follows behind me and shuts off the lights. My heart feels dead inside me as I hear him pull her door closed.

It's almost 3:00, and I have to ask Tim for yet another favor. I need a babysitter for Rosa while I meet with the Elders. He, of course, agrees and I hurry out the front door with no clue as to what this meeting could be about.

*****

It's a short lonely walk to the U.R. I watch the bushes for movement, some sign of Matt, but I don't see him. At the U.R., I am ushered right into the Elders' meeting room as soon as I arrive. All of the Elders except for Mr. Terrell are already here. Even Frank Hosch, who was absent at the last meeting, has put aside his honeymoon to be here. Instead of the formality of last time, this gathering seems confused and chaotic. I don't think any of them know why we are here either. For once, I'm not out of the loop.

We are all waiting for Mr. Terrell to arrive and explain why he called this emergency meeting. In the middle of the table sits whatever Mr. Terrell had under his arm earlier today. I have no clue what it could be, still wrapped in the green checked tablecloth. Is anyone else dying to peek inside that gingham wrapped mystery? I sit in the same chair I sat in last time and try to catch the Elders' whispered conversations to each other.

Several of them walk over to me and give heartfelt condolences over the loss of Aunty. She was a very important part of this community. Though she often ruffled the feathers of the men in this room, I'm touched that every one of them liked and respected her. Rev. Depold comes over and sits down next to me. He starts to offer his condolences, but he is interrupted by an angry shout from outside of the room. Everyone looks up in confusion; and, at the sound of approaching feet, we all turn towards the door expectantly.

Mr. Terrell enters first, followed closely by Captain Andrew Markowitz and the guard Anthony. The two guards have a squirming Chuck Fox handcuffed and locked tightly in their grasp. When Chuck sees me, he tries unsuccessfully to pull out of the strong hold the guards have on him. I'm completely confused.

"I'll get right to it," Mr. Terrell announces.

Direct as always.

"Mr. Fox has been with us for only a short time. In recent weeks he hasn't been feeling well, and he started seeing Dr. Markowitz. Unfortunately, he didn't realize that what he was suffering from was a recurring of LS.

Hale shared his concern over Mr. Fox's condition with me. The loss of his Healing gave me more reason to suspect him. His behavior and demeanor had already seemed odd to me. He made no secret of the fact that he was interested in Colleen from the first time he saw her. Then today when her death was announced in the morning meeting, I watched him. He didn't shed a tear. He smiled and visited with people during the greeting time. He didn't seem like a man who had lost someone he cared about. I left during the sermon and inspected his apartment."

At this Chuck shouts, "You had no right to go in there! This is still America! I still have rights! How dare you trespass on my property? You can't stand there and condemn me of sin when you're a trespasser and a thief!"

Andrew pushes a Taser into Chuck, and Chuck shakes violently in his chair, his muscles locking and his face stretched in pain and fear.

The entire room erupts as several Elders call for some explanation, and others shout for Andrew to stop.

Mr. Terrell ignores their shouts and walks closer to the table, leaning over and lifting the tablecloth off of his mystery item to reveal a black—something. I don't really know what it is. It looks like a black and gray box with a flashlight on top. Or maybe something they used to film old movies?

The Elders all look shocked. They seem to know what the small black box is and what it means. No one says anything; they just look sadly at Chuck.

The room is still when I ask quietly, "What is it?"

Mr. Terrell looks woefully at me and says, "It's a Polaroid Camera, Ivy."

I'm slow to process that. Trying to understand what Chuck Fox has to do with the camera that took a picture of me that was given to a zombie. My stomach plunges painfully when I realize Chuck is the one who did it. Chuck is working with the zombies to hurt me. Mr. Terrell said Chuck didn't even care about Aunty. Chuck was trying to get to me from the beginning.

I am filling up with fury. I feel it boiling in me, rushing quickly to the surface, about to pour out in rage and words that I shouldn't say—especially in front of the Elders. All of the last few weeks of fear and sadness have somehow morphed into one big storm of anger. My hands are shaking as I glare with hatred at Chuck. He looks cowardly and despicable, handcuffed and slumped in the chair. Still recovering from the Taser's shock, Chuck shivers and starts to cry.

"They took my wife!" he wails. "They were going to kill her if I didn't help them! What could I do? I couldn't let them kill her if I could do something to save her. I didn't know what else to do," he sobs.

He gives me a pleading, pitiful stare. I don't know if he wants my forgiveness or my surrender. My anger is barely restrained; I feel no pity for this manipulative man who pretended to love my Aunty. To think I had encouraged this hoax, had considered a future where Chuck was a part of our lives. Aunty's gifts of wisdom and discernment had kept us safe again. She had no interest in this viper; a true wolf in sheep's clothing. Walking around among us while working for Pravda!

The Spirit tries to whisper to my heart of forgiveness and pity. I swat the encouragement away like a pesky fly. I want to feel angry. It feels so much better than sad and scared. I want to hold on to it forever. Chuck's tears do nothing to move me. They only disgust me. No one else seems to pity him. The Elders sit in stunned silence, glancing back and forth between me and Chuck. I'm at the center of all of this. My future will be decided by what this crying man knows. If he'll tell us.

I try to be calm, but there are still sparks in my eyes when I look up and ask, "Are they still after me?"

I had hoped, after talking with Jack, that maybe they didn't find what they wanted, maybe I was already safe.

Chuck nods pitifully in the affirmative.

I feel cold and numb.

They still want me.

My life is over.

Rev. Depold speaks with an authority that still contains traces of his trademark kindness, "We need to know everything Chuck. Start from the beginning. You owe Ivy that much."

Chuck nods pitifully again, sighs and begins. "Nancy and I are from South Carolina. About a year ago we met a missionary from Texas. He told us about God; and, after we got Life, we wanted to go tell Theo, Nancy's sister. Theo lived in Gainesville, about an hour from here. We didn't find her there, but we thought maybe she'd be with her son, so we come up this direction. Theo's son lived out in the country near here, a farmer. We were camping in a field just outside of Toccoa when they surprised us at night. Some thugs from Pravda. Beat me up and told me they'd kill Nancy if I didn't do what they asked. Said there was a girl named Ivy in this town that they wanted. I told 'em 'no'! Then they -" he pauses apparently overwhelmed with grief, "- they cut off Nancy's hand! In front of me!"

He drops his head into his handcuffed hands and wails a pain-filled cry of complete agony. The sound hurts me, and I know I'll never forget it. That wail, that agony, will follow me from this room and haunt my dreams until Jesus comes for me. My anger cracks slightly, and small drips of sadness start eking out, forming rivulets on the dam walls around my heart.

Andrew nudges Chuck roughly. Chuck lowers his hands and stares at me with tears on his cheeks. I stare back, unable to look away as he continues his gut wrenching tale.

"I didn't have a choice. I couldn't watch her die! They dropped me off down the road from your gate. I wanted to find a way to tell you without getting Nancy killed, but I just couldn't figure my way out." With shame on his face he says quietly, "I met with them at the fence a bunch of times. I told 'em it was too hard. That you weren't ever alone and I couldn't do anything about it! I was stalling. It was killing me. I knew they'd kill Nancy easy if I didn't hurry up and give 'em something. So I took the picture to prove I was working on it. I found that camera in an empty apartment in my building. I gave em the picture and they gave me," he swallows another sob, "Nancy's ear. Said if I didn't deliver you, they'd give me the rest of her—in tiny pieces next time."

He sobs into his arm again; and, this time, everyone lets him cry in peace. We're all being moved to compassion, despite our anger and betrayal. This broken man has been through so much. I'm sure every man in the room is wondering if he would've done the same for his wife. Would we have the strength to say no if our dearest loved one was being threatened and abused and we had the power to make it stop? I'm finding compassion that comes from God and not from me. Chuck is my enemy, but I'm supposed to "bless those that curse me" and "turn the other cheek." So much harder than I thought it would be when I read those verses in naivety and said, "No problem, Lord, anything for you."

Chuck collects himself again and continues—speaking quickly—pushing to get to the end of his traumatic tale. "I heard you two were going out of town to shop. I wasn't supposed to meet them again for two weeks, and I didn't know what to do. I left the compound with a fishing pole, told the guards I was going fishing. I walked to one of their blood centers. Got a mask off of a—a dead guy in the street. Nobody stopped me. I told the Pravda guy at the blood center that you were important to Pravda and that you were going to be in Commerce the next day. I had another picture, I had taken three pictures that day. I gave it to a Pravda worker, and then I came back to the community and waited.

"When you came back safe, I knew I was in trouble. I mean, I was real glad you were okay. I didn't want anything bad to happen to you. I just didn't know what to do you know?" he looks down at his feet in shame. "I'm supposed to bring you with me next time I meet them. Supposed to be tomorrow. But I already decided I wasn't gonna do it!" he says loudly.

He hasn't earned any trust with this story, and I don't believe him. By the condemning looks on the Elders' faces, I'd say they don't believe him either. Mountain Man Jack said it's all about blood. They think my blood is special enough to go through all of this. All the trouble to Chuck and his wife, all of the weeks meeting at the fence and the attempted kidnapping. All of this for one person?

Me.

What will they do to me if they get me?

"Is Ivy in any danger from anyone else in the community?" Mr. Terrell asks.

Before I can even be nervous about that possibility, Chuck shakes his head "no," and I sink back in my chair relieved. Then Chuck stares into my eyes, and in a low voice he says, "But she's in terrible danger from the rest of the world." A shiver shakes my whole body when he says even quieter, "They want 'er real bad."

Chapter Forty-Three
Aunty's Admirers

We bury Aunty today. Rosa and I are sitting on my bed, ready too early for Aunty's funeral. Rosa still hasn't spoken, and I don't know how much she understands. Though I haven't cried yet today, she seems to know that I am sad because she sits close to me and pets me sweetly. I hope she and I will see happier days together. I know she has already seen way too much sadness in her short life. I want to show her happiness. She came to me in one of my darkest times, and I find it hard to give her more than an occasional smile. She must think that all of life is hard and tragic. I wonder what that must do to her little personality. I hope that she isn't too damaged by life already.

Rosa surprises me by crawling across the bed to the nightstand and pointing at Aunty's Bible. She wants me to read to her? I already devoted myself this morning before waking her, but this morning's Bible reading didn't bring me comfort. I can hardly remember now what I read. I pick up the Bible, but then decide to read first from the little daily book that I skipped this morning. I read out loud to Rosa:

> *"Give up the illusion that you deserve a problem-free life. Part of you is still hungering for the resolution of all difficulties. This is a false hope! As I told my disciples, in the world you will have trouble. Link your hope not to problem solving in this life but to the promise of an eternity of problem-free life in heaven. Instead of seeking perfection in this fallen world, pour out your energy into seeking Me: the Perfect One. It is possible to enjoy Me and glorify Me in the midst of adverse circumstances. In fact, My Light shines most brightly through believers who trust Me in the dark. That kind of trust is supernatural: a production of My indwelling Spirit. When things seem all wrong, trust Me anyway. I am much less interested in right circumstances than in right responses to whatever comes your way."*

The recommended reading at the bottom is Psalm 112:4,7. I look the verses up in Aunty's Bible and read them out loud too:

> *"Light arises in the darkness for the upright; He is gracious and compassionate and righteous... He will not fear evil tidings; His heart*

is steadfast, trusting in The Lord."

Rosa looks up at me when I finish reading and smiles at me encouragingly. She can't have understood any of that. I'm still not sure she even understands English. But she looks at me like, "See? It's going to be okay." I smile at her and hug her close. It's time to go say goodbye to Aunty now.

*****

I walk across the street, Rosa's little hand in mine. I'm happy to have her with me. The new responsibility is not a burden but a comfort. I feel less alone, and I thank God in my heart for sending her. It was so good of Him.

Tim is waiting outside in the cold morning air for me. I am relieved to see him. He came over last night to check on me, and I told him all about Chuck. I suspect he had already heard about it from Andrew, but he let me tell it all as though it was new to him, patiently listening. I am surprised to discover that he is suddenly my closest friend. I wouldn't be in my right mind right now if he hadn't carried me through this.

I feel somehow like it honors Aunty, too. She saw before I did what a good man Tim is. I still feel strongly attracted to Matt. I don't want to marry Tim. I'm sure I'll never get to marry anyone. Our time on earth is almost up, and I'm being hunted by zombies. The odds of me living long enough to marry someone and have a "normal" life are zilch.

The viewing feels like ten hours instead of one. I sit with Rosa near the front of the U.R. meeting room, across from the wooden casket. It's a simple casket, nothing pretty about it. It is raw wood, hastily constructed, without even a coat of stain. It seems almost an insult to bury her in it. I can't help but wonder if Jamie's dad intentionally didn't make something nice because everyone thinks I'm a problem lately.

I look down at my feet and avoid looking at the ugly casket or at her. I've already said goodbye; once when she left me, and then again as I prepared her body to go. I'm here today because it's what she would think is proper. I speak to as few people as possible. Only looking up when they linger near me and it becomes rude to avoid them.

In the short line of well-wishers, Harmony is the first to sit down next to me. I'm too dead inside to make effort towards our broken friendship. She is too awkward to know how to fix it on her own. She sits for a minute, neither of us speaking, the awkwardness increasing. I find anger building inexplicably inside me again. When I think I might not be able to hold it in any longer, Harmony chokes on a sob and surprises me with a kiss on the cheek. Then she's gone. My anger evaporates leaving only footprints of minor irritation. I go back to my quiet staring at the floor.

Jose and Ellen come separately, each taking a turn away from Thomas' bedside. Ellen tells me that they told him and that he cried for me. I guess he had to find out eventually. I wish he didn't have to know and be sad.

Dr. Markowitz stands next to my chair for a long time, his hand on my shoulder. Each time I look up at him to see if I should say something, he doesn't look at me but continues to stare silently at Aunty. Then, without any words, he squeezes my shoulder and walks away. I'm relieved because I have nothing to say. I never realized that there were men who cared deeply for her. Mr. Terrell seems to have been carrying a secret torch for her as well. I suspect that he cared a lot. That his suspicion of Chuck may have begun with jealousy over the attention Chuck was flaunting at Aunty.

I think Dr. Markowitz may have cared for her more deeply than just normal friendship, too. Her passing matters more to them than I would have ever realized. I wonder if she cared for them the same way. I'm ashamed that I have no idea. I feel guilty when I think about how much time we spent talking about me. I wonder if I really knew the real Aunty. I wonder if anyone else knew her, really knew her, better than me? If there was someone she confided in, would I long to know all that she shared or would I be jealous that it wasn't me?

If Mr. Terrell hadn't discovered Chuck's secret life yesterday, I'm sure Chuck would be here. Fake crying and making a show. Trying to figure out how to kidnap me. I think they have him in one of the cells where Matt was held. I barely slept last night thinking about Chuck and his wife. Part of me wonders if I should give myself up to save her. My anger from yesterday is mostly gone. I feel bad for him. He never wanted anything to do with me. I tell myself it's my love for Rosa that keeps me from suggesting I trade myself for Nancy. But I know it's cowardice, too.

I can vividly imagine what they would do to me. I have this horrible picture in my head. I see myself lying on a cold steel table, strapped down. I'm in a dark room with bright lamps shining down on me. I can't see into the shadows around the room, and I know they are there, staring at me. I'm wearing only a paper cloth across my body and there are needles in both of my arms, draining me of my blood. In this disturbing vision I know that they are draining me dry, not just taking small amounts. I know I'll die on that cold table alone.

I shiver, lost in my morbid fantasy. Rosa pulls on my arm and brings me back to reality. Reality is barely better. I ask her if she needs to go potty and she nods emphatically. I lead Rosa down the center aisle. Everyone stares at me as we slip through the doors at the back of the room.

*****

Rev. DePold's sermon is short. He speaks of what Aunty did for the community and how she loved me. He reads about Heaven from the Bible and reminds us of how beautiful it will be. Staring straight into my eyes, he reminds us that we don't grieve as those who have no hope. We'll be with Aunty again soon. His quote at the end is the only part that I'll remember. It's beautiful. He quotes the author C.S. Lewis:

"If I find in myself desires which no experience in this world can satisfy, the most probable explanation is that I was made for another world."

*****

At the small cemetery behind the old Methodist church building, there are only a handful of people. Tim and Rosa stand close to me, seeking warmth in the cold wind. Mr. Terrell stands whispering to Dr. Markowitz. Rev. DePold and a few other Elders and their wives make up the rest of who Aunty counted close.

It's less than I thought there would be. I guess Aunty didn't really make many close female friends either. We lived for each other and our work here. Was it enough? Were we right to seclude ourselves? Now, with her gone, I'm lost. She felt that way driving home from Commerce. I saw it in her eyes that day. She was terrified that someone had tried to take me. She didn't know how to live without me either. And now, somehow, I have to be the one who figures out how to survive alone. At the last minute, Ellen, Harmony and Sherry quietly join us. It fills the small group out a little and makes the gathering feel more complete. I'm thankful that they came.

As they lower my Aunty into the cold ground, I turn away. It hurts unbearably to see her drop from my sight for the last time. With my back to the grave, I see someone watching us, standing close to a tree at the far end of the field. He doesn't hide when I turn, but lifts a hand of greeting and friendship. A gloved hand. It's Matt. He came. I turn back around quickly as Tim starts to lean past me, interested in what I'm looking at. He doesn't see Matt but steps close to me and puts his arm around me in comfort. I cringe away slightly, knowing that Matt is still watching.

Mr. Terrell picks up a hammer and begins to pound a simple wooden cross into the ground to mark her grave. Someone has crudely etched her name into the front. The echoey sound of the hammer hitting with each swing reminds me of the Jesus movie. The horrible sound as the soldiers swung their hammers and nailed him to the cross. I had to turn away during the movie, unable to watch, even though it was just an actor. It felt real and I knew it was real. My Jesus had been nailed to a cross for me so that I wouldn't have to die. Aunty is still alive. She isn't really dead. I wish that my certainty could alleviate some of the lung crushing grief I am drowning in.

I must look awful because Tim offers to take Rosa for the afternoon so I can sleep. It's true I've had very little sleep in the last few days. I give in and accept his help again. The way we pass Rosa back and forth and share responsibility of her, it's starting to seem like we are married, and Rosa is our child.

We leave the gravesite as a group, and Rev. Depold steps alongside me. "Ms. Scott will be taking over the Inn, Ivy. You are welcome to stay there for as long as you need; Julia would probably love some help learning the ropes."

I don't know what to say. I hate the thought of anyone else running the Inn—especially the cold fish, Ms. Julia Scott. The Inn needs someone kind and good with people; someone with the gift of hospitality. Ms. Scott is hard working, but she couldn't come close to replacing Aunty. I have no desire to live there with her. I'll show her around and pack my things and go. I'm not sure where I'll go. But I won't stay there.

"When will she be moving in?" I croak. It's been hours since I've used my voice, and those hours have been filled with more crying.

"Tomorrow."

"Okay."

There's nothing else to say. I don't need permission to leave, and I don't want to be told where to go. Let him think I'll stay there for now.

Before stepping away from my side, Rev. Depold says, "I have a word for you Ivy. I read it this morning and I believe God wanted me to give it to you. Just to you. It's another quote from C.S. Lewis. He's one of my favorites. It's this: 'God, who foresaw your tribulation, has specially armed you to go through it, not without pain but without stain.'"

Not without pain but without stain.

I definitely get the pain part.

Chapter Forty-Four

How Many Pints for a Pair Of Pink Mittens?

I finally slip into a deep sleep, alone in my bed at the Inn.

I'm awakened sometime later by the sound of rain. As I become more aware, I realize it's not rain hitting my window. Something else is tapping. I suddenly know it is Matt. Throwing on my shoes, I hurry to the back door.

Matt is standing by the back door when I open it. How he knew I would open it at that moment amazes me.

"I saw you there," I say appreciatively. His intense stare makes me look uncomfortably at my feet.

"I came to make sure you were okay. It looked like you had all the comfort you needed, so I didn't stick around to shake hands afterward."

"Tim is a friend," I say defensively.

"That's not what he thinks. I need to show you something," he says, changing the subject with his typical abruptness. "We'll be out a little longer this time."

Matt and I walk in silence. It's a comfortable silence between us but also a necessary one. There is no U.R. meeting to ensure we'll have the streets to ourselves like last time. We watch carefully for anyone who may be out this afternoon. Our route to the hidden tunnel takes us past Harmony's apartment. I watch her windows closely and feel nervous when I see her curtain flutter.

Matt grabs my hand and I forget my nerves, thinking about the freedom I feel when I'm with him. A block later, I glance behind us and see someone turn quickly into a side alley. Are we being followed? Chuck is safely behind bars, and he assured us that no one else in the community is a danger to me. I'm just being paranoid. At the entrance to the tunnel, Matt disappears down into the hole. I take a quick glance around to be sure that no one is watching; and then, without hesitation, follow him into the darkness.

We feel more free to talk when we're underground. Our conversation is lighthearted and I'm surprised to find myself capable of smiling. He holds my hand again and leads me through the cramped tunnel. I am less nervous this time and don't really need his hand, but I don't tell him that.

"You were pretty dressed up today," he says with strange humor in his tone. I feel certain he's making fun of me somehow, but I can't figure out why.

"Funeral?" I say perturbed, an obvious given for my attire.

"I just thought since it was a special occasion you'd be wearing those pink heels again."

He is mocking me.

I can't see him well enough in the dark of the tunnel, but I'm fairly certain he is laughing silently at me. I should be offended at how light he makes of my loss. He has no sympathy for what I've just been through. But honestly, it's a relief to smile. I find myself giggling with him. I don't want to be low when I'm with him.

We haven't known each other long, but I have already stored up plenty of embarrassing moments with him. I acted like such a naive pouting princess that day we met. I must have looked so ridiculous—the heels, the myriad of necklaces, the mismatched new clothes. I blush just picturing my three weeks ago self.

Intent on not being that girl again, I respond to his antagonism with playfulness. "You are awfully fashion conscious for a guy. Most guys I know are too masculine to pay attention to a girl's shoes. I guess you're more in touch with your feminine side," I say sarcastically.

"Touchy," is his response. Of course, do the guy thing and act like *I'm* hormonal.

Trying to turn the conversation back to him I ask, "Don't you dress up at a funeral?"

"Haven't been to one since I was a kid."

"You're fortunate not to have lost anyone lately." I think it's a little strange that he hasn't lost anyone, especially out there where zombies are dropping like flies.

"I've lost a lot of people," he says matter-of-factly, "we just don't do funerals anymore. Too many people dying. No place to put them all. Most people have evolved, Ivy. They are smart enough to know that it's just a dead body and there's no point in being sentimental or emotional about it. Life goes on and soon it'll be me and that's just how it works."

When we get to the other side, he once again easily pulls me up out of the hole and into the basement. There are piles of stuff all over the place. The piles seem to be organized into food, clothes and guns. The gun pile makes me nervous. I'm not at all comfortable with weapons. There are large ones that look like military guns and small ones that would fit in a man's pocket. I stand on the other side of the hole opposite of the intimidating pile.

"Why is all this stuff here? Are you moving in?"

"Just trying to be prepared," he says simply. Like having this many weapons is a normal part of everyday life. "Here, put these on."

He tosses me a black ski mask and a pair of pink mittens. I didn't realize he intended to leave the cellar. Nothing he could say will convince me to go out there on the other side. I am regretting coming with him. He just doesn't get it. I'm not safe out there.

I shake my head "no" and take a step back towards the hole.

While I'm standing there, strongly considering jumping back in and running home, a loud noise echoes beneath. I shriek and jump away from the hole.

"Jumpy." Matt says condescendingly. "It was probably just a big rat."

"A rat?!"

"There are lots of 'em down there. Huge ones. Look, if you could walk through the rat filled tunnels with me, I think you can handle a leisurely stroll to see something magnificent."

He says the word "magnificent" with mysterious excitement, and I find myself wanting to know what it is he has to show me.

I don't like either of my options. I don't want to go down there with whatever large creature made that noise, but I don't want to step out into his world either.

"It's completely safe," he says confidently. "No one comes out this way; I've never seen anyone over here." Then with a manipulative pout on his face he says, "I had to look ten different places to find you those pink mittens. And they weren't free. Come with me?"

If they weren't free, it means Matt had to pay for them. He had to give his blood for them. I'll never get used to the new currency. I wonder how much he had to give to buy these for me.

It's so wrong.

And so romantic.

I pull on the ski mask, and it feels strange to be covering my face. I look like a bank robber from an old movie. I actually love the mittens, but I plan on giving the mask back as soon as possible. I feel like a traitor to my people. Chuck mentioned putting on a mask when he left the community. I hope God won't be mad at me and take away my healing. It's just a walk. It's probably not my wisest choice, but I don't think it's actually sin.

We walk up the old wooden stairs and through the abandoned house. Old moldy furniture is strewn about, and there are scary blood stains on the walls. Something bad happened here. Through the jagged holes in the dirty windows, yellow sunlight pours in and tries to pretend that this is a cheerful place, but I'm not fooled. An involuntary tremble of nerves runs through my body. Matt kindly pretends not to notice.

Once outside, I can see why no one has found this place. It sits in the middle of an overgrown clearing, completely surrounded on all sides by trees. If there was a driveway leading to the house in the past, it is gone now, covered by trees and Kudzu and thorny blackberry bushes. I think this house was abandoned long before the disappearances and the disease.

I walk behind Matt as he picks our way through the brush. We come out onto the road and the nervous warning in my heart hammers even louder.

It's still daylight.

Anyone could see us.

I have no protection out here.

My face is covered by the traitorous mask, but I feel even more vulnerable with it on. As though I'm denying Him by wearing it. He said if anyone denies Him, He would deny them before his Father. Will He let me get caught because I'm wearing the mask? I should turn back and go home. I feel a panic attack coming on. My steps slow and come to a stop. I am looking frantically around and over my shoulder as I take my first step backwards to retreat.

Matt sighs and turns back to see me wussing out. He doesn't wear a mask; and, though it's a little hard to see out of the holes in mine, Matt's green eyes suddenly fill my view.

"Ivy. I promise you are totally safe. It really isn't that bad out here. Your whole experience is based on what happened in Commerce and the sickos who hang out near the fence to scare you. Not everyone is bad. Am I a monster?" he asks stepping closer to me.

My pulse is racing, but not from fear. Matt is so close to me and his eyes—oh his eyes! They do things to me. I breathe short little breaths as he reaches out to take my hands. I think about what it would be like to kiss him. The mask and a few inches of space are the only thing between his lips and mine.

"Can we please enjoy our second date?" he asks sweetly, stroking my pink mittened hand with his shiny black gloved thumb.

Our second date?

I didn't realize we'd had a first date. I guess anytime I walk down the tunnel of love with him he's considering it a date. I've never been on a date, and I already missed enjoying my first one. I will enjoy every moment of my second date. I nod, and we resume our walk in the sunshine. Still holding hands.

*****

"Leisurely stroll" was a bit misleading.

We are literally walking around the small city of Toccoa, following the path of our fence from several blocks away. As we start down a huge hill, I realize where we are. We are only a few hundred feet from the West Gate. Not far at all from the Inn. This is the direction that Matt went the morning that Aunty and I walked him to the gate. The day he ate most of my syrup. I smile at the memory now. I was so disgusted with him that day. I hated him. I would gladly give him my last morsel of food now.

As we walk down, down, down the huge hill, I think it's strange that I've never been this way. After all these years of living only a half mile from where we are now walking, I'm on an adventure. I could be home in five minutes if I walked directly to the Inn, but I might as well be in another time and place. The route we are on feels that new and foreign.

My world has been too small and sheltered for too long. We pass an old cemetery, and it's run down walls and gravestones remind me of Aunty. The grand tomb stones and little marble temples draw my thoughts back to this morning and the rough wooden cross marking Aunty's resting place. No marble angel watches over her. Loneliness fills me again as we walk in silence.

"I saw you that day," he says.

I have no idea what he's talking about.

"When Tom and I left."

I remember that day with its sadness and regret.

"We didn't go straight to the tunnel. We had to walk towards the gate so you wouldn't figure out my way in. When we came around the bend, I made Tom hide in the bushes with me."

"Of course," I say jokingly. He loves a good shrubbery.

He laughs and then continues. "You came around the bend not two seconds after we were hidden. You had that coat," he pauses then adds softly, "and you were crying. I've thought about that day a lot. You looked so sad that we were gone. Were you sad about Tom leaving? Or about me?"

I blush under my mask, glad he can't see my face. "Well I had just met you," I say, hoping he'll assume that means my answer is Thomas. "And you were really irritating."

"So it was me. That's what I thought," he says, full of egotistical confidence.

"I didn't say that!" I punch him in the arm.

"Yeah, you did," he says smiling. "And who taught you how to punch? That was weak! We're going to have to work on your defensive skills."

I'm glad my horrible fighting skills have turned the subject away from my vulnerable display of emotion that day. I'm not comfortable with him knowing just how interested I am. He can't know how much I want to be with him. The small amount of wisdom that I possess warns me to keep my feelings to myself.

When we reach the bottom of the colossal hill, there is another hill rising ahead of us. My muscles are starting to burn, and I'm nervously wondering how long this "stroll" is going to be. Matt and I exchange jokes and sarcasm and meaningless flirtatious banter while we walk. He has never let go of my hand, which I am thoroughly enjoying.

Now that we're walking up hill, I'm letting him pull me along. I don't have his stamina. Only part way up the next hill we turn to the left. Walking down a side road, we enter an old compound of some sort. I look curiously around, and Matt answers my thoughts.

"It's an old college campus."

"Oh. Why are we here?"

"You'll see."

"You're sure it's safe?"

Matt smiles and pulls me a little closer. It has the necessary affect, banishing my worries and leaving me reveling in his closeness. We pass empty dark buildings of different sizes. Each of them seemingly built in different eras. Some buildings look relatively new, and some are very old. Most of them have a plaque or sign, naming them after different people from the college's past. Probably the names of the rich people who paid to have them built.

Matt weaves through the buildings, confident of where he's going. After a short walk through what proved to be a small campus, we stop in front of a decorative iron gate. It hangs, rusted on its hinges, partway open. Matt leads me between the tight gap in the open rusty gate and down a path that runs beside a brook that babbles cheerfully alongside of us.

I haven't seen a stream in years; and the sight of this place, tucked away from the world, is awe inspiring. We are surrounded by forest on all sides as we follow the shallow, gurgling creek that flows steadily over rocks and around bends. Ahead, I hear the water getting louder. I don't really know what to make of it.

Rounding a bend in the path, we come out into a cove surrounded by cliffs and winter bare forest on all sides. Straight ahead is the most beautiful waterfall I've ever seen. The grandeur of it takes my breath away. True, I've never seen any other waterfalls in real life, but I'm sure this one must be one of the prettiest He made. It's taller than the tallest trees, reaching up into the blue sky like a skyscraper. White water falls in long tendrils that weave in and out of each other, racing each other, until finally splashing down into the gray pool at the bottom.

The cliffs on either side of the majestic falls are orangey stone with gray patterns throughout. Standing still, drinking it in, I have this wonderful feeling of steadfastness—despite the changing world outside the cove. The waterfall stands in its place, always moving but never leaving, showing the beauty and power of God's creation.

I've been staring, lost in thoughts of my Creator, when I realize Matt has disappeared. My eyes sweep over the secluded area anxiously. Matt suddenly reappears high on a boulder that juts out near the pool at the base of the falls. I pick my way around the smaller stones near the bottom and find a path up to where he sits.

At the top, another glance around dispels all fear. From this height I can see the entire cove easily, and we are completely alone. I take my mask off and use it for a pillow as I lay back and look up into the sky far above the falls. We lay there together, resting and admiring the spectacular view.

This is definitely better than I could've imagined for a second date. The sun is starting to sink, and the first colors of sunset are showing behind the cliff at the top of the falls. It's not yet dinner time, but the tentacles of evening are already starting to wrap themselves around the day. The clear blue sky is starting to take on orangish hues near the horizon. Tonight's sunset is going to be beautiful.

The best part of the date has just begun, and I realize with a twinge of sadness that it will be the shortest part. We shouldn't stay here long. The hike back will take time, and I need to be home before dark. Tim will be bringing Rosa back to me sometime in the evening. I don't want to think about Tim or how mad he would be if he knew where I was.

"What do you do in Atlanta?" I ask. I want to know more about Matt, and I'm also hoping this question will lead to some explanation of the illusive topic that is Jesse. I've been hoping she is someone he works with, not someone he lives with. I know how different we are. Nice as he may seem, he doesn't believe the way I do. He wouldn't see anything wrong with living with Jesse, loving Jesse, and being on this date with me. I'm desperate for him to not have someone else, but it's probably foolish of me to hope. I don't think there are many virgin zombies.

"I'd rather not talk about that," he answers cryptically.

"You are the most mysterious zombie I know."

"Zombie?"

Shoot!

I sit straight up. I can't believe I let that slip! "Oh, yeah, sorry. That's what I call you. I mean them!" I'm cringing at my stupidity and hoping he isn't offended.

"Where did you come up with that flattering name?"

"Harmony and I found a movie once, in one of the abandoned apartments in her building. It scared me to death and—well, I couldn't help but make the comparison. You know, eating people and rotting body parts -"

"You watch movies in God Town?"

"Yeah. The kids mostly. The adults don't really have time for them. Do you ever see movies?"

"I do."

I can't help but assume that the movies he watches aren't old Disney movies. I'm afraid his kind watches the type of movies that Aunty thought I didn't know about. Naked people and all that stuff.

"Seen anything good lately?" I ask nonchalantly.

"Nothing you'd like," he says with a strange look on his face.

I like it that he's uncomfortable talking about it with me. It proves there's a conscience buried somewhere in that handsome body.

"What do you do in God Town?" he asks, changing the subject.

I don't love the title he's given our haven, but I suppose it's less insulting than what I call him. "I'm a secretary. And I clean the Inn. And pretty much anything anyone needs me to be. That's how we work. We all take care of each other."

"Sounds nice," is his halfhearted reply. "I help people too. For a small price. Pravda isn't interested in the poor, only the rich have a future in this country. My occupation evens things out a little."

"So you're like Zombie Robin Hood?"

He laughs out loud at this new title, his smile promising me that he likes the connotations of my new pet name.

“Something like that.”

We talk and watch the clouds go by for what I’m sure is too long. The blue sky is disappearing into dark pinks and purples, and the clouds are radiant white with silver. I need to get back for Rosa. The thought of Tim starting a search party makes me stand to my feet and stretch.

“Getting sick of me?” he asks.

“No!” I blurt out too quickly. “I just have to get back to Rosa.”

“And Tim?” he asks with more sincerity than sarcasm.

I pull my mask back on before he can read my face. I don’t want to feel anything for Tim, but he has been such an amazing friend. The least I can do is not leave him standing at the Inn worrying.

Chapter Forty-Five

Benjamin Franklin Does Nothing for Me

On the way back up the huge hill, I'm finding out just what kind of shape I'm in. Not great. I can't talk; I'm so out of breath. To my surprise, without my nervous chatter going on and on, Matt tells me more about himself.

"I've always been responsible for Tom. Ever since he was born. Our dad skipped out and mom worked. So Tom was always with me. The day they gave the shot in school, I was in 6th grade. But I wasn't in class when they locked the doors. I was hiding in the bathroom, smoking. It's funny because they told us smoking would kill us, but smoking probably saved my life.

"I heard gunshots and I knew something bad was happening. I climbed out the bathroom window and ran the couple blocks to Tom's school. He was in 1st grade at the elementary school. There were cop cars and army jeeps everywhere. I snuck around and found the windows to Tom's class. I looked in just as they were holding him down. I watched them stick a needle in his head while he cried. I banged on the glass and yelled at them to stop, but then they were coming after me.

"I ran like four miles to my mom's work. She called the school, but they wouldn't let us go get him. Said everyone had to ride the bus home like normal. When he got home, he was so shook up. I felt like it was my fault. I hadn't taken good enough care of him. Neither of us ever went back to school again.

"My mom got the shot the next day at work. She didn't even fight it. I think she did it to show Tom it would be ok. And she didn't want to get fired. Anyway, she died a couple years ago. She was real bad with the disease. Infection ended up killing her. I've been taking care of Tom by myself since then. I found a way to make credits and help people who can't help themselves at the same time. It's a win-win."

Finally cresting the top of the huge hill, I get my breath back as Matt is finishing his story.

"I don't tell very many people that story." he says, making me one of the privileged few. "So, now you know me."

I have a feeling that there is still a lot more to know.

"So you were smoking in 6th grade?" I ask.

"That's what you got out of my life story?" he asks in mock surprise. "I was a tough kid, okay?" He sounds proud of his younger rebellious self. "When did you try smoking?"

"Never." I say simply.

"You've never smoked?"

"Nope. Never tasted alcohol. Never tried drugs."

"You're kidding me?" His voice is full of disbelief and shock. "Is everyone in God Town as sheltered as you?"

I shrug. They wouldn't be in "God Town" if they weren't.

He still doesn't get it at all. How do I explain it?

"Some of them might have done those things before they got Healed, but after you're Healed, you just don't want any of that."

"Don't want it? Or aren't allowed because your God is a dictator?"

"He's not a dictator. If He was, we'd all be healed."

"If he was a dictator, we'd all be better off? That sounds ridiculous, you know that right?"

"No, it's just—if He was the boss of everyone, we'd all do exactly what He wanted, and there wouldn't be a disease. The disease is because He lets people make their own choices." I walk a few steps and then ask him, "If you had the magical power to make everyone love you, would you feel loved by them? If you made them love you, would it be love?"

I'm afraid my question is too confusing, but he seems to follow and answers, "No, they'd be slaves."

"Exactly. If God made everyone love Him, it would be pointless. He wants us to love Him because we want to. Does that make sense?"

"Parts of it. But I can't believe in God, Ivy. If there was a "God" -" he makes air quotes with his fingers again "- up there watching us, He wouldn't let people suffer like this. I've seen people eat babies, Ivy. I've seen drug addicts rape little girls and then kill them. There is just too much crap out there to believe what you're selling. An all-powerful God who made everyone and loves everyone who sat there and let it all turn to crap. I'm sorry. I just can't buy that. How is He loving that little girl who got raped and killed?

Who had no way to protect herself? Tell me, please, I'm all ears."

"We brought this on ourselves, Matt. He made the world perfect and people chose to sin."

"Come on, Ivy," he sounds so disgusted with me. "The 'Eve Ate The Apple' story? That's supposed to explain all this?"

"I know it sounds—hard to believe, but that's why it's called faith, Matt. I can't understand how you can see me, the Living proof, and not believe. I believe in God, and I'm Healed. How is that confusing?"

"So if I just say, 'I believe in God' this nightmare gets all better?"

"No, you have to do more than believe."

"I knew there'd be a catch. There always is."

"I'm not trying to sell you a car, Matt. This is important!"

"Calm down, Ivy," he says, trying to be congenial. "We're just having a friendly hypothetical conversation. Okay, so what else do I have to do other than believe? Swear myself to the church or something?"

"Ugh. You are so exasperating. Do you think the devil believes in God?"

"I don't believe in the devil. People are evil all by themselves."

"Now THAT makes no sense. Your reason for not believing in God is all the evil in the world. You think that a good God can't exist if there is so much bad. So, how can you not believe in the one who makes all the evil? It's easy to see him everywhere!"

"Fine, I'll pretend for the moment that you've won that point, and I'll say I believe in Satan. What of it? I don't worship Satan."

"My question was, if both God and the devil exist, does the devil believe in God?"

"Can we be done with this discussion yet?"

"The Bible says that the demons believe in God, and they are terrified of Him. So, is belief enough to have God's favor?"

"I guess not."

"Exactly!" I'm hoping he's starting to get it. "I believe that Benjamin Franklin was a real person. I believe he invented electricity. But Benjamin Franklin doesn't know me or have anything to do with my life today. You can believe in something without being intimately connected to it."

"I'd like to be intimately connected to you," he says pulling me closer to him—trying to fluster me and change the subject.

Our argument has been going on while we walk, and we are almost back to the house. As we turn the last bend in the road, we are suddenly within yards of a huge crowd of zombies.

Chapter Forty-Six

Raising the Dead

Matt had been holding my hand, despite our heated debate, but now he drops it. He whispers quietly, his tone full of the danger of our situation, "You have to follow me through. If we turn around now, they'll think we have something worth stealing. You have a mask, it will keep you safe. Walk now."

Matt starts forward towards them, but I stand frozen like Lot's wife, turned to a pillar of salt for disobeying God. I shouldn't have come.

Is this my punishment?

Matt said he's never seen them on this road. Was he lying?

I am so stupid!

These zombies will either take me to Pravda or tear me apart because of my own foolishness. I ignored wisdom, and now I'll pay for it. Matt, several yards away now, hisses over his shoulder at me, "Now, Ivy!"

I take a halting step, then another—lifting my legs like the Tin Man right after a long season of petrified rust. I can't think of another option. I have to make it back home. It took longer to walk back than I thought, and it's almost dark out. I've probably already been missed. I pray for safety and beg silently for forgiveness as I try to find my courage. Matt is getting farther ahead of me forcing me to hurry towards the swarming horde. I'm so scared that I am trembling all over as I lunge awkwardly towards Matt. Moving forward is my only option, and I know I can't walk through this crowd of zombies without him.

They don't seem to notice us as we are absorbed by the crowd. Once surrounded, the smell is nauseating. I'm afraid I'll puke. They reek of body odor and infection and poop. It's the most disgusting trifecta of smells I've ever encountered. They are all talking at the same time, shouting to each other and to no one. I've walked into an angry mob of infected, psychotic mental cases. It's literally like being in hell. This is my hell.

I keep losing sight of Matt. My panic is overwhelming. I can't breathe! The gasping breaths I'm taking bring me more of the foul stench and make me retch. I will myself not to throw up inside my mask. In my head I'm screaming Matt's name, and I clamp my teeth on my lower lip to keep the scream inside. I catch glimpses of his unmasked head as he moves steadily ahead of me.

What is his problem!

What if I fall behind?

Would he even turn around and notice?

One of the zombies turns around and screams in my direction. I freeze and bite through my lip. I taste blood in my mouth as I peer through the eye holes of my mask—looking my death in the face. Death wears the plastic mask of a green bogey-monster. The masked goblin suddenly lunges towards me, and I close my eyes waiting for the attack. Shouts are going up all around me. I'm knocked roughly to the pavement.

When seconds go by and I'm not assaulted, I open my eyes. A fight is going on just to the left of me. The goblin is clawing and thrashing with two other masked monsters. Matt lifts me by my coat and pulls me through the rest of the crowd. I start to pick out and understand some of what they are shouting. This is a gang with a purpose.

Their purpose is our destruction.

They are talking about what they'll do when the fence goes down. How they'll kill, what they'll do to people before they kill them, how long it's been since they've had healthy meat.

We break through on the other side, and Matt slows our pace, trying to look unhurried and nonchalant. My feet can't stop hurrying, but I keep his slow pace so it feels like I'm running in place. When we put enough distance between us and them, Matt pulls me into the brush and leads me towards the little house. I pull my hand away from him and sit down defiantly in the dead foliage. I'm not taking another step until my questions are answered. I won't go any further with him until I know the truth.

"Are they planning an attack?" I ask shrilly, still fighting hyperventilating.

He turns and sees me sitting. I'm certain of what I heard, but I'd still love for him to tell me I'm wrong. Tell me this is normal and they always hang out in droves near our fence, armed to the teeth, talking about murder.

His shoulders fall slightly, like he's surrendering information he had hoped not to give. "Yes, I think they are."

I put my head between my knees, and tears begin to wet the scratchy mask against my warm cheeks. I struggle to speak. I need more answers this time. I won't put up with vague anymore.

Matt volunteers the answers in my silence, "It's one of the reasons I brought you out tonight, but I didn't think we'd run into them. I've never seen them on this side of the fence before, I swear. I just wanted to show you it's safe out here and that I can take care of you. I've been hearing a lot of rumors when I'm at the compounds. I am pretty sure Pravda is riling them up on purpose. Now you've seen for yourself why I have to get you and Tom out as soon as possible. They aren't normally this well-armed, Ivy. I think Pravda is turning the mob into an army. From what I can gather, they are after something your people have in there."

He squats down in front of me and gently lifts my chin with his gloved hand. I try to resist, but he says my name softly, "Ivy?" and looks into my eyes again. I must get better at resisting this tactic. His face is so close to mine in the last glow of twilight.

The husky way he says, "I need you to want to come with me," makes me sure that I will go with him. "Will you help me get Tom out when the time comes?" he asks.

He begs me with rare transparency in his eyes, their vivid green tint still flashing in the last light of day. My face is hidden behind the ski mask giving him no way to read what I'm thinking.

"I'm not sure I should."

"Ugh!" He stands up and takes a step away from me. "Ivy, why are you so stubborn? That mob we just saw was a small part of a large group intent on raping and eating you and your friends. How can you still think you are safe in there? You will die if you stay!"

"I won't," I look down at my feet and finish, "because I'm the thing they are looking for."

Matt looks impatient and irritated, turning to and fro in the small cleft of space between the blackberry bushes we're sheltered in. "Is this about what happened in Commerce? That was just some drug addict, Ivy. There's no conspiracy to capture you. Something bigger is happening here. I've known Pravda a long time, and I've never seen them this desperate. Your people must be hiding something important."

I feel belittled and embarrassed. I know what I know, but I don't care if he believes me. I've seen what I needed to see tonight. I have to warn everyone. The missionaries were right. We have to leave as soon as possible. I don't have time to explain about Chuck and his deal with Pravda. Matt might not even believe me if I did tell him. I stand up. I have to get back home. Matt doesn't say anything, but turns to lead the way back to the house.

We are almost through the dense brush around the yard of the old house when I hear a scream. Matt waves violently at me conveying the clear message *Get down and be quiet*. I crouch in obedience. Matt creeps through the overgrown thicket moving out of my sight. I hear more cries and muffled screams. The fear and familiarity in the girl's voice sends a chill through my pounding heart. I fall backwards at the loud bang of a gunshot.

Someone shot him! Matt could be dead!

I'm out here alone!

How will I get back to the tunnel?

Maybe it's Pravda—maybe they've already found the tunnel!

When Matt's familiar voice calls me out of hiding a minute later, my eyes flood with tears of relief. I run through the rest of the thorny branches, scraping my neck, and come out on the shaggy lawn. Matt is near the house crouched over two bodies. I run to him, relieved, but still worried that he could be hurt. I stop a few feet away as the shocking sight of Harmony, covered in blood, fills my view.

How can she be here? What happened to her?!

I hear myself drawing in ragged uneven breaths. My body is lead, and I stand gaping as Matt lifts her gently and listens for breath. He holds her neck and searches for her pulse. He looks up at me with eyes that beg for my forgiveness.

She is dead!

Harmony's eyes stare lifelessly into the darkening sky. Her full lips hang open from her last scream. Her arms hang limply from her tiny frame. Her shirt is soaked with blood around the dark red hole that is torn through her chest. The cross necklace I gave her hangs near the horrible wound.

Best friends.

Matt has blood on his hands and arms, but it's Harmony's blood not his own. A small gun from Matt's pile in the basement lies next to him in the grass. Matt was the one doing the shooting, he brought a gun with him on our "date."

I lose it.

"You killed her!" I scream, oblivious of the dangerous zombies who are still too close by. "Why is she here?"

Horror and panic are pulling me over the edge of reason.

"It was her. In the tunnel. Not a rat. She must have followed us," he says with too little emotion.

It wasn't rats we heard in the tunnel? It was Harmony?

She must have seen me with Matt and followed me. And then somehow this zombie found her. Maybe she had gone through the brush to the road looking for me and was spotted.

I have led her to her death!

This is my fault. And Matt's.

I look at him with terror and hate in my eyes. I want to die too. I can't live with Harmony dead because of me. Ever since meeting Matt the people I love are dying. There might not be much sanity in that connection, but it feels like truth.

"Ivy, I'm so sorry. I couldn't see well enough. He was hurting her, so I shot him; but the bullet went through and hit her! I was trying to save her," his voice is pleading, "please believe me!"

I pull the stifling mask off my face, and cold air hits my fevered cheeks.

And then the world changes again.

As suddenly as the hate and panic took hold, a new feeling comes. It's not of me. My whole being is suddenly full with Him. It's surreal, indescribable. The anger and fear vanishes as I feel Him fill me up, and I know the Peace That Passes Understanding. My legs crumple under me, and I fall to my knees in reverence to His unseen presence. His Spirit alive in me, I know what I need to do.

I crawl forward to my lifeless best friend.

God wants to heal her.

I know it with every fiber of my being, with every piece of my soul. He is calling me to pray for her, and the urge is so strong I don't question myself. It's not my idea, it's His. I wrap my arms around Harmony and lay across her bloody form.

"God! Please!" I call out. I don't have an eloquent prayer, and I know an eloquent prayer has no place here. The Spirit in me is praying; it's not even my words.

Matt tugs on me, asking me to forgive him and whispering that she's gone. I hear him saying we have to go, but he sounds so far away. I ignore him and wrap myself tighter around Harmony.

"God!" I cry louder. "Please!" I beg Him.

But it's really His Spirit begging Himself through me. This prayer is so different from the selfish prayer of fear and need that I prayed over Aunty just two days ago. I had been desperate for God to heal her. I didn't want to live without her. I was afraid to be alone. The prayer was for me.

I know God didn't mind my selfish prayer; it wasn't why He answered "No." I know His heart broke for me, and He held me in His arms when he took my Aunty. He didn't want to break my heart, but Aunty was meant to go home. This prayer for Harmony, so full of God's peace, is different. I know for certain that He wants to restore Harmony, and I wait patiently for His power to come. It has nothing to do with me or my words. It just IS.

Harmony moves in my arms, and I look down at her face. My prayer of faith answered, tears spill down my cheeks onto hers, and she blinks and looks up at me. A scream leaves her lips, and I cover her mouth. I hold her close and whisper words of comfort. When I look to Matt for help getting her up, he is several feet away—sitting on the ground leaning away from us in fear and awe. When I see Matt's face, I realize fully the amazingness of what just happened and how truly different he and I are. I want to help him understand. Maybe now that he's seen, he will change. I suddenly remember that we aren't safe in the open. We need to get back in the tunnel.

Chapter Forty-Seven

Friendship Bites

At the bottom of the steps in the dark, cold cellar, Matt lunges at Harmony. I can't fathom why he is attacking her, and I try to push him away. Matt has hold of her shirt, and he rips it open down the front.

What is he doing?!

Harmony is screaming again in the terrified grips of another assault. I wrench her from Matt's grasp and hold her close to me. But before I wrap her in my arms, I see what he saw. Her sports bra is stained bright red with her blood, but there is no wound on her chest. Matt backs away and paces back and forth in a state of obvious agitation.

"She was dead," I hear him mutter.

Harmony is sobbing. I try to sooth her and reassure her that she's safe now. That Matt doesn't want to hurt her. He's not helping. He looks angry and menacing. It's dark outside now, and I know how late it's getting. I'm in huge trouble. I need to get Harmony home.

I find a shirt in the piles of stuff Matt has stashed in the dark basement. Harmony cowers in a corner and trades the torn, bloody shirt for the new, too big T-shirt. I leave Matt to his mental breakdown and help Harmony into the tunnel. We hurry back through the oppressive darkness to the entrance to our safer world. I've never gotten up the ladder on my own, and I'm not sure I can do it. I'll have to help pull Harmony up too.

I put my hand on the lowest rung of the ladder and take a deep breath. Suddenly, Matt is there next to me. Harmony shrieks again, and it echoes through the tunnels like a banshee's cry. Matt and I both turn impatiently and shush her. She covers her mouth with her hand and looks fearfully back at us. Matt lifts himself easily up the ladder and reaches to help me. His warm hand grabs mine, and I notice he's taken off the bloody gloves.

The physical touch between us does what it always does to me. It boosts my confidence exponentially, warms me with intimacy, and confirms in my heart that I want nothing more than to be with him. Our second date has been fraught with catastrophes.

Would I walk through the tunnel again for a third? Absolutely.

I'd take on the world with him. Harmony stands at the bottom, unwilling to take Matt's hand. I coax her to take one of my hands and one of his. We lift her small frame easily up to ground level without her even having to climb the ladder.

I take her hand to lead her towards home, and Matt grabs my arm gently, holding my attention for one more warning, "Don't let her tell anyone about this."

Harmony barely looks at me during our short, speedy jog. She lets out little sobs between panting breaths as we run. She's desperate to get home and get away from me. I won't leave her alone; I go with her to her door before running to see how much trouble I'm in. I try to reason with her and explain the importance of keeping the tunnel a secret. She doesn't give any indication that she's listening or that she'll comply. I don't have time to beg, and I wouldn't dream of threatening her. Her hands shake as she unlocks her door and ducks inside without a word. She slams and re-locks the door behind her.

"Bye," I mumble to myself and run the last block to the Inn.

I can see Tim pacing outside the back door as I run up the alley behind the Inn. I've left Matt frustrated and Harmony terrified to hurry back to Tim who is furious. I'm not doing great with friends right now. Tim barrels towards me and grabs me by my shoulders.

"Where were you?" he demands, worry and anger fighting for victory over his facial features. I meet his scowl with needy, emotional, tear-filled eyes—desperately hoping that worry will win out over anger. I can't take anymore tonight. I'm completely spent emotionally. If Tim starts yelling at me, I don't think I'll be able to keep myself together.

"I went for a walk?" I mumble as a tear breaks free in the corner of my eye and plunges down my sweaty cheek.

"You've been gone for hours! I looked everywhere. You weren't at the grave, you weren't at the U.R. Where were you?!"

"Tim, I'm sorry. I didn't mean to worry you. Where's Rosa?"

He nods impatiently towards the back door, and I see tiny Rosa sleeping sitting up against the door, bundled in her little jacket.

I feel terrible. I promised to take care of her.

How long has she been huddled there in the cold?

I've hurt three of the people I love with my foolish choice to follow Matt tonight. But was it foolish? It may have been very necessary.

"You're hurt?" Tim asks with concern, gently touching the bloody scratch on my neck where the briars caught me.

"Tim. I can explain, but right now I need you to do something," I wipe my nose and steel myself for the inevitable. I need his help, and that won't come without his anger—without hurting him.

His hands now on his hips, he puts his head back and looks up at the night sky, both frustrated and worried, trying to calm himself.

"I need you to go to the Elders tonight and tell them we're all in danger. The missionaries were right. We have to move as soon as possible. There are gangs of armed zombies gathering around the fence. They are planning to attack us. You have to tell the Elders tonight. I don't know how long we have."

"You were walking the fence? Alone? After everything we learned from Chuck? Are you an idiot, Ivy? Do you have a death-wish? What were you thinking?"

"I wasn't alone," I blurt and then deeply regret.

"Who were you with?"

When I don't immediately answer, Tim looks darkly at my face, my traitorous tattle-tale face, and figures it out. He knows it was Matt. I look down at my shoes, ashamed, testifying that he has indeed guessed right. He steps back from me disgusted and furious.

Anger has won.

Worry never had a chance.

Tim doesn't say a word. He stalks down the driveway without looking back at me. I've hurt him. I don't know if the damage is repairable, and I genuinely hope it can be. I care about him. He's been so good to me, and I hate myself for stabbing him in the back. Matt was right, Tim may have just gotten his first glimpse of the real Ivy.

"Please Tim!" I yell after him. "Tell the Elders tonight! We are in serious danger!"

No indication that he hears or cares.

I pick Rosa up, and she opens her sleepy eyes and smiles at me. Her smile is precious, and I'm thankful for her unconditional love. I hug her tight and take her inside.

*****

Rosa is back to sleep, tucked in my bed. I'm absolutely exhausted. Physically and emotionally drained dry. Before I climb in next to her though, I have to pack. I am thoroughly convinced that we have few days left here in Toccoa. The attack could come at any time. Hopefully the Elders will listen and decide to move us all before it's too late. If we leave as a community, I'm sure I'll be able to take at least one suitcase. If we leave in a panic in the middle of the night however, I'll need to be able to carry my bag and Rosa.

That's the bag I'm packing tonight; a backpack of the most important things. I pack: a change of clothes for Rosa and I, extra socks and underwear, Rosa's Mickey Mouse hat, a toothbrush and a bar of soap. I fill the front pocket with Gov Bars. I'm almost out of room.

What else can I not live without?

Oh, my Taser and my flashlight. And hair bands. I tuck the drawing that Matt made of me in between the pages of Aunty's Bible and add it to the backpack. I have just enough room for the little devotional book that has helped me the most lately. I can't think of anything else that I need or want. I zip the backpack and lay it next to my shoes by my bedroom door. I can leave fast if I need to.

I climb in next to Rosa; and, though I'm exhausted, sleep won't come. I wonder if Matt is sleeping. I wonder if Harmony is okay and if she understands what happened tonight. Did she know she died? Did she feel Him raise her? It was the most incredible thing He's ever used me for. If He never did anything noticeable in my life again, that moment alone will be enough for me to know who He is—how awesome He is—for the rest of my life.

My tired eyes tear up again just remembering how it felt to be so full with Him. That must be what heaven will feel like. To be that closely connected to our Source. Aunty has that now. Tears fall and quiet sobs shake my tired body and make my stomach hurt.

What about Tim? He must hate me. I wonder if I'll ever see him again. I know I have a choice to make. Matt has asked me to go with him "when the time comes," and I know the time is coming fast; if not tonight, then maybe tomorrow. I wonder where we'll go. I know Matt lives in Atlanta, but I can't go there. That's Pravda central. Ground zero. I wouldn't last a day there. Matt doesn't believe me though about how much they want me. What if I can't make him understand? What if I pick to go with him and miss out on leaving with the others and he still wants to go to Atlanta?

I have to think of Rosa, too. I know where I want to take her. A warm beach. I don't know how far away we are from a nice beach in Florida, but surely it can't be that far. Georgia is only one state away from Florida. I bet we could get there in a few hours. I think life would be so much more bearable if the weather was warm and hospitable. This awful cold is just one more reason to hate life. I can just picture me and Rosa and Matt and Thomas splashing in the ocean. Far from zombies. Far from Pravda. With the sound of the ocean in my mind, I fall into a fitful sleep next to Rosa.

Chapter Forty-Eight

This Is a First For Me

Rosa wakes me by tapping gently on my cheek. When I open my eyes she's just inches from my face. It's still dark out, but I can tell the sun is starting to rise. It is morning, and we made it through the night.

"Hi," I say with a smile and a yawn.

She smiles in response. She still hasn't spoken. She points at her open mouth to tell me she's hungry. I don't even know if she had dinner yesterday. I feel guilty again for making them wait hours for me last night.

I love waking up to guilt. It's such a great way to start your day.

*****

I make Rosa and I duck egg omelets with the last of the eggs and cheese. Aunty was in charge of trading for food and keeping the fridge stocked. I feel her absence everywhere this morning; her kitchen, her crocheted tablecloth, her bible verses on the fridge. She was memorizing the book of Revelation. Rosa waves for my attention; she wants me to blow on her bites. It's kind of amazing how easily we have fallen into this mother/daughter relationship. She wants to be taken care of, and I want to have something to live for, someone who needs me.

I don't know where Jack and Ben are or if they are even still staying here. I guess they've been eating their meals somewhere else. I try to tell myself that I can't take care of everyone; that Aunty would understand. I want to live up to what she wanted me to be, and I'm worried that I'm already falling short.

Rev. Depold said that Ms. Scott would be coming by sometime today to officially take over for me. If Tim took my message to the Elders, hopefully they are planning to move everyone. I'm worried that they won't take my warning seriously enough. I'm relieved that the attack didn't happen in the night, but I feel certain it's coming soon. If we are relocating, Ms. Scott won't be taking over the Inn. I think she would've been terrible at it anyway.

When the doorbell rings, I assume it's someone coming to tell us what the Elders have decided. Through the leaded glass door I see Jose standing outside. I hope nothing is wrong with Thomas as I hurry to unlock the door and let Jose in.

"Hello, Ivy."

"Hi. Is anything wrong with Thomas?"

"No, he's doing great. Actually, I'm here because Ellen and I were hoping you'd keep him company during the meeting today. Ellen thought maybe you wouldn't mind missing it; and she and I both want to be there."

"Oh. Sure. When is it?"

Jose looks suddenly uncomfortable when he realizes this is the first I've heard of the town meeting. I guess he's worried he's told me something I wasn't supposed to know.

"It's okay," I try to sound nonchalant. "I knew there'd be a meeting, I just hadn't heard what time."

I don't even consider this a lie. I'm more "in the know" than anyone at this point. I wonder if they asked Tim to tell me. That's a good possibility and a likely reason for my ignorance. He's probably really mad at me.

"I'd love to watch Thomas. I don't need to be at the meeting."

"Oh. Are you sure?" Jose looks like he'd like to back out of his request.

"Totally. I'll have Rosa with me if that's okay? What time do you want me at your house?"

"Uh, 11:45 would be great. Thank you."

Rosa has been hiding behind my legs peeking out at Jose. She suddenly sneezes and Jose squats down to her eye level and says, "Dios te bendiga."

Rosa smiles shyly at him and looks up at me with bigger eyes than normal. I think she understood him.

"¿Estás bien?" Jose asks her.

I don't speak any Spanish. I have absolutely no idea what he said. But it's one of the happiest moments I've had in ages when I hear Rosa's sweet little voice respond quietly, "Sí.."

I laugh and pick her up and hug her close. Jose stands back up and turns to go. He has no idea what an important thing he's just been part of.

"Jose!" I call out as he is stepping back outside. "Can you tell her that I love her? Please? Can you tell her for me that I'll always take care of her?"

Jose studies me for a moment. He looks skeptical. He's probably worried about promising this sweet little girl something that neither of us have true control over. Only God can make such promises. I know that, but I want to say it anyway. Is that stupid? I think it's the kind of thing a mom promises her little girl, even if it's not always kept. It's still what my heart wants.

Jose reaches out and takes Rosa's little hand. They have the same skin tone and similar eyes. He speaks quietly with sincerity, "Ivy te ama. Ella quiere cuidar de ti."

I can't be sure of what he said to her, but she looks sweetly at me and then hugs my neck. Jose has already stepped outside and pulled the door closed behind him. I spin Rosa around and around in the foyer until we are dizzy. We fall on the carpet laughing and she climbs into my arms for a snuggle.

*****

A few hours later, Rosa and I arrive at Jose and Ellen's a little early. I brought our bag of belongings with me. I plan to keep it on me wherever I go now. I hope Matt will find me and give me some warning when it's time to leave. But I'll be ready to go no matter what. I also decided to bring the bag of toys for Thomas that I've had in my closet. I should've sent them to him days ago. He's been stuck in bed with so little to do. I just never thought of it in all the chaos that has been my life this week.

I take Rosa in to meet Thomas while Jose and Ellen finish getting ready. He's sitting in a wheelchair this time, and I'm happy to see him out of bed.

"Wow! You're looking great kid!"

"Thanks," he nods happily, "I'm getting better."

"This is Rosa," I say introducing her. "Tom," I say looking at Rosa and pointing to Thomas. Now that I know she's capable of speech, I'm trying to remember to point to things and say their name. At home, after Jose left, she followed me around the house and listened to me point to different things and name them. She never tried to repeat me, but she smiled the whole time and wanted the new game to go on and on. Even on the walk to Thomas' she pointed at houses and trees, looking to me for each word.

"Hi Rosa!" Thomas says sweetly. He's more kind and gentle than other boy's his age and I can tell he likes her already. "Where did she come from?"

Thomas asks.

"I don't know very much about her. One of the missionaries brought her. He said he rescued her near Atlanta."

"Just like me!" Thomas proclaims.

I hadn't even thought of that connection. Thomas will probably love Rosa even more for that.

"Was it Harvey?" Thomas asks. "Harvey was great with kids."

I don't want to tell Thomas that Harvey didn't come home for the homecoming. It seems Jose and Ellen haven't told him.

"No, a missionary named Jack. He looked like a wild mountain man when he showed up at my door. I thought he was Big Foot or something!"

"Big Foot?" Thomas asks, too young to have heard of the old legend.

So much has been lost in the decline of civilization. Kids his age used to know all about Big Foot and the Abominable Snowman and the Teenage Mutant Ninja Turtles. Now, with no television, and most of life being a constant survival situation, the heroes and monsters that were common knowledge when I was a kid are dead.

"Never mind," I say with a smile.

I reach up and rub my hand over the stubble of Thomas' buzz cut. I miss his cute curly locks. The stitches on his head look much better and the cut on his face is healing fast. Last time I was here, his arm was in a sling. Today it's propped up on a small pillow on his lap, no sling, wrapped in layers and layers of gauze.

"How's the hand?" I ask when he sees me looking at it.

His sunny face gets cloudy, "Pretty ugly. Mom re-bandages it every day. It keeps getting infected. The Doctor found me some Penicillin, but it didn't make it all better. Mom puts herbs on it and they help. It still hurts." Then, in a conspiratorial whisper, he asks, "Does Matt know about it?"

I guess Thomas has figured out that I'm not supposed to see Matt but that I do. It's nice to talk about Matt with someone who is happy hearing his name. I'm used to hiding him. I choose my words carefully, not wanting to say something that would upset Thomas or get me into trouble with Jose and Ellen.

"Yes, he does. Actually, I need you to keep another secret. Can you?"

He nods "yes" emphatically; thrilled to know anything that has to do with his big brother.

"He gave me something to give to you." I pull the glove out of my bag.

I remembered to pack it this morning after Jose stopped by. Before we left the Inn, Rosa pulled it out of the top of my bag and slipped her hand inside. The glove has technology that responds to human flesh. When Rosa put her hand in, it tightened around her hand and filled in the rest of the fingers it thought she was missing because her hands are so tiny. She made a nervous little squeak and pulled it off quickly. Now, handing it to Thomas, he looks just as uncomfortable with it.

"I don't want that."

I hold it out to him, but he doesn't reach to take it.

"Matt thought it would help you use your right hand again," I say with fake encouragement.

To be honest, I don't much like the thing either. I feel nervous holding it out to him, knowing Jose or Ellen could walk in at any moment to say they are leaving. I tuck it back into my bag.

"You can just think about it while you get better. Matt doesn't understand how we are different. I understand why you don't want it; it's their thing. But you might decide it's useful someday."

"Do you think Matt will decide to follow God?" he asks with concern lining his young face.

"I really hope so." I answer with full sincerity. "I want him to be healed as much as you do."

"You like him, huh?" Thomas asks, a little disappointed.

I don't know what to say. I know Thomas has the whole "puppy love" thing going on.

"I like him almost as much as I like you," I say, rubbing my hand over his shaved head again.

Thomas' smile spreads over his face again. He whispers, "I tried to tell Matt about God when we were together, but right when he started to listen and ask me about it is when we got attacked."

Matt has never told me about what happened after he left here with Thomas. He doesn't like to talk much about serious things. Especially serious things that make him feel feelings he doesn't want to feel.

Jose is suddenly standing in the doorway and I wonder how much he heard. He asks me to speak with him in the hallway and my stomach twists. I can already tell what's coming. Jose whispers that I'm not to talk about sad or frightening things with Thomas. Especially not about Matt.

What can I do but agree to follow their rules?

I nod my consent, avoiding Jose's eyes. I think Thomas deserves to know what's going on.

Ellen goes over a few instructions for me as they are leaving, "Thomas can have one Tylenol if he starts to hurt more. He doesn't need his other medicine until tonight and we plan to be back within two hours."

"We'll be fine," I promise.

Shutting and locking the door behind them, I walk back to Thomas' room and find Thomas and Rosa playing together. I show Thomas all the cool toys we brought for him and help him open them. He lets Rosa strum the guitar with him. He's most excited about the skateboard and can't wait to get well enough to start "doing cool jumps and riding it down hills." I bet you two pints of blood Jose and Ellen aren't going to let that happen.

*****

I have had a lot of firsts lately. First love. First date. First child, kind of. Jose and Ellen have only been gone twenty minutes when another first happens. For the first time in the five years our community has been living here, the warning alarms start to sound.

Chapter Forty-Nine

The Tunnel of Love

As prepared as I thought I was for this, it's super scary. Rosa and Thomas look up at me, confused about the loud noise but unaware of what it means.

Thomas can tell something is wrong and he yells, "What is it Ivy?"

Thomas's house is close to the fence, and the alarms are deafening. I have to shout back, "It's an attack! We have to get out of here!"

I run to the window to see what's going on outside. No one is in sight out there, no infected and no Living either. I have to get the kids out of here and to the tunnel. Turning back to face Thomas in his wheelchair, I'm not sure how I'll do it.

Then suddenly Matt is there. I can't believe how I feel when I see him stride confidently into Thomas' room. I'm instantly calmer. He's here now. He cares for Thomas and, for some reason, he cares for me. He is here and nothing can hurt us. I feel safer with him because he's one of them. I know we don't believe in hurting them or fighting them. And I totally agree with that. I don't want to hurt anyone. But is it bad that I feel safer with Matt because I know he would stop at nothing to make sure we're okay?

Matt goes straight to Thomas. He hasn't seen him since he carried him bloody and dying into the compound. He wraps him tenderly in a hug made awkward by the wheelchair. I can see both relief and guilt on his face. Will he ever forgive himself for letting Thomas get hurt? And can he keep us safer this time? There are even more of us. We can't live in the tunnel. Where can we go to be safe?

"What's happening?" I shout at him over the scream of the sirens.

"We have to hurry," he yells, close to my ear "They came in on the other side. I did some scouting last night, and you were right. They are here for you. Everyone has your picture and Pravda is promising a lifetime of happiness for whoever brings you to them alive."

Hearing Matt say "a lifetime of happiness" plants a seed of doubt in the pit of my gut. I can't help but wonder if I can trust this boy that I've been falling for. He doesn't believe. He doesn't follow the path of righteousness. He is one of the most attractive men left of their kind. Surely he could have anyone he wanted. I'm not naive enough to think that he loves me and that love is enough.

What is to keep him from turning me in? Buying freedom for Thomas?

That's his greatest desire isn't it? To live his life with his little brother in safety.

He walks towards me, and I shrink back—overwhelmed with my precarious predicament. There are hundreds of zombies hunting me out there. Matt holds his hands up in front of himself to show me he's not trying to touch me or take me. He comes close to me and looks into my eyes. Like pulsing emerald stones, his magical eyes cast their spell. I relax in his closeness and take a deep steady breath.

He leans close to my ear, his cheek against mine, and says, "I'm going to keep you safe. I know I told you not to trust anyone, but you CAN trust me."

His breath against my ear is intoxicating. He puts an arm behind me and pulls me even closer to his lips. His arms are comforting, but different than Tim's. They feel tense like iron even though he holds me gently.

His lips brush my cheek as he promises, "I hate Pravda and everything they stand for. They are my enemy as much as they are yours. I promise to get you out of here. Will you come with me?"

I love him for asking me nicely and not trying to boss me. I nod that I will go with him. I had no idea he hated Pravda that much, and I want to know why.

Our mutual enemy?

No time to give heed to these new questions—right now, we have to run.

"I'm all ready," I say grabbing my bag. Rosa is standing near me, surprisingly calm, and as always, ready to follow me anywhere.

Thomas on the other hand is not ready. He's in a wheelchair, no shoes on, no bag packed, wounds that need constant care, and medicines that I don't know how to find. Matt pulls the blankets off of Thomas' bed and throws a pair of pants on the bottom sheet. I see what he's doing and hurry to help. I go quickly through Thomas' dresser and find the Steelers' sweatshirt and the Steelers' jersey right next to each other. No time to worry about embarrassing Thomas, I find his underwear drawer and throw a few pairs on the bed.

Leaving Matt to pull the rest together, I go to the kitchen with Rosa in my arms. Ellen told me where to find the Tylenol, and I'm desperately hoping to find his other meds there, too. I grab the painkiller and the two other bottles sitting with it and tuck them in my bag. Back in Thomas' room, I find Matt lacing up Thomas' shoes for him. I don't even know if Thomas is up to walking.

Matt has grabbed the four corners of the sheet and tied them up, making a sack of Thomas' things. One more glance around the room to make sure there isn't anything else we should take. I'm sure there are a lot of things he will wish we had grabbed for him; such is our occasionally rotten life.

We have to get to the tunnel before the mob makes its way over to this side of the compound. Throwing the sack on Thomas' lap, Matt wheels him out of the room. Thomas is asking for Jose and Ellen as we hurry from the house. Neither Matt nor I say anything. There is little chance that we'll ever see them again.

The tunnel entrance is only a short distance from Thomas' house—if you go through yards. Wheel chairs aren't ideal for yards, ditches and low laying shrubs. Thomas winces in pain over every jolt. Matt's face is grim as he hurries us over the shortest distance, hating how much he is hurting his Tom. But fear of worse injury drives him forward.

The sirens are screaming, and it feels like my eardrums might burst. Outside of the house and this close to the fence, the volume is maddening—driving all other thoughts out of my head. I can't think. I just want relief from the panic-inducing, repetitious blaring. As we dart past a clearing, I see the North gate about two blocks away. For the first time since the fence was put up, the gate is hanging open and unprotected. But there isn't an infected soul to be seen anywhere on the other side. They truly are all on the other side of the compound.

Searching for me.

Killing my friends.

The mind bending siren, the panic and pressing fears, all of this has kept me from processing what's really happening—until now. Tim. Harmony and Sherry. Rev. Depold. Mr. Terrell. Dr. Markowitz. Dr. Talmurf. Jose and Ellen. Frank and Jean Hosch. They may all die because of me.

Agony hits my soul with so much force that I stumble and my legs buckle. My eyes are an ocean, and the watery blindness brings my panicked getaway to a full stop. If I went back now, could I save anyone? Would the onslaught cease when they found me? I know I won't be able to live with myself if I don't try. But then Rosa is pulling on me. I blink the tears away and look into her young, innocent face. She understands who we're running from. She has been running longer than I have. I can't let them kill her. Would Matt take her for me? Protect her?

Matt has reached the tunnel. He looks up to see me across the yard standing still. Our eyes meet and he knows what I want. Somehow he knows. He angrily shakes his head "no." Leaving Thomas sitting in his wheelchair next to the hole in the ground, Matt runs back towards me glaring and yelling over the siren's screams. I can only make out every other word in the minuscule pauses between the steady beats of the blaring noise.

"You—save them—vy!" he yells, "- too late! Please—, I need -. Tom—Rosa need y- Stay—me! Help me!" He's run close enough for me to make out most of his words. "I can't get Tom through the tunnel without you. Save us!" he screams. "You can't save them!"

He points away towards the rest of town, and I follow his finger. The sky is full of black smoke. They are burning the town down. I pray for God to forgive me as I hurry to help Matt with Thomas.

Matt goes down first, and I toss down all of our things. Then I gently ease Thomas out of the wheel chair and help him sit on the edge of the hole. He grimaces in pain but doesn't cry or complain. I hold under Thomas' good arm and half lift/ half push him into the opening. Matt catches him at the bottom, and Thomas cries out in pain.

I try to hand the wheelchair down to Matt, but it won't fit in the hole. It takes me several moments of tears and frustration to finally fold it and shove it down to Matt. I lift Rosa down next; and, finally, jump in myself.

Matt climbs back up the ladder and pulls the heavy piece of wood over the opening, sealing us in noisy darkness.

Thomas is crying. Rosa is crying. I'm crying. All the people we've lost swim before my tear filled eyes. The world is broken and wrong. Everyone we know may be dead. They will wake to the sweet peace of eternity. We are still stuck here in Hell.

Matt doesn't give us long to cry. He lifts Thomas into the wheel chair and grabs the sheet full of belongings. I pick up Rosa and carry our bag, trying to follow close behind Matt. The wheelchair barely fits through the tunnel. Matt has to crouch behind it and push it through with laborious, back-breaking shoves. The pipe we traverse is completely round with no flat surface for the wheels. It's a slow process, slogging our way through the dark. My feet keep stumbling, despite how many times they've traveled the pipe, because I feel dead inside and disconnected.

When we get to the other end of the tunnel, Matt says we should rest for awhile before trying to lift Tom and the wheelchair up into the shelter of the little house. I don't even know how we'll do it after we rest. Thomas must weigh around a hundred pounds. If Matt goes up the ladder and leans down for him, he'll have to grab him by his arms which will definitely reopen Thomas' wounds—if we haven't reopened them already. I don't have the strength to lift him even half way up. We may have to stay down here in the rat filled tunnel for days. I'm so despondent, I can't muster any hope that Matt can come up with a solution.

Chapter Fifty

God Gives Me More

We sit for a long time. The siren is muffled on our far end of the tunnel, but it still rattles my soul. Matt goes up into the house and brings down blankets and Gov. Bars. The kids eat; and, after we make them a soft spot on the ground with blankets, they fall asleep together. I marvel again at how unique Thomas is. Rosa is a shy little girl, untrusting of most everyone. But there she lies, cuddled close to Thomas not long after meeting him. To know Thomas is to know sweetness and innocence.

Matt sighs as he sits down next to me and searches in the dark for my hand. His touch gives me comfort and lifts me a few degrees out of my despair. I find God there, hovering above my self-loathing darkness. He was politely waiting for me to turn to Him; sitting quietly in my spirit until I was ready to talk. I don't really pray or form any requests in my head, I just let Jesus give me the peace and comfort of His presence. I know He has a plan, and I hope I haven't messed it up too badly.

Am I supposed to be here?

Matt caresses my hand with his thumb, and I feel the attraction stir again. I feel guilty for having those feelings right now. I wonder wryly if this counts as our third date. After all, we did walk through the tunnel again. I think it's safe to say that I have bad taste in men.

After what feels like hours of sitting in the dark with Matt's arm around me, new sounds start to echo down the tunnel. Something big is coming towards us. I'm scared that it is giant rats and even more scared that it's not. Matt shushes me and climbs over me, putting himself between me and whatever is noisily approaching. A soft sound like someone crying carries to where I sit. Then I hear Harmony quietly call my name.

"Matt, it's Harmony!" I jump up and hit my head on the pipe.

In the blind darkness, bright colorful lights fill my vision. Matt catches me as I stumble and sits me down gently.

"I'll get her," he says, brushing my forehead with his lips.

Several feet down the pipe I hear Harmony demand in a quavering voice, "Where is Ivy? Do you have her?"

"I'm here," I call.

She stifles a sob and follows the sound of my voice until she stumbles on top of me. I feel her thin arms around me, and I hurt for her as I feel her whole body shake with silent sobs against me.

"They're all gone!" she wails in the darkness, and her voice echoes down the tunnels.

"Ivy, she has to be quiet!" Matt insists.

I shush her and hug her tightly.

"Did you re-cover the hole?" Matt asks impatiently.

I wish he could be a little more sensitive. She's been through so much in the last twenty-four hours. She's fragile, and this is too much for her. I feel Harmony shake her head "no" on my shoulder, and I purse my lips. I know Matt is going to be mad.

"She couldn't have reached Matt; and she wouldn't have been strong enough if she could reach."

"I'll be back," he says flatly.

I know Harmony wasn't part of his plan. He had a hard enough job getting me, Rosa and Tom to somewhere safe. Adding delicate, terrified Harmony to the list of his charges is not what he wanted.

When Matt comes back from recovering the hole, he is quiet. I can tell, even in the dark, that he's angry.

"Who did you tell!" he finally demands, his tone full of hate and disgust.

"What are you talking about?" I bristle.

"Not you, her," he accuses. "She told someone. There were people calling for you up above. Very near the tunnel."

"Who?" I ask excited and hopeful that some of our members still Live. "We have to go help them!"

"No."

"What do you mean, 'No!' Of course we have to! They'll be killed if we don't!"

"And we'll be killed if we do. First of all, if any escaped it was intentional. Pravda hasn't found you, and they'll follow those poor bastards right to us.

She's put us in way more danger than you realize. Second of all, suppose we let some of them down here? You think they're going to let you and Tom go with me? You think they will follow me and elect me their new leader?"

My silence answers him.

"No. They won't. We'll be lucky to not be found now. I pulled some brush over the wood cover. It's getting dark; I don't think anyone will find the tunnel tonight. But you can bet Pravda will have people scouring every inch of ground when they don't find you tonight. We can't stay here long."

"I'm sorry, Ivy." Harmony whispers.

"There's nothing to be sorry for!" I assure her quietly. "I'm so glad you're safe. I wouldn't change it for the world."

I remember the look in her eyes last night when she sat back up, dead and then suddenly alive again. There is a plan here. God is orchestrating something big. I'm comforted every time I think of how He leads and directs me. I hope I'm in His plan now. I hope I've followed wisdom and not my fears or my hormones. I think I'm supposed to be here now; but, if I'm wrong, then I'm probably guilty of the murder of a lot of Saints.

"What if my mom got away? What if she's up there? We have to go see who it is Ivy!" Harmony begs.

"How many people did you tell," I ask her gently.

"Everyone," she says softly.

"What does that mean, 'everyone?'" Matt asks, still furious.

"I went to the meeting. Everyone did. They were trying to decide if they should move the whole community somewhere else. I stood up to testify that we were unsafe. I told them about following you and about the tunnel. They sent Captain Markowitz and me out of the meeting so I could show him where it was. We were walking to the tunnel when the alarms went off. He—he left me."

I feel her shiver in my arms, and I picture her out in the streets alone with the blaring alarms. In the dark, I can visualize the terror that must have been on her face.

"He told me to go home, and he ran back towards the U.R. I went home like he said, and I saw it all out my window. They surrounded the U.R. and brought everyone out. They were searching through the crowd for someone and -" Harmony's voice catches. "They killed almost everyone," she sobs.

Her weeping fills the echoey tunnel. I feel like I was there with her because I can see it all happening. She recounted the story, but it might as well be my own memory. I've been dwelling on my own imagined images since abandoning my friends and climbing down in this hole to hide like a coward.

"Then they set the U.R. on fire and the Inn."

I choke back a sob. The Inn, my life with Aunty, is burning out there; being wiped from the earth as though those sweet years never happened.

"I saw them split up in groups and start out towards the other buildings. I knew they'd find me, so I went out the back and ran here. I didn't know where else to go."

Harmony and I cry together and eventually my tears run out. She continues to shake and sniffle in my arms. After a few minutes of listening to her cry, I suddenly know what to do. The idea gives me sudden hope and strength.

"Matt, you can go get a car."

"Where am I going to get a car, Ivy?" he spits the words, still angry.

I don't like being talked to like that, but I'm going to ignore it for now.

"We have cars in the compound," I explain coolly. "Working cars, full of gas. I can tell you where they're kept and where we keep the keys. They won't suspect you. You can walk right in and take one!"

He silently considers this and begrudgingly admits my brilliance, "Ok, it could work. Where are they?"

I smile with satisfaction in the dark. "Your favorite place. They are in the lower garage level of the old police station. The keys are in the office right down the hall from the cell where Captain Markowitz kept you."

Chapter Fifty-One

A Declaration of Love

Matt has been gone for a long time. The gun he insisted on leaving with me lies next to me like a piece of ice against my leg. There are no circumstances under which I will use it. I let Matt leave it for his own comfort, but it is anything but a comfort to me. Harmony is holding Rosa and talking quietly with Thomas. They've both just lost their loved ones. I sit down the tunnel a ways and let them share their grief. I've always considered myself stronger than Harmony; but, as I watch her, I realize I was wrong.

When I was attacked, it rocked my whole world. Then I lost Aunty two weeks later. This has been the hardest month of my life. Harmony went through all of that and more in just twenty-four hours. She was attacked, shot, brought back to life and then lost her mom, her town, and her whole world the next day. And she is sitting there caring for Thomas and gently petting little Rosa, her spirit still intact. Harmony is still herself. I almost lost myself in my trials.

God has kept her here with me for a reason. Last night, after the miracle, I thought that His reason was Matt. God showed His Glory magnificently to Matt, and I thought it was so that Matt would believe and find Life. Then, when Harmony came down the tunnel tonight still alive, I thought He must have an awfully special plan for her. But now—I wonder if he brought her because I need her. I need her example. I need her friendship. I need her solid consistency. She is stronger than me.

I am worried about Matt. I've prayed fifty times for him to make it back to us with a car and no more complications. I hope nothing went wrong. We can't get out of the tunnel without Matt, and we need him to survive. If he doesn't come back for us—We might as well have died with our friends.

I need him.

*****

After hours of waiting and worrying, I fall into a nightmare filled sleep. In my nightmares, there is no plot, no conversation, just violence and terror. I see the people I knew laying slain in the streets. I stumble over a body, and I find that it is Aunty. She is old and bloody and something has torn her apart.

I shriek and scream as her blue eyes fly open and lock me in an icy gaze. I feel more eyes on me, and I run because I am being hunted. There is no comfort in this dark world; no friend and no God. I'm alone. I hear them coming, I hear their voices.

I gasp, suddenly awake, because the voices are here, and they are real. The siren has finally stopped. In the new silence, I hear noises above us in the cellar.

Talking.

More than one person.

More than one voice.

Urgent, angry whispers and the creaking of the old wooden stairs. We are in real trouble now. Matt isn't back, and I'm the only one who can protect us. I feel my way over to Harmony, Thomas and Rosa. I whisper to them, trying to wake them, and I feel in the dark for their faces. Putting my hands over their mouths, I try to make them understand that they have to be quiet.

I remember the gun. The thought of it sends a shiver through my arms. I could just hold it. It would look intimidating. I could never pull the trigger. I crawl back to where I had been sitting and feel around in the dark for the icy metal. My hands rub through the dirt and muck that lies in a crust along the bottom of the pipe. Disrupting the filth sends foul odors to my crinkled nose.

I long for light and simultaneously thank God that I can't see. I brush against the gun in the darkness and send it skittering against the pipe where it makes a dull chime. I cringe and reach for it again, this time enclosing the barrel with my shaking hand. It is heavy as I fumble to hold it correctly.

I don't know what to do now. Should I lead Harmony, Rosa and Thomas back through to the other side? Could I push the wheelchair through? More danger waits back on our side of the tunnel. We could try one of the other tunnels, but I have no idea where they would lead us. We could get stuck at a dead end, trapped and alone with the rats.

I pray.

Lord, you are with me. You've brought me this far. That dark world of my nightmares doesn't exist. There's nowhere I can go that You won't be with me. Please help me protect them, Lord. I don't know what to do.

There are footsteps above, and they get closer.

Someone is looking down into the hole.

"Ivy?" Matt whispers my name.

I squat in silence, hoping that Harmony and Thomas will stay silent. I don't allow myself to feel relief at Matt's voice.

Who was the other person?

I know for certain that we can't trust one of them. I'm gold to them. I question my decision to go with Matt for the thousandth time tonight.

Maybe I did choose wrong.

Maybe God wanted me to stay up there and give myself up to save the others.

How many people have I killed by trusting my untrustworthy teenage girl heart?

Then I hear the other voice, and the new voice knows my name too.

"Ivy?" Tim's baritone voice fills the darkness.

"Tim?" I call back hesitantly from the shadows.

"It's okay, Ivy, you can come out. It's just me. I'm here."

And I'm crying again. Crying in relief. Crying because Tim is okay. Crying because I still feel so guilty about everyone else. I drag myself over to the light pouring down through the hole and look up into their flashlights. They are both there, peering down at me. In the same moment, they both reach a hand down to help me up into the cellar. It's probably awkward and strange for them, but I'm relieved beyond words to have them both.

I cast the gun aside and give them each one of my hands. Matt and Tim pull me up out of the hole. I stand still for only a second, and then I hug them both. First Matt—just a short quick hug. Without looking at Tim to see his reaction, I put myself into his arms next. I hold Tim just a few seconds longer and whisper "I'm sorry" into his ear as I cry. He returns my embrace, and I hope it means that he's less angry with me.

Pulling away from Tim, I turn again to Matt. "What happened? What took so long? Did you get a car? How are you here?" I finish with my last question directed at Tim, relief and happiness filling my face and voice.

They both start talking. Tim is more of a gentleman—*understatement*—so he motions for Matt to go first.

Before Matt begins answering my long list of questions, Harmony calls out from the tunnel, "Can we please get out of here?"

The guys help Harmony and Rosa up into the cellar, and then we coordinate how they'll get Thomas out.

Tim is a miracle in more than one way. With him here now, I'm sure we'll be able to get Thomas out of the tunnel without causing him too much pain. Matt goes down in and gently lifts Thomas up in his arms and then slowly up over his head, proving the strength of his muscular arms. Tim lies on his stomach and reaches down into the hole and takes Thomas from Matt. Harmony is sitting on Tim's legs to help him lift with leverage and not fall down into the hole himself. I sit ready next to Tim; and, as soon as Thomas is high enough, I reach out and help pull him the rest of the way out.

It took all four of us, but praise God we did it. We were so gentle that Thomas never even winced. Matt tosses up all of our belongings before coming back up himself. The gun that he left with me glints from where it is tucked into the back of his pants.

We stand and look at each other. We are such an unlikely group; one zombie, one Spanish speaking innocent, and four Living. We range in age and in belief. We actually have little in common. But we are suddenly a family. We need each other. These faces are my whole world now.

I ask Matt again, "What happened?"

After lighting several lanterns and dousing his flashlight, Matt sits down on a blanket and everyone but Tim follows suit. Tim leans against the wall, probably not as happy as I am about his new "family."

"It took me a while to get around to where they broke in. I didn't want anyone to see me leave this house, and I didn't want to be seen skirting around the fence. I couldn't risk anyone following me so I took my time; staying out of sight."

I picture him familiarizing himself with every bunch of shrubbery between here and the West Gate. I smile at him, and he winks at me in the low light. He knows what I'm thinking as usual. I like that we have our own private joke.

"I went in where they took out the fence, right near the gate by the Inn. It's like Mardi Gras in there now. They have bonfires everywhere and they're just standing around partying and watching the town burn. I didn't see any Pravda workers anywhere. Which is bad. It means that they interrogated enough people with the same story, and they know you aren't there anywhere."

"What do you mean? How could they know that?"

Matt tilts his head towards Harmony. "She just finished telling the entire town that you come and go when you want through a secret tunnel. Pravda probably interrogated a handful of people and all of them gave up the same story."

He keeps saying interrogated, but I know he means tortured. They wouldn't have just given me up like that unless they were being hurt or watching their family members get hurt. Just like Chuck Fox. When someone you love is being hurt and you can make it stop, you tell the bad guys what they want to know. I feel sick. I haven't eaten since this morning, but I feel vomit in my throat. Our people went through agony because of me.

Matt continues softly, "So, I pretty much walked right in like part of the crowd. I wore a mask, figured I'd fit in even better. I found the cars right where you said, but there were only a couple of them there. I don't think Pravda took them because there were lots of keys in the office. I think maybe some of your people got out. Maybe some of them knew how to hot wire a car, maybe they had extra keys. Either way, there were way more keys than cars. I grabbed all the keys, and went to take the largest car left. I made the mistake of taking off my mask in the garage. That's when I picked up the extra baggage." He jerks his head at Tim. "Guess he figured his girlfriend would be with me," Matt says too lightly, his antagonism intentional.

Tim doesn't respond. He stares down at his feet, and his face burns with the heat of barely restrained anger. I feel terrible. Tim feels betrayed by me. His dad and brother are gone, and he probably blames me. I know I would. I won't ask him again how he made it out. He has every right to ignore me.

"What now?" I say out loud to everyone.

Matt answers, "I think we need to leave as soon as possible. I had planned on staying here a day or two, but I don't think we can risk Pravda finding this house or finding the tunnel. They are looking for it as we speak. We should leave Toccoa tonight."

"And where do you plan to go?" Tim asks with restrained hostility.

"I'm taking Tom and Ivy, and I guess Rosa, to Atlanta."

"What!" Tim and I exclaim together.

"Matt, I can't go to Atlanta. That's Pravda headquarters. I want to get as far away from Atlanta as possible. You know they're hunting me. Surely you understand we can't go there? I was hoping for a nice beach in Florida somewhere."

"You aren't taking Ivy anywhere. Not to Atlanta, not to a beach," Tim says with a wilting look of irritation thrown in my direction, "she is staying with me!"

Matt is sitting with his back against the wall, his knees are up in front of him with his forearms resting on top of them and his hands folded. He looks at his gloved hands and then up into my eyes. "Ivy, do you know a man named Frank Lusato?"

My breath catches in my throat and my heart stops beating. "How do you know that name?"

"Who is he?" Matt asks, still staring at me.

"My dad. That was my dad's name." I say it as though my dad is dead. I've believed my parents to be dead for a long time. They would've come for me by now if they weren't dead. They loved me.

"Ivy, your dad is in Pravda's prison in Atlanta. I know this because I met him. I was in the cage next to his for about a month."

"Ivy isn't going to Atlanta!" Tim says again angrily. "I'm tired of your lies and manipulation!"

Matt stares into my eyes, ignoring Tim. "He was still alive last year when I broke out. I have a friend on the inside, and I think we could get your dad out too."

Tim pushes away from the wall and strides across the room to me. He bends down in front of me, blocking my view of Matt's penetrating eyes. "Ivy? Please? Please stay with me? Atlanta is the most dangerous place in the world for you. My brother was living there, and he told me they slaughter the Living on sight. There aren't any safe communities like Toccoa. There isn't anyone left Alive there. You would be taking Rosa to her death. Please don't let him trick you? I love you, Ivy. I will take care of you. I'll take you to the beach, and we can give Rosa a life there."

I'm speechless. I knew Tim cared for me a lot. I had guessed that he loved me. But to hear him say it—no to hear him plead with me because of it—I am completely torn.

If Matt is right and my dad is alive, how can I not try to find him?

Why does Pravda have him in a prison cell?

Could my mom be alive somewhere too?

It's beyond my wildest dreams that I could actually see my family again, but I made a commitment to care for Rosa. Atlanta is so dangerous. If I took Rosa there and she was killed or hurt -

How could I trade Rosa for the hope that Matt is right about my dad?

And I have to decide right now because every minute we wait brings Pravda closer to finding us.

Dear God, what do I do? Which path do I pick?

I am terrified to make this choice. I feel like Tim is the good angel on one shoulder and Matt is the devil on my other shoulder. And they both sound right.

Matt speaks again quietly, out of my view behind Tim. The cellar is small and the sound of his husky voice carries well. We all hear Matt intone, "Your dad talked about you and your mom. And your sister. You have an older sister don't you, Ivy? She ran away a long time ago and your parents blamed themselves."

Still crouched in front of me, blocking my view of Matt, Tim's shoulders fall visibly, and he closes his eyes. I just told him about Hazel. He knows Matt is telling the truth. Matt really did meet my dad.

Matt says, "I think you have more family than you realize, Ivy. There was an old woman there too. I heard your dad talk to her a lot. Do you know someone named Betty?"

I can't hold back the audible gasp that escapes my lips.

Aunty Betty!

"Tim!" I can't help how excited I sound, "It's my Aunty Betty! The woman in the picture next to Aunty Coe. You know? The silver frame by Aunty's bed? We thought she was dead! Tim, I have to go. You understand that don't you? If it was your family, you'd go," I plead.

"Even if you go with him, how will you get to them? Get yourself captured too? What about Rosa?" Tim's words are full of wisdom and responsibility.

He's right. How would I get to them?

Matt answers Tim's charge for me. "I was in there myself, and I know how to get them out. I have a friend inside of Pravda who will help me for a price. Credits talk. I can get them out. You can be with them again, Ivy."

"Tim, please? If it was your dad, I know you would go. You are honorable and brave and you would go for your family. I have to go if there's a chance that I can get them out; a chance to see my dad again."

Tim's slight nod is barely noticeable.

"Please come with me?" I plead with watery eyes.

At this request, Matt is up off the floor and fighting for my line of sight.

"Absolutely not, Ivy. I am taking you and Tom and Rosa and that's it. I never offered to bring anyone else. I'm not jeopardizing Tom by bringing them. It's too many people. I'll never get us all safely into Atlanta. I'm already bringing Rosa for you!"

"I won't go without them."

I desperately hope he doesn't call my bluff. I'm pretty sure if he refuses and leaves me here I'll die. I need to be with him. And he's the only way I'll ever find my dad. I am clinging to the chance that Matt feels something strong for me, too; that he needs me as much as I need him. I cross my arms where I sit resolutely, Tim still crouching in front of me. They have both seen my stubborn side before.

Matt's voice is almost whiny, "Ivy, you know how I feel about you, don't you? I care for you. I want to take care of you. I think you feel the same way about me. Why are you asking me to bring Lover Boy? He'll just be in our way!"

I'm embarrassed about how plainly Matt is speaking in front of Tim. That feeling that I've let Tim down—that he is judging me—comes over me. When Tim is around, I doubt the wisdom of having feelings for a zombie. But it's why I need Tim to stay with me. He's like my conscience. I know I won't do anything too stupid if he comes. I know I shouldn't be alone with Matt, with only children for accountability. It will be hard to say no to anything without Tim and Harmony there. If those green eyes asked me to jump into hell, I might. With other Living ones there, I'd be ashamed of myself for even the smallest sin. Even the miracle of reuniting with my family isn't worth the risk of losing my soul. Aunty warned me about Matt. My heart warns me now that I need everyone in this room to stay together.

Resolved, I say again, "If they don't come, I don't come."

Matt makes a disgusted sound and stalks away up the stairs. We hear the old door upstairs slam as he goes outside.

Tim looks beaten as he slumps down to the floor. "He's a killer, Ivy, a murderer. You know that right? He's even a criminal with his own kind! Why was he in Pravda's prison? If the lost think he's bad—he is!"

"How can you know that for sure?" I ask.

"He ran over two people on the way over here!" Tim says in loud disgust. "Go look at the car! You can see where he smashed into them. There is blood all over the bumper!"

"Ivy," Harmony speaks up for the first time, probably more comfortable now that Matt is gone. "How can you even ask that question? You know he's a murderer. He killed me!"

"What!" Tim asks with confusion and anger.

So she did remember. She knows what happened.

"He didn't mean to Harmony." I plead with her to understand that. "He was trying to save you."

"What do you mean 'he killed you?'" Tim is yelling now at Harmony.

She doesn't respond well to yelling, and she shrinks back into silence.

I tell the story, emphasizing Matt's heroic efforts and downplaying my part in the whole thing. I don't mean to speak lightly of what God did for Harmony; I just don't want to claim any of the glory for myself. It wasn't anything I did. God did it.

With this new information, Tim sits quietly thinking.

Finally he speaks. "Okay. We'll go."

I'm confused about how that story, which involved Matt and guns and

Harmony dying, has somehow changed his mind. I look at him quizzically.

Tim answers my questioning eyes, "God doesn't work in someone who is out of His will. He wouldn't have used you to bring Harmony back if you were living outside of His plan for your life. He only does big things like that in people who are fully His. This must be His plan for you, Ivy. I don't think you should go with Matt alone. If you want me to come, of course I will stay with you. I meant what I said."

He's referring to his admission of love, and I blush and look down at his reiterated commitment.

"Don't I get a vote?" Harmony finds the courage to speak again. "I don't want to go with him!"

Thomas has been sitting quietly while we argued. His angelic voice chimes in now, trying to convince Harmony. "Please come with us, Harmony? My brother isn't bad. He just doesn't know God yet. He's really great when you get to know him."

"Please, Harmony," I plead with her, "I need you. Don't you feel it? Can't you tell God wants you to come with us?"

She doesn't answer. She puts her head down on her knees, and I think maybe she's praying.

Chapter Fifty-Two

Zombie Robin Hood Boosts A Wagon

I decide to go look for Matt. We need a plan, and he needs to know that Tim is coming. I know Harmony will come too. In all honesty, she's just too chicken to stay here by herself. There is safety in numbers. It's best that she stay with us.

It's dark outside. It was midday when the alarms went off and we climbed down into the tunnel. Time is catapulting forward and pulling me along with it. The car Matt and Tim brought back is parked right outside the old house. I wonder how Matt got it here through the thick forest of weeds that surrounds us. I'm glad he found a way in, but I'm sure it left an obvious trail. Yet another reason why we need to leave here as soon as possible.

I find Matt sitting in the dented car. The front fender has indeed been damaged. It's too dark to see any gore, but I'm sure I can trust Tim's story—Matt mowed some zombies down on his short drive over here. Tim called Matt a killer. Why do I feel so certain that my life and Matt's are supposed to intertwine?

Matt chose a car I haven't seen before. It's smaller than the SUV that Aunty and I always drove. I mentally count the seats to see if we'll all fit. It has a large bench seat in the front, another bench in the back, and a big open area in the rear. I think maybe it's called a station wagon. It looks really old and dated, and I hope it's reliable. I know I won't find a little note on the dash from Maintenance proclaiming their blessing on our trip and promising the car will run great. I climb in the front seat and sit quietly. I feel like it's Matt's turn to say something.

"You're killing me, Ivy."

"Sorry."

"Are they both coming?"

"Yes," and then I add "Please?"

He sighs a long, tired, grumpy "I give up" sigh, and I'm relieved to hear him surrender.

"Thank you," I say, and I spontaneously lean over and kiss his cheek. I don't know why I did it, I've never kissed anyone but family. It's a big deal to me, but it doesn't seem to mean much to him. He just nods.

"You better go round them all up. I'm leaving here in fifteen minutes."

When I get out of the car, Tim is standing by the front door of the old house. Did he see me kiss Matt? Is he going to follow me everywhere and stare at me all the time? I look down instead of at him when I walk past him into the house. He's announced his love for me, unabashedly. If I want him to come with us, I'm going to have to live with the fact that he jealously wants my undivided affection.

As I walk past him into the dark house, Tim says my name quietly, like a question, "Ivy?"

I remember my strange feelings for him. I remember seeing him in a towel the other day and the surprising amount of attraction I felt. I'm still touched by how gentle and caring he was while I sat and cried for Aunty. He looks half decent when he takes off those awful glasses. He's a very good man, and I know that I can count on him for anything. He wants me even though I've been a backstabbing brat. A very small, minuscule, part of me kind-of wants him back.

I reach for Tim's hand in the dark and he squeezes my hand. I feel like a lunatic.

"Matt says we're leaving in fifteen minutes."

"Okay."

I pull away from Tim and walk back down the old stairs into the cellar. I jump with surprise as a dark figure emerges from the tunnel. Before I can let out a warning cry, Tim bounds past me, pulls his brother Andrew to his feet and embraces him. Captain Markowitz has found our secret cellar. This is a new complication.

Should I go get Matt?

Andrew looks around and clears his throat when he sees me. I feel deeply guilty of everything he's thinking and probably some things he isn't thinking.

"Where's Matt?" Andrew demands.

He's older than all of us, and he has lived through terrible experiences that have given him wisdom and authority. Our status here in the house just went from independent grownups to children. Matt was right about any of my people joining us. Andrew isn't going to let Matt be the leader. He will try to keep me and Rosa and Harmony and Thomas from going with Matt. And I'm sure Andrew won't let Tim to go, even if we do.

"Are you alone?" I ask instead of answering him. "Is anyone else safe?" I'm still clinging to the desperate hope that some of our people could have survived.

"I'm alone," he says sadly. "I wasn't at the U.R. when they came through the fence."

"Yeah, Harmony told us." I tip my head towards her, still sitting in the corner. She looks up but doesn't smile or speak.

"I couldn't do anything to save them. There were too many of them. I think some of our people did get away though. Harmony told me enough on the way to the tunnel for me to find it myself. It took me awhile to get here without being seen. I recovered the entrance; you had it fairly well concealed. I don't think they'll find it tonight, but we can't stay here."

"We aren't staying here. We're going to Atlanta," Tim states with no hint of doubt and no desire for permission.

"I see. May I ask why?" Andrew asks his younger brother with quiet respect.

I'm shocked.

Andrew treats Tim like an equal? He isn't going to say no?

I decide to let Tim handle his brother, and I sit down on the bottom step hoping for the outcome I desperately need—the six of us leaving here together ASAP.

"Ivy's father and Colleen's sister are in Atlanta, inside Pravda. Matt met them in *prison*," Tim says with too much emphasis on Matt's questionable criminal character, "and Matt says he knows someone who can get them out."

"So they are believers?" Andrew asks.

"Matt didn't say. I guess I'm assuming they are based on the fact that they were in Pravda's prison," Tim says with a shrug.

"In a cell near Matt?" Andrew asks, eyebrows raised, pointing out the obvious. Matt isn't Living. They might not be.

"Yeah, I guess we don't know if they are." Tim looks concerned as he realizes that we don't know anything about them or why they are being held by Pravda.

Listening to their concerns, I'm afraid for the worst. I hadn't really thought about Dad and Aunty Betty being one way or the other. When I last saw them, they had the disease but no symptoms. I was picturing them healthy because my last memories of them are when they were healthy. But really, I guess I don't know.

This new fear weighs on me. I need an answer, and I know where I can get one. Right now. I stand slowly and tiptoe back up the stairs to find Matt. If Tim and Andrew notice me leaving, they don't call me back. It's time Matt knew about our newest complication anyways.

Chapter Fifty-Three

And We're Off

I physically bump into Matt at the top of the stairs. We are alone in the dark, standing so close that our bodies are touching. The sound of Matt breathing fills my ears in the silent old house. He sounds so sturdy and strong. I feel my breath catch raggedly with the anticipation that comes from being so close to him. The attraction I feel for him consumes me like nothing I've ever experienced. Desires I've never felt are waking up in me for the first time. I forget why I came up the stairs, and I stand still, wanting to be close to him like this for as long as it can last.

An involuntary shiver of excitement runs through me. Matt rumbles a chuckle in my ear, and I'm suddenly embarrassed. I must seem like such a little girl to him; so inexperienced with guys; so overly excited by just being near him. The haunting thought that Matt has probably been with a lot of girls sweeps over me and steals my eagerness. The breathy moment is over, and I step around Matt and walk a few feet away. I feel depressed and frustrated and it's too much emotion in too short a time.

My feelings spilling out in my words, I sound flat and angry when I speak. "Andrew, Captain Markowitz, is here. He found the tunnel. He came alone. He said he re-covered the entrance well, and he thinks we are safe for tonight."

I can't see Matt's face in the darkness, and he doesn't immediately speak so I don't know if he's angry. I figure he will be. Andrew Markowitz has to be one of his least favorite people. Andrew kept Matt locked up while Thomas hung on the edge of death.

Matt steps closer to me, and the moonlight filtering through a broken window shows me his face etched with confusion. That isn't the emotion that I was expecting to see. "Why did you move away? Are you mad at me?" Matt asks with quiet, genuine concern.

I don't know how to answer him. I'm still embarrassed by my lack of experience; still frustrated that I don't know enough about him. And we are so different. I know he couldn't possibly understand any of that. If I told him that I wanted to be special to him, to know that he would love me faithfully, forsaking all others, and ideally marry me—I'm pretty sure he'd run away from the crazy girl from God Town. I suddenly remember the other reason I came looking for him.

"I need to ask you something."

"Anything," he states openly, wanting to please me.

"My dad and Aunty Betty—were they like me?" I pause, "Or like you?"

"They were like you," he says evenly.

I feel my shoulders relax in relief, and two tears spill down my cheeks from out of nowhere. They are Alive! Even if I can't ever get to them, I'll see them soon. We'll all be together soon no matter what.

Matt sighs and asks, "What if they hadn't been immune like you? Would you have cared less for them? Are we really all that different, Ivy?"

He reaches out and takes my hand and I notice he isn't wearing his gloves. The feel of his warm rough skin against mine brings back the confusing feelings again, though not as strongly as before.

I don't answer his question, unsure what answer would be the right one. Instead I ask another question, "Why were they there then? Why were you there?"

"I was there for my own reasons," he says, vague as always. There is more mystery to him than I'll ever be able to figure out. "They were there because Pravda was, uh, interested in them scientifically."

"You mean experimenting on them?" I ask horrified.

"Yeah."

"And it's why they want me, isn't it?" I must be stupid. It took me this long to reach that oh so obvious conclusion. It is no coincidence that Pravda has my family locked up and also happens to want me.

"I think so. There is something very special about you Ivy. You are really incredible, you know. What you did the other night -" he trails off, leaving a heavy silence between us.

I think he means what happened with Harmony. He thinks I did something incredible. Once again, he has completely missed the truth. Thomas' healing, Harmony's healing, how can a person be so blind?

"Ivy?" Tim's voice and shadow are suddenly in the room with us. He must have been worried that Matt would be angry about Andrew.

"So, how many more of your people are going to make themselves at home in my hideout?" Matt asks, almost good-naturedly.

I try to pull my hand away from Matt, but he holds onto it tightly, almost painfully. I'm sure Tim is as surprised as I am about Matt's seeming indifference to Andrew's presence.

"Actually, he is just passing through," Tim says sadly.

"I don't have to come up with free food and shelter for him too?" Matt asks sarcastically.

I hadn't thought about our group as dependent on Matt. Four more mouths to feed, and no credits to our name. And none of us can go give blood; we are wanted criminals now. Matt can't give enough blood to keep us all fed. We have a lot to figure out.

"No." Tim doesn't sound as appreciative as I feel. "He used the tunnel to get out of the compound, but he's not coming with us."

"Where will he go?" I ask softly.

It must be very hard for Tim to say goodbye to his only family. Their dad is probably dead, thanks to me. Tim still wants to come with me, even now when he could leave with his own brother. His love is overwhelming. I'm choosing my family over everyone else by daring this trip to Atlanta for a rescue that may not even be possible. As usual, just being near Tim makes me feel guilty.

"He isn't sure. Probably our grandmother's cabin."

"You don't want to go with him?" I ask.

I can't understand Tim picking me over his family.

"If you don't want me to come with you Ivy, I won't." Tim says with strangled emotion.

I sense that he's trying not to cry, and I feel terrible. I didn't mean for my question to sound like it did. He took it like I wished he'd go with Andrew.

"No!" I say quickly backpedaling. "I want you to come with us!"

Matt finally drops my hand. He draws phlegm up in his throat with a disgusting loud noise and spits on the floor. His disgust with my desire for Tim to come is all too clear.

"We're leaving in five minutes," he says tersely. "Make yourself useful, and help me haul everything to the car."

I'm pretty sure Matt was talking to Tim, but I hurry down the stairs to start the moving process—partly just to get out of the darkness and away from our uncomfortable threesome. Everyone but Thomas starts hauling armloads of stuff to the car. Andrew is a huge help, and I can't help but be impressed by the graciousness that Dr. Markowitz instilled in his two sons.

Little Rosa is asleep again, and Tim carries her up the stairs and gently sets her into the back seat of the old car, tucking blankets around her. Matt hauls the guns himself; none of us feel comfortable touching them. I watch him place them strategically throughout the car. One in the glove box, one under the driver's seat, one under the back seat. When he bends to lay the last couple in the back of the car, the gun I held in the tunnel glints in his waistband. I wish it was overkill; but, from what I've heard about Atlanta, I find myself wondering if it will be enough.

The basement emptied, we stand at the car and look at each other under a star filled sky. Matt has loaded Thomas' wheel chair in the back with the rest of the supplies, and Thomas is sitting in the front seat with the door open.

Andrew clears his throat, breaking the silence, "I'd like to pray for you before you go."

Without a word, Matt walks to the driver's side, gets in and shuts his door. The rest of us glance awkwardly at each other; and, when Andrew starts praying, we bow our heads. Tim reaches out and takes my hand, and I assume he is also holding Harmony's hand. We often hold hands and pray in groups at the U.R.

"Father," Andrew says loudly into the night sky. His voice catches for a moment, and I imagine his thoughts have drifted to his earthly father, who is now in heaven with his Heavenly Father, and my Aunty. "Lord," he starts again, "protect them. Guide them in your will, make their paths clear. We know you are coming soon. May they accomplish what you have planned for them in the short time we have left. You are good, always good. Thank you for healing us, for saving us. Bring everyone here safely into your great kingdom."

This last request, though he prays for all of us, was mostly for Matt. I'm humbled and thankful for this good man's prayer over the one I love. I hope Matt will find the truth before it's too late.

"Amen," Andrew says and we each echo the closing word.

When I look up, I see that no one else is holding hands; just Tim and I. I look over my shoulder and see Matt watching us. I drop Tim's hand, and Tim looks sadly away from me.

With nothing left but to get in the car, Tim, Harmony and I turn to find a seat. I'm not sure where to sit. Rosa is sleeping in the back, and she is my responsibility. But with Thomas and Matt both in the front, there is only one seat left there; and I know neither Tim nor Harmony will want to sit there. Tim sees my dilemma and solves it by sliding into the front seat. So it's guys in the front and girls in the back.

Andrew leans down and embraces Tim before shutting the front passenger side door. Andrew nods politely at me and pushes our back door shut. Matt cranks the car, and the old engine roars to life. Tim starts to roll down his window for one more farewell word to his brother, but Matt steps on the gas, kicking up dirt and stones, and we're away. Tim, Harmony and I turn around in our seats to look behind at Andrew standing alone in the starlight. It must be gut-wrenching for Tim.

The car plows through the thick underbrush, bumping and jostling us as the bottom scrapes over the rough, dead vegetation. Then we are through the weeds and out on the road and driving towards tomorrow. The small town of Toccoa is quickly behind us, and I doubt I'll ever see it again. When I glance back to say my own private goodbye to the place I've called home, I see billows of smoke rising from the center of town—and I know it's all my fault.

*****

Ivy's adventure continues in Book Two—IMMACULA†E
Available wherever fine books are sold.

*****

Elizabeth Forkey

Elizabeth Forkey is a Christian blogger, novelist, and an award-winning creative writing teacher (she has a keychain to prove it!). Her debut novel INFEC†IOUS is a Christian Post-apocalyptic Zombie Love Story and is the first book in The INFEC†IOUS Series.

The next book in the series, IMMACULA†E is available now; and, the final installment, IMMANEN†, is expected to hit the shelves Spring of 2016. Elizabeth is also an award-winning sugar artist and cake sculptor and the mother of two very adorable, outspoken daughters.

Made in the USA
Charleston, SC
24 March 2016